Praise for

FINDING FLORA

"Historical fiction readers will love this fascinating, incredibly researched story of survival and courage honouring the strength and resilience of early female pioneers."

Genevieve Graham, #1 bestselling author of *The Secret Keeper*

"When we think of pioneers and homesteaders, women are normally relegated to the sidelines. Elinor Florence's new novel upends this narrative. You can't help but cheer for the resilient women of Ladyville who are not only lovable characters but also reflect the grit, hardships, and societal tensions that helped shape Canada as we know it today. *Finding Flora* is an engaging and educational read, rich with shifting fortunes and trouble brewing at every turn."

Ellen Keith, award-winning author of *The Dutch Wife*

"Elinor Florence has vividly captured a time in Canadian history when life for so many people was physically very hard and rigid demarcations separated both class and gender. The struggle of her female characters to forge a life for themselves against daunting odds grabs our sympathy and doesn't let go until the totally satisfying ending. They are women I, for one, would love to hang out with."

Maureen Jennings, award-winning author of the Murdoch Mysteries books

"A gorgeously written and researched story of love and survival following a plucky Scotswoman fleeing her abusive husband and a powerfully diverse group of women homesteaders on the prairie in the early 1900s. You will fall in love with the prairies and this wonderful book."

Maia Caron, author of *The Last Secret*

"I was swept away to the wild and wide-open spaces of Alberta, circa 1905, by the magic of Elinor Florence's writing. I cheered for Flora every step of the way in this epic tale as big as the prairie sky."

Leslie Howard, bestselling author of *The Brideship Wife*

Also by Elinor Florence

Bird's Eye View

Wildwood

FINDING FLORA

Elinor Florence

Published by Simon & Schuster
New York   Amsterdam/Antwerp   London
Toronto   Sydney/Melbourne   New Delhi

SIMON &
SCHUSTER
CANADA

A Division of Simon & Schuster, LLC
166 King Street East, Suite 300
Toronto, Ontario M5A 1J3

For more than 100 years, Simon & Schuster has championed authors and the stories they create. By respecting the copyright of an author's intellectual property, you enable Simon & Schuster and the author to continue publishing exceptional books for years to come. We thank you for supporting the author's copyright by purchasing an authorized edition of this book.

This book is a work of fiction. Any references to historical events, real people, or real places are used fictitiously. Other names, characters, places, and events are products of the author's imagination, and any resemblance to actual events or places or persons, living or dead, is entirely coincidental.

This Simon & Schuster Canada edition April 2025

SIMON & SCHUSTER CANADA and colophon are trademarks of Simon & Schuster, LLC

Simon & Schuster strongly believes in freedom of expression and stands against censorship in all its forms. For more information, visit BooksBelong.com.

For information about special discounts for bulk purchases, please contact Simon & Schuster Special Sales at 1-800-268-3216 or CustomerService@simonandschuster.ca.

Interior design by Erika R. Genova

Manufactured in the United States of America

10 9 8 7 6 5 4 3 2 1

Library and Archives Canada Cataloguing in Publication
Title: Finding Flora / Elinor Florence.
Names: Florence, Elinor, author.
Description: Simon & Schuster Canada edition.
Identifiers: Canadiana (print) 20240352335 | Canadiana (ebook) 20240352343 |
ISBN 9781668058916 (softcover) | ISBN 9781668058923 (EPUB)
Subjects: LCGFT: Historical fiction. | LCGFT: Novels.
Classification: LCC PS8611.L66 F56 2025 | DDC C813/.6—dc23

ISBN 978-1-6680-5891-6
ISBN 978-1-6680-5892-3 (ebook)

To Jessie McDonald, my Scottish-Cree great-grandmother
We carry within us all the ancestors who came before us.

FINDING FLORA

BOOK
ONE

CHAPTER ONE

Bracing herself against the jerk and pitch of the train, Flora leaped into the darkness.

Her long skirt billowed in the icy updraft. For several seconds she was airborne, trapped between her past life and an unfathomable future. Then her left foot struck the ground with such force that her ankle bent like a green twig and she screamed with pain, the sound lost in the thunder of the wheels. She tumbled down the steep gravel bank and landed on her back in a shallow pool, shattering a thin crust of spring ice. There she lay rigid and gasping, terrified that someone had seen her shadow cross the lighted windows.

Flora clenched her chattering teeth and forced herself to play dead. Steel screeched against steel as the massive steam locomotive groaned around the curve and picked up speed. The ground vibrated, the boxcars creaked, and the wheels clattered across the cracks in the rails. Eventually the caboose rolled past and disappeared. The rhythmic chuffing of the engine faded, and the earth fell silent.

Only then did Flora struggle to her feet, the ice beneath her breaking into shards as sharp as needles. Her hat had vanished, and her hair hung heavy and wet over one shoulder. Although her new tweed travelling suit and tartan shawl had saved her skin from abrasion, one side of her face throbbed with pain.

Flora had heaved out her calfskin valise before jumping, had watched it bounce once before it was swallowed up in the black night. After an unsuccessful attempt to wring the water from her sodden skirt with numb hands, she limped along the ditch, searching for the bag, straining her eyes in the gloom. Her left ankle was on fire.

For a moment she regretted her trunk, locked in the baggage car, rushing away in the opposite direction. With a sense of urgency, she fumbled for the leather pouch strapped around her waist and gripped it for reassurance. Inside were her identification papers and her life savings. Safely sewn into the seam of her petticoat was her secret treasure. Now that the contents of the trunk were gone, everything else she owned in the world was in that valise. Flora bent over and renewed her desperate search.

The heavy clouds parted, and moonlight flooded the prairie. She spied the bag wedged under a clump of willows and gave a small cry of relief. Clutching it with one hand, she clawed her way up the bank with the other. The steel rails looked like two silver threads stretching away to the horizon. Flora hobbled a few steps and halted, her treacherous ankle pounding, as she came to the bitter realisation that she couldn't walk all the way back to Calgary. Nor could she remain beside the tracks and wait for help, since she knew there wouldn't be another train for three days.

Balancing on one high-heeled shoe, Flora scanned her shadowy surroundings. She was no stranger to the empty sweep of the Highland moors, but this landscape was an alien creature, bristling with hostility. Patches of stubborn snow lingered between the spiky blades jutting from its broad back. Even the air was thin and harsh and stung her panting lungs. Through the silence came an eerie howl. Flora started so violently that she bit her own tongue and tasted blood. Surely setting off into this savage wasteland was an act of suicide.

While she stood motionless, almost stupefied with shock and fear, something caught her eye. A yellow glow winked once, winked twice. Flora stared into the shadows, wondering if it were a star, unsure where the black earth met the black sky. Then she glimpsed it again, a tiny beacon that flickered and faded.

Flora slid down the bank and wrenched a sturdy branch from the underbrush. Wedging her makeshift staff under her left armpit and hoisting the valise with her right hand, she set out across the cold, dead plain toward the light.

CHAPTER TWO

Flora inhaled an unfamiliar smell. It wasn't the acrid odour of soot from the train's smokestack, but the fresh, sweet fragrance of resin. When she tried to open her eyes, only the right one responded. She found herself lying in a bed, facing a wall of round peeled logs, as golden as boiled toffee.

Still half-asleep, she became aware of another scent, the comforting aroma of simmering parritch. It reminded her of mornings in her father's stone house, watching her mother tossing a chunk of peat into the fire, hearing the clatter of hooves on the cobblestones outside.

Flora awoke with a surge of panic. Where was she? And why couldn't she see properly? Reaching up to her face, she touched her left eye with her fingertips and flinched. It was swollen shut, the flesh around it puffy and tender. Rolling over, she scanned her surroundings with her good eye. A young woman in a shabby dress stood at a cookstove in the corner, stirring the contents of a blackened pot and holding a baby in one arm.

The woman glanced back at her and smiled. "How are you this morning?" She lay the baby in a wooden cradle and sat down on the edge of the bed.

"I'm all right, I think," Flora croaked in a strange, hoarse voice. She dimly recalled someone peeling off her wet clothes, chafing her with a rough towel, and dragging a cotton nightgown over her head. "Thank you so much for taking me in."

"Nobody turns away visitors out here." The woman paused, obviously curious.

Flora struggled into a sitting position, inhaling sharply as her bruised muscles contracted. It didn't come easily to break the ninth commandment by telling an outright lie, but that's what she did.

"Ach, I did something stupid, to be sure. I fell off the train." She swallowed, and the motion hurt her throat. "I was crossing the open platform between two cars when it gave a lurch and I lost my balance. Tumbled right off the side. I saw yon light, so I came here."

"Mercy me!" the woman said. "It's a good thing you fell when you did, because the train enters the Rockies not far away. You might have gone straight off a cliff!"

Flora pictured her broken body lying at the foot of a crag, never to be found. On the other hand, maybe that would have been a preferable fate.

"Was anyone travelling with you?"

Flora shook her head. She would have to lie again. "I was alone. I landed in Montreal only a few days ago. Someone told me the weather is warmer on the West Coast, so I bought a ticket for Vancouver. I was hoping to find work there."

"So nobody knows where you are?"

"I don't even know where I am." This time she told the truth.

"We're twenty miles west of Calgary, as the crow flies. I'm Lydia Prince, and my husband's name is Joseph, and that's our little Lizzie." She nodded toward the cradle with a loving smile.

"I'm Flora Craigie." She used her maiden name without thinking, then mentally castigated herself for an eejit. She should have created a false one.

"Pleased to meet you, Miss Craigie. I've hardly spoken to another woman in the last four years, ever since we moved out here from Ontario and staked our claim."

Flora looked around the room. The cabin reminded her of a humble crofter's cottage, but this one was made of logs rather than stone. A table and two chairs stood beside the stove, a rag rug covered the plank floor, and a flowered teapot sat on the windowsill. There was only one bed. "Where did you sleep?" Flora asked.

"I sent Joe out to the barn to bed down in the hay. I crawled in with you. We couldn't let you lie on the floor in your condition, poor thing."

"That was verra kind of you, Mrs. Prince." Flora tried to smile. "I'll leave as soon as I can."

Yet where could she hide? The terror, so strange and unfamiliar, rose again in her chest.

"Well, you can't go anywhere yet," Mrs. Prince said. "You must have landed on the side of your face. It's so bruised you look like a rutabaga. The district nurse will be here in a few days to check on Lizzie's cough, and she can take a look at you."

She rose to her feet. "Let me help you outside to the Parliament Building— that's what we call the toilet. I'll heat some water so you can have a wash."

After the kettle boiled, she filled an enamel basin and gave Flora a bar of yellow soap. Mrs. Prince and the baby went out to the field to bring lunch to her husband, whom she said was picking rocks. Flora wondered why he needed the rocks, but decided not to ask.

Alone in the cabin, she lifted her nightgown. Her left side was stained and mottled, the blood pooled beneath the skin, and her ankle swollen to the size of a small tree trunk. She hopped over to the mirror hanging above the basin and examined herself with one hazel eye. She was barely recognizable, even to herself. A dark bruise covered her left cheekbone, and her auburn hair was tangled and matted.

Painfully aware of her aching throat, Flora pulled down the ruffled collar on her high-necked nightgown. When she saw the angry red marks, she stepped back from the mirror, gasping. She couldn't seem to get enough air into her lungs.

Her first impulse was to take the train back to Montreal and return to Scotland, but she had no family there, no livelihood. If she stayed here, how would she support herself? Her savings would last for some time, but not indefinitely. She needed to work, yet it occurred to her that she must keep away from established settlements. Although Flora tried to think rationally, it was no use. Every ounce of her bruised body screamed out to run away and hide. She raised her good eye to the tiny window beside the mirror and felt slightly reassured by the sheer emptiness of the surrounding terrain. Surely there must be no better place to disappear than in this vast wilderness called Canada.

Flora awoke two days later with the same rush of sickening dread. She was still stiff and sore, although her ankle felt slightly less painful. After breakfast, Mrs. Prince helped her outside to sit on one of the family's two wooden chairs.

From where the cabin stood on a slight rise, she saw the broad sweep of the prairie, stretching away to a line of violet foothills in the west. Drenched in bright sunlight, the country still looked strange and desolate, but far less threatening. Life was stirring in this dead landscape. The heavy brown grass was flushed with spring green, as subtle as a woman's blush. An indefinable hum filled the air, a sense of awakening that throbbed from every swaying blade.

Flora lifted her battered face to the healing sunshine and breathed deeply. A warm breeze carried the metallic odour of melting snow and the fresh scent of budding leaves. It smelled so different from her own country, with its dank, peaty moors and salty sea breeze. A yellow-breasted bird flitted past with a twig in its mouth, and Flora felt a primeval response within her own breast. She simply must survive, reinvent herself, build a new life in this unfamiliar land.

But where should she go? She was aware that her presence must be a burden for the Princes. Her only contribution was to mind the baby while Mrs. Prince worked outdoors with her husband. She knew nothing about babies and was frightened of dropping it. The child, who was suffering from a nasty cough, screamed in such a way that Flora wanted to scream herself.

Yet the Princes were obviously happy. Mr. Prince came in from the barn each day at dawn, kissed his wife with gusto, bolted his breakfast while bouncing Lizzie on his lap, and left the cabin whistling to begin his long day's labour.

Mrs. Prince, too, sang as she washed the dishes and tidied the cabin, chatting away as if Flora were an old friend. "This will be our first crop on land that is truly our own, Miss Craigie, and there is no better feeling in the world. For a joke we call each other Dolly and Dusty, after the horses. The team pulls together, and so do we. Now, if you don't mind watching Lizzie, I'll help Joe carry the biggest stones off the field. We can't afford to break another ploughshare."

Flora didn't envy Mrs. Prince for the husband, or the baby—quite the opposite—yet when she looked around the cabin, a wave of yearning washed over her. It seemed that she was not destined to obtain the one thing she had always wanted: a home of her own.

She could hardly wait until bedtime, when she huddled under the woollen comforter to ponder her uncertain future. Lying awake on the third night, she heard the mournful sound of the train whistle and began to tremble so violently that Mrs. Prince roused and asked if she were unwell.

The nurse, whose name was Grace Godwin, arrived in a horse-drawn buggy, accompanied by her little brown-and-white mongrel Rags. She was older than Flora had expected. Her bony face and her dark hair, twisted into a tight knot, looked as if they were carved from granite. No doubt accustomed to people with hideous injuries, the nurse was expressionless when introduced to Flora, whose black eye had become even blacker, although she could now see through a slit that had opened in the swollen flesh.

The nurse first examined Lizzie and pronounced her cough much improved. Mrs. Prince then took the baby outside to play with Rags while Flora lay on the bed and the nurse probed her with firm hands, manipulating her ankle until she cried out.

"It isn't broken," she said. "You've twisted it badly, but you should be able to walk without limping in a few days. The rest of your bruises will soon fade. They appear worse because your skin is so fair."

She took Flora by the chin and turned her head from one side to the other, studying her swollen cheek and the marks on her throat. "Would you care to tell me what happened?"

Flora steeled herself to lie once again, but the nurse's gaze was so penetrating that she simply couldn't do it. Her words came out in a rush.

"I married a wicked man, Nurse Godwin. That's the truth of it."

The nurse's voice was calm. "You wouldn't be the first. Go on."

"I met him nought but four weeks ago. Hector Mackle is a land agent with the Canadian Pacific Railway, and he was in Scotland selling farms. I didn't have time to discover his true character, because his ship was ready to sail. We hardly spoke on the passage, either, because he was so ill."

"Seasick, I suppose?"

"Much worse than that. He had a fever and sore throat and a rash all over his body, even the palms of his hands and the soles of his feet."

Nurse Godwin drew her heavy eyebrows together. "Was he seen by the ship's doctor?"

"Aye, the doctor gave me a jar of mercury ointment for his rash. That did help a mite." Flora wondered why she was asking about Hector's illness.

"I'm surprised he was allowed into the country."

"He's a grand actor, he is." Flora grimaced, remembering how thoroughly she had been deceived by her husband. After the ship docked, she helped him dress, covered his scabrous hands with a pair of gloves, combed his hair, adjusted his fedora, and supported him with one arm while he leaned on his gold-headed walking stick with the other. Thanks to Flora's elegance and Hector's eloquence, the immigration authorities allowed them to pass.

"What happened then?"

"After we boarded the train to Vancouver, he took straight to his bunk and stayed there until we reached Calgary." Flora stopped and took a shuddering breath.

The nurse reached for her hand and pressed it. "Go on, my dear. You'll feel better if you tell me the rest."

It was such a relief to unburden herself that Flora kept on telling the truth. "Shortly after we left Calgary, he tried to . . . to force himself on me. We hadn't consummated the marriage, you ken, because of his illness. We struggled, and he fell backward and knocked himself unconscious."

Her voice began to rise. "Nurse Godwin, I was so feart! I had to get away before he woke, so I jumped from the train!" Her tears overflowed and stung the swollen flesh around her eye.

The nurse pulled a clean handkerchief from her pocket and handed it to her. While Flora wept, the nurse stared at the floor.

"Was there any other physical contact . . . of an intimate nature?"

Flora answered through her sobs. "He reached into my blouse and grabbed my breast, but that's all."

"I think you've had a narrow escape in more ways than one. The symptoms you're describing sound like syphilis."

"Syphilis?" Flora repeated the word. She had heard it before but wasn't sure exactly what it meant.

"It's an incurable disease, often fatal, transmitted by sexual intercourse."

Flora was so shocked that she stopped crying. She had discovered too late that her new husband was a reprehensible character, but never had she imagined he would knowingly infect her with a deadly illness. She buried her face in the handkerchief. What a boorach she had created, and no one to blame but herself.

"The question is—what's to be done with you now?" Nurse Godwin asked. "Do you have enough money for your passage back to Scotland?"

"Yes, but I don't want to go back. My parents are dead, and I left my position as a lady's maid to marry that awful man. I want to stay here, if I can find somewhere to hide!"

The nurse's penetrating eyes were fixed on her, as if she were analysing Flora's mental state as well as her physical condition. There was a brief pause before she spoke again. "Have you ever considered homesteading, Miss Craigie?"

"Nay. I canna qualify for a homestead on my own." This much she knew from Hector. Single women, unless they were widows with minor children, were ineligible for the free one hundred and sixty acres offered by the federal government.

"Such a ridiculous law." The nurse glowered. "A healthy young woman is just as capable as any man. Even the American government understands that. South of the border, thousands of single women are claiming homesteads."

Flora blotted her eyes, hoping the nurse might have another suggestion. There was silence for a moment while the older woman ruminated, tapping her foot. Then she turned her sharp eyes on Flora again.

"Miss Craigie, let me ask you this. Suppose you did manage to acquire a homestead. You would have to live there for three years, under some draconian conditions."

Flora lowered the handkerchief and stared. "Forgive me, Nurse Godwin, but why do you ask?"

"I'll tell you why. During the South African War, seven thousand Canadians volunteered. After it ended, our veterans were granted land scrip coupons entitling them to claim a homestead of three hundred and twenty acres, double the usual size. Since most of them have no interest in farming, they're selling their coupons. And there's no law against selling them to single women."

Flora blinked rapidly, bewildered. "But how does that help me? I dinna ken any veterans."

Nurse Godwin smiled for the first time. "My dear girl, you're looking at one."

CHAPTER THREE

In one short week, the landscape had come to life. It was in constant motion, dappled with sunshine and shadow, both grassland and clouds galloping before the wind. The pure air filled Flora's lungs and stirred her blood. As the buggy jolted down the muddy trail, putting more distance between herself and Hector Mackle, her spirits rose by the minute.

With Rags at their feet, Flora and Nurse Godwin were heading toward Airdrie, the nearest whistle stop along the two-hundred-mile railway spur line running from Calgary north to Edmonton, the end of the steel. Halfway between those two cities was the town of Red Deer, where the nurse lived and worked. There, Flora would file on her homestead.

Flora felt as though she were being plunged into a warm bath of hopefulness, followed by an icy shower of terror. The word *homestead* thrilled her to the marrow of her bones. Yet when she beheld this untamed wilderness, she couldn't help asking herself whether she had the courage to undertake such a venture.

How she envied those rare women who appeared to have boundless self-confidence. Where had it sprung from? Like Flora, they had been born into a world where men were considered the lords of creation, sovereign over women in every way. And, in truth, Flora secretly agreed. Throughout the centuries, it was men who were the thinkers and doers. Surely the historical record could not be so far wrong.

She tried to recall the names of fearless women but was hard-pressed to come up with more than two or three examples. Her namesake, Flora MacDonald, had smuggled Bonnie Prince Charlie to freedom after the Scottish rebellion was crushed. Grace Darling had braved the stormy seas in her little lifeboat to rescue stranded shipwreck survivors. In modern times, the English suffragette Emmeline Pankhurst was organizing demonstrations, battling for women's right to the vote.

And the stern figure beside her, perhaps.

Flora stole a glance at the nurse, sitting ramrod straight, gripping the reins in her strong hands. "Nurse Godwin, did you consider claiming your own homestead?"

"No, Miss Craigie. My calling is to care for the sick and the injured."

Flora admired this woman who understood herself so well. She had never experienced a strong desire for any profession, and that included motherhood. Undoubtedly Hector had expected her to bear his children, but she had avoided thinking about it.

"When did you first experience this calling?" she asked.

"As early as I can remember, playing nurse with my dolls and pretending to be Florence Nightingale. After leaving school, I trained at the Montreal General Hospital. When the South African War began in 1899—for the usual idiotic reason, man's lust for gold—twelve of us nurses volunteered to join the Canadian troops. The Brits and the Boers spent three long years shedding each other's blood, while we did our best to stem the flow. Even worse than the battle wounds was the lack of clean drinking water. It caused enteric fever—you may know it as typhoid, Miss Craigie. It carried off our boys by the hundreds."

Flora marvelled at the dedication that led twelve women to risk their lives in this fashion. "The Canadian government must have appreciated your sacrifice, since it rewarded you as well as the soldiers," she said.

Nurse Godwin snorted. "That was a simple oversight on their part. Believe me, the enlisted men valued our efforts far more than did our own government."

"What made you move out here, to the North-West Territories?"

"Because of the influx of settlers, medical help is desperately needed. I've accepted the position of matron at the new Red Deer Memorial Hospital. It's the first hospital between Calgary and Edmonton, dedicated to four young soldiers who lost their lives in South Africa."

She negotiated a pothole in the trail before changing the subject. "Miss Craigie, I would be remiss in my pledge to improve the health and welfare of this new territory without asking: Are you truly prepared to take on the prospect of starving and freezing and working harder than the horse pulling this buggy for the next three years? Homesteading requires not only a strong back, but an iron will."

"I'm not afraid of hard work." Flora was definite on that point, recalling the hours spent scrubbing stone floors on her knees, scouring blackened pots and pans with sand until her wrists ached. "But Nurse, what I ken about farming might be engraved on the head of a hatpin."

"You won't be at a greater disadvantage than most other homesteaders. It appears to me that the principal markers for success are determination, plus a willingness to learn. You strike me as a young woman who could accomplish much if you put your mind to it."

"Do you really think so?"

"I do." Her voice rang with conviction.

"Thank you, Nurse Godwin." Flora smiled and sat a little straighter.

"In my observation, people choose the hard path of homesteading for many reasons. Some are desperate to escape the trap of poverty; some are weary of doing the bidding of others—yet all are souls who want to sail against the tide. Do you belong to that gallant company, Miss Craigie?"

Flora thought about it. "I dinna ken, Nurse Godwin. I've never seen myself in that light."

"You risked everything to marry a man you scarcely knew and accompany him to the new world—not to mention jumping from a train, rather than submit to his abuse. I would say, Miss Craigie, that you have a stiffer backbone than you have been led to believe."

A flock of migrating geese flew north, darkening the enormous blue sky as they passed overhead, filling the air with a wild, exuberant honking. Flora's heart lifted as she watched the weightlessness of the birds. "You are the first person ever to tell me so, Nurse Godwin."

The women fell silent. Rags pressed against Flora's knee, and she stroked his shaggy head while she considered the nurse's words. No one had ever encouraged her to achieve anything on her own hook. Certainly not her softspoken father, John Craigie, a chemist in the Highland town of Dornoch. Flora suspected that he wished she were a son, trained to take over the family business he had inherited from his own father.

Her mother, Isobel Mackay, had plenty of fighting spirit, but never had she urged Flora to do anything but find a rich husband. She had spent her lifetime raging against the Sutherlands, the titled landlords who had evicted her own parents from their croft during the Highland Clearances. They had been forced into a stone hut on the rugged coastline, where they barely survived on herring and kelp pulled from the sea.

Thanks to her auburn-haired beauty, Isobel had caught the eye of the local chemist and married him. But it was a bitter blow when she discovered that her husband merely leased his two-storey stone house from the hated Sutherlands. "Flora, you must marry a man with a muckle of gold," she often repeated. "Only then will you be safe from the evil Sassenachs who can steal your home in a heartbeat."

When Flora was twelve years old, her mother stepped on a rusty nail and died of blood poisoning. For the next six years she attended school, kept house for her father, and helped in the shop below their living quarters. Nobody ever suggested that Flora pursue higher education. Her teachers ignored the lasses, even the clever ones, and devoted their attention to the lads. And the strict tenets of the Dornoch Cathedral across the street, where Flora sang in the choir, preached masculine superiority. There was no conceivable way for a woman to advance without marrying up, as Isobel herself had done.

Now Flora asked herself for the first time whether her mother might have been wrong.

She was brought back to the present by the nurse's words. "Miss Craigie, let's talk business. You agreed to buy my scrip for fifty cents an acre. That's one hundred and sixty dollars."

"Aye, and I'm extremely grateful to you, Nurse Godwin."

"May I ask how much money you have altogether?"

With true Scottish thrift, Flora had saved sixty pounds from her wages, amounting to three hundred Canadian dollars. "After I purchase your scrip, I will have one hundred and forty dollars." She heard the satisfaction in her own voice. It sounded like a small fortune.

But the nurse was shaking her head. "Oh, my dear. I'm afraid that won't be enough. You must build a house; that's one of the requirements for proving up. You need to buy tools and equipment and horses. And although you're strong and healthy, you can't do the hard labour alone. Even a single man needs an extra pair of hands to get started."

Flora's spirits plunged again. "How much money would I need?"

"Let me think." While the nurse made her calculations, a heavy cloud drifted over the sun and cast them into shadow. A chilly breeze whistled across the open prairie, and the gooseflesh rose on Flora's arms.

"If you had another five hundred dollars, you could probably scrape by."

Flora's tiny flame of optimism flickered and almost died. But she had one last hope, the treasure sewn into her petticoat.

After dropping off the rented buggy in Airdrie, the two women boarded the northbound train. When it pulled into Red Deer, Flora was struck again with the raw newness of this country. No stately hall or steepled church marked the centre of the community. The main street was nothing more than a wide dirt road lined with wooden boardwalks, precisely intersected with other dirt roads that simply disappeared into the horizon.

However, this brash young settlement was obviously booming. Wagons, buggies, and riders on horseback jockeyed for position on the main road, Ross Avenue. An oddly shaped structure that the nurse called an elevator stood beside the station, storing grain to be shipped to market. Boxes and bundles were piled on the platform, even a wicker basket filled with clucking hens.

As they walked along the street to the Alexandra Hotel, a simple two-storey brick rectangle, a whirlwind forced the women to hold down their skirts. Outside the front door, Flora removed her hat to shake out the dust. Lydia Prince had given her a man's brown felt hat with a wide brim and draped it with mesh mosquito netting that passed for a veil. Flora re-pinned her hat onto her coronet of braids and arranged the veil to hide her bruised face.

"Goodbye, Miss Craigie. I'll be here tomorrow morning to learn your fate." Nurse Godwin shook her hand and strode away, Rags at her heels.

Flora limped up the steps into the lobby and requested a room. From where she stood, she could see through the arched doorway into the long, narrow dining room lined with flocked wallpaper and lit with a fringed glass chandelier. A man wearing a fedora sat at the front window, reading a newspaper. Flora experienced a jolt of fear before she realised he looked nothing like Hector. Nevertheless, she requested that dinner be sent to her room.

That night Flora was wakeful, wracked with reservations, her confidence ebbing and flowing with the force of the North Sea tide. Should she abandon this wild notion and return to Scotland? Perhaps she should sail for England instead, lose herself in the sooty metropolis of London. But what could she do there, except work as a servant?

Finally, she tossed aside her covers and groped her way to the window. The glass panes were as dark as the walls. The overcast sky obscured the stars. Red Deer had not yet installed streetlamps and no light was visible, not even the flicker of a candle. She held her hand inches from her face but could see nought. She was invisible even to herself.

Yet as she stood there, an insignificant wraith in the night, Flora recalled the nurse's encouraging words and a warm glow ignited in her breast. Nurse Godwin believed that she was capable of homesteading. Here was a woman who had indeed gone against the tide, all the way to South Africa and back into the western wilderness. They might be as rare as freshwater pearls, but such women existed.

Flora wasn't sure if she were one of them, but there was only one way to find out.

After choking down a hasty breakfast of tea and toast, Flora dressed in her tweed suit, sponged and mended following its encounter with the ditch; donned her hat and veil; and limped along the boardwalk to a two-storey frame building. Above the storefront on the main floor were twin windows hung with lace curtains that indicated living quarters, not unlike the building where Flora had spent her childhood. An oversized replica of a pocket watch hung from a swing-ing metal sign that read HAROLD J. SNELL: WATCHMAKER, JEWELLER, OPTICIAN.

Flora pushed open the door. Ticking timepieces of every size and shape covered the walls. An ornate grandfather clock stood in the centre of the room, and a row of gramophones with polished brass speakers shaped like trumpets lined one wall. Glass cases shimmered with sets of silverware and fine china, watches, and jewellery.

Behind the counter was a young man in a blue suit. His tawny hair was freshly cut, his face and neck burned red by the sun. The skin on his nose was peeling. "Good day to you, madam. May I help you?"

Flora was taken aback to recognise his familiar Scottish accent. "Happen you can. I want to speak to the owner, please."

The young man came around the counter and offered his hand. "Mr. Snell is busy just the noo. I'm Alexander Mitchell. Do I detect a wee hint of the heather in your speech?"

"Aye," Flora said. "I've come from Aberdeen. My name is Flora Craigie." She bit her lip, annoyed with herself for once again using her real name. She could have at least called herself Flossie, a childhood nickname, or used her middle name, May. Well, it was too late now.

"Aberdeen, is it! And my hame is in Auchenblae, not thirty miles away!"

Flora smiled under her veil. Thirty miles was a great distance in Scotland, but here it seemed no more than the toss of a caber. "What brought you here, Mr. Mitchell?"

"I finished my seven-year jewellery apprenticeship last month and set out to make my fortune in Canada. This is my first week on the job. What do you need, Miss Craigie? Perhaps a set of china, or a silver teapot?"

"Nay, thank you kindly. I'm here because I have something to sell."

"I'll fetch Mr. Snell. He does purchase items from time to time, mostly watches or wedding rings. Some newcomers lack the funds to go on with, you see. I'll be back in a tick. That's what we say in our business." He laughed at his own joke and passed through a doorway behind the counter, hung with a heavy brocade curtain.

In a moment Mr. Snell emerged from the back room, a jeweller's loupe on his forehead. He frowned when he saw Flora's veil, no doubt wondering why she was concealing her face. She was glad he couldn't see it. This morning her cheekbone was yellow edged with green, like an unripe plum.

"Good morning. I understand you have something to sell?"

Flora pulled off her white cambric gloves, one fingertip at a time. She drew a piece of black velvet from her reticule and laid it on the counter, smoothing it flat before reaching for a small leather pouch. She removed an object from the pouch and burnished it between her warm palms to make it shine before laying it reverently on the fabric.

It was a beautiful thing, large and lustrous against the velvet, slightly heart-shaped, gleaming with a pale pink colour as if blushing at its sudden exposure to the morning light.

Mr. Snell did not seem particularly impressed. "And what is this item?"

"It's a freshwater pearl."

He didn't bother to examine it before shaking his head. "I'm sorry, that's not the sort of thing we carry here. I have no idea how to value it, and the market would be limited."

For one awful moment, Flora feared she might burst into tears. She swallowed hard, thankful her face was covered.

"If you will excuse me, madam, I'm in the midst of a difficult watch repair. Good day to you." Mr. Snell nodded to Flora and disappeared behind the curtain.

As Flora reached for the pearl, speechless with disappointment, the young man spoke. "Before you put it away, Miss Craigie, may I take a gander?"

He pulled a magnifying glass from below the counter and bent to examine the pearl, turning it in his fingers and studying it from all sides. "It's an excellent specimen. Where did it come from?"

"It belonged to my father." Flora repeated the story he had told her. Years ago, the daughter of a local pearl diver was dying in great pain. Since the diver couldn't pay for a doctor, her father gave him a bottle of laudanum to ease the little girl's suffering. A few months later, the diver returned to the shop and repaid his debt by presenting his benefactor with this pearl that he had pulled from the River Oykel.

"That's a grand story, and a lovely thing to own." He gave the pearl a lingering caress before setting down the magnifying glass. "I'm verra sorry to disappoint you, but Mr. Snell has the last word. I don't know the local clientele like he does."

Not trusting herself to speak, Flora picked up her treasure and placed it back in the pouch. "Thank you for your time," she managed to whisper before leaving the store.

Flora set off toward the hotel, heedless of her surroundings. Her ankle burned and she stopped to rest for a moment, leaning against the nearest rough wooden wall as she remembered her father's last words.

She hadn't even been aware of the pearl's existence until he lay dying of Bright's disease. One evening, after she had spooned fish soup into his mouth and washed his grey face, he presented her with the leather pouch.

"Flora, it's a hard life for a lass. I've nay much to leave you, and you'll have to work for your bread until you can find a husband. I want you to have this. It's your dowry, and I pray to our Heavenly Father that it will help you attract a man of means."

Flora knew the gem was valuable. She had watched the divers, men and women and children, wade into the local waters day after day with their forked sticks and glass-bottomed jugs, forcing open the twisted black mussel shells that lined the riverbeds. Perhaps only one in ten thousand shells held the glossy treasure, and few were the size of this one.

Flora hadn't replaced her gloves, and now she plucked her pearl out of the pouch again. It felt hot in her throbbing palm, like a tiny beating heart. This was her treasure, her talisman, the only thing of value that she owned. Yet in this foreign place it was as worthless as a pebble on the beach.

Could she take the train back to Calgary and sell it there? That bustling city was filled with men of wealth and purpose. Surely she could find a buyer among them, a gentleman who would like to transform this lovely gem into a ring or locket for his wife.

Then she gave an involuntary shudder as she dismissed the idea of returning to the first city where Hector would search for her. Her time would be better spent running for her life. With a groan Flora straightened up and began to walk again, her ankle more painful than before. She wanted nothing more than to lie face down on her hotel bed and weep with frustration.

She had almost reached her destination when she heard a shout.

"Miss Craigie!"

She turned to see young Mr. Mitchell running down the boardwalk toward her. He was panting with exertion but grinning all over his red face. He caught up with her, pausing to catch his breath before he spoke.

"I mustered my courage and had a chat with my employer. You see, Mr. Snell was unaware of the value of freshwater pearls until I explained it to him. He was quite impressed to learn that the Crown of Scotland at Edinburgh Castle is adorned with them, and that Queen Victoria herself had a weakness for Scottish pearls. I convinced him that yours is a particularly fine example."

Flora squeezed the pearl in her fist as she waited.

"It's true there is little market here for such an item, but I assured Mr. Snell that my former employers in Scotland would be happy to purchase it for a tidy sum."

Flora swallowed, trying to control the tremor in her voice. "Does that mean . . . Are you saying that Mr. Snell is prepared to make me an offer?"

The young man sounded apologetic. "Well, I wouldna want to raise your hopes entirely. He won't give you what it's worth, in my opinion."

Four horses pulling a wagon trotted past, raising a cloud of dust that almost obscured Mr. Mitchell's shiny red face. He took out his handkerchief and wiped his brow before he spoke again. Flora had been holding her breath so long that she felt faint.

Her hand clenched the pearl more tightly than any mussel shell. In the back of her mind, she was screaming: five hundred dollars, five hundred dollars, please make it five hundred dollars!

"Would you be willing to take six hundred dollars?"

CHAPTER FOUR

That night, Flora knelt beside the bed in her hotel room and prayed that her father would forgive her for using her dowry not to find a husband, but to lose one.

She scrambled under the covers and pulled them up to her chin, shivering at the thought of Hector's rage when he had found she was missing. Then she chastised herself for her own weakness. This blind fear was clouding her judgment. She must force herself to think rationally about what steps he would take. Her very survival might depend on it.

The Pacific Express travelled through the night from Calgary to Banff, Laggan, Field, Golden, Glacier, and Revelstoke, where it stopped for breakfast. Hopefully Hector had remained asleep until the next morning. He might have wasted an hour or two searching the train. Once he realised she wasn't aboard, he would likely telegraph down the line to discover where she had disembarked. And there would be no word, no sign of her.

Flora was positive that Hector would continue his journey. Three days after arriving at the coast, he was scheduled to meet with his employers at the Hotel Vancouver, one of the luxurious railway hotels springing up across Canada to shelter wealthy travellers. "William Van Horne, the Chairman of the Board himself, will be there!" Hector had told her more than once, rubbing his palms together.

Hector had praised this paragon so often that Flora had almost tired of hearing about him. The man was larger than life in every sense of the word, a transplanted American with a ferocious drive to succeed and a staggering abundance of energy. He enjoyed the biggest and the best of everything. His art collection was the foremost in Canada. He played the violin like a maestro. He had not only built the transcontinental railway, but designed a string of palatial hotels along its route, their magnificence rivalling the castles of Europe; and founded a line of steamships that crossed both the Pacific and the Atlantic Oceans.

Not even for a missing wife would Hector relinquish his opportunity to meet this captain of industry. But after the meeting, what then?

She reflected that Hector didn't know her very well. During their brief courtship he had talked only about himself, heedless of Flora's own hopes and dreams. Although she was too inexperienced to judge, she suspected that most wives understood their husbands more fully than the reverse.

However, fathoming your spouse's nature took some time, and time was what Flora had lacked. She had failed to discern his true character until it was too late. With her own highly developed sense of right and wrong, Flora's discovery that her new husband was prepared to lie and cheat to make his way in the world was the most shattering blow she had ever experienced.

But she knew exactly why Hector was so keen to marry her. He had been told by his employers in no uncertain terms that marriage would benefit his career. Van Horne was a devoted family man, and he made it clear that he wanted to build his railway empire with the help of others like him.

"You're exactly what I'm looking for," Hector told her, counting Flora's assets on his fingers, "single, attractive, educated, no family ties, and willing to emigrate." He beamed as if he had paid her a tremendous compliment. It had never occurred to him to ask why she wanted to marry him.

However, his ignorance of Flora's own motives could work in her favour. Hopefully he would conclude that she was too timid to stay in a strange country alone and would head straight back to Scotland. He might board the eastbound train, checking every stop between Vancouver and Calgary. If he continued his search all the way back to Montreal, that would buy her some time. Perhaps he would review the departure lists of passengers sailing to Britain, and eventually realise that her name wasn't present.

What if he reported her as a missing person to the Royal North-West Mounted Police? Aware of Hector's massive ego, Flora thought that would be a last resort. Her disappearance might be made public, and Hector would hate to admit that his new bride had deserted him. Still, she couldn't be sure.

For a moment she toyed with the notion that he might assume she had plunged off the train to her death somewhere in the Rocky Mountains, but quickly realised that was wishful thinking. He probably wouldn't be satisfied until he laid eyes on her lifeless body.

Flora well knew that Hector wasn't a man to give up easily. It wasn't until after the wedding ceremony that her new husband told her what she immediately recognised was a cautionary tale. A barking dog had kept him awake while he was on a business trip in Glasgow. He had spent the next day combing the neighbourhood, searching for the dog—and when he found it, he had kicked it so hard that he broke the poor animal's ribs. He grinned with satisfaction as he watched her horrified reaction, his deceptively innocent blue eyes alight with revenge.

Flora's own ribs now ached in sympathy with the dog. She moaned and pulled the blankets around her chin, determined to leave Red Deer as soon as possible. She estimated that it would take Hector fourteen days to exhaust all the obvious choices. It was nine days since she had jumped from the train. She must get away from these busy rail line settlements and lose herself in the open countryside while there was time.

Before she fell into a fitful sleep, she remembered what Nurse Godwin had said about Hector's illness, that syphilis was sometimes fatal. She moaned again, aghast at her own thoughts. She refused to wish for anyone's death, even Hector's.

But perhaps it wasn't unchristian to hope that his poor health might delay the search.

The morning air was heavy with the green fragrance of spring, enriched by the smell of fresh horse manure steaming in the dirt, as Flora and Nurse Godwin walked down the main street. Every living thing was in motion. Shopkeepers were sweeping the boardwalk outside their front doors, washing their windows, arranging their wares. A boy ran past them, late for school, his books tied with a leather strap. Riders waved and hallooed to each other, and even the horses tossed their heads and kicked up their heels.

The most attractive structure on the street was the flat-topped two-storey Greene building, constructed of pale golden sandstone and featuring Italianate arched windows. On the ground floor was the Merchants Bank, where Flora changed her pounds into Canadian dollars before they mounted the narrow wooden stairs to George Greene's law office.

The paperwork didn't take long. Mr. Greene prepared a bill of sale transferring ownership of the South African Scrip Coupon to Flora, and she counted her unfamiliar cash three times before handing it over. Flora May Craigie was now the proud owner—not of land, not yet—of a coupon entitling her to file a homestead claim on three hundred and twenty acres.

Mr. Greene's expression was kind. "If you don't mind my asking, Miss Craigie, where are you planning to file your claim?"

"I'm not sure." She tucked the coupon into her reticule and buttoned it. "I understand that the staff at the Dominion Lands Office may assist me."

He leaned back in his chair. "Allow me to offer you a little advice. I don't believe you should trust the clerks to choose the best land for you."

Flora's confidence retreated once again. How was she to leap this next hurdle without the faintest idea of what she was doing? She clutched her reticule, wondering whether she had made a terrible mistake.

The lawyer swivelled in his chair and observed the bustling street below. "Did you ladies know that one million settlers have already arrived in the west? Red Deer has recorded a higher number of land claims than any other office in the country. Unfortunately, that means many of the best homesteads are taken."

He reflected for a moment. "I understand why you might wish to remain close to town, Miss Craigie, but if you are prepared to go farther afield—"

Flora leaned forward so abruptly that she nearly fell off her chair. "Believe me, Mr. Greene, I'm quite willing to go anywhere."

"In that case, I hear that excellent land is available east of Lacombe."

"La-COMB." Flora repeated the unfamiliar word. "Where is that, please?"

"Take the train twenty miles north to the next station. From Lacombe, the route eastward is by horseback or wagon, along the Buffalo Lake Trail. The lands office staff can tell you which quarters are available."

Flora smiled. "I'm verra grateful, Mr. Greene. I shall take your advice."

Back on the street, Nurse Godwin extended her hand. "Best of British luck, as they say! Miss Craigie, please write to me care of the hospital, and tell me how you are getting on."

"Goodbye, Nurse Godwin." Flora gripped the nurse's hand. She wanted to embrace her but feared that would be overly familiar. "Ach, how can I ever thank you?"

"You can thank me by proving up. And by the way, Miss Craigie, we nurses are accustomed to hearing personal confessions. I sincerely hope that a certain gentleman never comes looking for you, but if he does . . . rest assured, my dear, that your secret is safe with me."

Flora dared not waste another hour. It was imperative to file her claim and get out of town. She hurried down the street to the Dominion Lands Office with all the speed her ankle would bear. As the lawyer had warned, a long queue of men was already waiting outside the double doors of the three-storey brick building. They were a motley collection, young and old, some wearing suits, others in scruffy work clothes.

One lone woman was conspicuous in the middle of the line, a curly-haired bairn in her arms. A scrawny lad stood beside her, and a lass with braids clung to her skirt. Flora gave the woman a curious glance. She must be waiting for her husband.

As Flora walked to the rear, the men either ignored her or stared, although a couple of them doffed their hats. Flora took her place behind a youth wearing a striking outfit: a black woollen shirt with pearl buttons, a purple silk bandana knotted around his neck, and a pair of leather chaps buckled over his trousers. On his head was an oversized white Stetson with a towering crown, the brim turned up at the front, tied under his chin with leather laces. Even in his high-heeled boots, adorned with chased silver spurs, he was shorter than Flora.

She assumed he must be holding someone's place, since he was obviously too young to claim a homestead. The minimum age was eighteen. The youth touched the brim of his huge hat, and she nodded in return. A man with a handlebar moustache stepped up behind Flora and growled, "These men are waiting for homesteads."

"So am I," she said.

He mumbled something unintelligible.

Flora settled herself to wait, putting most of her weight on her good foot.

The men at the front went through the doors, sometimes two or three at once, and emerged smiling and jubilant. The sun grew hotter and the line grew longer, snaking down the block and out of sight. Flora fidgeted and shifted on her throbbing ankle. She saw the young lad who had been standing with his mother walking down the line toward her. When he reached Flora, he stopped. "Please, ma'am, are you willing to help my ma for a few minutes?"

She hesitated, reluctant to lose her place.

"You step right along," said the man behind her.

Flora was afraid he wouldn't let her back into line. She was opening her mouth to refuse when the youth in the white hat spoke. "Don't worry, ma'am, I'll hold your spot."

Flora hurried up to the woman, anxious to finish the task, whatever it was. The baby was howling. "Thank you, my dear, for coming to my aid," the woman said in a musical accent, which Flora recognised at once as Welsh. "It's time to nurse my babby."

She darted a glance at the burly man behind her and lowered her voice. "I can't leave the other children alone or they'll be pushed aside. Will you be kind enough to stop here for ten minutes? I'll come back as quickly as I can."

"Aye, but please hurry." The woman darted around a corner of the building.

Flora stared at the boy and the girl, and they stared back at her. Since becoming an adult, her life had been remarkably untouched by children, and she had no idea how to talk to them. However, she felt obliged to say something.

"I believe you must be Welsh, am I correct?"

The boy answered. "Yes, ma'am. We're from Swansea."

"And, er, where is your father?"

"He died last year in an accident, down the mine."

"I'm very sorry to hear that. How old are you?"

"Eleven last week." Flora was no judge of children's ages, but she had assumed he was much younger.

"And your sisters?"

"Nellie here is almost nine, and baby Jewel is six months. My name is Jack Penrose."

Although widows with children were allowed to homestead, it seemed the height of folly to do so with children so young, one of them still at the breast. Whatever was this poor misguided woman thinking? About fifteen minutes later she scurried back, a sleepy baby draped over her shoulder.

"Ta ever so much," she said. "My name is Margaret Penrose. My friends call me Peggy."

Flora didn't presume they were friends. "How do you do, Mrs. Penrose? I'm Flora Craigie." The two women shook hands.

"Are you here with your husband?" Mrs. Penrose asked.

"Nay, I purchased South African Scrip for three hundred and twenty acres."

Her eyes widened. "You're that fortunate! Two whole quarters! Where do you mean to stake your claim?"

"I'm not sure, but I've been told there's good land east of Lacombe."

"That's where I'm headed! If you file next to me, we could give each other a hand."

Flora studied her. A slight woman, with wispy fair hair straggling from under her sunbonnet, she didn't look strong enough to peg a load of wet sheets on the line, let alone manage a homestead. Flora had no intention of hitching her wagon to this funny little Welsh woman with her working-class accent and her gaggle of children. They probably wouldn't last a month.

"Have you already selected your quarter?" she asked, silently vowing to stay well away from them.

"I have indeed." Mrs. Penrose pulled a piece of paper from her bag. "I hired a land locater, and he showed me where to file."

Flora had heard of land locaters from Hector. He found it hilarious that one of them had shown the same quarter to ten different men and collected a dollar from each of them, although the quarter had already been claimed months earlier.

"Can you trust him?" she asked, feeling new sympathy for this simple soul.

The widow lifted her chin. "I'm not that gormless, Miss Craigie. The man came with good references. We spent two days driving around the area, and I chose the perfect spot."

"Where is it?"

"Ten miles east of Lacombe. Mr. Cook told me that's farther from town than most people want, but it's a flat piece with a creek running through it and plenty of bush. That's what you want: fresh water, and trees for firewood and fences. Oh, it's a lovely piece of land. And the one next to it is every bit as nice."

Apparently the little widow already knew more about homesteading than she did, Flora thought, which wasn't surprising. Her ignorance settled on her shoulders like a lead weight.

"I'll make a note for you," Mrs. Penrose said. "Every quarter is marked with an iron stake, flattened on the top, and the land description is chiselled right into the metal so there can't be any mistake. They're Roman numerals—trust the government to make it complicated—but I copied them ever so carefully, and Mr. Cook translated them into plain English."

She pulled a pencil stub from her bag and tore a corner off the paper, scribbling three numbers: the section, township, and range. "Make sure you file on the two quarters bordering mine to the south. Hopefully they haven't taken up yet."

"Well. I'll find out what's available. Thank you for the suggestion."

Flora took the note, said goodbye without glancing at the children, and hurried away. To her relief, the young man tipped his big white hat and ushered her into place. She heard a mutter of disapproval from behind.

At last, the Penrose party mounted the steps. They were inside for a long time, but when they emerged, the widow was beaming. They headed toward Flora.

"Dear Lord, that man grilled me as if I were an enemy spy! He only signed my certificate because Jewel started to fuss. We'll be on the morning train to Lacombe, if you want to come along."

A stiff breeze fluttered the brim of her sunbonnet. Holding it down with one hand and clutching baby Jewel with the other, Mrs. Penrose bustled off, the other children close behind. Flora held the scrap of paper bearing the land description, and she noticed the man behind her craning his neck, trying to see it. She crumpled it into a ball and shoved it into her reticule. She would toss it away later.

The line ahead grew shorter and the hot sunshine beat down on Flora's felt hat. She drew a handkerchief from her sleeve and blotted the perspiration from her forehead beneath her veil. Finally, the boy in the white hat mounted the steps and went inside. Five minutes later, he came out empty-handed and walked away, his head hanging.

It was Flora's turn. She stamped her good foot to bring back the circulation, limped up the steps, and pushed open the double doors. The sunlight shone dimly through the dusty windows, and she blinked to adjust her vision after the bright glare outside. The room smelled of dry paper and fresh ink. Oak filing cabinets with brass drawer pulls lined the walls, and a raised counter divided the room. Five clerks stood behind it, four of them engaged in conversation with customers.

The fifth man beckoned to her. He wore a brown woollen suit and a white shirt with a high collar. Like almost every man in Canada old enough to grow whiskers, he sported a full glossy moustache. He raised his eyebrows when she handed him her scrip coupon. "Where did you get this?"

"I purchased it from a Boer War veteran."

"I need to see proof of that."

Flora drew out her bill of sale and presented it to him. He studied it closely before picking up a magnifying glass and examining the signatures and the seal. He wet the tip of his forefinger and tested the dried ink. "You're welcome to contact the lawyer if you don't believe me," Flora said. "Mr. George Greene drew it up this verra morning."

"Wait here," he said. Carrying both the bill of sale and the scrip coupon, he went into the glass-fronted office behind him where another man was seated. The gold lettering on the door identified him as the Registrar. A lengthy discussion ensued, as they examined the paperwork and glanced toward Flora through the glass.

The registrar made some remark to his clerk, and both were laughing as he returned to the counter. Without speaking, he pointed to the map spread out before them. It was composed of tiny squares and looked like a jumbled crossword puzzle. Flora bent over it, hoping she could decipher its meaning.

Western Canada was surveyed in a grid pattern, with townships of thirty-six sections, each measuring one square mile and containing six hundred and forty acres. These were further divided into four smaller squares called quarters, measuring one-quarter mile on each of the four sides, amounting to one hundred and sixty acres.

Flora could see that the red squares were thickest around settlements, and grew increasingly sparse with the distance from civilization. "The quarters shaded with red pencil have already been claimed," the clerk said. "Those crossed out with an X belong to the railway company or are set aside for schools."

This system seemed perfectly logical on paper. But what made it so difficult for the observer, Flora thought, was the fact that the patchwork of geometrically perfect squares had been laid down without regard for climate, topography, or soil quality.

"This would suit you," the clerk said, indicating a piece of property west of Red Deer, bumping against the foothills of the Rocky Mountains. Flora had overheard the men behind her talking about how the western reaches would be the last taken up, because of their uneven terrain and distance from the railway.

"I would prefer something east of Lacombe," she said.

"These two quarters haven't been claimed yet." He pointed to the map again.

Flora studied it. "Aren't they covered with lochs?" She could see the irregular bodies of water outlined in blue ink, leaving little space around them.

He didn't answer. "Here's another empty pair." This time, he tapped a spot to the north, closer to Edmonton than Lacombe.

The man was being deliberately obstructive. Unless she could provide him with a land description, she was at his mercy. She pretended to study the map, but she was so distraught that the squares blurred before her eyes. The clerk drummed his fingers and looked pointedly at the clock hanging on the wall.

Flora unbuttoned her reticule and withdrew the crumpled paper that Mrs. Penrose had given her. "What about here?" She smoothed it out and read the numbers aloud.

His fingertip traced a straight line east of Lacombe and came to a stop. To her relief, those two quarters were blank, surrounded on three sides by red squares. One of them must belong to the widow Penrose.

The clerk pulled a leather-bound ledger toward him and consulted it before heaving an ostentatious sigh. He dipped his fountain pen into his ink bottle and passed it to her, together with a blank certificate titled "Application for Entry for a Homestead."

With great care, she printed her name, Flora May Craigie. This was a gamble, but other than her marriage licence, the only identification papers she owned carried her maiden name. She noted her last address, previous occupation, and country of birth. She affirmed she was a British subject. She filled in the date: May 9, 1905. Finally, she signed her name, rounding her letters so deliberately that her signature resembled a child's handwriting.

"That will be ten dollars." He took her crisp new salmon-coloured ten-dollar bill and put it into a cash box. A revolving wheel held several rubber stamps with wooden handles. He selected a stamp, inked it, and banged it onto the certificate as though he were killing an insect. He initialled the paper, studied it for a long moment, and held it out. Yet when her fingers closed on it, he refused to relinquish his grasp.

For a few seconds, they froze in a brief tug-of-war. Flora yanked the paper so hard she was afraid it might rip in two. The man opened his mouth and shut it again. He released the application and stepped back, shaking his head. Flora heard him utter one word under his breath. "Landgrabber!"

She didn't know what that meant, but she could guess it was derogatory. She gave him a withering look through her veil. Frankly, she didn't care what names he called her. She had her Homestead Application at last.

Flora stepped outside into the hot sunshine, clasping the precious paper to her breast. She was glad of the veil then, because it hid her tears. She didn't want to be seen in public greeting like a babe.

CHAPTER FIVE

Not until the wagon was bouncing along the rugged Buffalo Lake Trail did the land locater inform Flora and Mrs. Penrose about their neighbours. "I have a fine surprise for you!" Matthew Cook said. He was a gnomish creature, with sandy hair that rose from his scalp in spikes. His grin was a snowy crescent in a face as bronze as a polished saddle. "I'll bet you never imagined that the neighbours right next to Miss Craigie would be two ladies, just as genteel as yourselves!"

"Ladies!" Mrs. Penrose and Flora exclaimed in unison. They were perched on the high wooden seat, one on each side of him. Jewel lay sleeping on her mother's lap, while the other two children sat in the wagon box behind them.

"Yep, it was all part of my plan." He winked and tapped his finger alongside his nose, like a character in a Dickens novel. "That's why I kept this property under my hat. I was waiting for the right person to come along. Believe me, some of the oddballs I seen out here would make you fear for your life and limb! When Mrs. Penrose happened along, I knew it was Providence. Now all you ladies can keep each other company!"

Flora inwardly lamented this unwelcome information, although the jovial

Mr. Cook obviously believed he had done them a great favour. Not only would she have the Penrose brood on one side, but two strange women on the other side. Heaven knows what Mr. Cook defined as genteel ladies. Back home, the daughter of a respected chemist would barely have a nodding acquaintance with a coal miner's widow. However, there appeared to be little adherence to class in this new country.

Flora told herself that she wasn't an elitist, but she had nothing in common with Mrs. Penrose. And she wasn't interested in associating with other women, no matter how refined. She didn't want to be blethering and exchanging recipes and having tea parties. She wanted to be homesteading.

Moreover, Flora suspected that Mrs. Penrose would need her help with the children, and that was something she absolutely would not do. She glanced back at them. At least they didn't natter and shout and flail about like other children.

"Mr. Cook, who are these neighbours?" Mrs. Penrose asked, leaning forward. "What do you know about them?"

"I haven't made their acquaintance myself, but they're a little older than you young ladies. They come from down in the States somewheres. They aren't homesteaders, so they don't have to prove nothing to nobody. They must have money of their own, because they bought their quarter outright from the last farmer. His wife give up the ghost and went back east, so he pulled out. Anyhoo, they arrived last year and built a real nice house. They're raising chickens. Folks call them the Chicken Ladies."

"Chickens!" Mrs. Penrose and Flora said in unison once again, like a comedic duo.

"It ain't such a far-fetched notion. There's a market for hen fruit around here. Most bachelors buy them, and the general store sells eggs to those who don't want the bother of poultry."

Mr. Cook reached inside his lapel to scratch his chest. He wore an unusual garment, a jacket woven from native grass. He did so, he had informed them, to demonstrate what grew on this fertile land—the grass so heavy it could be woven into fabric. It looked extremely uncomfortable. "You won't meet them for a whiles yet, because their hired hand took them into Calgary. They visit the big smoke once or twice a year, keeps them from getting bushed."

"Whatever do you mean?" asked Mrs. Penrose.

"Happens when people spend too much time alone, they start to lose their faculties. First comes the loneliness, and then they start talking to themselves and seeing things that aren't there. When they get to that sorry state, the Mounties take them away. It seems to affect womenfolk the worst. I got six daughters myself, so I reckon I understand the need for female company. That's another reason I put you ladies together."

Flora was silent as she thought about this. She had never experienced a single day in her life without speaking to another human being. What if she became bushed? Which faculties would she lose first? Perhaps there might be some advantage to having neighbours after all—especially when she viewed her surroundings.

The landscape unrolled before them like an endless bolt of coarsely woven cloth. Nestled between the sloping hills were small bodies of shining water that Mr. Cook called sloughs, but he pronounced them slews. He continued to enlighten his listeners.

"A lot of newcomers prefer the bald prairie, where it's so doggone flat you can see an antelope's tail bobbing five miles off. But this ain't prairie, this here is parkland." Flora, whose idea of parkland was manicured lawns, looked at him sideways.

Mr. Cook waved his whip around his head. "I'm dead serious, Miss Craigie! You have everything here a man could want, or a woman. Fresh water flowing from the ground, grass as high as your stirrups, and trees to shelter you from winter's blast. This here is God's country."

Just then, one wheel dropped into a pothole with such force that they were nearly knocked off their perch, and Flora bit her tongue.

"It's unfortunate God didn't provide anything like a road in his country," Mrs. Penrose said dryly.

"It's rough going, especially during the spring thaw. Bushwhackers cleared this trail with axes in the olden days, must be a good twenty years ago now. The trail runs all the way to Buffalo Lake, so-called because it's shaped like a buffalo hide stretched out to dry. Don't you worry none, the trail's a lot easier between your place and Toddsville. That's where you'll go to get your necessities."

"Well, that's one blessing," Mrs. Penrose said.

"Joseph and Cynthia Todd come up from Michigan a few years ago with their five daughters in a prairie schooner, that's a covered wagon. He's a far-sighted man who had part of his homestead surveyed for a town site."

"Is Toddsville a large town?" Flora asked.

"I wouldn't call it a town just yet, but I guess it's going to stay put. Some places spring up and disappear almost overnight. One settlement already had twenty buildings when the railway came through five miles away. Folks picked up their houses and hauled them to the new site. This one old gal refused to budge, so they hitched up the team and put the whole shack on skids, with her inside. She boiled the kettle and made tea on the stove while she was riding along to her new home!" Mr. Cook threw back his head and laughed. The story was so unbelievable that Flora assumed he must be jesting.

A small bird with two black bands around its white breast flew across their path. "That's a killdeer, makes a sound like its name." Mr. Cook gave a shrill cry that startled the horses, and it took him a minute to get them under control again.

The wagon now approached a mudhole so wide that tree trunks had been laid side by side across the muskeg to form a platform. The wagon wheels lurched and banged over the logs while everyone gripped the sides of the wagon.

"That's why you always carry an axe, in case you need to cut down a few trees and build a corduroy road." Mr. Cook turned and spoke to the children in the back. "They're called riprap roads, that's the sound they make when the wheels roll over them."

If he hoped to get a smile out of them, he was mistaken. Nellie and Jack stared around with unblinking interest. Another bird, this one fat and speckled, fluttered up from the grass. "That there was a prairie chicken," Mr. Cook told them. "Anybody who can shoot will never go hungry in these parts. This young man needs his own twenty-two, that's for darn sure."

"What's a twenty-two?" Mrs. Penrose asked.

"Twenty-two calibre, ma'am. It's a nice light rifle, perfect for him." From the corner of her eye, Flora saw Jack's delighted grin.

The horses dragged the wagon up a long incline, and they emerged with a view that stretched for miles. Mr. Cook drew the team to a halt. From here they could see not only the full sweep of the landscape, but a few scattered remnants of human encroachment—rectangles of weeds, still showing the marks of a plough; two or three decrepit shacks like stars floating in an empty galaxy. A trail of smoke arising from one or two of these lonely dwellings showed they were inhabited, but this was no source of comfort. Flora made an involuntary sound of dismay. Mr. Cook misunderstood her reaction and grinned at her.

"Pretty country, ain't it? The land out here is nigh empty except for Percy Buckhorn, he lives three miles south of your place. He's considered an old-timer around these parts. He come up from Montana on the Fort Benton trail and headed to the Klondike, looking for gold. He didn't find the motherlode, so he stopped here on his way home ten years ago and stuck fast. They call him Sourdough because he never has a smile on his danged old face."

He scratched his armpit with one hand, clucked at the horses, and they went on. The wagon began a gentle downgrade. Other, fainter trails were visible, meandering around sloughs and clumps of trees, crisscrossing the Buffalo

Lake Trail and braiding each other. Mr. Cook told them that these paths ran between impassable creeks and abandoned homesteads.

They approached one derelict cabin now, the door hanging open, bearing a crudely lettered sign: HAVE GIVE UP THE STRUGGLE. HELP YOURSELF TO ANYTHING INSIDE. Not far away stood two simple crosses made from sticks wrapped with twine. "Them two kiddies died of smallpox last month." Mr. Cook removed his faded cloth cap. "Their folks waited until the ground unfroze to bury them, and left the same day."

Mrs. Penrose gasped and hugged Jewel to her chest, while Flora said a silent prayer for their little souls. As if reading their mood, Mr. Cook spoke again, this time warningly. "Ladies, homesteading ain't for everyone. The failure rate is near fifty per cent." The two women avoided each other's eyes, but Flora knew they shared the same thought: If the odds were only even for the men, what chance did they have?

By the time he swung the team to the right, Flora was feeling bruised both in body and spirit. "This here's the fork in the trail. Your land is one mile to the south." The new track was almost invisible. Flora looked behind and saw the grass separate when the wheels passed over it, and draw together again with barely a ripple. How would they ever follow this trail in broad daylight, let alone the darkness of a prairie night?

But her fears were forgotten moments later when the wagon stopped at the summit of another long hill. "Here we are, ladies!" he said, flourishing his whip like a ringmaster. "Your land is dead ahead, Mrs. Penrose, and yours is across the creek to the south, Miss Craigie." The women craned their necks while Nellie and Jack stood up in the wagon box behind them.

Below them was a scene of breathtaking beauty. The hill descended to a flat, grassy bench dotted with bluffs of poplar and willow. Relief surged through Flora's limbs when she saw that her land consisted of a lush open space backing onto a thick wall of trees. Mrs. Penrose's claim was much the same, mixed meadow and bush. A band of sapphire water snaked between the two properties, reflecting the vivid sky overhead.

Near the southern edge of Flora's land, a sturdy clump of poplars stood on a slight rise, their white trunks streaked and spotted with black. When the breeze touched them, their branches waved a leafy welcome. Flora envisioned her own home nestled beside them, overlooking a field of golden grain.

Mrs. Penrose, too, was contemplating her land with a rapt expression. "I'll put my house there, not far from the bank." She pointed to a flat area beside the creek, about half a mile away from Flora's chosen spot. At least they wouldn't be living cheek to jowl.

The team proceeded down the hill and pulled up beside the Penrose quarter. A red bandana fluttered from an iron stake. "There you are, Mrs. Penrose, exactly as you left it."

Mr. Cook turned to Flora. "I suggest you mark your own boundaries the same way, Miss Craigie. Sometimes people wind up farming the wrong quarter altogether!"

Flora visualised the map she had viewed at the lands office. Mrs. Penrose's quarter was on the north side, Flora's two quarters lay in the middle, and to her south was the quarter belonging to the Chicken Ladies. The faint, grassy trail they were following ran along the frontage of all three farms. Flora had asked about her other neighbour, the mysterious third X bordering her property on the west, but Mr. Cook didn't know anything about him.

"Ma, may we please get down?" Jack's voice was eager.

"You may. But don't go near the creek!"

The children scrambled out of the wagon and ran through the grass, shouting with glee. Flora wanted to join them, so eager was she to see and touch her own land. She was breathless with excitement as they climbed down.

Almost immediately Nellie fell into the creek, which fortunately was shallow, and soaked herself to her waist. "I suppose you'll dry off," said Mrs.

Penrose in a resigned tone. "Give me your stockings and I'll hang them on this branch."

She set Jewel on the grass so she could wring out Nellie's stockings. The baby snatched a handful of berries from a nearby bush and crammed them into her mouth. "Jewel, don't eat those! They might be poisonous." She ran her finger inside the baby's mouth to remove the partly chewed berries.

Honestly, these children were nothing but a nuisance. "I'm going to walk over my land," Flora said, loving the sound of her own words. She jumped across the burn at a narrow place, reminding herself to call it a creek, and plunged into the deep grass. It was so thick and tangled that she had to take plunging steps to get through it, lifting her skirt up to her thighs.

She climbed onto the rise where she thought her house should be situated and revolved in place, looking at her view in all four directions. It felt so strange, and yet so familiar, too. She was standing under the same sun that shone on Scotland, on the same earth that houses us all. She unpinned her hat and lifted her face to the sky, feeling the warm breeze ruffle the hair at her temples, and experienced such a swell of optimism that she could scarcely breathe. Three hundred and twenty acres of her own. Back home, people dreamed of owning ten acres.

After revelling in her newfound satisfaction, Flora returned to where her companions were seated beside the creek. The widow was nursing Jewel, and the other children were eating bread and cheese. Mr. Cook had removed his scratchy jacket to reveal a blue cotton shirt and red suspenders. He was asleep in the shade of the wagon, his cloth cap covering his eyes.

Flora had felt sick all day with nervous anticipation. Now that she had seen the place, the relief made her ravenous. She drew out the packed lunch of biscuits and boiled eggs and dried apples provided by the hotel and ate with gusto, all thoughts of Hector forgotten, already planning where she would stake out her house and plant her garden.

Before climbing into the wagon for the long ride back to Lacombe, the two women stood together beside the cold, clear, spring-fed creek. "I'm reminded of Psalm 23," Mrs. Penrose said in a solemn voice. "'He maketh me to lie down in green pastures: he leadeth me beside the still waters.' Here we have both green pastures and still waters."

Turning to Flora, she asked, a little anxiously, "What do you think, then?"

Flora took a deep breath of the crystal air, scented with the promise of spring, and smiled. "Mrs. Penrose, I think it's the bonniest land I have ever seen."

CHAPTER SIX

The amber sunshine poured through the windows of the H. A. Day General Merchant store in Lacombe the next morning as the eager homesteaders arrived to buy their supplies. They were accompanied by Mr. Cook, who had attached himself to them like a fatherly barnacle. Flora could barely restrain her impatience. Standing at the front counter, her feet shuffled of their own accord, as if they wanted to start walking to her new home.

It didn't take long to order the familiar household items: kettle, frying pan, enamel plates and cups, cutlery, water bucket, sealing jars, tin tub, washboard, broom, washbasin and soap, coal oil lamps, candles, kerosene, and matches. Mrs. Penrose reminded Flora to buy a chamber pot. "The sooner Jewel starts using one, the better," she said. Flora flinched at the notion of dirty nappies.

The widow had one advantage over Flora: she had brought her settler's effects from Wales, two trunks crammed with linens and clothing. Since Flora possessed only the meagre contents of her valise, she selected two cotton sheets, four woollen blankets, and a pillow stuffed with straw.

She refused to waste any time buying clothes. Aside from the tweed suit, ivory silk blouse, and tartan shawl she had been wearing when she jumped from the train, her valise contained two serviceable woollen skirts, one brown and one grey; three cotton shirtwaists; her nightgown, and her underclothes. Mr. Cook insisted that she buy work boots to replace her dainty shoes, and leather gloves to protect her hands. This wardrobe would last for the summer. Beyond that, her imagination faltered.

As the store grew busier, the bell on the door tinkled every few minutes. What if Hector had already reported her missing? Would anyone recognise her description? Flora tried to hide behind Mr. Cook, hunching her shoulders and bending her knees under her skirt to make herself shorter. It was a habit she had acquired while working for the diminutive Mrs. Galt, who was unreasonably irritated by Flora's height.

She forced herself to concentrate while they ordered their grubstake, the bulk goods that would last for several months: flour, sugar, lard, salt pork, rice, potatoes, oatmeal, tins of salmon and sardines and beans, raisins and prunes, yeast and baking powder, tea and coffee, salt and pepper and spices.

"You can grow your own vegetables," said Mr. Cook, "but don't get carried away like some tenderfoot and plant them too early. The frost won't be out of the ground until June." Flora fidgeted while he selected several packages of seeds.

Since the women had only a vague notion of what tools were required, Mr. Cook chose the essentials: handsaws, hammers and nails, chisels and mallets, spades, pitchforks, and axes. Flora tried without success to picture herself using any of them.

But the most daunting purchase was yet to come. Neither woman had ever fired a gun. Flora thought she might manage a rifle, but Mrs. Penrose said grimly that she would be more likely to hit something with a shotgun. Three firearms, including a Browning shotgun, a Winchester repeating rifle for Flora, and a smaller twenty-two calibre rifle for Jack, went onto the pile.

The next stop was Fortune's Livery. The women had agreed in advance not to buy a breaking plough, since the task of driving this implement through the virgin soil was beyond their physical strength. However, they had decided to share the cost of a two-horse team and wagon, for carrying their goods and grain and themselves. Choosing the wagon was easy. Every homesteader had the same heavy wooden box with running gear underneath, spoke wheels, and a spring-loaded seat that marginally reduced the bone-jarring discomfort.

Selecting the team took longer. The stable owner produced a couple of horses that danced sideways at the sight of them. Mrs. Penrose cowered against the stall and kept the children behind her skirts, but Mr. Cook came to the rescue. "These ladies don't want any wild mustangs, nor some old nags that are on their last legs! You find them a nice team that's broke to harness and won't give them no trouble!"

When Bessie and Bob were led out, a dapple grey and a muscular bay, Flora stepped forward and patted their noses, hoping Mr. Cook would make a quick decision. He asked about their age and state of health, forcing open their rubbery lips and inspecting their teeth, before giving a curt nod. Since Flora knew how to ride, thanks to Mrs. Galt's habit of taking a turn around the park every Sunday, she had elected to buy her own saddle horse. Mercifully Mr. Cook approved of the first horse brought out, a pretty roan filly named Felicity. Mrs. Penrose said she had no intention of getting on an animal's back and would take the wagon if she needed to go somewhere.

Along with the three horses came a staggering amount of equipment: halters and harnesses and hobbles, saddle blankets, curry combs and brushes and files for their hooves, chains for dragging trees out of the bush, and a lady's saddle for Felicity. By this time, Jewel was wailing, and Flora's nerves had reached the breaking point. It was arranged that the supplies would be delivered to their homesteads on the following day.

Flora counted out her precious dollars. She had crossed the Rubicon. She no longer had enough money for a return passage to Scotland.

"They're coming; they're coming!" Jack and Nellie shouted. Four wagons appeared over the hill, silhouetted against the red dawn, each pulled by a pair of speckled Percherons and driven by two men seated on a towering load of lumber.

Mr. Cook had accompanied them to their homesteads the previous day in the new wagon, leading Felicity and his own saddle horse, Dapper. The little man seemed reluctant to leave them alone. "I can't help picturing my daughters in the same boat as you ladies," he said. "I doubt they could manage." But finally, after unharnessing the team and giving the women a few final instructions, he had departed for Lacombe.

They watched without speaking as his horse climbed the hill. At the summit, he waved his cap farewell and disappeared. When he was out of sight, Mrs. Penrose heaved a great sigh and clapped her hands. "Well, starting the work is two-thirds of it, as they say back home. Jack, Nellie, gather some dry twigs and we'll make a fire."

The women boiled the kettle for tea, and fried bacon and beans for supper, before hanging blankets from the wagon box and anchoring them with rocks in a futile attempt to protect themselves from mosquitoes. Shifting on the hard ground and slapping at the insects, the little widow told Flora her sad story.

"Alwyn, that's my husband, he worked in the pit alongside his father. His da was already old before his time, all bent over and wheezing from the dust in his lungs. When the blast happened, he couldn't run."

Her voice quavered. "Alwyn stayed behind to help him, and the roof collapsed on both of them. They were killed instantly."

The silence was broken only by the whine of mosquitoes before the widow spoke again. "The company paid me Alwyn's death benefit and his father's, too. It wasn't much, but I sold everything we owned and made a little extra. We sailed steerage to save on the fares."

Flora remembered the dark, damp hold in the ship she had travelled on, where the economy passengers were crammed together like pickled herring. At least Hector had spared her that.

"My sister told me I was daft, so did the neighbours. They were sure I would cause the deaths of myself and the children." Flora secretly sympathised with them. She didn't believe the family would last until the first snowfall.

As though noting Flora's silence, Mrs. Penrose's voice hardened in the darkness. "Nought will make me send Jack down pit. Twelve is the age they start. They leave their books and go underground, wriggling into the narrow holes where the men can't fit. It would break your heart, Miss Craigie, to see them coming home at the end of the day, their little faces blacker than pitch. God help them, Sunday is the only day of the week they feel the sunshine! When I heard there was free land in Canada, I knew it was my boy's salvation."

"What about the girls?" Flora asked.

"Jack will take care of his sisters, come what may, but I trust they'll find good husbands here. Back in Swansea, they had no choice but to marry some poor lad and sit at home worrying, along with all the other wives and mothers."

Now the men unloaded the wagons and began with Flora's shack. After placing four flat stones from the creek bed for the foundation, they built the floor, a platform of wide planks. Four walls of overlapping boards called shiplap went up next. Sheets of tarpaper—black paper impregnated with waterproof tar—covered the cracks, followed by another layer of boards. A roof, sloped to keep off the rain and snow, was finished with rough-hewn shingles.

Daylight entered this crude wooden box through two single sheets of glass in wooden frames—one beside the door, and one on the creek side. The door opened to the east because, as the foreman informed Flora, she could use the morning sunshine to warm the shack following a cold night. The hinges swung inward so the drifting snow couldn't trap her inside. Flora's eyes widened in disbelief when she heard that, but there was worse to come. "Bank up the foundation with dirt to keep your shack from blowing away," he told her. She had a vision of Dorothy, cowering in her farmhouse as a tornado whirled it into the sky.

While the roof was being shingled, two men shovelled a deep hole and erected a crude structure above it—Flora's first outdoor toilet.

Inside the shack, the men hung a single wooden bed frame from one wall on leather straps. They knocked apart a couple of packing crates and built shelves along the opposite wall. Flora carried in her three pieces of furniture, a wooden table and two chairs. The final addition was a cast-iron cookstove with a stovepipe leading through the roof.

When the stove was operable, the women opened a dozen tins of beef stew and Mrs. Penrose fried potatoes while Flora baked bannock for the hungry men. That night, the workers slept under their wagons before moving on to the Penrose house, identical except that Flora's dwelling was ten by twelve feet, and theirs was twelve by sixteen. Mrs. Penrose would share a bed with Nellie, Jack would have his own, and the baby would sleep in a hammock hung from the rafters.

By sunset on the second day, the second crude wooden structure was complete. Flora and Mrs. Penrose thanked the men, and Jewel bestowed on them one of her radiant toothless smiles.

"You're quite welcome, ladies!" the foreman said, touching his finger to his cap as he accepted their wages. "Looks like you have everything you need for the job ahead."

The women smiled, warmed by his praise.

"You should see some of the danged things we've hauled out for people—pianos, oil paintings, golf clubs, even a canary in a cage." He shook his head. "Had a feller last week who shipped his entire library from England. Three thousand books, packed in crates. But winters are long, so mebbe he knew what he was about after all."

As they approached the horses, Bessie rolled her eyes and bared her huge yellow teeth. Flora extended her arm to full length and patted the horse's nose with her fingertips, but Bessie tossed her head, forcing her to duck away. A blow from that massive skull could knock her off her feet. Both animals appeared larger and more menacing than they had in the livery stable. Flora was supposedly the expert, but she had no experience with work-horses.

The two women had watched Mr. Cook as he showed them how to harness the team, but he had done it so quickly, drawing the straps between their front legs, over their backs and around their bellies, under their tails, and then buckling together this complicated contraption, that they had lost the plot. The horses stood motionless while he worked. "They're as gentle as lambs!" he said. It wasn't clear whether he was talking about the horses or the ladies.

Flora guessed she might have better luck with Bob. She murmured to him as she fitted his bridle and slipped the bit under his large grass-stained tongue—she knew how to do that much—before heaving the padded leather oval collar over his head. Mr. Cook had explained that the collar allowed the horse to use his full strength, pushing forward with his heavily muscled forequarters rather than pulling with his neck. Attached to this collar were hames, two curved lengths of wood; and from these, leather straps called traces led back to the wagon shafts.

With Mrs. Penrose's help, Flora untangled the heavy harness and pitched it onto Bob's back. She drew one strap between his front legs, reached under his belly, and buckled it to the shorter side straps. Cautiously, she lifted his heavy tail out of the way and pulled the strap around his hindquarters. Bob stamped his hooves and Flora leaped backward, afraid he might step on her foot. Perspiration was trickling from her temples. "I think this strap is supposed to go all the way around, but it isn't long enough."

They dragged off the harness, repositioned it, and tried again. Bessie snorted, and even Bob showed the whites of his eyes.

"Go around to the other side and I'll pass the strap underneath," Mrs. Penrose suggested. "Will it reach that bit hanging down?"

It would not. They were on their third attempt, so intent on their task that they jumped and the horses shied when a voice boomed, "What the bloody hell are you doing?"

They whirled to see a mountain of a man bearing down on them, well over six feet tall and heavily built. His black beard was streaked with grey and his greasy hair hung to his shoulders. It was his expression that was the most alarming. His dark eyes positively glittered with rage. He looked capable of murdering them both, and the children as well. Flora's first thought was to run to her shack for the rifle, but it was too late.

They stood frozen while he approached with long strides and shoved Flora aside with one brawny arm.

"Gawd Almighty, I wouldn't wish the care of a cat on you people!"

His voice changed as he spoke to the horses, placing his large, dirty hands on Bob's neck. "All right, all right, calm yourselves. I don't blame you for wanting to run away."

Neither Flora nor Mrs. Penrose dared to object while this towering hulk, with a few deft moves, fastened the harness into place. When he finished and turned toward them, Mrs. Penrose clung to Flora's arm.

"I heard there was a passel of women and children living here. What the devil is the government thinking, giving land to the likes of you? It's enough to make a man sick!"

Although it was a withering experience to be shouted at, Flora stood her ground. "We have every right to be here. And we'll learn how to harness the team and everything else as well as any man. The only thing we lack is brute strength—and I do mean brute!"

He didn't answer, but stood with his fists on his hips, glaring first at Flora and then at Mrs. Penrose. He looked at the children seated on the grass and shook his head. Jewel screwed up her face and began to cry.

Flora spoke in a commanding tone, hoping not to enrage the man any further. "Thank you for harnessing the team. We don't require any further assistance."

His only response was a grunt. He spun on one enormous, booted heel and stomped across the yard to where his sorrel was waiting, the biggest riding horse Flora had ever seen. He swung himself into the saddle and rode away without a backward glance.

The two women locked eyes. Flora's knees were trembling, but she tried to pass it off as a joke. "I assume that was Sourdough Buckhorn."

She wanted to make light of his words, but she couldn't help seeing what he saw—two timid women, a skinny young boy, a little girl, and a crying baby. None of them with the least experience in this new country. What business did they have here if they couldn't even harness the team?

She looked at Mrs. Penrose. There was fear on her face, too. Both women had been filled with optimism, but it had all drained away under this man's attack. Flora had supposed that all she lacked was strength, and manpower could be bought and paid for. But what about the myriad things they had never been taught or shown because they were women?

Then Jack spoke up. "Don't worry, Mum," he said. "We can do it. I'll help you." He was standing as tall as he could, sticking out his bony chest. His mother's expression softened, and she lifted her small chin.

"Very well!" she said in a ringing tone. "Let's take a good look at this harness and memorise every strap and buckle so we know exactly how to put it on and take it off. Nellie, you watch, too. We need to practise until we can do it with our eyes shut."

That night Flora lay on the hard bench hanging from her wall while she gazed around her shack in the dusky twilight, admiring every rough-hewn inch. It was smaller than the oriental carpet in Mrs. Galt's parlour, but she had her heart's desire at last.

Her own roof over her own head. She could scarcely believe it. Flora had wanted this since the day of her father's funeral, when she had found an eviction letter tacked to the door. The Sutherlands had rented the building to another chemist. Flora had tossed the letter into the fire and sunk to her knees, weeping with grief and despair.

From that moment, her mission in life was to secure a home of her own.

The next day, she answered an advertisement for a lady's companion. A note arrived from Mrs. Euphemia Galt of Aberdeen, who was visiting friends in Dornoch. Flora spent an uncomfortable afternoon being cross-examined by the old lady, whose bright eyes scrutinised Flora's hair, bound in the tightest chignon she could manage, her shoes, her handkerchief, even her fingernails. She grilled Flora on Scottish history and asked her to read aloud from the Bible. The wages were only twenty pounds a year but included food and lodging. Three days later, they left for Aberdeen in Mrs. Galt's carriage.

Flora had never imagined living in such a grand place. Westburn House was built in the Greek Revival style and faced with white stucco, which was highly unusual in a city carved from granite. A twenty-acre park surrounded the home, landscaped with gravel walks and geometric flowerbeds.

Her new employer was a wealthy widow, the last surviving member of a newspaper family. Like all Scots, she had a keen eye for every sixpence and intended to have her money's worth from her new companion. Flora not only answered Mrs. Galt's letters and accompanied her on social calls, but weeded the kitchen garden, baked her favourite tea cakes, ironed her silk dresses, polished her extensive silver collection—in short, did everything that Mrs. Galt didn't trust the other servants to do properly. And the old lady was not a trusting person.

While she laboured, Flora reflected that Mrs. Galt's financial independence was possible only because her husband was dead. According to the cook, Mr. Galt had been a ruthless taskmaster who presented his young wife with a list of daily duties and demanded total obedience. Did his bride consider it a fair trade, Flora wondered, sacrificing her youth in return for a mansion like this one, anticipating that after his death she would have it all? Flora looked around at her opulent surroundings and thought Mrs. Galt had struck a pretty good bargain.

For six long years, she did not allow herself the smallest luxury. Lying bone-weary in her narrow bed each night, she fantasised about her "wee hoose among the heather," in the words of the popular song by music hall performer Harry Lauder. She planned it to the last detail, mentally choosing the curtains and cushions and rugs, imagining the precise location of every teacup on every shelf.

It wasn't until the seventh year approached that Flora realised her dream would never come to pass. No matter how carefully she saved, she couldn't make enough money on her own.

There was only one solution: she must marry a wealthy man.

CHAPTER SEVEN

A scarlet glow lit the eastern sky as Flora set out on horseback for Todds-ville. She was on a vitally important mission to find the muscle they so badly needed: someone, anyone, willing to break their land.

The women were acutely aware of the government's conditions. The first year, break five acres; the second year, seed the first five and break the next ten; and the third year, break the final fifteen acres and seed the first fifteen. The result: thirty acres broken, with fifteen in crop.

Flora couldn't even visualise thirty acres until she paced it out. It was a staggering size, the equivalent of eight cricket fields. If they were to reach their first five-acre milestone this summer, they had no time to waste.

She mounted the hill and headed north toward the Buffalo Lake Trail. When she reached the fork and turned Felicity to face the dawn, the prairie loomed before her like an inland ocean with no visible shore. She looked over her shoulder. She could no longer see her shack, or even a trace of smoke from her chimney.

For the first time in her life, she was utterly alone.

Flora's heart began to pound with fear. The cavernous sky was greater than the earth below, and she no more than a dust mote. She felt as if she might drift upward with the breeze, as weightless as thistledown. She shut her eyes as a wave of vertigo washed over her, clutching the reins to keep herself from wafting into the huge blue dome overhead.

The dizziness lasted only seconds. Opening her eyes, she saw the flat black horizon line surrounding her, as if a gigantic hand had placed a water glass upside down on a table and trapped her beneath it. Now her perspective shifted again and her body grew heavy. She felt the sky pressing on her, forcing her down into the waves of thick grass that were writhing and tossing in the wind, changing colour from rose to gold as the sun climbed higher.

Sensing her rider's reluctance, Felicity slowed her steps and stopped. Flora squeezed her eyes shut and sat very still. This time she was afraid to open them. She recalled being caught in the undertow while swimming in the North Sea and experienced the same terrifying pull now, a mighty force dragging her into the depths. Flora fumbled for the buttons on her high-necked blouse, opened her collar, and took several gasping breaths. If she lost her way, if she fell from her saddle into that sea of grass, she would never be found. Nobody would hear her call for help. She screamed aloud. Even her voice was tiny, carried away by the stiff breeze.

The horse nudged Flora's leg with her nose, reminding her that she wasn't alone. She had Felicity. She pressed her face against the mare's neck, drawing warmth and strength from the animal, inhaling her familiar fragrance.

Not daring to raise her head, she opened her eyes and saw a splash of colour like a drop of purple blood, almost buried in the grass beside the trail. It was a clump of amethyst blossoms that Mr. Cook had called Shooting Stars. In the middle of each fragile bloom, a cluster of yellow stamens converged to a point, resembling the tail of a burning comet.

Flora fixed her gaze on these gallant little wildflowers, flourishing in the tough prairie sod, until her heartbeat slowed and her body weight settled into the saddle once again. She nudged the horse with her leg, and they moved forward.

That curious sense of dislocation didn't return. After some time, Flora was able to forget her trepidation and admire the sweetness of the air and the majestic clouds drifting across the hard bright sky overhead. Still, the hours seemed long until she spotted several small rectangular shapes in the distance. She uttered a cry of joy and urged Felicity into a gallop.

When they reached Sims Livery at the near edge of the village, Flora dropped to the ground, stiff-legged. Her lower back ached from riding such a distance in her sidesaddle. She didn't wish she were a man, at least not often, but she envied them many things—one of which was their ability to wear breeches and ride astride.

Flora arranged her veil before leading her mare into the stable, wary of being seen in public, although Toddsville was a long ride from Lacombe. It was almost inconceivable that Hector would seek her here, but it was best to be cautious. While the owner pitched forkfuls of hay into the manger, Flora asked him about hired help.

The grizzled old gent was sympathetic. "Sorry, miss," he said. "The men are working their own fields."

Well, she would have to make the attempt. She left Felicity crunching oats and headed down the main street, no more than a dirt road sprinkled with grass and weeds, leading from the livery stable at one end to the hotel at the other. A few solitary horses, hitched to wagons and buggies, waited for their owners.

Toddsville was even smaller than the settlements seen from the train. It looked like a toy village, with painted wooden boxes lined up in two facing rows. The street between them was wider than the boulevards in Aberdeen, demonstrating a courageous confidence in the future, as if the inhabitants anticipated that their village would someday become a metropolis.

She walked along the dirt footpath worn beside the road—no boardwalks here—past the blacksmith shop, bank, and post office, repeating the same question and feeling more defeated each time she heard the word *no*.

Here was the newspaper office where the *Toddsville Free Press* was printed. Flora stepped inside and made her request at the counter. A man in a green eyeshade, who introduced himself as the editor Charles Frederick, shook his head.

"You're welcome to put a help wanted advertisement in the paper," he said. "One cent per word, and the paper comes out every Friday."

As she opened the door, the editor seemed to relent. "Miss, you might as well save your money. You won't find anybody around here, not if you took out a full-page advert."

Flora thanked him and left the office. Standing in the shade of the building, she tried to gather the fortitude to continue her mission. The sun was high and perspiration trickled down her spine. Glancing around to make sure she wasn't being watched, she lifted her skirt and flapped it vigorously to get some air movement around her legs before setting out again.

When Flora reached the Imperial Hotel at the far end of the street, the only brick structure in this village made of wood, she made her request to the proprietor behind the front desk. The expected answer came: "No, nobody." The lobby was cool after the afternoon warmth outside, and she stood there for a moment, reluctant to leave.

The door to the tavern opened—she reminded herself that here it was called a beer parlour, or a beverage room—with a burst of men's laughter and a blast of smoky air. A man emerged and staggered down the front steps. In this country, only men were allowed in drinking establishments. Flora wondered how long their wives and children and horses would have to wait for them.

Crossing the street, she headed back toward the livery stable and noticed a doctor's office on the ground floor of a two-storey building. A sign on the window read: DR. SAMUEL FARRADAY. OFFICE VISITS: FIFTY CENTS. RURAL CALLS: ONE DOLLAR. Flora hoped she would never have occasion to pay.

Next was the general store. She pushed open the door. The air was thick with smoke, noxious after the freshness of the outdoors. A pot-bellied stove stood in the centre of the room, and an open sack of unshelled peanuts beside it. Several elderly men were seated on boxes and kegs. As she entered the room, all conversation stopped. One fellow, sporting a grey beard streaked with brown tobacco juice, spat noisily into a brass receptacle.

Self-conscious under so many appraising eyes, Flora blurted out her request, "I'm looking for a man." The room erupted with noisy laughter, and her cheeks burned beneath her veil.

Only one individual didn't laugh. He was younger than the others, as skinny as a sapling, in a black suit that hung from his scrawny limbs. A matching bowler with a rolled brim perched on his bony skull, and his face was cadaverous. His pale eyes raked her from hat to boots.

"You one of those gals took up a claim west of here?" the grey beard asked in a gravelly voice.

"Aye. My name is Flora Craigie. I'm seeking to hire someone to break ten acres—five for me, and five for my neighbour."

The thin man spoke then. His voice was unusually high, almost feminine. "You're wasting your time, madam. Pack your bags and get on the next train."

Rage surged through her body like a rogue wave. Her muscles were stiff, and she was hot and tired and parched. At the very least, these dunderheads could show her some common courtesy. Heedless of being identified, she threw back her veil and drew herself to her full height. "Thank you verra much for your helpful advice, but we have absolutely nay intention of leaving. Good day to you, gentlemen." She glared into the thin man's pale eyes while she emphasised the word "gentlemen."

A couple of the oldsters shifted in their chairs, but the thin man held her gaze and his lips formed a smirk as he registered the insult. Flora turned to leave. She wanted to make a dignified exit, but her skirt caught on a nail and she had to jerk it free, ripping a three-cornered tear in the fabric. To compensate, she closed the door behind her with a loud and satisfying slam.

The earth now exploded with green vegetation in an outpouring of fertility that seemed to mock the women. Just three weeks into their three-year challenge, and it was painfully obvious that they could not do this alone.

Flora slumped at her small table, her head in her hands. She wished they could approach Mr. Cook for help, but he was away on a scouting expedition. Should she visit the neighbours? She remembered the network of faint trails meandering around the prairie and despaired of finding any other inhabitants without becoming hopelessly lost.

She had little appetite, but she picked up her spoon and swallowed her last bite of parritch, reminding herself to call it porridge. She was determined to lose her accent, one more characteristic that set her apart. She was rinsing her bowl in the blue speckled enamel basin when she heard a man's baritone.

"Damn and blast, get along there!"

She dashed outside to find Sourdough Buckhorn leading two heavy horses into her yard, dragging a wooden platform on skids called a stone boat. On this platform sat a breaking plough. He charged toward Flora, his features as furious as the first time they had met, wearing the same filthy denim overalls and plaid shirt, enveloped in a cloud of stale sweat. Flora wondered if he had taken off his clothes since then. A flap of dirty underwear appeared under his collar, from whence dark, curly hair sprang out like bedsprings.

Was he about to shout at her again? She tensed her body, forcing herself not to shrink away. Behind him, she saw the entire Penrose brood splashing through the creek at a dead run, coming to her rescue.

"Good morning, Mr. Buckhorn." Her voice was faint, almost a whisper. "What can I do for you today?"

"You can do nothing for me!" he bellowed, as if outraged that she would suggest such a thing. "I came to save you half-wits from yourselves!"

Mrs. Penrose arrived, panting with the exertion of carrying Jewel. The whole family cowered behind Flora as the aptly named Sourdough turned his angry red glare on them.

"I'll do your breaking for a dollar a day, take it or leave it!"

There were a few seconds of stunned silence.

"We'll take it," Flora said.

He advanced toward her, fists clenched as if he were trying not to lash out with them.

"I'll work this field first, and then that one." He gestured across the creek. "Stay out of my way. And keep those brats away from me too!" he yelled at Mrs. Penrose, spittle flying through the sunlit air. Jewel shrieked and buried her face in her mother's shoulder.

The women and children retreated under the trees, watching as Sourdough led his team into the meadow behind Flora's shack. The familiar Scottish Clydesdales were gargantuan animals, their backs taller than her head. Their mahogany coats were groomed, glossy and shining. Clearly their owner cared more for his animals than for himself.

He lifted the heavy plough off the stone boat as though it weighed no more than a sack of flour and hitched it to the team. Ignoring the rock piles that Flora had collected, marking the corners of what she had estimated were five acres, he drew a ball of twine from his pocket and paced out the field. Flora was relieved that he didn't move her rocks, at least not by much.

Sourdough marked the first furrow by pounding in a row of sharpened stakes that he fetched from the stone boat. There was one for every fifty paces—Flora counted his steps as he marched down the field.

When he was finished, he positioned his team at the stake nearest the shack.

"Mr. Buckhorn! Wait!" Flora called as she ran toward him.

He watched her approach with a terrific scowl. "What the devil do you want?"

"Would you mind . . . it won't take but a moment of your time . . ."

"What is it?" he roared.

Flora gathered her courage. "I want to hold the plough when you make the first cut."

His snarl was unintelligible, but he moved his filthy hand from the wooden handle on the left, and she grasped it. It was warm from the sun.

He lowered the triangular metal blade and yelled at the horses, "Gee, you rascals!"

Their massive hooves, covered with shaggy hair, began to plod across the meadow. The plough scraped and bounced along the surface for a few feet, then suddenly the metal bit deeply into the thick sod, bound together with the roots and remains of grasses and flowering plants, wild roses, yellow buffalo beans, and prairie crocuses.

The earth opened in a black wound, and Flora felt a pang of sorrow. The sod had been here for thousands of years of rain and snow and sunshine, ever since the retreat of the glaciers. It was like slashing open a living thing. The handle jerked under her hand as the blade fought with the force of the resistance below. *The word* break *is a good one*, Flora thought, *since the earth is literally breaking in two.*

Not wanting to try Sourdough's patience, she walked behind the plough for only a few steps before releasing her grasp.

"Are you finished?" he growled. "Now, make yourself scarce!"

"Thank you," she said, and darted to one side, watching the man and his team perform. The first roll of soil peeled back, clean cut with the sharp knife of the ploughshare, as black as a raven's wing. A fringe of coarse grass clung fast to the edges, as though the two could not bear to be parted after all these centuries together.

The horses found their rhythm and walked abreast at a steady pace, their mighty shoulders quivering with strain as they dragged the blade through the reluctant soil. They came to the end of the first row, and their eight hooves swung around in unison as if they were on a parade ground. By the time they returned to their starting point, both man and horses were running with sweat.

The Penroses had gone home. Flora fetched one of her wooden chairs and sat in the shade beside her shack. The smell of the moist earth filled her nostrils. There was something mesmerising in the way the sod rolled over. Yet even Sourdough, his brawny arms like hairy hams, needed a tremendous amount of strength to keep the furrows straight. Whenever the plough struck a rock or a root, the blade bounced from the ground. Dozens of times he stopped the horses and lugged a rock to one side.

Flora recalled Mr. Cook telling them about a crooked land locater who had hoodwinked an unsuspecting client by ploughing a strip of sod the previous day and pushing the furrow back into place so the waving grass covered the join. When he placed the blade in the cut furrow to demonstrate, the soil parted as if he were slicing butter.

"Whoa!" Sourdough walked ahead of the team and lowered himself to his knees before clambering to his feet, holding a bird's nest in his big hands. He carried the nest some distance away and tucked it into the grass before returning to his team. Flora felt a tendril of affection for him, until he blew his nose with his fingers and wiped them on his overalls.

When the sun was blazing overhead, Flora started a fire and prepared a huge meal of sausages and fried potatoes. She opened a tin of baked beans and stuck one of her two spoons into it. After filling the enamel pitcher with cold tea, she carried everything to the field.

Sourdough snatched the pitcher and drank deeply but said not a word of thanks before beginning to shove the food through a hole in his ragged beard, dropping bits down his chest. Several beans stuck in his whiskers and clung there, quivering. Flora had to look away.

"The horses," he said, and she ran to and from the creek with her bucket a dozen times until the Clydesdales had drunk their fill. Flora returned to her shack. Since the stove was still hot, she used one cup of her precious sugar to bake oatmeal cookies. In the afternoon she returned to the field with three salt pork and mustard sandwiches, plus a dozen cookies.

In her absence, Sourdough had removed his shirt and was naked to the waist. Flora had rarely seen a shirtless man. Even the pearl divers in the rivers around Dornoch wore singlets on their upper bodies. She was shocked by the springy hair covering his chest and stomach and wrapping his back. He resembled a woolly black Aberdeen Angus bull.

Flora handed him the food with her eyes averted. Sourdough led his horses to the creek and allowed them to graze while he wolfed down the sandwiches and all twelve cookies. After a short nap in the shade, he rose and sharpened his ploughshare with a file until the sparks flew around his head in a shower of fireworks. The team and their owner returned to their labours.

As the sun touched the tip of the tallest spruce at the far end of Flora's property, two dozen rows of thick chocolate ribbons edged with green covered the meadow.

Sourdough said just three words before he left, his voice hoarse from shouting at the team. "That's two acres."

Flora calculated that a man walks five miles back and forth in the ploughing of one acre. Sourdough and his team had walked ten miles, and there were still three acres to go.

CHAPTER EIGHT

Seated at her table in a shaft of sunlight, mending the tear in her skirt with invisible stitches, Flora spotted a horse and rider at the crest of the hill. With dismay, she recognised the skeletal figure from the general store, looking like a monstrous spider on horseback. She dropped her mending and shut the door, hoping he would ride past.

No such luck. Peeping through her front window, Flora watched as he rode to the stand of poplars beside her shack and unfolded himself from the horse, his pant legs flapping in the breeze. She ducked below the sill, wishing she had somewhere to hide.

The man tied his horse to a tree and stepped forward to study the shack as if examining it for flaws. He pulled a notebook and pencil from his pocket and scribbled a few words. Whatever was this black-hearted skinny-breeks doing here? Bracing herself, Flora flung open the door.

As before, the man surveyed her from head to toe before fixing his pale eyes on her chest. Flora resisted the urge to raise her hands and cover her bodice.

Without shifting his eyes, the pupils such a light grey they appeared almost white in the strong prairie sunshine, he asked, "Are you Flora Craigie?"

"You ken that I am," she said. "I introduced myself at the general store."

He removed his bowler to reveal long, stringy hair, the colour of sand. "My name is Sterling Payne. I'm the homestead inspector for this region."

Flora felt the shock physically and caught the doorframe with one hand for support. This was the inspector himself, the one man with the authority to approve or deny her application. And he had already told her once to pack her bags and leave!

He smiled, revealing a row of small childlike teeth, openly enjoying her discomfort. "I'm aware that you graciously provided those present with a name, but I require proof of your identity."

If he was the spider, she was the fly.

"Of course," she said, struggling to keep her voice even. Once again, she felt helpless in the presence of a man with more power than herself. "I'll fetch my papers." She had planned to leave him outside, but he followed her through the open door.

"I need to examine the interior," he said. "The regulations demand a habitable dwelling."

Her shack was even smaller than the traditional Scottish but-and-ben, with one room in the front and one in the back where people slept. This simple rectangular box did triple service as parlour, kitchen, and bedroom. As his eyes travelled around the room, Flora felt embarrassed by this disagreeable man's presence in her sleeping quarters. Her lace-trimmed silk chemise was lying on the bed, and she stuffed it under her pillow, but not before he had seen it.

Surely her tiny home must be considered habitable. Her blue-and-green Clan Mackay tartan shawl covered the table. On the shelf above was her copper pot, a pair of blue enamel mugs, and the only two books she owned: her childhood Bible, and the copy of *Great Expectations* she had been reading on the train. Her meagre wardrobe hung from nails on the wall behind the door. Payne peered at everything. He took the liberty of opening her Bible and examining the inscription from her father, written on her twelfth birthday. An unpleasant odour of must emanated from his black suit, the smell of menace.

"Hmm. Well, let's see your papers." Without being invited, he sat down on one of her wooden chairs. Flora pulled the leather pouch from under her bed, withdrew her scrip bill of sale and Homestead Application, and handed them to Payne.

"Take a seat, if you please." He gestured to the other chair as if he were the host. Flora perched on the edge while Payne peered at the documents.

"Are you single, Miss Craigie?" He emphasised the word "Miss." His moustache was thinner than the thin lips below.

"Aye."

"No children?"

"Nay." The question was insolent, since she had told him she was single, but she tried to speak in a pleasant tone. She hoped he couldn't see her rapid heartbeat through her pink cotton shirtwaist.

"What about your family? Do you have a father or brother, or any male relative with an interest in this property?"

"No one. My father is dead, and I am without brothers."

"What do you intend to do with this land, in the unlikely event that you succeed?"

This was none of his business, but she tried to answer courteously. "The same as everyone else, to make my home here."

"The purpose of the Dominion Lands Act is to create permanent settlements. There have been far too many cases of people claiming homesteads for the sake of getting their hands on free land, and decamping for the West Coast or other parts as soon as they secure their title."

"That is not my intention, Mr. Payne."

"Do you have sufficient financial resources to carry out this endeavour?"

"I believe so." Flora sounded hesitant, and he darted a sharp look from his pale eyes.

"Are you familiar with the terms of your contract with the federal government to break thirty acres and have fifteen in crop within three years?"

"Certainly. You can see for yourself that my first five acres are already broken." Flora breathed a silent prayer of thanks for Sourdough.

"Miss Craigie, let me be perfectly frank." He raised his sparse eyebrows, a few straggling hairs in each one.

"The federal government's intention is to transform western Canada into a British colony, settled by white families. By staking your claim, you are effectively stealing two quarters from a man who would turn them into a prosperous farm."

Flora was truly frightened now, and she spoke in a pleading voice. "Mr. Payne, please believe me, I fully intend to make this land productive."

"Be that as it may, there's a greater issue at stake. Your primary duty is to help a man in his endeavours, to bear his children and instil in them the values we hold most dear. It's true that you aren't English, but at least you speak English. Well, a form of English." He chuckled at his own joke. "Do you understand what I'm telling you? As a white woman, you have a moral obligation to propagate our race."

Flora was aghast. She didn't know how to respond, so she said nothing.

He smiled a sickly smile. "Really, my dear young woman, why don't you give up this mad notion? I can see from your lovely hands that you were made for finer things."

Flora clasped her hands on the table to hide her palms, which were covered with blisters.

"You shouldn't labour in the field like an ignorant savage. Only the Ukrainians and the Poles treat their women as if they were beasts of burden."

"I don't mind working with my hands, Mr. Payne," she said. She swallowed, trying to bring some moisture into her dry throat. "In fact, I quite enjoy it."

"Why don't you make yourself available to a man, and become the mother of his children, as our Lord intended?"

How dare he quote the Bible to her? "Mr. Payne, I am verra familiar with the Scriptures, and I don't believe it is the Lord's plan to do as you suggest. I believe my future is here."

When Flora heard her own words, she was struck with their inescapable truth. Like Nurse Godwin, she had discovered her calling at last. It was almost ironic that having found her rightful place in the world, this odious man should be questioning her motives.

Payne scrutinised her papers again, shaking his head. "I don't understand by what fraudulent means you managed to get your hands on this property."

"Ach, no fraud was involved!" Flora took a deep breath and moderated her tone. "I purchased scrip, the same as hundreds of others."

He tilted back on his chair legs and studied Flora's face, fingering his sparse moustache. "Are you aware, Miss Craigie, that your fate as a homesteader rests with me?"

"Yes, Mr. Payne."

"We could come to a private arrangement, one that would benefit both of us."

Flora was confused. "What sort of arrangement?"

Mr. Payne reached out and covered Flora's hand with his own. She forced herself not to snatch it away. His touch caused her flesh to creep like the damp chill of a Scottish morn.

His eyes went to the bed and he stared at it for a moment, then looked back at her and cocked one skimpy eyebrow. What on earth was he suggesting? Surely he didn't mean . . . Flora leaped to her feet and her chair fell back with a crash. Her cast-iron frying pan was sitting on the stove, and she longed to crack it over his skull, but she dared not alienate the man any further, let alone land herself in jail.

She turned and took two steps toward the door, trying to collect herself. Forcing a smile that felt more like a grimace, she whirled to face him. She decided that wilful ignorance, coupled with a bland, deadly courtesy, was her best defence. "Mr. Payne, if I meet the conditions outlined in the Homestead Act, I trust that you will approve my claim based on your honesty and your integrity as a representative of His Majesty's Crown."

Payne's thin eyebrow hairs drew together. He rose to his feet, his obsequious expression replaced by an ugly scowl. "I'll be watching you closely, Miss Craigie. If I find one infraction, you'll be gone before the first snowfall. And that goes for your neighbour, too. She has no more right to this land than you do. Unfortunately, our elected officials sometimes make mistakes, and innocent men must pay for them."

He clapped his bowler on his stringy hair. "The simple fact, Miss Craigie, is that the government doesn't want you here. And neither do I."

With this parting shot, Sterling Payne stalked to the door and slammed it behind him, a pointed reminder of the way she had left the general store. Flora sank onto her cot, the perspiration breaking out on her scalp.

There was no law against purchasing scrip, married or single. But she had signed her maiden name to her Homestead Application and listed her occupation as "Spinster." If this repulsive creature discovered her marriage, her claim would be void.

Flora had almost despaired at finding a rich man when Hector Mackle arrived in her life like the proverbial knight in shining armour. In theory, she had few qualms about marrying for money. In her favourite novel, *Pride and Prejudice*, the character Charlotte Lucas agrees to wed the unattractive Mr. Collins in exchange for a comfortable home. Flora found her decision perfectly sensible. In Charlotte's own words: "Not all of us can afford to be romantic."

The problem was that Flora didn't meet any rich men, attractive or not. Mrs. Galt's cousin showed her marked attention whenever he came to call, but he was already married. Another woman might have considered becoming his mistress, but the teachings of the kirk were so powerful that Flora would never consider living in sin, not even for a palace.

One wet day in April, she visited a print shop on Bond Street to fetch new calling cards for Mrs. Galt. She had collected her package and was about to unfurl her umbrella before stepping into the rain when the door opened and a man appeared out of the mist.

"Hello, my good man, my charming lady," he said, bowing and doffing his fedora. "I need to reproduce this poster," he said to the shop owner. "Are you able to print fifty copies by tomorrow?"

The owner held the poster up to the window. Its bright colours glowed in the murky light from the rain-streaked glass. Flora paused to admire the painted illustration, a pastoral scene with white farmhouse, crimson barn, and golden fields sweeping away to a cobalt sky. On a hill overlooking the farm stood a man and his wife, who was wearing a white dress and cradling a bouquet of roses. In the distance, a train smoked along the horizon. Across the top of the poster in large type were the words: CANADA: THE RIGHT LAND FOR THE RIGHT MAN. And across the bottom: APPLY NOW TO YOUR CANADIAN PACIFIC RAILWAY AGENT.

"I can have them ready tomorrow, if you're willing to pay extra for a rush job."

"Thank you kindly. I want to put them up around the city before my lecture on Thursday. I'm Hector Mackle, land agent for the Canadian Pacific Railway, here to inform the good people of Aberdeen about the splendid opportunity awaiting them in the new world."

He gave Flora a winning smile. "Perhaps you'd be interested in attending, dear lady, with your father or your brother, or perhaps your husband?"

"I'm not married, and I have nay kin," Flora said, studying the poster, "but your lecture does sound verra intriguing."

Mr. Mackle beamed. "Excellent! Won't you join me in a cup of tea, so we can discuss the matter further?"

Flora tore her eyes away from the farmhouse in the illustration and looked him over. His embroidered waistcoat and gold watch chain indicated a man of means. He was not unattractive, slightly shorter than Flora, with a stocky build and flaxen hair. His blue eyes were wide and guileless, and his manners were excellent. She hesitated only briefly before accepting his invitation.

Over three cups of tea, Mr. Mackle did most of the talking. He explained that the Canadian government had granted his employer tracts of land the size of small European countries in exchange for building the country's coast-to-coast railway. Although free homesteads were available, the Canadian Pacific Railway was selling this land outright to people who had the cash and didn't want to spend three years and untold labour earning their title. He made it sound as if the company were doing them a huge favour.

And then, he produced a hand-tinted photograph of his home in Vancouver, British Columbia. It was a graceful stone house overlooking the ocean with a turret on one side. Roses climbed the walls and framed a bay window, while frothy waves lapped at the seashore below.

"That's a braw house," Flora breathed, enchanted.

"I travel so extensively that it stands empty most of the year. Poor old Sunnybrae is sorely in need of a mistress."

Flora heard her mother's words as distinctly as though she had whispered them into her ear: "Marry a rich man, and you'll never be homeless."

Mr. Mackle's hand was lying on the lace tablecloth, his fingernails manicured and buffed. His gold ring bore a large diamond.

"I believe I shall attend your lecture, Mr. Mackle," Flora said. As she handed back his photograph, she smiled at him as charmingly as she knew how.

Remembering that dismal day, Flora ground her teeth in frustration. She stood up and wiggled the loose board in the wall over her bed until it came free.

Behind it was hidden the single piece of identification that bore her married name: her marriage certificate.

A few embers glowed in the stove from her morning fire. Flora opened the lid and thrust the certificate inside, watching it burst into flame. She stood at the stove for a long time, stirring the ashes with a poker until they were as cold and dead as the marriage itself.

Only one person in the world would be overjoyed to inform Sterling Payne that she was married—and she feared that he was still on the hunt.

BOOK TWO

CHAPTER NINE

Flora consulted the calendar tacked onto the wall above her bed. Mr. Cook had warned them not to plant their gardens before the first of June, but it was time to start preparing her plot.

Donning her leather gloves, she emerged into the sweetness and freshness of this new world and paced out an area in the yard, reflecting that the word "yard" was a quaint Canadian colloquialism for the sea of wild grass that surrounded her shack right up to the doorsill. Pushing her spade into the earth with her foot, she wriggled it loose, lifted the heavy, root-bound clod with an effort, and hacked it into pieces with the blade.

After an hour of battling the stubborn sod, she stopped to rest and wipe her forehead with the tail of her shirtwaist. The sun was a burning ball in the bright blue sky. Flora untied her braid and allowed her thick hair to tumble onto her shoulders. The breeze lifted and separated the damp strands with gentle fingers. She placed her hands on the small of her aching back and inhaled the richly scented air.

Believing herself to be alone except for the host of songbirds that serenaded her from every shrub, Flora was startled when two fashionable ladies appeared around the corner of her shack. Hastily she tried to brush the dirt off her skirt, mortified by her own outlandish outfit. Her blue-and-white striped cotton shirtwaist had rings of perspiration under her oxters, armpits as they were called here. Her corset was long gone, abandoned in her haste to leave the train, and beneath her shirtwaist she wore only her silk chemise. Tired of dragging her way through the grass, she had tacked up her brown woollen skirt and several inches of bare leg showed between her hem and her boots.

In contrast with Flora's dishevelled appearance, the taller of the two women wore a well-cut navy skirt and a blue shirtwaist, her brown hair in a neat chignon. The soft tie around her throat was held in place with a monogrammed gold pin.

"Good morning," she said. "We are your neighbours to the south. I'm Roberta Edgar, and this is my friend, Henrietta Greenwood. We arrived home from Calgary yesterday." Her accent was unmistakeably American.

"How do you do?" Flora said. "My name is Flora Craigie." She held up her dirty palms. "I'm afraid I'm not fit to shake hands."

"Miss Craigie, we're sorry to interrupt your labours!" The shorter woman also wore a simple skirt and blouse, but her light brown hair was dressed in puffs and curls, and a pair of crystal drops dangled from her delicate earlobes. She smiled, showing dimples in her cheeks. "We know how busy you must be, but we do hope you have time for tea this afternoon."

"That's most kind of you, Miss Greenwood."

"Please, call me Wren." She did remind Flora of a little bird. Her head bobbed up and down and her brown eyes twinkled. "Do come, just for an hour. We want to hear all about you, and Mrs. Penrose, too."

This was what Flora had feared, being drawn into a circle of women who gossiped and wasted their time instead of working. And she would have to be careful not to reveal too much about herself. But her curiosity was aroused. What were these elegant ladies doing here? They would have been more at home in Mrs. Galt's parlour than the Canadian wilderness. She couldn't resist the chance to learn their story.

"Thank you, I would be verra happy to come."

"Isn't it wonderful that we are all living so near each other? We're just tickled!" Wren clasped her little hands together. Miss Edgar's expression didn't change.

"Aye, I was surprised as well!" Flora said, reflecting that dismayed would be a better description of her feelings. She watched as they tripped off toward the Penrose cabin, holding their skirts above their ankles, an incongruous pair in their dainty shoes and straw hats.

Anxious to erase their first impression of her as a clarty wench, Flora bathed in the creek before donning her ivory silk blouse and grey skirt. At three o'clock she followed the faint trail that ran past her property and continued south. She had never yet ventured in this direction.

Passing the heavy bush that lay between their farms, she walked from one world into another. The lane leading to their farmstead was lined with double rows of young but flourishing Manitoba maples as tall as Flora's head. These framed a charming house with a front verandah, and twin gables set into the red shingled roof. The clapboard siding was painted buttercup yellow, and two rocking chairs stood on either side of a crimson door. Overhead was a crescent-shaped stained glass window in shades of yellow and green and red like a winking cat's eye.

Dotting the area around the house were several dozen fluffy, copper-coloured chickens, pecking in the grass, eating the fat grasshoppers that were too lazy to avoid their fate. Behind the house and off to one side was a barn and a chicken coop, both painted red with white trim, and a log cabin that Flora guessed was the original homesteader's dwelling.

Beside the cabin, a youth was splitting firewood. Flora recognised his high-crowned white hat—it was the same boy who had held her place in Red

Deer. Today he wore a navy double-breasted flannel shirt and a yellow paisley bandana.

Wren answered the door and invited Flora inside, fluttering around like her namesake. Flora barely glanced at her. She was too busy admiring her surroundings.

The ladies were seated in a large open room—Miss Edgar in a green plush armchair, and Mrs. Penrose in one of two slat-backed Morris chairs upholstered in maroon brocade. An oval braided rug covered the wooden plank floor. A second room was visible through an arched doorway, a spacious kitchen with a double porcelain sink and cookstove. A staircase in one corner rose to a landing and out of sight.

One wall in this delightful room was lined with bookshelves. Flora eyed them with longing, having now read *Great Expectations* three times. An easel standing in front of the window bore a half-finished watercolour, and several pastel landscapes in gilt frames hung on the walls. A glass-fronted cabinet displayed china ornaments, a shell-covered box, and a velvet pincushion. On the top shelf, a gold clock with revolving balls gave out its merry tick-tock like a beating heart.

It was exactly the sort of home that Flora had pictured in her imagination.

"Ach, what a bonnie hoose!" she exclaimed.

"We think so too!" Wren said, showing Flora to the other Morris chair before seating herself in a rocker with a needlework cushion. "We're snug as the proverbial bugs, but it's lovely to have company! We've been here more than a year and scarcely another soul except Beau has crossed our threshold!"

"And who is Beau?" Flora asked, as she took her seat. She glanced at Mrs. Penrose, who was sitting erect, her knees and feet pressed together, holding a teacup with her little finger extended. A plate of sliced scones, spread with crimson jam, sat on the side table.

Wren poured the tea into a delicate flowered cup and handed it to Flora.

"Our hired boy, Beau Henderson. He came out from England alone, just imagine. He's only sixteen years old! Back in the old country, some unscrupulous land agent—honestly, those men are nothing but crooks—told him he could qualify for a homestead but failed to inform him that he had to be eighteen! So here he is, counting down the days and wishing his life away."

"Oddly enough, I met him in Red Deer, standing in line at the lands office," Flora said. "I recognised him just now by his hat."

Wren chuckled. "You see quite a number of those young dudes in Calgary, strutting around in their big hats and fancy spurs. Did you notice that he flips the brim back to show his face? That's the latest fashion. It's called the Fort Worth Flare."

"Does he live here?" Flora asked.

"Yes," Miss Edgar replied. "He sleeps in the old settler's cabin. He cuts our firewood and cares for the horses in exchange for his room and board. Since we aren't cultivating our land, we don't have enough work for him, so he hires himself out here and there to save money for his own homestead. He can help you and Mrs. Penrose, if you need any odd jobs done."

Wren broke in. "And he takes such good care of my hens!"

"I saw them in the yard. Splendid specimens indeed," Flora said.

"Three dozen of the finest Buff Orpingtons, all the way from England! Why, they've seen more of the world than we have!" Wren showed her dimples again.

Flora glanced over at Mrs. Penrose, who was apparently too intimidated to utter a word, while Wren elaborated on her chickens. "A man from Orpington, Kent, created the breed and named them Black Orpingtons. He bred them with black feathers to hide the London soot. Wasn't that clever of him? And since then, he has developed another two breeds, the Blues and the Buffs. They are the dearest pets! So quiet and so affectionate!"

"Wren is exceedingly fond of her hens," Miss Edgar said dryly. "So much so, that she sometimes forgets they are here for the purpose of making money."

"That doesn't mean I can't love them!" Wren exclaimed. "I've named every single one. They're wonderful layers, but of course we can't live on eggs alone. Dear Robbie has another source of income—she translates historical documents from the original Greek for a professor at Harvard University. She's terribly clever!" Wren beamed at her friend.

Both Flora and Mrs. Penrose turned to the older woman, who looked somewhat embarrassed.

"Wren is being far too modest," she said. "She has a classical education as well. We taught together, at a private girls' school in Boston." She gestured toward the easel. "She's also a fine watercolourist."

"Why did you choose to come here, so far from Boston?" Flora asked.

"We were tired of city life," Miss Edgar replied. "Besides, we were feeling the constraints of our profession. Most of our students had no interest in higher education. They attended college only to enhance their marriageability. We decided to strike out for somewhere completely unknown."

Her tone was somewhat stiff, and Flora wondered whether there was more to the story. "Didn't you want to claim a free homestead in your own country?" she asked. "It's wonderful that your government allows single women to qualify."

"We have nothing but admiration for those women, although not everyone agrees that they should be allowed to farm," Miss Edgar said. "Back home there's a derogatory term for them—Lady Honyockers, meaning 'hayseeds.' At any rate, we didn't want the hard work of proving up. We aren't wealthy, by any means, but we saved enough to buy this quarter and build our own house."

Wren, who had been silent during this explanation, changed the subject. "Won't you have a scone?" She passed the plate of fluffy creations to Mrs. Penrose, who mumbled her refusal. "Mrs. Penrose, I insist! I want your opinion on my homemade jam." It was obvious that Wren was trying to coax the other woman out of her shyness.

"Thank you." Mrs. Penrose was forced to speak at last. She helped herself to a scone and took one ladylike nibble.

"I'll show you where to find my special strawberry patch," Wren said. "The wild fruit simply flourishes here. You'll see for yourself in a few weeks."

Flora looked at the widow, wondering how to draw her into the conversation. "Mrs. Penrose and I have hired a neighbour to break our land. Perhaps you know him. His name is Mr. Buckhorn."

"Old Sourdough! I'm surprised he agreed to work for you," Wren said. "He has the reputation of hating all women, and most men, too. He's always angry at someone, usually the government."

Miss Edgar set down her teacup. "He came to my aid one day when my horse Posy went lame," she said. "He allowed me to ride his big sorrel, Champion. It was like sitting on an elephant. I clung to the beast's mane for dear life, afraid every minute that I would fall and break my neck. Sourdough walked beside me all the way home, leading Posy and complaining bitterly that we should be taken to the nearest railway station and sent back to the States."

Wren laughed. "And Sourdough is an American himself, or rather, he was. He had to become a naturalised British subject in order to file his claim."

"Another reason we chose not to homestead," Miss Edgar said. "We didn't wish to renounce our citizenship."

Wren nodded in agreement. "Sourdough was one of the earliest settlers around here. Of course, the sooners take a rather jaundiced view of the laters, always suspecting them of being landgrabbers—those folks who cut and run as soon as they earn their title."

So that's what the lands office clerk meant when he called her a landgrabber. Annoyed at the memory, Flora bit down hard on her scone and the jam spurted between her teeth.

Miss Edgar raised one elegant hand. "In fairness, Mr. Buckhorn has earned the right to his opinion of latecomers. He's an excellent farmer. He proved up his own homestead several years ago and bought the quarter next to it."

Wren leaned forward and lowered her voice. "He may be a good farmer, but you'd never guess it from his living quarters. When he throws something away, he opens the door and flings it out. The area around his cabin is littered with rusty tin cans and animal bones. And there's no sign of an outhouse! I shudder to think where the man goes to relieve himself."

All four women laughed, even Mrs. Penrose. To her surprise, Flora found that she was enjoying herself.

"And what about our neighbour to the west?" Flora asked, wiping her fingers on an embroidered napkin. "He's been elusive so far."

"Miss Craigie, we thought you knew!" Wren said. "The owner of that land is another woman. Her name is Jessie McDonald. We've caught sight of her in the distance a couple of times, riding her mustang at a tremendous gallop, but she never acknowledges us. We have walked over to her cabin twice, but there was no answer when we knocked."

"We were told she is of mixed blood," Miss Edgar said. "She inherited two hundred and forty acres from her father, who was granted Half-Breed Scrip by the federal government. Aside from that, we know nothing about her. And she, apparently, wants to know nothing about us."

CHAPTER TEN

Miss Grace Godwin
c/o Red Deer Memorial Hospital
Red Deer, North-West Territories

Dear Miss Godwin:

I am writing, as you requested, to update you on my situation. My homesteading days have begun in earnest. I was fortunate enough to find a choice piece of property west of Lacombe. My house has been erected, and a helpful farmer broke my first five acres. I spend my days working the soil, preparing to plant my garden. In short, all is well.

My congenial new neighbours will post this letter for me. I can be reached at General Delivery, Toddsville, but I beg you not to write unless it is an urgent matter, as I would prefer not to receive any mail. My intention is to venture into society as little as possible, for reasons known to us both.

Thank you again for selling me your scrip, and I shall do everything in my power to justify your good opinion!

With every wish for your continued health and success.

Yours most gratefully,
Flora May Craigie

CHAPTER ELEVEN

Flora thrust her spade into the earth and stepped back, surveying the patch of lumpy soil. Was this area large enough for her vegetables? Below ground: potatoes, carrots, turnips, and beets. Above ground: squash, cauliflower, cabbages, onions, beans, peas, and tomatoes. It would have to suffice. She couldn't waste another precious day.

Flora smiled grimly as she recalled what gardening meant to Mrs. Galt and the other fine ladies of Aberdeen—sauntering around with a trug over one arm, pinching off dead petals with gloved fingertips, clipping a few sprays for the hall table. Anything that produced muscles would jeopardise their womanhood. Well, Flora's femininity had already been sorely compromised. No doubt the sight of her bulging arms would revolt any gentleman, accustomed to those limp, boneless creatures with flesh like pastry dough.

"Ouch!" She slapped a mosquito that was feasting on her bare calf, and her palm came away wet with her own blood. Her arms and legs were a scarlet network of mosquito bites and scratches from the sharp grass. She recalled a naughty advertisement in the *Lacombe Globe*:

Overalls beat any tweeds.

They cut the wind and spurn the seeds.

Overalls don't pick up burrs,

That plague all men and cows and curs.

Overalls repulse spear grass,

Protecting legs and arms and a—.

How her desires had changed in a matter of weeks! Not long ago she had yearned for a silk dress. Now she coveted a pair of men's overalls, no matter how indecent her appearance. There was little chance any male would see them except Sourdough, and she could sink no lower in his esteem. Besides, she would need to protect her legs when slashing the shoulder-high grass called orthodox hay that grew in the dry slough bottoms, gathering enough winter feed for the animals. For now, the horses were dining like royalty on wild pea vines and clover.

Felicity even had her own wee hoose. After hearing stories of livestock freezing upright on their hooves and turning into grisly white statues, Flora and Mrs. Penrose hired Beau to build them each a log barn. He felled the trees and snaked them into the yard before erecting four walls on a dirt floor. Flora cut the heavy sod into squares with her spade and handed them up while he fitted them together to form an earthen roof. This shelter would keep Felicity alive during the cold weather, he explained, but only if the walls were chinked.

There was no help for it. Flora collected horse droppings in a bucket and mixed them into a sludge with creek mud and water. As she poked the disgusting mixture into the cracks with her bare hands, she remembered the old saying about "the girl so pure that she couldn't say manure." Was there no end to the indignities of pioneer life? Nellie and Jack chinked the larger barn at their place, and Flora reflected that the children might be good for something after all.

As she raked the roughened earth, she heard a small voice.

"Excuse me, Miss Craigie."

An odd little creature stood behind her, looking like a Scottish bog fairy except this one was wearing a blue sunbonnet. It was Nellie. Every inch of her bare skin was smeared with a layer of mud to keep off the mosquitoes. The whites of her eyes were luminous in her brown face. The effect was so ridiculous that Flora was hard-pressed to keep from laughing.

"My ma sent over this bread for you. She just baked it." Nellie held out an oblong object wrapped in a gingham tea towel.

"Thank you," Flora said, as she took the warm loaf from Nellie's dirty little hands with her larger, dirtier ones. "That's very kind, but please tell her not to bother. I can bake my own."

Mrs. Penrose was a generous soul, but she would prefer not to owe her any favours. And Flora definitely didn't want the young Penroses dropping by. They had already named the path between their homesteads Buffalo Bean Boulevard and placed a row of stepping stones across the creek. Flora was sorely tempted to remove them.

The next day, it was their mother who crossed the creek. Flora was kneeling in the dirt, placing her seeds in precise rows. She was dressed in her usual work clothes, but she had followed Nellie's example and swabbed every exposed inch of skin from her neck to her ankles with mud. When she saw her neighbour approach, her first impulse was to hide behind the shack. She didn't care what Mrs. Penrose thought of her appearance, but she was determined to squash any further attempt at familiarity.

The rippling of the waist-high grass behind Mrs. Penrose showed that she was accompanied by her unkempt border collie, his fur clotted with knots and burrs. Sourdough had dropped off the dog in his usual graceless manner, claiming it would keep away the wolves. Wolves! Flora envisioned the wolf packs in folk tales that attacked Russians riding in sleighs over the frozen steppes and tore them into bloody pieces. She doubted this ragged mutt, named Taffy, would be a match for any wolf.

"Morning, Miss Craigie."

Flora nodded and kept on with her work. "Good morning, Mrs. Penrose."

"And how are you this fine day? You have a nice piece of garden here."

"I'm well, thank you. May I help you with something?"

"Perhaps you may."

Flora waited for the dreaded request.

"Would you be wanting to buy my milk and butter? I bought a cow and calf yesterday from a farmer four miles up north. I need milk for my own brood, but Blossom is such a good milker I have plenty left over. I'm churning my own butter, too."

Flora dropped another cabbage seed into the waiting soil while she considered. She wanted to refuse, but the notion of fresh milk for her porridge and butter for her bannock was irresistible. "How much are you charging?"

"Two cents a quart for the milk, and fifteen cents a pound for the butter. I asked the Chicken Ladies, too. They might be gentry, but they aren't high cockalorum, so I guess we'll get along fine. They ordered two pounds of butter every week. So did Sourdough Buckhorn, although he complained about the price."

"I'll take a pound of butter and a quart of milk," Flora said. "I'll come and fetch them every Saturday." Surely there could be no harm in a commercial transaction.

"I'm going to do Sourdough's washing as well," Mrs. Penrose said. "When I walked over to his place to ask about the milk, I noticed a shirt and a pair of trousers floating in the creek. He told me in his usual angry way that's how he washes his clothes—ties them to a branch and throws them into the water for a few days, then fishes them out and dries them on a stump."

Flora laughed in spite of herself. "That explains his appearance."

"That's not the worst of it! When I asked if he washed his sheets the same way, he said he never washes them at all! I peeked into the open door and saw his bunk with the linens all crumpled into a rat's nest, the colour of egg yolks and stiff with dirt!"

Flora grimaced. "He really is the most repulsive man."

"That he is. I stood right up to him and told him to give me that bedding and Jack would bring it back before dark. He was in such a rage I was afraid he might strike me! And then, without another word, he rolled them into a ball and handed them over. Told me he would pay me twenty cents a week, not a penny more. And I was about to ask for ten!"

"You'll earn every cent, doing laundry for a man as filthy as Sourdough."

Mrs. Penrose shrugged. "I've spent my life washing coal dust out of men's clothes and there's nothing nastier. But arian is the key that opens all locks, as they say back home, arian being the Welsh word for money. I'll not keep you from your work any longer. Thank you kindly, Miss Craigie."

She turned and trotted back across the creek, Taffy at her heels. Flora acknowledged a grudging admiration for the little widow. Mr. Cook had told them that homesteaders raised cash however they could, trading everything from pails to pillows, even farming out their own children to work. Mrs. Penrose had already found a way to make some arian. She was more resourceful than Flora had guessed.

Sitting down to eat her supper of sardines and canned peas that evening, Flora jumped when she heard a knock. She peeped through her front window to see a scrawny man with a bedraggled grey moustache, fingering a disreputable felt hat.

She opened the door a few inches. "May I help you?"

"How do, ma'am. I surely hope you may." He licked his lips and swallowed. "The name's Royal Dunne. I live six miles yonder, on the way to Lacombe."

He pulled an envelope from his breast pocket and spoke without taking a breath. "I got back from the lands office yesterday. This here's my deed; I'm all proved up. I got twenty acres to crop and two horses and two cows, and this summer I finished a real good house."

He paused and took another deep breath. "What I need is a wife, and I heard you was a spinster. I thought we might get hitched, join forces, you might say. It's lonesome out here for a single man, especially since I ain't much of a cook. I wondered if you would have me."

During this speech Flora's jaw had fallen open, and now she snapped it shut. "Mr. Dunne, I don't even know you!"

"I already told you everything there is to know. I got two horses and two cows and a good house and title to a quarter section."

The man was so earnest that Flora almost regretted dashing his hopes. She tried to sound pleasant. "Ach, Mr. Dunne, I appreciate your offer, but I'm not wanting a husband. I intend to prove up my own homestead. Good luck, and I hope you find someone who, er, deserves you."

"A good evening to you, ma'am. If I'm still single when you change your mind, the offer stands." Flora watched as he rode away, reflecting with some bitterness that even Mr. Dunne would make a better husband than the one she had chosen.

The next day, when she fetched her milk and butter, she couldn't resist telling Mrs. Penrose about her proposal.

"Miss Craigie, he came to me with the same offer! And he told me straight out that he had already asked you, and both of the Chicken Ladies! I would have liked to see their faces! He was that disappointed when I refused him. He was sure that one of us would jump at the chance to marry him!"

The widow was laughing so hard that she had to wipe her eyes on her apron. "And then, if you please, he said, 'Well then, if you won't have me as your husband, will you do my washing? I hear old Sourdough has an arrangement with you, and I'll have the same. And I'll take a pound of butter a week, and two loaves of bread if you have a mind to bake extra.'"

Flora couldn't resist laughing with her. "It seems his visit was a blessing in disguise."

"'The bud may have a bitter taste, but sweet will be the flower,'" Mrs. Penrose quoted, as she handed Flora a pound of butter wrapped in cheesecloth. Then she became serious. "Miss Craigie, for one brief moment I considered whether to accept his proposal. Maybe it would be best for the children to have a roof over their heads that's free and clear. But I'm powerful determined that Jack must have his own place."

As if flaunting its fertility, the entire country now became one gigantic flower garden. The meadow blazed with yellow buttercups and buffalo beans, masses of purple and blue vetch. Pink prairie roses perfumed the air and mingled with the scent of the golden flowers growing thickly on the silver-leafed shrubs called wolf willows. The fragrance was so overpowering that it coated Flora's nose and throat.

For the third time this morning, she knelt beside her garden, searching in vain for signs of life. Why was everything on God's green earth growing except her garden? Had she planted her seeds too deeply? Was the earth too cold for them to germinate?

As she stood and whacked the dirt off her knees, she noticed a trail of smoke rising above the heavy bush that bordered the back of her property. Jessie McDonald must be at home. She had a sudden urge to find out where this mysterious neighbour lived.

Flora walked along the bank of the creek until she reached the bush. These woods were lighter than the heavy forest that grew in the Scottish Highlands. The trunks were smaller than her waist and their branches, although thick and full, were no bigger than her wrist. The greatest obstacle to walking was the tangled undergrowth.

Taking one last look behind her, Flora plunged into the bush and ploughed along for several hundred yards, leaving a trail of flattened grass and broken branches, until she came to a clearing. In the centre stood a log cabin.

Flora stopped and stared. Here was the typical rustic structure, not unlike Felicity's barn, made from tree trunks covered with bark, and chinked with mud. What made this one different was the triangular rack of peeled saplings beside the front door, draped with strips of drying meat; and the silvery wolf pelt nailed to the wall.

Nearby was a log rail corral where four nervous horses were stamping and tossing their heads. A fifth horse, coal black and shining, grazed beside the cabin, untethered. He eyed her while he crunched the fresh grass with his strong teeth.

Without warning, two dogs rushed from behind the cabin and bounded toward her, barking furiously. They were large animals of an indeterminate breed, mottled in colour. Flora snatched up a stick, holding it like a cricket bat with both hands, her pulse racing as she imagined herself going down, her flesh tearing under their sharp fangs.

The cabin door flew open and a man emerged. He put two fingers to his mouth and whistled. The dogs dropped to their stomachs as if they had been shot, watching Flora warily, lips curled back from their teeth.

So her neighbour wasn't single after all.

With a sudden indrawn breath, Flora realised that the figure was a woman. A dark braid hung over one shoulder. She wore a fringed buckskin jacket and leggings, moccasins on her feet. Strapped around her slender waist was a hunting knife in a leather sheath.

The woman whistled again, and the dogs came running. Without speaking, she pointed to the ground, first on her left and then on her right, and the animals stationed themselves on each side of her. The buckskin-clad figure beckoned to Flora with a single gesture.

Flora approached and stopped a few yards away, and the two women studied each other.

This unusual individual had high cheekbones and a strong jawline, her skin the same colour as that of any tanned white woman. She held herself erect, her chin high, as if she were looking down her nose at Flora, although they were the same height. Her eyes were a startling light-grey colour.

"Hello," Flora said. The other woman didn't respond. Perhaps she didn't speak English.

Flora tried again, forming her words slowly and carefully. "I live in yon house, to the east." She pointed in what she hoped was the general direction. "I'm your new neighbour."

The woman gazed at Flora without expression. "I know where you live." Her voice was low and mellow, and she sounded like every other Canadian Flora had met.

Flora was unsure how to continue. "I wanted to introduce myself since we live so near each other." She stepped forward and held out her hand. "My name is Flora Craigie." The other woman continued to stare at her, motionless. Flora's hand fell back to her side.

"I saw you come, you and the others," the woman said. "Where are your men?"

"Er, we don't have men. I mean, we aren't married. I'm on my own, and Mrs. Penrose lives with her three children. We've taken up homesteads. The other two ladies, Miss Greenwood and Miss Edgar, live in the yellow house. They're raising chickens."

The woman made a sound of disgust in her throat. "First the white men come and take the land, and now it's the white women!"

Apparently someone else didn't want her here. Flora tried again. "You're a woman too. Do you have a husband?"

"I don't need a man!" The woman struck her chest with her fist. "I can feed myself. I hunt and fish and live off the land. You people don't know what you're doing. That settler and his wife only lasted one winter. You will either starve or freeze to death."

Flora was silent as the woman's words struck home. It was true that she had no idea how to live off the land. Her education, her father's position, her ability to embroider a fine seam or polish a cruet—all these things were useless here. When it came to self-sufficiency, social class had no meaning. She was at the bottom of the heap. Feeling she should make some response, she retorted, somewhat feebly, "I'm going to break my land and grow grain."

"Break! The land doesn't need breaking!" The woman's eyes flashed. "The whites say the Indians waste the land, but the Indians only take what's on the surface. They don't plough it to ribbons, kill everything that grows on it, and drive away the game! At least the ranchers and fur traders use the land without destroying every living thing on it, but you farmers are the worst!"

She raised her hands to waist level, palms toward the sky. The dogs scrambled to their feet and bared their teeth, growling. "Go away and leave me alone!"

Flora didn't wait to be told twice. She turned and plunged headlong into the bush.

CHAPTER TWELVE

The nights were so short now that Flora fell asleep while her shack was filled with twilight and woke to find dawn breaking. In Scotland this was called simmer dim, the dusk that never becomes dark. The sunset filled the western sky as if some great fire were burning on the other side of the world, and the morning light rolled across the landscape in a golden flood.

When the first shoots emerged in her garden, Flora wanted to fling herself on the ground and embrace them. She watched them as closely as the Buffs minded their chicks, measuring their height with a piece of string, lugging buckets of water from the creek. She even sang to them, hymns she knew by heart from her years in the church choir.

Unfortunately, the weeds grew as quickly as the vegetables. Flora spent her days in a fierce battle with these pernicious pests. When her back gave out, she knelt. When her knees stiffened, she squatted and took frog-like jumps along the rows.

One afternoon, as she was plucking weeds and singing "Work, For the Night Is Coming," she noted with satisfaction that her pea pods were plumping out. The lettuce leaves resembled lacy flower petals, and the red-veined beet leaves were as full and feathery as a lady's fan.

At the end of the row she stood to stretch, marvelling at the great snowy masses of sharp-edged clouds against the brilliant sky. A few minutes later, she glanced up to see them rising higher and higher, mounting each other until they formed a giant wall of white boulders, moving as quickly as a galloping horse. Flora went back to work, pausing when a shadow blotted out the sun. The clouds were directly overhead. The breeze dropped, and the air became deadly calm.

Abruptly, the wind struck like a whip. A small white stone hit the ground at Flora's feet as if it had been shot from a pistol and bounced into the air, higher than her chimney. With a cracking sound, another pebble struck the shingled roof of her shack, followed by a dozen more. One of them smacked into Flora's upturned face and stung her cheek.

She ran toward the shack as more began to pelt her head and body. Hurling herself inside, she slammed the door as hundreds, then thousands, plummeted from the sky. The first missiles were the size of marbles, but they soon swelled to the size of eggs. From her windows she could see them rebounding crazily off the ground, rising to smash into the wall of new stones on their way down.

Flora cried aloud but couldn't hear herself above the roar of the hail. It sounded as if a thousand men were beating their hammers on the roof. Her knees gave out, and she fell onto her cot and buried her face. There was nothing to do, nowhere to hide.

The stones rang against the glass panes, rattling in their flimsy frames, until the front window shattered, sending shards of glass flying across the room. A flurry of hailstones invaded her home and piled up in glistening heaps against the legs of the furniture. Flora pulled her blanket over her head but could feel them hitting her through the fabric. She screamed into her pillow.

As suddenly as it had arrived, the bombardment ended. The world fell still again, except for the odd hailstone banging against the roof like a farewell fist. Flora shook the stones from her blanket and rose on unsteady legs. Picking her way among the broken glass and slippery pellets, she stepped outside.

Only minutes had passed, yet this was a different world. Where once there had been birdsong, now there was a morbid silence. The earth had been churned as if it were butter. Grass and mud clung to her door, thrown up by the force of the hail. The leaves were shredded on their branches, the spruce trees stripped bare of their needles. A musty smell filled the air.

Sick with apprehension, Flora raced around the corner of the shack. Her garden lay in ribbons. She fell to her knees and tried to lift a few plants out of their earthy graves, but they came apart when she touched them. Nature, so beautiful and bountiful, had betrayed her. She put her filthy hands to her face and wept.

But what about her neighbours? Flora flew across the creek to find the Penroses standing outside their front door, their faces pale and drawn. Nellie's eyes were swollen, and the baby was hiccupping with sobs, but the Penrose garden had been saved.

"The storm wound through here like a snake," Mrs. Penrose said in a hushed voice. "It hit the cabin first, then changed direction and crossed the creek." She pointed at the path of the hail, the grass beaten down as if a giant slug had rolled over the earth. "We were afraid for Taffy, but when we called him, his head popped out of the woodpile. He had burrowed himself right into the middle."

"We must go and check on the Chicken Ladies," Flora said.

Flora and Mrs. Penrose, together with three frightened children, walked along the grassy trail and down the lane to the yellow house, picking their way between streams of mud, small lakes of water, and piles of glistening hailstones.

Aside from the obvious damage surrounding them, it was as peaceful as though the storm had never happened. The air was cool and fresh, fragrant with the perfume of wolf willow and wild roses, the sky once again deep blue and cloudless.

When they came into the yard, they found both ladies standing in a sea of mud between the house and the chicken coop. Wren was sobbing, her hair loose and falling down her neck. Miss Edgar had one arm around her shoulders.

Surrounding them lay the bloody, beaten bodies of two dozen Buff Orpingtons. Feathers clung to the grass and mud, while a couple of them floated in the air. One hen's head had been torn off and was lying some distance from its body.

"Oh, what a terrible shame!" Flora exclaimed. "Can we do anything to help?"

Miss Edgar shook her head. "Not much, I'm afraid. I'm going to take Wren inside and give her a shot of brandy. Perhaps you need one too."

Everyone trooped into the house. Miss Edgar led Wren to the rocking chair and poured her a glass of amber liquid. Wren had stopped crying, but she was staring fixedly at the wall. "The poor thing is in shock," Miss Edgar said. "You know how she loves those fowl."

Mrs. Penrose turned to the children and whispered, "Jack, Nellie, leave the baby here. Go and pile the dead chickens behind the coop, out of sight."

The children went off to perform their grisly task.

Flora went to Wren and knelt beside her. "I'm so sorry, Wren."

The other woman raised her tear-stained face. "My poor chicks. We tried to chase them inside, but they were so confused, they ran every which way. If only Beau had been here." Her eyes widened with a look of horror. "Beau! He's on his way home!"

Just then they heard a shout from Jack and hurried to the door. Beau rode into the yard, hugging his pinto's neck. His hat was battered to a pulp, his emerald-green shirt torn to shreds. He slid off the saddle and was surrounded by the women and children.

"I'm all right, ladies, but it was a close call. The first sign I had was when a hailstone the size of a baseball bounced off the ground in front of my horse, so I dug in my spurs and rode hell-bent for leather. We nearly outran it, too, but it caught us where the trail forks. My back took the brunt of it."

The ladies exclaimed over his back, covered with round red marks between the fabric remnants. "Poor Sadie here was pretty scared, but her hide is a lot tougher than mine." He patted the frightened horse. "I think my hat will recover with a good brush and steam. I sure hate to lose my new shirt, though."

"Go into the house, Beau, while I look after Sadie," said Miss Edgar. "Wren can take care of your injuries."

She spoke to the others. "Thank you for coming. You'll be wanting to tend to your own homes, I'm sure." She lowered her voice, checking to see that Wren was out of earshot. "Take a few chickens with you. The meat is fresh, and you can make use of it."

Flora walked home holding a dead Buff Orpington. Jack carried one in each hand.

"I'm going to pluck and clean these birds for supper," Mrs. Penrose said, when they reached the path to Flora's property. "Miss Craigie, won't you join us? There's nothing you can do about your garden. As they say in Wales, it's a lang road that has no turning. We might as well break bread together and count our blessings."

All at once Flora dreaded returning to her lonely shack, filled with broken glass and melting hailstones, seeing her devastated garden. The Penrose family were not the companions she would have chosen, but they exuded warmth and kindness. Her eyes filled with tears of gratitude.

"Thank you, Mrs. Penrose. I would be pleased to accept your invitation."

Two days later, a sorrowful Flora was raking her dead plants into a pile when Sterling Payne came riding over the hill in his long black coat. The massacre of her garden had left her in a state of mourning. Having Payne appear like an unwanted guest at the wake was almost too much to bear.

Abandoning the ragged remains of her vegetables, she hurried inside to hide her few personal items and shove the chamber pot under the bed. She watched through the window as he tied his horse to the nearest tree, slapping it viciously in the face with his reins when the poor beast tried to back away.

When his knock came, she counted to ten before opening the door. It gave her a tiny measure of satisfaction to make him wait.

"Miss Craigie." He took off his bowler and smoothed his thin hair with one hand before pushing himself forward, so that she was forced to step aside to avoid touching him. "I see that you lost your garden in the recent hailstorm. Another reason you should abandon this mad quest of yours."

"Ach, I'm not ready to give up yet, Mr. Payne."

"It's only a matter of time," he said in his reedy voice. "Let's have another look at your paperwork."

"Mr. Payne, please. You've already inspected my papers."

"Just a formality."

"Won't you have a seat?" She had no choice but to agree.

He pulled out one of the wooden chairs and sat down, leaning back on two legs. At first Flora hoped they wouldn't break, and then hoped they would.

"I see you lost one of your windows," he said, pointing to the empty frame. "That must be replaced." Flora had tacked a flour sack over the opening. It made the light inside the shack dim, almost intimate. She went to the door and opened it, trying to lessen the effect of being closeted together in such a confined space.

Payne watched while Flora pulled her leather pouch from under the bed, trying to kneel sideways without presenting her backside to him. She opened it and placed her Homestead Application on the table.

He turned it this way and that toward the sunlight streaming through the door.

"Do you have anything that proves your identity?"

Flora reached into the pouch and withdrew her birth certificate. Her hand was steady, thankfully, but she prayed that he wouldn't ask for anything else.

He read the certificate, his lips moving. "You are twenty-four years old. Most women your age are married by now." He gazed at Flora with narrowed eyes, as if studying her for hidden flaws. "You appear to be healthy, and you're not unattractive. Why are you still single?"

Flora's jaw tightened, but she answered truthfully. "I suppose I lacked the opportunity to meet potential husbands during my previous employment as a lady's companion."

He grinned, showing his small teeth. "You don't have that problem here. Women are in great demand, even the ugly ones. You could have your pick of husbands."

She didn't answer him.

"Anything else? Anything to prove you are single?"

"Mr. Payne, be reasonable." Flora forced a false smile, although her heart rate quickened. "How do you expect me to prove that I'm not married? I've already sworn on my Homestead Application that I'm a spinster. I have nothing else to show you except my school leaving certificate."

She withdrew the document and laid it on the table rather than pass it to him, anxious to avoid the touch of his hand. Scotland had a high standard of public education, and Flora had graduated at the head of her class. Her certificate cited "With Honours."

Payne's face was impassive. "Do you have anything more recent?"

Flora did not. She pretended to search her pouch again, stalling for time.

With a rush of relief she remembered a card in the side pocket. "I don't have anything except this, but it's dated only six months ago."

With a flourish, she presented her Aberdeen Public Library Card, listing her name as Flora May Craigie. He examined the date and handed it back to her. "When did you enter this country, Miss Craigie?"

"Three months ago, on April 24, 1905."

"You must have been granted entrance by the authorities. Where are your immigration papers?"

Flora struggled to keep her face expressionless. "I'm afraid they were lost when my trunk was stolen from the train. That's why I have so few possessions." She gestured around the room. He must be aware that even the poorest settler arrived with trunks full of belongings.

"I trust your financial situation was not affected by this mysterious theft."

Flora guessed he was trying to calculate how much money she had. "Fortunately, I carried my savings with me. However, I lost my entire wardrobe and a number of personal items which had great sentimental value." She spoke with such feeling that Mr. Payne must hear the ring of truth.

After placing his bowler on his head, he walked to the door and turned back, his eyes roving around the room one last time. Flora held her breath, waiting for some further intrusion on her privacy, some question she was unable to answer.

His skimpy eyebrows drew together, and he glared at her. His high-pitched voice sounded like a fingernail on a frying pan. "Miss Craigie, let me remind you that misrepresenting yourself to a government official won't just result in the cancellation of your homestead. It's a criminal offence, punishable by jail."

CHAPTER THIRTEEN

Flora pressed a sheet of newspaper, liberally slathered with flour-and-water paste, to the wall above her bed. The papers were passed along from Miss Edgar, an avid reader who took the dailies from Edmonton, Toronto, and Boston, plus the weekly *Lacombe Globe* and *Toddsville Free Press*.

"By the time the papers get here, the news has whiskers on it," she said, "but we want to know what's happening in the outside world, even if we don't care to be part of it."

Flora read every word several times, although the people and places outside her own small sphere had shrunk into insignificance. Sometimes she was even able to forget Hector for a brief interval—although the memory always returned with the force of a blow.

When applied to the walls, the newspapers served a more practical purpose: they kept out drafts. They also provided visual interest, packed with illustrated advertisements offering everything from sewing machines to stomach remedies to horseflesh. Horses were the lifeblood of this new country, and horse trading was the liveliest of occupations.

"They say Matthew Cook never comes home with the same horse he left on," said Beau, who went into Toddsville every week to fetch the mail and the local gossip. He told them that Miss McDonald was earning quite a reputation as a horsewoman. Locals brought her their unbroken horses "to take the buck out of them." She also roamed around the countryside on her black mustang Tipiskow, the Cree word for "night," catching wild horses, breaking them to saddle, and selling them.

One sunny afternoon, Flora had seen an example of Miss McDonald's skills. She had been filling a bucket with plump purple saskatoons beside the creek when her reclusive neighbour emerged from the bush, leading a russet-coloured stallion. A strip of cloth covered his eyes. The horse was snorting and sidestepping, eager to rid himself of the strange leather apparatus strapped to his back. Shivers rippled down his hide from his neck to his hindquarters. Flora shrank behind the shrubs and watched.

Wearing her usual leggings and moccasins, Miss McDonald led the horse into a channel of the creek where the water flowed swift and wide. When she was up to her thighs in the muddy stream, she swung herself into the saddle. The horse tried to throw her off, but his lower legs were buried so deeply in mud that he couldn't buck. First he pulled his front left hoof out of the silt, then replaced it with his front right hoof. He tried kicking his back hooves, but to no avail. The water sucked and swirled around his belly while he tossed his head and whinnied with frustration. Meanwhile, his rider stroked his neck and murmured in his cocked ear.

Finally the stallion stood quite still, his flanks quivering. Miss McDonald pulled back on the reins and walked him toward the bank. As soon as the horse found himself in shallow water, he began to buck, arching his back and twisting his body into a crescent. His rider vaulted off the saddle with the grace of a bird in flight and led him back into the mud, where once again he found himself unable to move.

After this process was repeated three or four times, the stallion ceased his struggle. His mistress rode him onto the bank, still speaking to him in a low voice. Horse and rider disappeared into the trees at a slow walk.

Flora had also seen a man breaking his wild horse in the corral next to the Lacombe livery stable. She was shocked by the way the man had beaten the animal with a crop and how it had thrown itself against the wooden rails of the enclosure until its sides were bleeding. Miss McDonald's method was so much gentler that Flora was filled with new admiration for her mysterious neighbour.

Along with horses and all manner of settler supplies, the local newspapers listed auction sales. Every week, failed farmers sold their belongings and moved away.

"Miss Craigie, you should attend an auction if you need anything," Miss Edgar said. "I hear things often go for a song." She drew Flora's attention to an upcoming sale two miles north of Toddsville.

The advertisement told the familiar tale:

> One Bay Mare with colt at foot; One Jersey Cow with calf at foot; One black Percheron stallion named Parsifal; One Sow with six Piglets; Family Buggy, little used. Household Goods: Kitchen Table & Four Chairs; Piano; "Home Comfort" Cookstove; Double Iron Bedstead; Washing Machine & Wringer; Commode; Butter Churn; Kitchen Utensils; and a Great Number of Other Articles.

"Beau says the family is leaving for the Coast, as everyone here calls it," Miss Edgar said. "The West Coast is the mecca for failed homesteaders. They can start a dairy farm or fruit orchard with less work, and in a more temperate climate. I sometimes wonder if we made the right choice in moving here."

"Do you think they might sell clothing?" Flora asked. It was August, and she was anxious about her scanty wardrobe. Her shirtwaists were patched at the elbows and both woollen skirts were showing signs of hard wear.

"Perhaps," said Miss Edgar. "One never knows until one arrives."

Flora fretted about whether to show herself at a public auction, but she decided to risk it. Early that morning she set off with the team and wagon. When she reached the homestead, she found the yard filled with dozens of wagons and buggies and horses tied to various fenceposts and trees. She drove the team efficiently under the farthest clump of poplars before arranging her veil over her face and joining the crowd.

The sale began with the livestock. Since Flora had no interest in animals, she walked around the yard, examining the sad jumble of possessions. A tea-kettle, a lamp with no chimney, a cracked chamber pot. A tennis racquet—she wondered who had assumed they would be playing tennis. Everything seemed so small and pitiful in this landscape of colossal proportions. She was momentarily intrigued when she found a box of books, but all of them concerned animal husbandry.

The weather-beaten homesteader was laughing and joking with the other men, bragging about how he would send them a box of apples from the Coast. His wife stood to one side, wiping her hands on her apron. Her face worked as if she were fighting back tears.

Flora was ready to give up when she spied a sleeve hanging from a wooden crate. She knelt on the grass and began to sort through the box with mounting excitement. Here was long underwear, a heavy tweed jacket, a pair of men's woollen breeks, and striped flannel pyjamas. Best of all, there was a pair of bib-and-brace denim overalls, only a little stained at the knees. She stood and held them against herself. They were too big, but she could make them fit.

As she folded them back into the crate, the homesteader's wife approached.

"Those belonged to my brother. He went home to England. I kept his socks, but everything else was too small for my husband. Do you want them for your own man?"

"Nay, for myself," Flora replied, dropping her eyes.

The woman seemed unsurprised. "There's plenty of material in those things if you're handy with a needle."

"Indeed, they're verra fine goods," said Flora. "Well, I wish you better luck at the Coast."

"No matter where we end up, it can't be worse than this place."

There was no answer for this, so Flora excused herself to check on Bessie and Bob. She ate her bread and hard-boiled eggs, drank tepid water from her glass jar, and returned to the yard. When the last piglet was sold, the auctioneer began with the implements. A group of men stood before him in a semicircle, raising their hands and hastening away with their purchases.

The crowd thinned out. It was late afternoon before the household goods were brought forward. It took a long time to sell the smaller items—a painted vase, a pair of ice skates—but at last the box of men's clothing went on the block.

"How much am I bid?" the auctioneer asked.

A man standing at the front shouted, "One dollar!"

Flora raised her hand. The auctioneer didn't see her at the rear of the crowd, so she straightened her arm and waggled her fingers. "One dollar and five cents!" she called.

The first bidder turned and glared at her. "One dollar and fifty cents!"

"One dollar and fifty-five cents!" Flora's voice was determined.

The remaining customers craned their necks toward her, and the auctioneer grinned. "The young lady here needs some new duds for her husband! Maybe she thinks he isn't smart enough!" There were a few scattered chuckles.

"One dollar and seventy-five cents!" shouted the man in front.

Flora opened her reticule and checked inside. All she had brought with her were two one-dollar bills, one nickel and two pennies.

"What do you say, miss? Do you want to bid a dollar eighty?"

Flora yearned for those overalls. "Two dollars and seven cents!"

This time the crowd broke into laughter.

"Two dollars and seven cents! Do I have another bid?"

Flora held her breath, but there was no response from her opponent.

The auctioneer tried again. "Sir, would you like to make a better offer?"

Her adversary turned on his heel and stomped away.

"Going once, going twice, sold to the young lady in the back!" The hammer fell.

Flora paid the auctioneer's assistant and lifted the crate to her chest. Two men offered to carry it to the wagon for her, but she refused.

"That's one of them lady farmers from east of town, I'll bet," she heard someone say. Disturbed by his words, Flora determined not to leave her property again. She could not afford to court any further attention. It was just too risky.

Flora picked and preserved three dozen jars of wild fruit, grateful that the cook in Mrs. Galt's kitchen had shown her how. She boiled batches of tiny, sweet strawberries and fat juicy raspberries. She experimented with several unfamiliar varieties—chokecherries, pincherries, and high-bush cranberries. The cooked rosehips formed a thick sludge until poured into glass jars and cooled, when they turned a lovely shade of amber.

These were her pleasantest days yet. The cool weather had ended the scourge of the mosquitoes, but the air was still warm. The meadow glowed with orange tiger lilies, golden sunflowers, Black-Eyed Susans, and bluebells. Flora ate all her meals outdoors. Seated on her wooden chair, she felt like a queen on her throne, monarch of all she surveyed.

Until Payne made another appearance.

He caught Flora in an undignified position, lying on her stomach and crooning "Wild Mountain Thyme" to her root vegetables. She had been overjoyed to discover that her potatoes, carrots, turnips, parsnips, and beets had survived the hailstorm, sheltered beneath the soil. Even the tattered leaves were showing signs of revival.

It wasn't until a narrow shadow fell across them that she realised she wasn't alone.

"Good morning, Miss Craigie."

She recognised Payne's tinny voice and scrambled to her feet.

He wasn't looking at her—his eyes were fixed on the twine strung from the shack to the nearest tree. On it, the clothes she had scrubbed early that morning on her washboard were drying in the breeze. The men's overalls, striped pyjamas, and long underwear waved their arms and legs merrily, as if mocking their unwelcome visitor.

He lifted his forefinger in the direction of his bowler without touching it and faced her with a triumphant smirk. "And whose clothes might these be, Miss Craigie?" he asked, emphasising the word *Miss*.

"They are mine, Mr. Payne."

"Do you honestly expect me to believe that? You must think I'm a fool."

Flora wanted to answer yes, but she smiled sweetly instead. "You may believe whatever you choose, but I assure you those clothes belong to me."

"It's obvious you have a man around here somewhere. If I find any sign of him, I'll cancel this claim so fast your empty little head will spin!"

He had never been this insulting before. Instead of the familiar fear, this time Flora felt nothing but rage. "You're welcome to search anywhere you please."

Payne walked straight into her shack. She heard him banging around and hated this intrusion into her personal space. Flora was happy that Beau had replaced her broken window, giving Payne one less reason for complaint. He emerged, strode past her without a word and went into the barn, where she heard Felicity give a nervous nicker. When he emerged, he set off toward the ploughed field. He bent and examined the single set of boot prints she had left earlier while removing her daily quota of twenty rocks.

"You haven't searched the root cellar," Flora called. Beau had dug a pit next to her door where her precious root vegetables, wrapped in burlap and buried in sawdust, would spend the winter. She had originally planned a shallow hole, but Beau set her straight.

"Miss Craigie, the frost line goes down to six feet, sometimes more."

"Nay, you canna be serious." Flora tried to imagine the earth frozen as solid as iron to a depth of six feet. It seemed unbelievable, but Beau shovelled a hole eight feet deep and four feet square, and covered it with a wooden lid. The cellar was accessed by means of a crude ladder, strapped together with leather thongs.

Payne threw open the trap door and peered into the cavern. He returned to her side, his thin lips twisted with resentment.

"Aren't you forgetting something, Mr. Payne?" Flora gestured toward the outhouse.

His pale eyes bored into her as he calculated whether she was canny enough to hide someone in this unlikely place, and then invite him to look. But he wasn't taking any chances.

He hurried to the toilet and hesitated before throwing open the door. Flora watched as he stepped inside and bent over the single hole before straightening up with a disgusted expression. Flora smothered a laugh.

He came toward her, his face twitching with anger. "You may think you're clever, Miss, but you'll find the government isn't so easily hoodwinked."

"I'm confident that the Dominion of Canada will treat me with the fairness it guarantees to all British subjects." She clung to the hope that Payne was answerable to a higher authority.

"What do you know about our government?" he snarled. "You probably can't even name the prime minister."

"Sir Wilfrid Laurier, of course." Flora tried not to appear smug. "The Liberal Party was re-elected last November for their fourth term. The prime minister himself is scheduled to visit Edmonton next week, to celebrate the inauguration of our new province, named after Queen Victoria's daughter, Alberta."

Secretly, she breathed a sigh of relief. She had been sadly ignorant of Canadian politics until she had read Miss Edgar's newspapers. As a new resident, she had been interested to learn that the federal government, reluctant to give the west too much power, had scrapped its plan to create one huge province called Buffalo, and instead carved the North-West Territories into two provinces: Alberta and Saskatchewan.

His high-pitched voice rose higher. "You're well informed, Miss Craigie. I suppose you're one of those women who think they should have the vote."

"I believe that women will be enfranchised in the very near future, Mr. Payne."

"You are wrong, quite wrong," he said. "Women have no place in politics. They should tend to the role assigned to them by our Great Creator."

Once again, Flora resented this reference to God. "Surely both men and women are capable of fulfilling more than one role."

"Time will prove that women are unfit to perform the duties of a homesteader. Our federal minister, Mr. Frank Oliver, agrees with me."

"I'm aware of Mr. Oliver's views on the matter," Flora said through gritted teeth. An ardent supporter of the West, Oliver was also a loyal Liberal who had been awarded two plum appointments after his party's recent victory: Superintendent-General of Indian Affairs; and Minister of the Interior, responsible for the Dominion Lands Act. He also published the region's first newspaper, the *Edmonton Bulletin*, and he made no bones about the fact that he was opposed to women farmers.

"I suspect that Mother Nature will accomplish what the law has so far been unable to do. Miss Craigie, I don't believe you've experienced a Canadian winter."

"You already know the answer to that, Mr. Payne."

"There's a reason that spring sees a mass departure of those poor souls who can't endure our harshest season. You'll be on the first train out after the thaw—if you're still alive."

CHAPTER FOURTEEN

Truly, Miss Craigie, how much firewood do you think we need?" Mrs. Penrose asked.

Flora had come to fetch her butter and milk, and the two women stood outside, inspecting the woodpile. Overnight, the first glittering frost had transformed the landscape into a spectacular fairyland. Flora had exclaimed aloud when she beheld the stunning beauty of the silver filigreed branches, but her initial delight was followed by one of those plummeting drops in confidence. The deadly cold was creeping closer.

Jack had been spending his daylight hours cutting wood. He was just strong enough to chop down dead trees in the plentiful bush, attach them to Bob's harness with a chain, and snake them into the yard. The straightest logs were stacked beside the barn, ready for the rail fence to be built next spring. The others would be burned to keep their hearts beating through the coldest months.

Nellie helped, too. Using the hatchet, she hacked the branches into kindling while Jack and his mother stood at each end of the crosscut saw, laboriously dragging the serrated blade back and forth across the trunks, cutting them into foot-long pieces and tossing them onto the woodpile.

For extra fuel, Nellie gathered "flops," the dried patties produced by Blossom and her calf Petal, that burned hot in the stove without any smell. Flora had once found the girls playing animal doctor. Each had a stick, and they were stirring the cow pies to unveil the colour inside. "If it's bright green, that means the cow is healthy," said Nellie with her usual serious demeanour. Flora was surprised to find Nellie at play. She was such a solemn little thing, like a miniature adult rather than a child. Jewel was the opposite, always beaming. She laughed and waved her stick cheerfully. Flora dodged as a dollop of wet manure missed her head.

Now Flora studied the pile, trying unsuccessfully to calculate what volume of firewood was required for the coming ordeal. "My pile isn't as big as yours, but of course my shack is smaller."

Mrs. Penrose frowned. "To be honest, I suspect that the old-timers are pulling our leg when they warn us about the cold. It isn't as though we're living at the North Pole. According to the map, Toddsville is almost as far south as Swansea!"

Flora wasn't sure. Hector had joked that the old country was referred to as Evergreen England, because it produced so many greenhorns. "It's the land agent's prayer: 'O Lord, give us this day our daily Englishman!'" And Mr. Cook had told them about two young bachelors who burned all their firewood and then every stick of furniture in their cabin before taking to their bedrolls, never to rise again.

"Perhaps we should err on the side of caution," she said.

Mrs. Penrose sighed. "Much as I hate the sight of coal, we could surely use some now."

Feeling something soft brush her ankle, Flora glanced down and saw the stray cat that had adopted the Penrose family. The children had named him, with a certain lack of imagination, Mr. Grey. He looked like a veteran of the North-West Rebellion. The tips of his ears must have frozen off, and his broken tail had healed with a crook in it. Mrs. Penrose allowed him to stay because he fed himself by catching mice in the barn.

As the women talked, a cloud of dust appeared over the hill, and within minutes Sourdough galloped Champion into the yard. When he dismounted, wearing his usual hostile expression, the ground seemed to shake under his giant boots. Flora took a step forward, refusing to be intimidated, while Mrs. Penrose took a step backward.

"You call that a woodpile?" he shouted. "That's no better than a heap of kindling!"

The women exchanged meaningful glances. Clearly this was another attempt to frighten them into leaving.

"You need at least ten cords!"

Flora had no idea how a cord of wood was measured, and she was sure Mrs. Penrose didn't, either. They were enlightened when he pointed at the woodpile and added, "You've only got half that much!"

He reached for the double-headed axe strapped behind his saddle, an awesome thing like a Viking's weapon. Flourishing it, he resembled a prehistoric warrior himself. All he needed was a horned helmet.

"You!" He roared at Jack, ignoring the women. "Sharpen your axe every night before you go to bed. It should be keen enough to shave with!" Jack nodded dutifully, although he wasn't nearly old enough to shave. Flora couldn't picture anyone shaving with an axe, least of all this wild and woolly westerner. Sourdough's beard obviously hadn't been touched in years.

With a graceful gesture, unanticipated in such a large man, Sourdough snatched a stick of firewood and split it in two with one blow before tossing his double-headed axe high into the air. The axe revolved several times, flashing in the sunshine, before he caught the handle in one hand and split the same log again, this time with the opposite blade. The women gasped in admiration, and Jewel laughed aloud, revealing two new teeth like tiny seed pearls.

Following this exhibition, Sourdough set to work in earnest. Stripping off his leather vest to reveal a plaid shirt full of holes, he grabbed his own saw from his pack. This was bow-shaped, designed for a single user. After slicing through the first trunk in ten strokes, he roared for another. Jack dragged the logs forward and Sourdough cut them into pieces as though he were dicing carrots.

Flora watched for some time before slipping away to her shack and climbing down into her root cellar, where she stored her butter and milk. The cellar was a most welcome addition to her household, as chilly as a cave, and sometimes on a hot day Flora went inside to cool off. With an abundance of caution, she had dug a hole in the earthen wall and buried the leather pouch containing her identification papers and her remaining cash, just enough to tide her over until harvest, inside a coffee tin.

She mounted the crude ladder and went into her shack, punched down the bread dough that had been rising all night, and popped two loaves into her oven. Two hours later, she left her crusty bread cooling in the open air and returned to see Sourdough's progress.

The pile of firewood had grown substantially. Sourdough paused to wipe the sweat off his brow with one dirty sleeve. It appeared that even this human sawmill was flagging. "Fetch your mother!" he roared at Jack.

The women and children gathered around him like biblical disciples while Sourdough shouted instructions. "Your woodpile is too far from the cabin. In a blizzard, you'll never make it back!" This time, Flora was positive he was exaggerating. The pile was no more than thirty steps from the door. "Stack your wood around the outside walls. That will keep the cabin warm, and you won't have far to go when you need more."

He pointed his sausage-sized forefinger at Mrs. Penrose, who didn't back down but clutched Jewel to her chest. "Make sure you always have dry kindling beside the stove. Don't run out of matches, whatever you do. And keep your axe inside, or it might disappear under the snow until spring!"

He turned to Flora. "As for you, that puny pile won't keep you alive until Christmas! I'll come over tomorrow and cut up some wood for you, too." Sourdough shook his head and muttered to himself, as if questioning his own sanity. "Damn and blast, I can't always be playing nursemaid to a bunch of simpletons!"

Almost overnight, autumn's beauty dissolved. The colour leached out of the landscape until the prairie grass turned dull and grey. The ground froze so hard that Flora's feet felt bruised through the soles of her boots. She had to break a hole in the ice to fetch water from the creek for herself and Felicity. The trees became naked black skeletons. At night they wore the stars on their branches like diamond earrings. Only the glorious blue sky remained, faithfully burning with scarlet fire at dawn and at dusk.

The regulations allowed homesteaders to live away for six months each year, but Flora wasn't going anywhere since this was the only place where she felt safe from discovery. The Penroses couldn't afford to live in town, although Jack's mother was concerned about his education.

"The lad will need to read and do sums when he starts farming," she told Flora. "Nellie doesn't need any more schooling. Better she doesn't learn about the frightful things happening in this old world." Flora opened her mouth to argue, then shut it again. The Penrose children were none of her business.

The Chicken Ladies had no desire to leave their comfortable house. It was built so soundly, the double walls insulated with sawdust and wood shavings, that it was cozy even in the coldest months. Jessie McDonald would remain here because she carried on her horse business year-round. The small community hunkered down and prepared for the worst.

Before the weather closed them off entirely, Flora, who hadn't left the farm for three months, dared to take the wagon into Toddsville one last time to purchase their winter supplies at the general store. The genial owner, Robert Sanderson—Sandy for short—offered his advice while she consulted her list. First she chose several items for warmth: a buffalo robe, a pair of fur-lined leather mitts, and two extra woolen blankets—one for Felicity, and one for herself. She gazed longingly at the yard goods, the bolts arranged diagonally on the shelf behind the counter to show their colours, cream and chocolate and plum. One day, perhaps, she could sew herself a new dress. For Mrs. Penrose, she bought an entire bolt of indigo wool, paid for with the widow's milk and butter money.

Then she stocked up on the usual staples and canned goods. How she longed for a juicy roast beef! After many hours of practice with her Winchester, she could send an empty tin can spinning into the air, but so far she hadn't killed any living thing. Sourdough had shown Jack how to snare rabbits. Their tender flesh was especially welcome now that Jewel was eating solid food, although her mother was trying to keep her on the breast as long as possible. Flora spent her own nickel to buy a bag of lemon drops for the children, and Mr. Sanderson helped her load everything into the wagon.

She wasn't far from town when the first snowflakes began to fall. At first these were graceful miniature lace doilies that covered her shoulders like fairy dust, quite different from the wet snow that blanketed the Scottish Highlands. Flora pursed her lips and blew at the flakes to see them sparkle and dance. However, it wasn't long before the wind strengthened, and these delicate fragments changed into stinging pellets. She pulled her tartan shawl over her head and urged Bob and Bess into a trot.

Within moments, they were enveloped in a cage of snow and the trail ahead was obliterated. Flora was unable to make out any demarcation between land and sky. Fighting a wave of panic, she decided to turn back, but when she looked behind her, she found that their tracks had vanished. Flora's blood literally ran cold.

Sourdough had told them that if caught in a storm, to give the horses their heads and they would find their way home. Flora loosened the reins and shouted, "Home, Bob! Home, Bessie!" She had to scream above the howling wind. The horses hesitated as they made some silent communication, and then picked up speed.

Reaching back into the wagon box, Flora pulled out her buffalo robe and draped it around her shoulders. The horses trotted into the swirling storm. Wherever there was a slight impediment to the blowing snow, a bush or even a clump of tall grass, the long tail of a snowdrift formed, and they had to break through it, dragging the steel-rimmed wagon wheels behind them.

Flora's hands grew numb inside her new leather mitts. Tying the reins to the rail on the wagon box, she stuck her hands inside the warmth of the buffalo robe, pulling it tightly around her head until she was peeking through a tiny gap. There was nothing to see but a milky whiteness. Her face was stiff with cold and fear.

She tried to remember what she was supposed to do if caught in a blizzard—turn the wagon over and take shelter underneath, try to stay alive until the storm passes, and whatever happens, don't fall asleep. Was she strong enough to flip the wagon? Dear God, how she wished she had listened more carefully. All the stories she had only half believed came flooding back—the man whose team brought home his body, sitting bolt upright and clutching the reins in his frozen dead hands. The woman who missed her own front door by three steps and wandered onto the prairie to die a lonely death. The remarkable number of people who had disappeared altogether, never to be seen again.

The drifts were growing thicker and denser. Whenever there was a lull in the wind, Flora caught a glimpse of the team's muscular hindquarters, surging ahead with stubborn determination, their flanks heaving with the strain.

The roar of the wind was oddly soothing, and Flora found herself getting drowsy. The revolving flakes made her feel so dizzy she was afraid she might fall from the wagon. They seemed to spin in a concentric circle that rotated to the left and to the right—and then shot outward in every direction as a fresh gust sent them spiralling.

The wind grew stronger, buffeting her head and shoulders. There was no reason to be sitting upright on the wagon seat. She crawled into the box behind and lay on her back, staring into the chalky sky. Fighting the urge to sleep, she fumbled her bare hand out of her mitt inside the buffalo robe and pinched her own breast, hard. Her flesh had so little feeling that it barely hurt. Her eyelids closed and her head lolled sideways.

When she felt the team falter, Flora jerked back into consciousness. They had encountered an exceptionally deep drift. The horses lifted their front hooves and plowed through it, but the wagon wheels jammed. Flora dragged herself to her knees and screamed with all her strength. "Gee, Bob! Gee, Bessie!"

The horses refused to give up. Again and again, they plunged and reared until the wagon gave a lurch. With one colossal heave, they pulled free of the drift and the wheels began to revolve again.

A foot of snow had filled the wagon box, and Flora slid back into its depths as if it were a feather comforter. The flakes fell on her numb cheeks and stuck in her eyelashes. She felt herself drifting into a white dreamland. She remembered her mother, her father, a doll she had once loved, a prize she had won in school, the sound of the rain on cobblestones, her own shimmering reflection in Mrs. Galt's silver teapot, the endless waves upon the Atlantic, the shifting ocean of prairie grass.

Then she saw, heard, felt nothing.

Flora's mind struggled to the surface only when her weight shifted. She was dimly aware that her feet were higher than her head. The wagon box was tilted forward at a steep angle. It was going downhill, moving faster than before. Had the horses lost their way? Were they seeking shelter in a ravine?

She closed her eyes, longing to drift into peaceful slumber, and then forced them open again. There was still nothing to see but the blurry white world above. With one monstrous effort, she gripped the edge of the wagon box with dead hands and raised her head high enough to peek over the edge. A rectangular shape emerged from the whirling snow.

It was the Penrose cabin.

The horses drew up next to the door, almost as if they wanted to go inside. Mrs. Penrose's face appeared in the lighted window. Her anxious expression changed to one of anguish when she caught sight of the empty wagon seat.

With her last ounce of strength, Flora lifted one leaden arm.

Mrs. Penrose and Jack hauled her inside on a blast of wind and snow.

"God be thanked! We've been on our knees this past hour, praying for your safe return!" She unwrapped Flora's outer things and led her to the stove, speaking to Jack over her shoulder. "The horses will find their own way to the barn, but unhitch the poor things and give them some extra oats. Miss Craigie owes them her life!"

Jack piled on his outdoor clothes. When he opened the door, the storm hurled itself into the cabin with a howl of rage. His form vanished as he gripped the rope leading to the barn. His mother forced the door shut with both hands. Sourdough had insisted that they connect their cabins and barns with ropes. Flora had secretly scoffed at this. She would never scoff again.

She collapsed into a chair beside the fire while Mrs. Penrose knelt before her, pulled off her boots, and chafed her feet between her warm hands. Taffy emerged from his blanket behind the stove and licked Flora's icy hand with his rough tongue as if he wanted to help. Flora gasped with pain as her chilled flesh began to thaw and burn. The girls were huddled together in bed, their faces pale against the dark boards, the nail heads around them dotted with frost.

When Mrs. Penrose looked up, Flora saw the same horror reflected in the widow's eyes that she was feeling herself.

"Oh, Miss Craigie, what have we done?"

CHAPTER FIFTEEN

Winter fell upon them like a starving beast, eager to devour them whole. Blizzards blew up in the blink of an eye and lasted for days. Between storms, the air was translucent and colder than anything Flora had ever imagined. An icy wind drove the powdered snow over the landscape in rippling sheets, through the cracks in her walls and down the stovepipe, hissing as it struck the fire.

It was six o'clock, and darkness had fallen two hours earlier. Flora lay in her cot, fully dressed and rolled so tightly in her blankets and buffalo robe that not a breath of cold air could enter her cocoon. After eating her bacon and beans, she had gone to bed because there was no better place to keep warm.

A frantic pounding sounded at the door. Flora untangled herself from her bedclothes and cracked it open to find Jack, crouching against the bitter wind. He lowered the scarf wound around his face and yelled, "My mum says please come quick! Jewel is sick!"

While Jack warmed himself beside the stove, Flora scrambled into her outdoor clothes, regretting that she knew so little about babies. She would probably be no help whatsoever.

They ran across the surface of the frozen snow and burst into the cabin to find Mrs. Penrose seated on the bed, holding Jewel in her arms. Swaddled in blankets, the baby resembled a wax doll. She was awake, but her beautiful blue eyes were dull, and she stared straight ahead as if she were in a trance. Her cheeks were as crimson as paint. Flora knelt beside them, her heart wrung by the child's appearance.

"Miss Craigie, she's burning up!" Mrs. Penrose's voice was shrill, on the verge of hysteria. "I beg you to ride for the doctor!"

Flora hated to deny her request, but she had no choice. "Ach, I would leave this minute if I could, but Felicity has a lame foot! She would never go the distance! What about Beau?"

Mrs. Penrose's face crumpled. "Miss Edgar needed the dentist, so he drove the ladies into Lacombe yesterday." She clasped the baby closer as the tears flowed down her cheeks. "My poor darling! We could harness the team and take her to town—but in this weather! I doubt she would survive the trip!"

Flora heard the baby's laboured breathing, saw her little chest rising and falling. Clearly the situation was serious. Her mind cast around for another option. She could think of only one, and the prospect wasn't hopeful.

"I'll ask Jessie McDonald," she said.

"Please, please hurry."

Flora left the cabin and ran clumsily over the rock-hard drifts beside the creek, with no sound but the crunch of her footsteps and her own panting breath. Twice she stumbled and fell. When she reached the trees, she stopped. The wall of bush resembled a forbidden forest. She looked at the sky, trying to note the position of the stars, and stepped into the woods. Within minutes she lost all sense of direction, turning this way and that as she struggled through the underbrush. The branches felt like the claws of animals, clutching and dragging at her legs. One of them whipped her across the face, drawing blood.

Flora had almost decided to retrace her steps when she broke into the clearing and the dogs began their savage barking. The door opened and their owner appeared, silhouetted in the lamplight. She spoke one word to the dogs in another language, and they dropped to their bellies.

"It's the wee bairn!" Flora called out. "The Penrose baby! She needs a doctor!"

Miss McDonald whirled and went inside, slamming the door shut behind her.

It was no use. She wouldn't help them.

Flora was about to turn back when the door opened again and the woman reappeared, shrugging into a fur-lined buckskin coat, holding a bridle and a blanket. She put two fingers in her mouth and whistled. Tipiskow came out of the darkness at a fast trot.

She shoved the bridle into the horse's mouth, threw the blanket over him, and swung herself onto his back. She clicked her tongue, and the mustang broke into a gallop. As they left the clearing, she appeared to be one with the animal, her black head bent low over his black neck, her calves gripping his black sides, her shoulders moving in time with the horse's strides.

Flora was still panting, and clouds of vapour swirled around her head. The perspiration was freezing on her body. Surely Miss McDonald wouldn't mind if she warmed herself inside. She opened the cabin door and shut it before the cold could rush in, drew off her mitts, and held her hands over the hot stove.

The cabin wasn't unlike her own shack, with the same three-cornered configuration of cookstove, bunk, and table. And like hers, this one was spotless. The stove was polished, the kettle gleamed, and a striped Hudson Bay trading blanket covered the bed.

There the similarities ended. Animal hides covered the walls rather than newspapers. A cinnamon-coloured bearskin lay on the floor, complete with a jaw full of pointed ivory fangs. Beside the stove was a rocking chair made from woven poplar branches bound together with leather sinews.

A book lay open on the table. So Miss McDonald could read. Flora chastised herself for her surprise. She knew nothing about the woman. She turned it over to see the title: *Gleason's Veterinary Hand-Book and System of Horse Training.*

On the shelf above the bed stood a framed photograph, presumably her parents: a bearded man with Jessie's eyes, and a woman with long dark braids.

Flora pulled on her mitts. She had been in the cabin only minutes, but she couldn't linger because Mrs. Penrose would be frantic. She inhaled the warm air, lightly scented with an unfamiliar herbal fragrance, and went out into the night again. This time the dogs didn't bark. She dashed back the same way, easier now that she had broken a path.

Flinging open the Penrose door, she slammed it behind her. "Miss McDonald has gone for the doctor!"

"Please God he gets here in time," Mrs. Penrose said.

The sheer magnitude of their isolation bore down on Flora. Even her small Scottish town had a cottage hospital and two doctors on call around the clock. Her father had installed one of the first telephones, and he rose at all hours to fill a prescription if needed. Some patients came to him for advice before they consulted the doctor.

The baby's blond curls were so wet with perspiration that they stuck to her cheeks. Flora remembered what her father had said about treating a fever. "Let's unwrap those blankets and give her a sponge bath. Maybe that will lower her temperature."

"Are you sure, Miss Craigie?" The other woman was doubtful. "I'm so afraid she might take a chill."

"I'm quite sure," Flora said, sounding more confident than she felt. It was very warm in the cabin and the surface of the stove glowed red-hot.

Mrs. Penrose lay the baby on the bed, unrolled the heavy blankets around her, and removed her flannel nightie. Jewel looked even smaller and more fragile without clothing. The women bathed her face and body with a cloth soaked in cool water. When Flora wiped her little hands, the baby's fist closed around her thumb, as if in gratitude. They wrapped her in a loose cotton sheet.

The other two children sat on the floor, Jack with his arm around Nellie. At one point their mother gave a harsh sob that was almost a groan, and then collected herself. "You two might as well crawl into bed," she said to them.

Nellie tried to stay awake but eventually fell asleep. Jack remained sitting up in his corner, silent and watchful. At intervals Flora stoked the stove with more firewood. There was little else to do but wait. If the doctor were out on another call, the situation was hopeless.

The clock on the corner shelf ticked down the hours. The women removed the baby's sheet and sponged her again. She was struggling for air and her rosebud lips had taken on a blueish tinge. When she inhaled, a hollow formed between her collarbones. At times she stopped breathing for a few agonizing seconds before taking another gasp. Her blue eyes were wide and unblinking. They seemed to be staring into the next world.

Flora had never felt so helpless. "Do you want me to hold her for a wee while?" she asked.

The anguished mother didn't take her eyes off the baby. "No, thank you, Miss Craigie." She whispered so the other children couldn't hear. "If she, if she . . . leaves this earth, I want my face to be the last thing she sees."

At that moment, if Flora could have sacrificed her own life for the precious bairn, she would have done so.

The cabin was silent except for the crackling of the fire and the wind howling around the windows. From time to time Mrs. Penrose murmured a prayer. She began to sing the old Welsh lullaby "Suo Gân," but her voice faltered and broke. In the stillness, the baby's gasps were very loud. It seemed that every breath would be her last.

All at once Jack cried out from his bed, "Listen! Hoofbeats!"

They strained to hear. The snow muffled the sound, and they couldn't tell if there was one horse or two. If Miss McDonald were returning alone, that meant her mission had failed.

The anxious mother rose to her feet and swayed as though she were about to faint. Flora ran to the door and stood ready. The galloping hoofbeats grew louder and drew to a halt. Without waiting for a knock, Flora flung open the door.

A tall man carrying a black bag rushed into the room, followed by Miss McDonald. "I'm Samuel Farraday. Where can I wash?" He stamped the snow from his feet, threw off his buffalo overcoat and dropped it on the floor.

"Over there, Doctor," Flora said. "Ach, we're so thankful to see you!"

Without answering, he ducked under the line of nappies hanging from the low ceiling. Under his coat he wore a charcoal tweed suit. He tore off his jacket and tossed it onto a chair, rolled up his shirtsleeves, and scrubbed his hands and forearms in the enamel basin. Only then did he take Jewel from her mother's arms.

"Aren't you a lovely baby?" he said. "Let's take a look at you." His voice was so tender and reassuring that tears filled Flora's eyes.

The doctor felt Jewel's hot forehead and cheeks with the back of his hand before laying her on the bed. While he unwrapped the sheet, he asked questions about her age and general health. He pulled his stethoscope out of his bag and listened to her tiny lungs, labouring for air. "We need to get steam into the room," he said. "The moisture will help her breathe."

Flora sprang to the stove and filled both kettle and saucepan from the water bucket.

Only then did she remember Miss McDonald, leaning against the door. The fur around the hood of her parka was rimmed with ice from her breath. Flora pulled a chair toward her. "Please, sit down. You must be exhausted." Twenty miles of hard riding in the cold and the dark—Flora could never have done it, not in any amount of time.

The other woman shook her head. "I must see to the horses," she said, and slipped outside.

The doctor drew a watch from his pocket and counted the seconds while he held the baby's wrist in two fingers, measuring her pulse. He felt the swollen glands below her ears. The women watched every move, waiting for his verdict.

Mrs. Penrose said in a quivering voice, "We tried to bring down her fever by bathing her in cool water. Was that all right, Doctor?"

He nodded. "Yes, indeed. You must keep it up, every hour."

"That was Miss Craigie's idea."

"It was absolutely the correct thing to do."

He tucked his stethoscope back into his bag before turning to the widow and placing his arm around her shoulders. Was he preparing to tell her what no mother wants to hear? Mrs. Penrose worked her hands as if she were kneading bread dough. Her face was ashen.

"Your little girl is in for a bad time, but she'll recover."

Her mother gave a strangled cry of relief, and Flora's knees went weak. She sank into the nearest chair.

"She has scarlatina, or scarlet fever. The fever has already broken, and tomorrow her body will break out in a rash. Her tongue will become red and lumpy, like a strawberry. She needs plenty of warm fluids, water or broth or milk. Are you still nursing her?"

"Yes, just the once at night."

"Give her the breast as often as she will take it. In a few days her rash will become extremely itchy, and her skin will start to peel. Bathing her in warm water with baking soda will give her some relief."

He glanced around the room. "I don't suppose there's any way to keep the other children away from her, so they don't catch it."

He spoke to Miss McDonald, who had come back into the cabin. "Have you had scarlet fever?"

"No," she said.

"Have you touched the baby?"

"No."

"You should be safe, if you leave now. Thank you for coming to fetch me, Miss McDonald. It was a brave thing to do."

Without answering him, she turned toward the door.

"I can't thank you enough!" Mrs. Penrose went toward Miss McDonald with outstretched arms, but stopped as if unsure whether her embrace would be welcomed.

The other woman placed her hand on the latch. "I hope your baby lives." She opened the door and disappeared into the night.

The room was cloudy with steam, and already Jewel was breathing more easily. She had closed her eyes and fallen asleep as if she, too, were comforted by the doctor's presence.

While he tucked her up in the sheet, he addressed Flora. "Are you a neighbour?"

"I live on the next quarter. My name is Flora Craigie."

"Have you had scarlet fever?"

"Never."

"Have you handled the baby?"

"Aye," Flora said.

"You might fall ill, although it's unlikely. Babies are especially susceptible."

He straightened up and looked at her for the first time. Flora suddenly became conscious of her own appearance. She was wearing her men's woollen breeks, pulled over her long red men's underwear. Her hair was uncombed and loose down her back. She knew she had an angry scratch across her cheek because it stung.

Sensing her discomfort, the doctor averted his gaze. Flora realised that he was a young man, perhaps no older than herself. Although there was a shadow on his strong jaw, he was clean-shaven. Moustaches and beards were so common that Flora found the sight of his naked lips almost shocking.

"Unfortunately, I must place you in complete quarantine, all of you. You need to post notices on your cabin doors. For the next three weeks you may visit each other, but no one else." He turned to Mrs. Penrose. "Do you have any idea where she could have contacted this?"

"The only visitors we've had this past week are the Hedley boys. They came to buy butter and milk. One of them complained of a sore throat." The Hedley boys were brothers in their fifties who were batching it, a new verb in Flora's vocabulary. In this country, all bachelors were referred to as boys, no matter what their age.

"I'll ride out tomorrow and make sure they go into quarantine, find out if they've been in contact with anybody else. I had scarlet fever as a child, so I'm immune. Now, Mrs. Penrose, I'll trouble you for a cup of tea, and then I must be on my way."

"Won't you spend the night, Doctor? You can have Jack's bed."

"Thank you, but I'm afraid not. One of my town patients is expecting her first baby tomorrow, and I swore to the poor girl that I'd be there."

Flora noticed the exhaustion on his face, the circles under his eyes. His dark brown hair fell unevenly over his collar, as if he had been cutting it himself.

"I'll come back in a day or two to check on the babe, but please don't be concerned. Most children recover with no lasting effects. I can tell this little one is a fighter."

"Doctor, I can't . . ." Mrs. Penrose's voice faltered. "I can't afford to pay you a dollar for every call."

"There won't be any charge. I need to ride out this way anyway, to visit another patient." He turned his back as he spoke, pulling on his tweed jacket.

Flora was fairly sure he was lying.

"The least I can do is give you a meal, Doctor. I can heat up some rabbit stew."

"That would be much appreciated, Mrs. Penrose."

"Oh, Doctor! May God bless you a thousand times for coming!" She snatched his hand and then, to his obvious embarrassment, raised it to her lips and kissed it.

"You're quite welcome, my dear lady." As he patted her back, his eyes met Flora's. They were very green.

CHAPTER SIXTEEN

Jewel broke out in spots as if she had been spattered with drops of blood. Her little bottom was so sore that she whimpered in distress whenever her nappy was changed. Nobody entered the Penrose cabin except Flora, but the Chicken Ladies left a pan of cinnamon buns outside the door, and Sourdough dropped off a haunch of fresh venison.

Even Jessie McDonald brought an offering.

"I could scarcely believe my eyes when I saw her!" Mrs. Penrose said. "She showed me how to roll the baby in a blanket and wrap the ends around my waist so I can carry her on my back. It felt odd at first, but it's such a treat to have my hands free, and Jewel goes right off to sleep. I take her to the barn when I do the milking. I can't let her out of my sight, not for a minute. And that isn't all." She pointed to a woven basket on the floor, filled with moss. "She told me to pack this inside Jewel's nappy, so she won't have a rash. It's muskeg moss, washed and dried before the fire. She gathered a great quantity for her own use."

"Why does she need it?" Flora asked.

Mrs. Penrose lowered her voice. "For her monthlies."

"Truly?" Flora was intrigued.

"I've already tried it on the baby," Mrs. Penrose said. "It soaks up everything. When it's wet or dirty, I throw it into the fire. And her rash is disappearing already. I told Dr. Farraday about it, and he said it's quite safe."

"I wonder how it works for, you know, the other thing." Flora had torn strips of cotton into long rectangles and hemmed them. It was a chore to rinse them in cold water and soak them in a boiler on the stove every month in a vain attempt to lighten the bloodstains. The other ladies did the same; she had seen the rags hanging like rusty flags on their clotheslines, frozen stiff.

"I'm sorely tempted," Mrs. Penrose said.

Both women looked thoughtful.

The doctor himself had returned twice in the past week. The first time he knocked, Flora was caught unprepared. She had risen late, a common custom among homesteaders who wanted to save their firewood. She hadn't even washed her face or brushed her hair. Assuming it was one of the children, she answered the door in her men's flannel pyjamas, her shawl thrown around her shoulders, to find the doctor standing on the frozen snow in his buffalo coat. He was even taller than she remembered.

"Good morning, Miss Craigie." He touched his fur cap, averting his eyes and gazing into the sunrise.

"Dr. Farraday, I wasn't expecting anyone, especially since I'm in quarantine." Flora clutched the shawl around her throat. He must think that she never dressed in proper clothing.

"I'm sorry to disturb you. I had another case of scarlet fever to the south, and I'm on my way back to town. I decided to drop in and visit the Penrose baby." His face was pale and tired. He probably hadn't slept, and he had a ten-mile ride ahead of him.

"How is she faring?"

"She's definitely on the mend, and it appears the other children have escaped. How are you feeling?"

"I'm quite well, Doctor."

"I mustn't keep you. It's far too cold to leave the door open. I'll be back in a few days."

Flora stood at the front window and watched with regret while he mounted his palomino quarter horse and rode away. She had wanted to invite him inside for breakfast, but she couldn't entertain a man in her pyjamas, and there was nowhere to change.

The second time he arrived, Flora was ready for him. She didn't want him to think that she always looked like a besom in men's clothes, her hair as wild as a thistle bush. She had risen early each day, pinned up her braids, and dressed neatly in a skirt and shirtwaist. Since she had no mirror, she examined her reflection in the blade of her butcher knife. Several times she asked herself why she was taking the trouble, but had no good answer.

When the knock finally came one afternoon, Flora patted her hair, glanced around her tidy shack, and opened the door. "Good day, Dr. Farraday."

He stepped over the threshold quickly to keep out the cold. His broad shoulders and his height made the room seem smaller. Flora didn't need to bend her knees beside this man.

"Please, sit down."

The doctor took one chair, and she took the other. He wore the same charcoal tweed suit he had on the other day, but he had added a blue tie, and his jaw was freshly shaven.

He was Flora's first real visitor, and she was proud of her miniature home. She had made such small improvements as she could afford. A square of practical yellow oilcloth covered the table, replacing her tartan shawl, and she had sewn curtains from a remnant of sprigged calico provided by Wren.

When the kettle sang on the stove, she poured boiling water into her teapot and produced a plate of buttery Scottish shortbread, freshly baked, wishing she had proper teacups rather than enamel mugs.

"How are you feeling, Miss Craigie?"

"I'm verra well, Dr. Farraday. My father used to say I was as healthy as a Shetland pony."

The doctor grinned, revealing one crooked tooth. Flora found it so endearing that she had to look away, reminding herself again that she was a married woman. She could not allow herself to forget that essential fact.

"Excuse me, Miss Craigie, I can't help smiling when you pronounce my name. It's your way of rolling the *r*."

"I'm trying to lose my Scottish accent," Flora said, hearing with annoyance the way she pronounced the word as "trrrying."

"An English accent is something of a liability in this country, since it often signifies more money than brains. I've seen help wanted signs in Red Deer saying, 'No Englishmen Need Apply.'" He smiled again. "However, your accent is very charming."

The doctor himself spoke Canadian, with no hint of the dreaded British vowels. He poured a dollop of Blossom's cream into his mug and took a sip before helping himself to a piece of shortbread and devouring it in two quick bites.

"That was delicious."

"Please, have another."

"Thank you." He took a second piece and ate it before drawing out his handkerchief and wiping his long fingers.

"It's none of my business, Miss Craigie, but I've never run across a single woman living alone on a homestead. Do you have a farming background?"

"Nay, not at all. I grew up in a wee Highland town, where my father was the chemist. My mother died when I was twelve, and I helped my father in the shop. I learned quite a bit about medicines from him. After he died, I spent six years as a lady's companion."

"How did you come to be here?"

Fortunately, she'd been asked this question often enough that she had a ready answer. "I was visiting friends in Red Deer when the chance arose to purchase South African Scrip. It was such a rare opportunity that I couldn't pass it up."

"It's quite a leap of faith to start farming with no experience."

"Aye, like so many others."

"How are you finding it so far?"

Flora considered. Certainly nothing had prepared her for the vastness of the landscape, the isolation and the loneliness, and her own complete ignorance of every aspect of farming—not to mention the deadly cold. Yet she knew the truth of the matter. "I love it," she said. "I love the newness of this country, and the sense of opportunity, the notion that one can change this place, and be changed by it."

Feeling she had revealed too much, she sipped her tea. "What is your background, Doctor?" she asked.

"I came from down east, as they say here, although my hometown is closer to the centre of Canada. I grew up in Port Hope, Ontario, and studied medicine at McGill University in Montreal. Like you, I wanted a new experience, so I came out west and spent a year at the Red Deer Memorial Hospital before setting up my practice in Toddsville."

"Do you serve a large area?"

"Too large, I'm afraid. Some fifteen miles from town in every direction. I keep Pal at the livery barn, ready to ride out whenever I have an emergency. Even then I can't always get there soon enough to do any good." A shadow crossed his face as if he remembered something painful.

Flora wondered if his duties were too onerous. "Is it what you expected, being a rural doctor?"

"Good heavens, no! I never imagined there were so many blessed ways to injure yourself. Just yesterday, I treated a farmer who rested the butt of his rifle on the ground, placed his palm over the barrel, and blew a hole through his hand."

"The poor man! One can see how easily it might happen, though, when people are forced to master a great number of skills in a short time." She'd already experienced a few close calls herself—nearly setting the roof on fire after putting too much wood in the stove, narrowly missing her ankle with the axe, slipping on a patch of ice between the shack and the barn.

"Exactly. Ignorance is fatal, especially out here. To give you one example, an entire family south of town perished with typhoid after drinking slough water. Nobody told them to boil it first. They had arrived at their claim just three days earlier."

"How dreadful!"

Seemingly encouraged by Flora's interest, he continued. "Even when I reach my patients in time, I often don't have the medicines. I pack my pills and powders with me. There's little point in writing a prescription when the nearest drug store is miles away in Lacombe."

Flora made a sympathetic murmur, remembering her father's well-stocked shop.

"My only anaesthetic is whisky. Last week I amputated a farmer's foot after he froze his toes and gangrene set in. I gave the poor sod as much liquor as he could drink."

"You perform surgeries, too?"

"I have no choice, Miss Craigie. I've operated on the kitchen table many times." Flora gazed at him in awe. This young man had faced challenges she never imagined, and had mastered them.

The doctor shook his head. "It's the women who have it the worst. They arrive here fearing the wild animals and the weather, but if they realised it, their greatest peril lies in giving birth. Young girls, far from their mothers, expecting their first babies—they have no idea what's happening to them, or what's about to happen. If they come from a sheltered background, they've never seen a baby breastfeed, or a nappy changed. Almost every family here loses an infant within the first week."

The doctor seemed to recall that he was speaking to a young unmarried woman. He took another gulp of tea. "I apologise, Miss Craigie. I shouldn't be telling you my problems. If you have any sense, you'll prove up and return to the city—especially if you plan to marry and have children of your own." He gave her a searching look.

Flora refilled his cup, unwilling to meet his green eyes. "Have you considered moving back to the city yourself?"

"Until we get another doctor here, these people have no one else. If only the steel would come out to Toddsville, I could send my patients to the new hospital in Red Deer. I put a couple of beds into the spare room over my office for the serious cases, but I daren't leave them alone for long. I haven't had a trip home in three years. My poor mother is quite distracted, worrying that I'm not taking care of myself."

Flora thought his mother was probably right to be concerned. He was slender to the point of thinness. She pushed the plate of shortbread toward him, and he took another piece.

"I hope I'm not giving you the wrong impression, Miss Craigie. Despite the drawbacks, my work is profoundly satisfying. If I had some help, I could settle down and be perfectly happy here. I feel the same way as you, that this is a country filled with opportunity and the kind of people who make their own luck. I consider it my privilege to keep these folks healthy."

Flora felt unaccountably pleased to find they shared such a similar opinion of their new home. "It's like having a ringside seat on history, isn't it?" she asked.

"Yes, indeed. I delivered a pair of healthy twins on September first, the same day that our province was born. The government sent them a rather unusual pair of gifts, set with gold nuggets—a brooch for Pearl, and a tie clip for Earl.

I want to be here to watch those little tykes grow up. It's our newest citizens and others like them who will determine the future of Alberta, of this entire country."

He drained his mug. "I must be off. Thank you for listening. I don't often have the chance to talk to such a sympathetic listener." There was that crooked tooth again.

"It was my pleasure, Dr. Farraday. Here, take the rest of the cookies." She wrapped them in a scrap of paper, and the doctor put them into his coat pocket.

"Good day to you, Miss Craigie."

She extended her hand, and he enclosed it between both of his. The warmth of his firm clasp ran up her arm and flew into her face, making her cheeks burn. She could only hope he would think she was overheated by the fire.

CHAPTER SEVENTEEN

January 4, 1906

Miss Flora Craigie
c/o General Delivery
Toddsville, Alberta

Dear Miss Craigie:

I would not write to you unless it were a matter of some urgency. Yesterday one of my patients requested a lawyer to attend her bedside in order to issue her last will and testament. No sooner was that painful task complete, than she went to her eternal rest.

The lawyer was Mr. Greene, who prepared our bill of sale. He informed me that he had received a letter from a private detective in Montreal who is searching for a Mrs. Flora May Mackle, also known as Flora May Craigie. The detective had written to every law office in the west, seeking information on your whereabouts.

I inquired whether the detective had provided any reason for his quest, but the lawyer said he had not. At this point, I told an outright lie: that after a few short weeks you had sold your scrip coupon and departed for the United States, lured by the promise of a free homestead. Miss Craigie, I think the Lord will forgive me in this instance. I was so convincing that Mr. Greene said he would reply to the detective with this new information.

I trust the trail will now go cold. I did feel, however, that I should warn you. Mr. Mackle has not given up the search.

With warmest wishes for your continued good health,
Grace Godwin

CHAPTER EIGHTEEN

Flora felt as if she had been kicked in the chest by a Clydesdale. Overwhelmed with her own struggles, she had dismissed the threat of Hector—a dangerous mistake that might yet prove fatal. Now she rebuked herself for her stupidity.

She knew the man's character only too well. Obviously the reason he had married her, to further his own career, was the very reason he would never allow her to vanish. She knew he had cabled his employers from Glasgow to tell them he was married. The humiliation of admitting that he had found a wife, only to lose her again, would be a bitter cup to a man like Hector. He could probably buy some time by pretending that he wanted to establish himself before bringing his wife out from the old country, like so many other husbands and fathers. But ultimately, he would have to produce a wife.

It was hearing about the professional detective that induced a state close to panic in Flora. She pictured a bloodhound like Sherlock Holmes, uncovering clues and connections that every other mortal had missed. How she blessed Nurse Godwin for directing the detective's attention south of the border. Since thousands of homesteads were being taken up in the western states, even

Sherlock Holmes would have his work cut out for him. She had read that Montana alone already had twice the population of Alberta.

Imprisoned by the weather, alone with her fears, there wasn't much else for Flora to do but think. Think, and try to stay alive. She had to wake twice each night to feed the fire, or risk not waking at all. Her blankets froze to the wall. She no longer visited what Wren referred to as the "death trap" after hearing that one settler had perished in an outdoor toilet. Instead she emptied her chamber pot in the nearby trees, kicking snow over the evidence, planning to bury it next spring.

When a blizzard raged, it worked itself into an insane fury, determined to tear her flimsy shack to pieces. On those days Flora dared not venture to the creek. She melted snow on the stove and lugged her bucket to the barn in the howling gale, dragging herself along the rope with one freezing fist. When she left, Felicity would whicker nervously as if she, too, feared for Flora's life.

During the daylight hours, when the shack was marginally warmer, Flora sat at her table wrapped in a blanket and studied pamphlets from the federal Lacombe Agricultural Research Station. Distributed widely to homesteaders, these contained useful advice about grain, vegetables, flowers, and shrubs. Flora distracted herself by imagining the splendid garden she would plant next spring. If the ink wasn't frozen solid in the bottle, she made lists and sketches and notes.

The frigid weather had one benefit. Sterling Payne stayed away, no doubt hoping she would either abandon her claim or perish. It was highly unlikely that Hector or his detective would be combing this hostile wasteland for her in the dead of winter. Of course, that meant nobody else visited, either. By nobody, Flora meant the doctor. She dreaded the thought of him saddling Pal in the night, riding out to some remote farm, battling the biting wind and the blinding snow. It was a testament to his dedication that he would risk his own life to save another. Flora couldn't help contrasting him with the man she had married.

The friendly calls between neighbours had mostly stopped. Even during the short time it took to walk from one place to another, it was too easy to become lost or injured, or freeze to death. Instead, she and Mrs. Penrose worked out a signal. Each evening at six o'clock, and again at eight in the morning, Flora raised and lowered her lamp three times to indicate all was well. Mrs. Penrose made the same response. It was a great comfort to see the light flashing thrice across the creek, crossing the gulf of isolation.

During one of their infrequent visits, Mrs. Penrose confided her fear of becoming bushed. "Beau told me that several of the mental patients in the Ponoka hospital are diagnosed as prairie women. Prairie women! That's the medical term for it, Miss Craigie! They're just ordinary folks, broken into pieces by the loneliness and the hardships. One prairie woman put a shotgun in her mouth and blew off her own head!"

Mrs. Penrose clutched her arm. Flora looked at her small hand with its ragged fingernails and rough skin. The touch of another human being felt so strange that for a moment Flora wondered if she herself were going mad.

"When a blizzard wails around the cabin like old Cythraul, that's when I'm most afraid for my wits! Miss Craigie, promise me you will care for my children if I'm taken away!"

What else could she do? Flora promised.

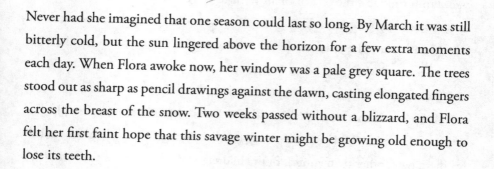

Never had she imagined that one season could last so long. By March it was still bitterly cold, but the sun lingered above the horizon for a few extra moments each day. When Flora awoke now, her window was a pale grey square. The trees stood out as sharp as pencil drawings against the dawn, casting elongated fingers across the breast of the snow. Two weeks passed without a blizzard, and Flora felt her first faint hope that this savage winter might be growing old enough to lose its teeth.

With the increased daylight, Mrs. Penrose asked the Chicken Ladies to give Jack lessons in reading and arithmetic. They agreed, but only on condition that Nellie be included. The children trudged past Flora's shack each day at nine o'clock and back again at noon, bundled up so well that they staggered along like miniature drunkards.

Late one morning, the wicked snow clouds began to gather in the eastern sky. Through a hole melted in the frost on her front window, Flora watched the monumental purple mass racing toward them. As the first flakes fell, she saw the children plodding home along the trail, followed by the faithful Taffy.

Opening her door a crack, she called, "Jack, Nellie! Come away now! Make haste!" No sooner had the door slammed behind them, than the blizzard struck with the force of a locomotive, howling down the stovepipe and rattling the panes. The world outside vanished.

"You'll have to bide here until after the storm," Flora said.

"What about our Ma?" Jack asked. "She'll be that worried!"

Flora's voice was sympathetic. "I'm sorry, but it canna be helped."

Taffy lay in the corner while Flora fed the children lunch: vegetable chowder made with fried bacon, potato, and carrots, seasoned with salt and pepper, and thickened with canned milk. Jack and Nellie ate with their best manners, sat on the bed and did their lessons, and played tic-tac-toe while Flora read an old copy of the *Toddsville Free Press*, known locally as the *Toddsville Distress*. From time to time one of them went to the creek-side window and gazed into the swirling whiteness. Flora knew they were imagining their poor mother, frantic with fear. She tried to divert their attention. "Do you ever miss your home back in Wales?" she asked.

"Sometimes I think of my mates," Jack replied, "but not often."

"I don't miss anything," Nellie said. Flora was surprised to hear this. She had assumed that both children were pining for their former lives. There was so little for here here, other than chores. Both children worked as hard as their mother.

"What do you like about living here?"

"The outdoors," Jack said without hesitation. "It's great fun, fishing and snaring rabbits and swimming in the creek. Mr. Buckhorn says he'll teach me how to drive his Clydesdales next spring."

"I love Taffy and Mr. Grey and Blossom and Petal," Nellie piped up. "We were never allowed to keep animals at home. And Miss Greenwood is teaching me to read. I'm learning poetry, Miss Craigie! Do you want to hear my verse?"

Flora had never heard her speak with such confidence. "I surely would."

Without missing a single word, Nellie recited:

My Little Doll

I once had a sweet little doll, dears,
The prettiest doll in the world;
Her cheeks were so red and so white, dears,
And her hair was so charmingly curled.
But I lost my poor little doll, dears,
As I played in the heath one day;
And I cried for her more than a week, dears,
But I never could find where she lay.
I found my poor little doll, dears,
As I played in the heath one day:
Folks say she is terribly changed, dears,
For her paint is all washed away,
And her arms trodden off by the cows, dears,
And her hair not the least bit curled:
Yet for old sakes' sake she is still, dears,
The prettiest doll in the world.

Flora clapped her hands with genuine appreciation. "That's grand, Nellie! And what about you, Jack? Do you enjoy your lessons?"

"Not so much as Nellie."

"He's good at sums, though," said his loyal sister. "He can do them in his head, ever so fast."

Their teachers had mentioned that Jack excelled at math, but it was Nellie who astonished them. "She's such a bright little spark!" Wren said. "Not ten years old, and she's writing a most edifying journal about pioneer life. She'll be an author someday! I told her mother, but she wasn't impressed in the least."

Secretly Flora agreed that Jack's skill with arithmetic was more important for a farmer than any knowledge of literature. Everything came down to numbers—bushels per acre, the price of grain, the cost of seed—his future revolved around making the numbers work.

The children fell silent again. In desperation, she offered to read aloud to them. Her only book was her well-thumbed copy of *Great Expectations*, which she had almost memorised before the Chicken Ladies began to lend her their novels. She was afraid it might be too advanced for the children, but after the first chapter—in which the boy Pip meets the escaped convict Magwitch in the marsh—they clamoured for more.

Darkness fell, and still the storm raged. It was awful to imagine Mrs. Penrose's terror, trapped in her cabin with baby Jewel, not knowing whether her other children were safe and warm, or their little bodies lying rigid under the snow. Flora fried sausages and pancakes for supper, but neither she nor the children had much appetite. Taffy ate the leftovers, along with a slice of bread soaked in grease.

At six o'clock Flora raised her lamp in the window three times, knowing that the light would be invisible, but wanting to make the gesture nevertheless. Nellie stared into the night for a long time, although there was nothing to see.

After Jack washed the dishes in melted snow water and Nellie dried them,

Flora battled her way through the storm to feed Felicity, and brought back a sack full of hay that she spread on the floor for her guests. They settled themselves for the night, Taffy snuggled between them for warmth.

"Good night, Miss Craigie," they chorused in unison.

Flora was unable to sleep, picturing the distraught mother. The children whispered and tossed in the hay. Nellie cried a little, trying not to make any sound, and Jack comforted her.

Sometime in the wee hours, the storm blew itself out. Flora was lying awake when the howling stopped dead, like a faucet that had been turned off. Her ears rang in the silence. She rushed to the window, thawing a hole in the frost with her palm. A lamp glowed from the Penrose cabin. Nellie and Jack hurried to stand beside her, shouting with joy when they saw the light. Flora fumbled for her matches and lit her own lamp. She raised it once, twice, three times. Immediately, a series of frantic flashes came in response.

"Mama, Mama!" Nellie waved and called, as if her mother could see her.

Flora wouldn't allow the children to leave until dawn's first light. As they scrambled into their coats, Nellie asked, "Please, Miss Craigie, may we come back and hear more about Pip?"

She opened her mouth to make some excuse, then surprised herself by saying yes.

It was the first of April, but winter still held the landscape locked in a death grip. Flora was seated at her table, making notes in her gardening journal and imagining the golden gorse blooming in the Highlands, when Beau knocked, wearing red woollen earmuffs under his big white hat.

"The ladies are inviting you to come over at two o'clock. Miss Edgar said it's important. I'm to fetch Mrs. Penrose and Miss McDonald, too."

Flora wondered what could be so important that the ladies were inviting their elusive neighbour. She hadn't seen her since the episode of the scarlet fever, although Miss McDonald had visited the Penrose cabin several times.

"She has a soft spot for the children," the widow said, "and she must get lonely, too."

Flora donned her obligatory five layers of clothing and headed for the yellow house. It had become the meeting place simply because it was the only home spacious enough to hold everyone. It was especially appealing because the Chicken Ladies always served the most delicious Indian tea in their Coalport china teacups.

She and Mrs. Penrose arrived at the same time, greeting each other as if they hadn't seen each other for weeks instead of days. But when Wren opened the door, she wasn't smiling. Miss Edgar was seated in her armchair, her reading glasses hanging on a chain around her neck. She was holding a copy of the *Toddsville Free Press*, and Flora noticed a tremor in her hand.

"Hello, Miss Craigie, Mrs. Penrose," Miss Edgar said. "Please, take a seat."

The visitors sat down in the Morris chairs while Wren assumed her usual place in the rocker. Miss Edgar took the lead, as usual. "Miss McDonald declined my invitation. Perhaps it's just as well. We found something disturbing that concerns us all. It's a Letter to the Editor." She lifted her spectacles to her face and cleared her throat before reading aloud:

"'Dear Editor, It has come to our attention that a group of women are pretending to farm east of town, thereby robbing our good British menfolk of the opportunity to establish themselves in this country. I put forward the following questions:

"'How do we know the Welsh woman is a widow? She supposedly meets the legal requirement because she has minor children, but how can we be sure there is no male figure lurking in the background?'"

Mrs. Penrose made a choking sound.

"'And how did the Scottish woman acquire South African Scrip? We can say with certainty that she is not a veteran of the Boer War. Under what unlikely circumstances was this single woman allowed to take precedence over her fellow man?'"

Flora swallowed, her mouth suddenly dry.

Miss Edgar glanced over her spectacles at Wren before she continued. "'As for the American ladies, one can't help but wonder why they didn't choose to remain in their own country, where homesteads are available for single women, albeit in a misguided policy by our lawless neighbour to the south. From what scandal are they fleeing?'"

Wren's face crumpled, and she raised her handkerchief to her eyes.

"'Finally, the presence of a Half-Breed rounds out this objectionable cadre. Our generous government distributed scrip to these unfortunate misfits in the absurd hope that they would make the land productive, but hers has yet to see the mark of a plough.'"

Miss Edgar raised her voice as a gust of wind moaned down the stovepipe like an evil spirit. "'A black cloud of suspicion hovers over the deplorable little community known locally as Ladyville, which this writer wishes to have cleared up, once and for all.' The letter is signed by Alice Hall Crofton Westhead."

Flora felt as if she had received a physical blow. Her shock was mirrored on Mrs. Penrose's face.

"Who is this awful person?" the widow asked in a tone of bewilderment.

"Alice Westhead, known as Alix to her friends, is a woman of long standing here," Miss Edgar said, removing her glasses and folding the paper with great deliberation. "She and her husband, Charles, arrived back in 1892 and founded a ranch west of town called the Quarter Circle One."

"How do you know so much about her?" Mrs. Penrose asked.

"We have a mutual acquaintance, a rancher's wife named Irene Parlby, who is president of the new Country Women's Club. Their first objective is to create a public lending library, and Mrs. Parlby visited us last fall to ask for a donation. We found her to be most congenial, didn't we, Wren?"

Wren nodded without lowering her handkerchief.

"Both Mrs. Parlby and Alix Westhead were Empire babies, girls raised in India who knew each other back in England. When Mrs. Parlby came out to visit her friend a few years ago, she ended up meeting her future husband, Walter, and now she's married with a little boy named Humphrey. However, the two women have little in common except their background. Mrs. Parlby is a bluestocking, a progressive thinker, and a great believer in women's rights. She is positively discouraged by the way Mrs. Westhead clings to the old hidebound class distinctions."

"It's shocking the way some people think they are better than others!" exclaimed Mrs. Penrose, forgetting how intimidated she had been by the Chicken Ladies when she first met them.

"You're right, Mrs. Penrose. Alix Westhead considers herself one of the community's leading lights, bearing the white woman's burden to an uncivilized world. She wants to create an idealised British colony here, and Ladyville, as she calls it, doesn't fit into her plan."

Wren sat up straight and lowered her handkerchief. "I wouldn't mind this place being called Ladyville if it were a term of affection, but she makes it sound like a brothel! Robbie, I know you don't like to gossip, but you haven't told them everything."

She turned away from her friend and fixed her gaze on the other two women. "Mrs. Parlby thinks that her friend is cleaving to the past because the Westhead marriage is not a happy one. Charles Westhead spends all his time drinking and ruining the ranch. If it weren't for his remittance money, they would have been bankrupt long ago. Of course, Mrs. Parlby is much too genteel to betray any confidences, but apparently this is common knowledge. Maisie Bell, the maid at the Westhead ranch, loves to tittle-tattle. And the ranch hands tell stories as well. As we all know, men are often worse gossips than women."

"What do you mean by remittance money?" Mrs. Penrose was asking all the questions, since Flora was in such mental turmoil that she had temporarily lost the power of speech.

"Some wealthy families in Britain send their black sheep to Canada or other parts of the world and pay them an allowance to stay away. They are called remittance men, and Charles Westhead is one of them."

"So they don't even work for their arian." Mrs. Penrose shook her head. "If that's the case, how much influence does she have?"

"Unfortunately, a great deal," Miss Edgar answered. "Her husband spends his money recklessly, endearing the Westheads to the business community. And she has the advantage of being the first white woman to settle here, which carries a certain cachet. She never lets anyone forget that fact."

"But she has no grounds for her complaints about us!" Mrs. Penrose said. "I know women can get into trouble for claiming to be widows under false pretences, but my husband is dead, God rest his soul. I saw him lying in his coffin. I have a copy of his death certificate." It sounded as if she thought the others might doubt that he was really dead.

Flora was still silent, her limbs paralysed with shock. She had read in the *Edmonton Bulletin* about a court case in which a woman claimed a homestead by pretending to be single. In vain did she argue that her husband was a beast who had broken her ribs, gambled away their savings, and taken a mistress. He walked away from the courthouse a free man. The battered wife went to jail for fraud.

"Robbie, what should we do?" Wren whispered.

"Do!" Miss Edgar said. "We shall do nothing!" She rose and stood behind Wren, gripping her shoulder with one hand. "We are no strangers to adversity, my dear. And these ladies have more than their share of difficulties. My advice

Elinor Florence

is that we maintain a dignified silence, and ignore 'the slings and arrows of outrageous fortune,' in the words of Mr. Shakespeare. We have committed no crime, and time alone will prove our worth."

Flora was still dumb with horror. What the others didn't know is that she had committed a crime. She'd misrepresented her marital status and perpetrated a fraud. And if Hector or his man Holmes got his hands on a copy of the local newspaper, he would learn that a single Scottish woman, possessed of South African Scrip, had filed on a homestead east of town.

He'd know exactly where to find her.

BOOK THREE

CHAPTER NINETEEN

Spring arrived with the speed and force of green lightning. One morning they were floating in a frozen white sea, and that same evening the earth showed its smiling face between the snowbanks as the warm wind greedily licked them away. The surface of the creek splintered into crystal shards, and the water gurgled and chuckled like a child. Flora's shack wept with joy as the ice poured off the roof in shining teardrops.

The weary farmers at Ladyville—they had agreed to change the insult into a joke—crept from their homes as if they had been released from jail, their clothes and hair smelling of woodsmoke, blinking at the unaccustomed sunshine, their eyes weak from reading in lamplight, feeble and pale and undernourished after a steady diet of root vegetables and canned food.

All their former trials were forgotten as the world came back to life. The black tree skeletons sprouted emerald buds. The first crocuses bloomed; fuzzy lavender petals unfurled in their sheaths of silver silk. The children were practically hysterical with glee when they heard mewing sounds coming from the barn and discovered four newborn kittens. Mr. Grey wasn't a mister after all, although nobody could remember to call her anything else. After that, the girls were rarely seen without a kitten hanging around their necks. Jewel had begun to walk, and she toddled everywhere while a watchful Taffy prevented her from falling into the creek.

Flocks of ducks and geese flying north were so plentiful that Jack could bring down two or three by firing the shotgun into their midst. Ladyville enjoyed the taste of roast meat once more. Flora's strength and energy swelled along with the sap rising in the trees.

When the earth had absorbed the heat of the sun, Sourdough arrived with a set of harrows, an implement bearing a row of circular metal discs, to prepare their fields for planting. The blades struck the clumps of earth with such force that daylight appeared between the metal seat and Sourdough's huge rump. He finished by plowing five rows around the circumference of the field which would be left fallow to guard against prairie fire. The sight of the cultivated earth, rich and ready for the living seed, inspired in Flora an unholy joy.

Since it was impossible to find help, the women sowed their wheat by hand. Flora strode from one side of the field to the other with a basket strapped to her chest, scattering handfuls of grain as evenly as possible. The pale kernels spangled the topsoil like stars. *The ancient farmers did it this way when Jesus was a wee laddie*, she thought, and then laughed at her own romantic notion. Across the creek, Mrs. Penrose planted her field from the back of the wagon. Jack drove the team, and she perched on the tailgate, her little feet dangling, flinging the grain from a tin washtub.

Only ten days later, Mrs. Penrose knocked on Flora's door at dawn. "Miss Craigie, come quick! The wheat is sprouting!" The two women ran outside to marvel at the green mist covering the black earth.

Flora volunteered to take the team to town and purchase their spring grubstake, just for the luxury of seeing the landscape reborn. The prairie resembled a living thing, rolling and rising and stretching after a long winter's slumber. The spring air was a magic elixir, so heavy and sweet that Flora wanted to cup it in her hands and drink it.

Nevertheless, she lowered her veil as she approached the livery stable. Her fear of discovery still burbled along in her subconscious like the creek below its layer of spring ice. Hopefully the detective was still combing the backwoods of Wyoming or Nebraska in his fruitless quest, but there was no need to attract the attention of strangers.

When she entered the general store, a bell jangled in the back room and the owner emerged, wiping his hands on his apron. "Good afternoon, Mr. Sanderson," she sang out.

"How do, Miss Craigie." His expression was stern.

"I have my list of supplies right here." Flora reached into her reticule.

He gazed out the front window as if he observed something interesting in the street. "I'm afraid, Miss Craigie, that I can't advance you any credit."

The smile dropped from her face. "Why not?" It was common business practice for farmers to run up their accounts in spring and pay them out following the harvest.

"Miss Craigie, I'm not a rich man myself. I can't be sure that you'll have the money when the time comes."

"I promise you, Mr. Sanderson, that I'm as reliable as anyone else—if not more so." The joy she had felt on this lovely spring day evaporated like the morning dew.

"I've been told that you ladies—you and the widow and those two Yanks raising chickens—aren't to have credit because you won't be able to pay."

"Mr. Sanderson, when our first crop comes off, you'll be the first creditor on my list. In fact, you're the only creditor on my list!" Flora heard the pleading note in her own voice.

"I'm afraid I can't accommodate you any longer, Miss Craigie. You'll have to take your business elsewhere."

There was nowhere that didn't require making the arduous drive to La-combe on a muddy trail that was virtually impassable in spring. "Please, Mr. Sanderson. You can raise the interest on my bill."

"It's cash on the barrelhead or nothing doing. I'm sorry."

Flora stood motionless, unwilling to give up the fight. She could probably eke out her soap and candles for a few months, and survive on her garden vege-tables and remaining canned goods. But she couldn't bake without flour, or pre-serve her fruit without sugar. And what about Mrs. Penrose and the children?

"I'm real sorry," Mr. Sanderson repeated, his mouth turned down at the corners as if he had swallowed something unpleasant.

She tried to keep her voice steady. "Please tell me who's casting doubt on our ability to pay."

"I'm sorry, Miss Craigie, that's confidential. If you'll excuse me, I have work to do in the back."

Flora couldn't come up with another argument. Her eyes overflowed as she left the store. Her vision was so blurred that she bumped into someone on the dirt path and almost fell.

"Miss Craigie! What's the matter?" Dr. Farraday gripped her upper arms to steady her, while Flora tried to collect herself.

"The store owner suspended my credit and refused to tell me why."

"That's not like Sandy Sanderson. There must be more to it." He still held her arms in his firm grip, and now he released her and stepped back.

Despite her distress, Flora was glad she had taken pains with her appear-ance for her trip to town. She had donned her tweed skirt and silk blouse, although she wore the old felt hat donated by Lydia Prince. She had tried to smarten it up with a pink ribbon from her camisole, and several tail feathers from Wren's rooster.

"I'm on the way to my office," the doctor said. "Won't you come inside for a moment?" Tucking her hand under his arm, he escorted her along the street.

Even in her misery, Flora was conscious of his physical presence. He opened the outer door, and she stepped into a room with a desk on one side and three straight-backed wooden chairs on the other. A door behind the desk presumably led to an inner examining room.

"Please, sit down. I'll fetch you a glass of water."

Flora dropped into a chair. She folded back her veil, drew her handkerchief from her reticule, and wiped her eyes. She was struggling to compose herself when the outer door opened again.

The stranger who entered wore a wine-coloured poplin skirt and matching three-quarter-length coat trimmed with black braid. A wide-brimmed hat with a black cockade on the front, like something belonging to a parade sergeant, rested on an elaborate arrangement of glossy brown hair. She barely glanced at Flora before addressing the doctor, who had emerged from the back room carrying a glass.

"Dr. Farraday. I need you at the ranch. Charles had another attack of gout. I sent my girl Maisie to summon you this morning, but she said you refused to come. I simply didn't believe her because she is so unreliable. I decided to check for myself."

"Good afternoon, Mrs. Westhead. You could have saved yourself the trip. Miss Bell was here. As I explained to her, I'm unable to attend your husband today. I have three calls to make this afternoon, and they can't wait."

So this was the famous Mrs. Westhead! Flora stared at her rigid back.

"You'll have to disappoint your other patients," the woman said. "My husband is in great discomfort. I warned him not to eat so much rich food last night, but he wouldn't listen." Without waiting for his reply, she turned to Flora. "And who might you be?" Her eyes raked Flora from head to toe, lingering on the disreputable hat.

Flora stood up and nodded politely, bending her knees slightly so that her hem would cover her dusty leather boots. "I'm Flora Craigie. How do you do?"

"Are you one of those dreadful women from Ladyville?"

The blood rose in Flora's cheeks. All at once she felt as if she were being scolded by her former employer. She opened her mouth but couldn't think of a suitable response.

The other woman curled her lip. "I suppose you're a suffragette or some such rubbish."

Flora stood a little straighter and found her tongue at last. "I do believe women should have the vote."

"Nonsense. The only people in favour of suffrage are long-haired men and short-haired women. Perhaps you're one of those man-hating types."

This was so outrageous that Flora gasped. "Surely that's my own business!"

"Just why did you move here, pray tell?"

"I claimed a homestead and I plan to earn my title."

The other woman sniffed. "You're here to get your hands on a piece of free land and sell it to the highest bidder. It's a moot point, anyway, since you'll never last for three years."

Dr. Farraday was watching this exchange with an increasingly horrified expression. "Mrs. Westhead, please step outside." He strode to the door and opened it with so much authority that she was forced to leave, sweeping her skirts to one side to avoid touching Flora. As Flora watched through the store-front window, they exchanged a few words on the street before the doctor came back inside.

"My apologies, Miss Craigie." He looked as upset as Flora felt. "She's an outspoken woman, to say the least, but that's no excuse for her rudeness."

"You have nothing to be sorry for, Doctor, but I don't understand her attitude. Why should she care about something that doesn't affect her in the slightest?"

"To put it bluntly, she believes that single women represent a threat to the government's goal of increasing the white population here in the West."

"Ach, there's nought I can do about my gender!" Flora was on the verge of tears again.

"Of course not, and I wouldn't want you to." He smiled, revealing his crooked tooth, and Flora's heart gave an odd flutter. "Nobody took you ladies seriously because you weren't expected to last out the first winter. But you did, and for that I congratulate you."

"Thank you," Flora said in a faint voice, warmed by his words. Her knees felt weak, and she sank into her chair again. The doctor folded his long legs and sat down beside her.

"I want to warn you, Miss Craigie," he said, his voice serious. "You've proven yourself to be stronger than many men, and Mrs. Westhead has you in her crosshairs. I suspect it was she who persuaded Sanderson to cut off your credit. Her word is gospel around here, and she has friends in high places, including Frank Oliver. She's always singing his praises because she thinks he's the epitome of an English gentleman."

Flora was distinctly unhappy to hear this. Oliver had so much influence in Ottawa that he had convinced the federal government to choose Edmonton as capital of the new province rather than the logical choice, Calgary—even though the southern city was much larger and located beside the transcontinental railway line.

"Oliver is a thoroughly unpleasant individual," the doctor said. "His rival newspaper, the *Calgary Herald*, calls him the meanest man in Canada. Not only is he opposed to single women homesteaders, he's openly contemptuous of anyone who isn't white. And his ethics are questionable, to say the least. According to various reports, he's been involved in some shady land deals. He's even carved away sections of Indian reserves and sold them to his friends. If he finds any way to force you off your land, he won't hesitate."

Mr. Sanderson not only cut off Ladyville's credit, but added injury to injury by cancelling his weekly purchase of Wren's eggs. Apart from Jessie McDonald, who didn't shop at the general store, the women met at the yellow house to commiserate. As Flora approached the yard, she saw the hens pecking in the grass while their rooster preened himself and crowed his superiority from the ridgepole. He reminded her of almost every male she knew.

Wren was distraught. "A few days ago, Mr. Sanderson told me my eggs were so delicious that several customers requested them specifically! I asked him why he had changed his mind, and he told me he had enough eggs. I know that is an untruth, because he refused to look me in the eye!"

"A lie is halfway around the world before the truth has its boots on," murmured Mrs. Penrose, who appeared to have a quote for every occasion.

Flora hated to be the bearer of bad news. "Mr. Sanderson isn't the problem." She described her encounter with the formidable Alix Westhead.

Miss Edgar snorted. "That woman sounds like the sort of person who drove the Americans to revolt. She simply can't comprehend that Canadians refuse to bow and scrape, since they don't give a toss about the British upper class. Mrs. Parlby told us that Alix Westhead has dismissed eight hired girls since she arrived. The latest one, Maisie Bell, is probably headed for the same fate—although in her case it might be justified since she's such a gossip."

"What will you do with your eggs now, Wren?" asked Mrs. Penrose.

"Beau can drive them to Lacombe. The hotels will take everything I can provide, but I'll lose a lot of them on those corduroy roads." Wren packed her eggs in sawdust, and they usually survived the journey into Toddsville. The trail leading west, however, could not be considered egg friendly.

"If only the railway would come out here," Miss Edgar said. "The newspapers are filled with rumours about which route the CPR might choose, but the company keeps its plans under wraps in an attempt to prevent land speculation."

"Would it help if we visited Mr. Sanderson and begged for mercy?" Mrs. Penrose asked.

Miss Edgar shook her head. "Once again, my advice is that we do nothing. Perhaps Alix Westhead is looking for a reaction, and we don't want to engage her in a fight we cannot win. It's best to keep our heads down. Miss Craigie, Mrs. Penrose, we can lend you enough flour and sugar to see you through until the harvest."

There was little more to be said. Always hospitable, the Chicken Ladies brewed a pot of their excellent tea, but it was a dismal tea party.

Back at her shack, even the sight of her wheat field, the sprouts as soft and thick as the hair on her head, couldn't console Flora. She sat at her table and pulled out the blank exercise book she used for her accounts. She couldn't sell eggs or milk, and she had nothing else to offer. Flora counted her remaining cash yet again, although the amount had not changed: $47.88.

She would simply have to tighten her belt, and pray for a good crop. Flora rose and went outside to her garden, comforted by the sight of her flourishing vegetables. She knelt and put her hands into the warm earth, as thick and black as molasses, connecting her to the land in a way that was visceral.

Surely the doctor was overestimating Mrs. Westhead's influence. Let her write letters and insult Flora to her face. Let her complain about Ladyville to her fine friends who had never worked a day in their lives. Flora tore out a stalk of pigweed and tossed it to one side. There was nothing else that appalling woman could do to them. Nothing at all.

CHAPTER TWENTY

The summer flew past in a flurry of long days filled with labour: gathering berries, cutting hay for Felicity, re-chinking the barn walls, and clearing rocks from the next ten acres of virgin sod that Sourdough would break before freeze-up. Flora even managed to bring down her first prairie chicken. Never had she felt so charged with energy and purpose.

Her chest expanded every time her eyes fell on her burgeoning wheat field, a waving green sea dappled with darker green shadows cast by the drifting clouds. The sun blazed overhead, but whenever Flora began to fret about drought, thunderheads formed and sent down a steady rain that fell in silver spears.

The doctor dropped in several times on his rounds but he, too, was overwhelmed with the demands of his profession now that homesteaders were pouring into the region and finding new and innovative ways to injure themselves. Although his presence had the usual effect on Flora, she did her best to smother her feelings. This was as futile as trying to stamp out a peat fire that smouldered beneath the surface.

Sterling Payne made six disagreeable visits. Each time he knocked, with his characteristic triple rap-rap-rap, Flora wanted to hide in her root cellar. He was obviously infuriated that she had survived the winter. It gave Flora great satisfaction to be seen wearing her overalls and plaid flannel shirt, the very clothes that had created so much suspicion. She stood by with a frozen smile while he inspected every inch of the premises and rode away after hurling insults in his high-pitched voice at her crop, her haystack, her horse, and once even the size of her cabbages.

Not that there was anything to criticize. The women stopped working only long enough to visit each other's gardens and admire their phenomenal growth. Today Flora was praising Mrs. Penrose's corn. Pulled from its leafy husk, each cob revealed neat rows of pale yellow kernels. Flora hadn't planted corn, but now she wished she had. Back home it was used for animal feed, but here people gnawed the kernels straight off the cobs, like beavers stripping bark from the branches.

As Mrs. Penrose piled a dozen ripe cobs into her arms, Flora noticed the widow's eyes were swollen. "Is anything wrong?" she asked.

"Ah, you can tell I've been weeping. I saved my tears for Blossom, but Nellie found me in the barn and it gave her such a fright I had to leave off. A mother isn't often allowed the comfort of a good cry."

"But what is it? Did something happen?"

"This is my fourteenth wedding anniversary. I was a girl of eighteen when we married, and it never entered my head that I would find myself alone in the world without Alwyn by my side—let alone in a foreign country."

"I'm so sorry," said Flora, surprised to find that Mrs. Penrose was thirty-two, only a few years older than herself. Nellie had asked her mother once how old she was, and she had joked, "Just as old as my little finger, and older than my teeth!" Flora had thought she was at least forty.

Hearing the compassion in Flora's voice, Mrs. Penrose's eyes filled again. "Oh, I do miss my husband!" she burst out. "I miss his strong arms around me, and the touch of his beard against my cheek! He was such an affectionate man, was Alwyn. He never went to sleep without telling me how much he loved me. And every Sunday afternoon, we sent the children outside to play so we could have some time to ourselves, if you take my meaning. Of course, you're a single woman, you aren't aware of that side of married life. Let me tell you, it can make up for a lot of things."

This was so alien to Flora's experience of marriage that she nearly dropped her armload of cobs. She couldn't remember her parents ever embracing, or even touching each other intentionally. As she walked back to her shack, she thought about the widow's words. She had actually enjoyed the marriage bed! Mrs. Penrose was hardly the stuff of romantic heroines. Her face was careworn, and her untidy fair hair was always escaping from its combs. But perhaps one's appearance had nothing to do with it.

Was it possible to take pleasure in what Flora had always believed was a wife's painful duty? She knew little about what went on between a man and a woman. In her experience, marriage was a straightforward arrangement— the woman attained financial security, more or less, and the man acquired a cook and a homemaker and a mother for his children. She had read about love matches, of course, but to her knowledge she wasn't acquainted with anyone who had married for love alone. She had assumed that was the stuff of fairy tales and cheap novels.

Flora pondered the unfamiliar sensation she experienced whenever Dr. Farraday took her hand. Her whole body engaged—her scalp tingled, her toes curled, and she got an odd jolt somewhere in the region between her hip bones. Her body was flooded with a sensation of weakness, as if she suddenly wanted to sit down. Or even lie down. How differently she had felt when Hector had clasped her hand in his moist one. She wanted to snatch it away and wipe it on her skirt.

And what about the time the doctor was bending over Jewel and Flora had an urge to touch his sturdy brown neck? So strong was this devastating impulse that she had put her hands behind her back. The sight of his legs, so long that he had to lower his stirrups to the last notch, made her feel slightly lightheaded. This must be physical attraction, the natural force that drives all living things. She had never realised that it could be so powerful. This was the most dangerous aspect of her whole enterprise. She was in no position to fall in love with Samuel Farraday.

Flora reached her shack and dropped her armload of corncobs on the table. She sank onto the bed and pressed her palms to her eyes as she recalled her only brush with sexual intimacy. Her wedding day had not been romantic in the least. She and Hector were married at a dingy registry office in Glasgow, and then sailed on the *Corinthian* with the evening tide. Flora stood at the rail, watching the others wave goodbye to their loved ones on the shore.

"Don't fret, lassie," said her new husband, putting his arm around Flora's waist with a proprietary air. She stiffened, trying not to shrink away from his unfamiliar touch. Hector believed she was unhappy to leave Scotland. In fact, she was secretly bursting with jubilation. No more waiting hand and foot on the parsimonious Mrs. Galt, counting every tuppence. She was on her way to a new country. More importantly, she would finally have a home of her own.

Her only concern was what shape her life would take, married to Hector. She had already discovered his inclination to be boastful, but this seemed a common male characteristic, easily tolerated.

"We'll return for a visit soon, depending on my good fortune," Hector said. "And you're going to help me with that, naturally."

"Aye, it will be my pleasure," Flora said. Once again, she imagined dusting her own furniture, laundering her own linen tablecloths, arranging the roses from her own garden. She glanced sideways at Hector, wondering how much time he would spend at home.

He gave her waist another squeeze before tossing his cigar over the railing.

"And now, dear bride, I'm going to have a kip. I've never been a good sea traveller. Mind you don't talk to strangers."

He did seem paler than usual. He removed his hat, and the ocean breeze lifted his carefully arranged hair, revealing a bald spot on his crown that Flora hadn't noticed before. By the time she came downstairs to their cabin an hour later, he was very ill indeed. And he remained that way for the entire voyage.

Flora, on the other hand, proved to be an excellent sailor. Since they were travelling first class, she ate at the captain's table and enjoyed every morsel. She was enchanted when the ship steamed past an iceberg that looked like a floating glass cathedral on the flat grey sea. Even when the waves were choppy, she walked the deck for hours, breathing the fresh salt air and contemplating her blissful future.

Flora was still a virgin when they arrived in Montreal, twelve days later. She had never been happier.

After they boarded the Pacific Express, it seemed as if their rail trip across the country would prove just as enjoyable. Hector's position with the company meant that they travelled in style. Each sleeping car had a separate compartment at one end called a drawing room, and one of these was assigned to the newlyweds. It was a snug little space, with mahogany walls, two bunks, a plush sofa, a writing desk, and a water closet.

As soon as they entered their private quarters, Hector crawled into the lower bunk without speaking and fell asleep. By now, Flora was becoming uneasy. What on earth was wrong with the wretched man? She took her copy of *Great Expectations* into the passenger car and found an empty seat, where she spent most of the journey.

For the first couple of days, she observed little except a thick forest, interspersed with glimpses of granite slabs and sparkling water. Flora had not imagined that there were so many trees in the entire world. The train chugged slowly around the curves of the Great Lakes. By leaning out the window, she could see the engine ahead, the smoke drifting back like a charcoal scarf. At times the train moved so slowly that one passenger won his bet with another by throwing his hat off the side, leaping down and snatching it from the ground, sprinting beside the tracks, and jumping back inside.

On the third day, the train broke out onto the prairies. This was what Flora had been longing to see—the verdant countryside described by Hector, dotted with farms and villages. "Where are we?" Flora asked the porter.

"We're approaching Winnipeg, ma'am."

So this was the heartland of Manitoba, supposedly so lush, so fertile. She could scarcely believe her eyes. It was a dun-coloured treeless plain. *Perhaps we haven't reached farming country yet*, Flora thought, but when the train left Manitoba and headed toward Regina, capital of the vast North-West Territories, the prairie landscape looked no different. Occasionally a shack appeared, like a cork bobbing on a sea of brown grass.

Judging by the murmurs from the other passengers, she wasn't alone in her dismay. She recalled the brochure that Hector had distributed in Aberdeen, bearing an illustration of a wagon with bright red wheels, stained by the juice of strawberries growing thick on the ground. A horrible suspicion grew that Hector had not told his audience the truth about the Canadian prairies. That meant he had been lying to her, too.

Flora struck up a conversation with a young woman who had been working as a housemaid in Toronto. She was disembarking in Moose Jaw to meet a strange man. She had agreed to marry him based on nothing more than one newspaper advertisement, one letter, and one photograph.

"If I have to cook and clean, it might as well be for a husband," she told Flora. "You know the saying: 'Go West, Young Man, To Find Some Land. Go West, Young Woman, To Find a Man.'"

Flora pitied her. No doubt the poor lass was destined to live in one of those miserable shacks, rather than the beautiful stone house that was waiting for Flora.

When the train approached Calgary, she returned to their drawing room and found Hector sitting upright on his bunk.

"Help me get dressed," he said. "We'll be here for six hours. I've got to see a man about a dog."

"A dog?"

"It's just an expression," he said impatiently. "Hand me my breeks, would you?" Flora helped him pull on his trousers. His rash had cleared up somewhat, thanks to her daily application of mercury ointment. He clamped his fedora onto his head and departed without saying goodbye.

Left to her own devices, Flora spent the afternoon wandering the streets of this brash young city. Everywhere was a contagious sense of excitement—brick and stone buildings springing out of the flat earth like mushrooms, high-spirited horses cantering down the broad streets, shop windows filled with colourful merchandise ranging from feather dusters to rock candy, and well-dressed ladies strolling arm in arm. In a restaurant near the station, she ordered her first Alberta beefsteak. It was delicious.

There was no sign of Hector when she boarded the train, and Flora began to feel concerned. At eleven o'clock the conductor shouted, "All aboard!" and the wheels started to revolve. Minutes later, the compartment door opened and he lurched inside.

"Thank goodness!" she said. "Ach, I was that worried!"

"Were you."

"Did you visit your friend in Calgary?"

"He's no friend of mine, but yes, I saw him. I lost five hands of poker to that bloody swindler." Hector's face was flushed and his eyes were glassy. A strong odour of smoke and whisky filled the compartment. Reaching into his coat pocket, he pulled out a flask, unscrewed the cap, and took several swallows.

"May I ask you something, Hector?" Flora couldn't wait any longer.

"Ask away, dear wife."

"Where are the farms that you described back in Aberdeen? I haven't seen anything except bald prairie, and not a single house."

Hector dropped onto the sofa and took another pull from his flask. "You're being far too literal. I'm not selling real farms, but a promise, a hope for the future. Those people can have their barns and their gardens and their picket fences, if they work hard enough. And in exchange for my services, the CPR pays me good money."

Flora was speechless. Her mind could scarcely absorb the magnitude of Hector's deception. She imagined the crushing disappointment that awaited thousands of innocent souls who had sold all their possessions and travelled across the ocean, expecting to find a Canadian garden of Eden.

Hector leered at her, his rosy lips wet with whisky. "And now that I have a charming wife, it will be that much easier to part the peasants from their pounds—especially when you go to work on the women."

Flora blinked. "You want me to help you? To persuade those poor wives to leave behind everything they hold dear, in exchange for no more than a promise?"

He took another swig and stared at her with an ugly expression. "Why the hell do you think I married you?"

"I thought you wanted me to be the mistress of your home!"

"And so you shall be, if you do your part. Until that happy day, we'll live in a boarding house."

Flora collapsed against the wall. "That house in the photograph. Sunny-brae," she whispered. "It doesn't belong to you?"

"If we convince enough people to buy land, you'll have another house, even grander."

A bitter taste filled Flora's mouth. She had been taken in as thoroughly as all his other victims. This villain was no better than the snake oil salesmen who tried to convince her father to buy miracle cures. And he was her lawfully wedded husband!

She would have to get one thing straight. "Hector . . . I canna lie to people. Lying is a sin."

His face turned a dangerous shade of magenta. "You'll do exactly as I say!" He started to unbuckle his belt. "And you're going to start right here and now! Take off your clothes!"

"Nay, Hector." She heard the panic in her own voice. "Please. Not like this."

He lunged at her and ripped open her blouse. Two buttons flew across the room. He grabbed her naked breast and squeezed it so hard that she screamed.

"Shut your mouth!" Hector hissed and drew his fist back. Flora turned her head and the blow landed heavily on her left cheek. In shock and pain, she retaliated instinctively by slapping him. His face convulsed with rage and his hands closed around her throat. Flora grabbed his wrists and tried to pull them away, but they were locked in place like a pair of pliers.

In the dim light from the gas lamp fixed to the wall, he was a gruesome spectre, his red lips drawn back from his teeth. His sour breath stank of whisky and smoke and sickness. Star shapes burned and turned in her peripheral vision, and the room began to darken. He's not going to stop until I'm dead, she realised with horror. She ceased clawing at his hands and shoved him in the chest as hard as she could.

Flora was young and strong, while Hector was drunk and ill and unsteady on his feet. He flailed his arms but couldn't save himself. He fell backward and his head struck the edge of the writing desk with a loud crack. He lay motionless, while Flora sobbed for breath. She wasn't sure if he were dead or alive. She wasn't sure if she cared. Suddenly, after one tremendous grunt, he began to snore.

At that moment Flora vowed that she would die penniless on the prairie rather than live with Hector for another day, and she had never regretted her decision.

But that didn't change the fact that she was still married.

CHAPTER TWENTY-ONE

The wheat rustled in the breeze, their heads bending toward each other like a great multitude of fairies whispering secrets. Flora broke off an ear of grain and ground it in her palm, blew away the husk, and examined the plump kernels. This was the miraculous new variety of wheat called Marquis, with a growing season ten days shorter than the traditional Red Fife. She popped the kernels into her mouth and chewed them, deliciously sweet and nutty, as she made her calculations. If her five acres yielded thirty bushels to the acre, and each bushel was worth one dollar, she would make one hundred and fifty dollars—enough to cover her expenses and purchase her grubstake for the coming winter.

Flora had gazed into the heavens so often that she had a crick in her neck. It was the third week of August, and the sky was blue and hot and cloudless. She turned back to her crop. Already it appeared fuller, as if ripening before her eyes. "One more week," she breathed, praying to the sun god above. No wonder ancient peoples worshipped the sun, the source of all living things. Miss Edgar referred to him by his Greek name, Helios. Flora wondered what the Cree called him. She would ask Miss McDonald when she saw her again.

Whatever his name, the sun god continued to smile until the last particle of green turned into gold. By this time, the women were on their own. Beau had left Ladyville for the next month, hired out to another farmer. Sourdough was busy with his own work—he had fifty acres sown to wheat and oats—but he gave them a hasty lesson in scything, shaking his head and warning them not to lose a toe.

"It takes a good man two days to scythe one acre," he warned. "You'll be at it until the snow flies!"

As usual, his words had the opposite effect, since both women were determined to prove him wrong. The next day Flora arose at dawn, bolted her bacon and eggs from the Buffs and fried tomatoes from her garden, and was poised to begin at the precise moment the morning dew had dried.

Following Sourdough's instructions, she swung the scythe carefully, relaxing her arm at the top of the swing and letting its weight do the work, rotating her body at the waist. At first her blows were choppy, but as she grew more proficient, the shining blade whistled through the air and the grain fell in neat rows before her feet. She felt almost sorrowful, mowing down her first-born infants like the Grim Reaper.

After one hour, her arm was throbbing.

After two hours, she stripped down to her sweat-soaked bloomers and chemise.

At noon, she staggered into her shack and wolfed two bowls of leftover duck stew as if she hadn't eaten for a week.

By mid-afternoon, her right arm was so weary that she could barely lift the scythe. She tried using her left arm, but couldn't find the rhythm on that side. Maddeningly, simple exhaustion forced her to stop while the sun was still high. She flung herself into the creek to wash away the dirt, stuffed herself on pork sausages and new potatoes, and crawled into her cot exhausted. The next day she worked more slowly, since her right arm burned with every movement. The stubbled area behind her was pathetically small compared to the acres of waving grain that lay ahead.

On the fifth day, Flora hit her stride. Her arm felt stronger, and she made good progress. She could see Mrs. Penrose across the creek, her sunbonnet bobbing above the grain, her blade flashing in the sunshine. Jack spelled off his mother at intervals. He was twelve years old now and had filled out in the last year. His slender arms were almost as muscled as Flora's. Taffy followed Jewel around to make sure she didn't get into mischief, while Nellie prepared their meals. At the age of ten, Nellie could bake bread as light and tasty as her mother's.

Never had the women worked so long and so hard. Gradually the stubbled area grew larger and the area of standing grain shrank. Three weeks later, as the sun was shedding its final glow over the landscape, both Flora and Peggy cut down their last rows.

One final task remained: to gather the grain in armfuls, tie the sheaves with twine and stack them upright in stooks, wedged together to keep off the rain. Only then could the weary homesteaders stand back and admire their army of amber triangles, lined up like rows of miniature tipis. Nothing could hurt the grain now, except the deadly frost.

Flora stood at the top of the hill, shading her eyes with her hand and praying for the sight of the threshing machine. A team of horses drew a steam-powered engine from farm to farm, accompanied by a crew of eight men. Four of them cut firewood and fed the boiler; the others tossed the sheaves into the thresher that separated the grain from the straw.

It should be here by now, but there was no sign of it.

Two days passed, then three. Everyone strained their ears, listening for the steam whistle that heralded its coming. Several times a day Flora climbed the hill, hoping to see movement on the horizon. Once she threw back her head and screamed with frustration, so loudly that she set Taffy barking across the creek.

On the fourth morning a skim of silver covered the grass. Flora dashed to the field barefoot to check on her stooks. She broke open a few heads of grain and examined the kernels. Thankfully, they were still plump and golden. The grain hadn't been harmed—yet.

Nearing a state of panic, the women dispatched Jack on a scouting mission. He left the farm on Felicity's back at a full gallop. While they waited for his return, the women busied themselves in the Penrose kitchen, preparing sauerkraut with shredded cabbage and vinegar. Mrs. Penrose dropped a canning jar and broke it, and a distracted Flora put six extra tablespoons of salt into the boiler. Every few minutes one of them would go to the door and stare down the trail. When at last Jack appeared, they ran into the yard, wiping their hands on their aprons.

"They've gone south, Ma," he called from the saddle.

"What do you mean, gone south? When will they be back?"

"They ain't coming back. They crossed the Red Deer River three days ago. They're probably halfway to Calgary by now."

Mrs. Penrose gasped in horror. "Did they forget about us?"

"They didn't forget, Ma. I talked to one farmer six miles south. He said the crew was told not to bother with those fools at Ladyville, they wouldn't pay and would be gone by spring anyway."

So, Mrs. Westhead had triumphed after all.

"My poor children! Whatever shall become of us?" Mrs. Penrose threw her apron over her face and began to cry, regardless of their reaction. When Nellie and Jewel heard their mother's unaccustomed sobs, both started to wail in unison. Even Jack buried his face in Felicity's flank.

Flora took two steps before her legs refused to support her body and she dropped to her knees on the grass. Her mind went blank, so shocked by this new obstacle that she couldn't even think logically. The murmur of the creek, the twitter of birdsong, the weeping children, Taffy whining in sympathy—all these sounds faded away as she knelt on the ground.

Finally, she raised her head and looked across the creek at her stooks, helpless and innocent in the warm sunshine. She couldn't bear to watch them freeze to death, buried under the snow, the golden kernels inside turning black and rotten and worthless.

This could not, would not happen. Flora struggled to her feet and faced the Penroses, her fists clenched.

"We maun do it ourselves," she said.

One frantic hour later, the women had shovelled the manure out of the Penrose barn and swept the dirt floor before laying down a sheet of canvas and anchoring it with rocks. Jack was dispatched to Sourdough's place for a couple of flails, each consisting of two pieces of wood connected by a short chain. These were in widespread use before threshing machines had arrived on the prairies several years earlier.

Beginning with the Penrose field, they tossed the sheaves onto the wagon with pitchforks and unloaded them on the canvas, spreading the stalks evenly about two feet deep. Then they beat the grain mercilessly, as if their lives depended on it—which wasn't far from the truth. Bessie and Bob helped by walking over the grain, crushing the stalks with their hooves. Even Jewel whacked at the pile with her little stick.

When they judged the grain to be sufficiently loosened, they removed the excess straw before lifting the canvas by its edges and bouncing it up and down. The remaining stalks flew into the air and left the kernels behind. A breeze coated them with chaff until they resembled a family of scarecrows. After scooping up the wheat with cooking pots and cups, they poured it into burlap sacks. Every precious kernel was picked off the floor with dirty, broken fingernails.

This work went on for several days. On Sunday afternoon, a visitor rode into the yard—Crawford Crawley, the young Anglican minister from Toddsville. Filled with missionary zeal, he had visited each Ladyville household in turn. The only one who had been happy to see him was Mrs. Penrose. Remembering her broken marriage vows, Flora had barely spoken to the poor young man.

The minister wore a disapproving expression. "Ladies, why are you working on the Sabbath? According to Exodus, 'You shall work six days, but on the seventh day you shall rest; even during ploughing time and harvest you shall rest.'"

Flora was too abashed to meet his eyes, but Mrs. Penrose answered in ringing tones, "That's true, Mr. Crawley, but remember Revelations: 'Take your sickle and reap, because the time to reap has come, for the harvest of the earth is ripe.'" The minister looked somewhat mortified at this. He dismounted and spent the rest of the day helping Jack fill the wagon while the women winnowed.

Miss Edgar and Wren appeared at the barn door one morning wearing their oldest dresses, kerchiefs covering their hair. They gathered Mrs. Penrose's vegetables, then headed to Flora's garden to do the same for her.

Ten days later, the last sack was filled. Before tying it shut, the exhausted women reached inside and allowed the Marquis kernels to slip through their filthy fingers, marvelling at their rich scent and glossy coats. Flora didn't think she could love them more than if they had been golden coins. She felt an unfamiliar sensation rise in her breast and it took a moment before she identified it as pride.

They had hoped for one hundred and fifty bushels, but each field had yielded an extra twenty-five. As Flora caressed the grain, she dreamed about how to spend her windfall. She would drink real tea rather than Lily White tea, as it was called here, the same leaves used until the water was clear. She would buy extra sugar and make a pan of Scottish tablet, or fudge, and give it to the children. And she would ask Wren, who had excellent taste in clothing, to choose a new hat for her in Red Deer—although nobody would see it, of course.

Unless she happened to run into the doctor.

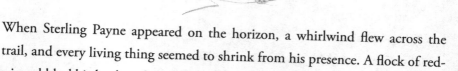

When Sterling Payne appeared on the horizon, a whirlwind flew across the trail, and every living thing seemed to shrink from his presence. A flock of red-winged blackbirds, their feathers glistening as if dipped in blood, took chattering flight as he rode up to the shack.

"Miss Craigie."

"Mr. Payne."

"I'm here to make my annual report. It's my duty to visit the homesteaders in my area after the harvest is finished and record their progress. Or lack of it."

"You're verra welcome to do so." Flora tried not to appear complacent. "I've met every condition to the letter."

"We'll see about that." Mr. Payne took a roll of twine from behind his saddle. He walked over to her field, pegged a stick into the ground, and began to unroll the twine.

Flora had paced out the field, and so had Sourdough. They had agreed that it was precisely five acres. However, she couldn't help feeling tense as Mr. Payne worked his way around the edges, writing in his black notebook. She refused to give him the satisfaction of holding the twine for him, although she worried that he might falsify the numbers. Perhaps she should have helped him after all.

The sweat had soaked the hatband of his bowler by the time he returned to Flora, who was seated in the shade. He had an unhealthy pallor and she wondered why his pale skin never changed colour, seemingly impervious to the sun and the wind. She stood up, brushing the grass off her seat of her overalls. "Well, Mr. Payne? I hope you're satisfied."

His thin lips parted in a grin, showing his little teeth. "I'm satisfied that your cultivated acres do not meet the minimum size requirement."

Flora took a step forward, ready to do battle. "I measured that field myself, more than once! And so did Mr. Buckhorn!"

"Ah yes, Miss Craigie, but I'm afraid you're forgetting something."

"And what's that?"

"The road allowance."

Flora stared at him in confusion. "What do you mean? What's a road allowance?"

"The government sets aside a strip along the edge of every section, for a future road. This one runs between your land, and the property belonging to those Yanks next door."

Flora's confidence evaporated. Naturally she had assumed that one day there would be roads rather than grass trails, but it had never occurred to her that the land for these roads had to come from somewhere.

"I know exactly where my land begins and ends," she said, her voice trailing away as she remembered searching in vain for two of her eight pegs. The survey crews left behind one metal peg and three wooden pegs to mark the four corners of each quarter. The wooden pegs sometimes disappeared, broken by the weight of snow, or lost under a blanket of grass.

On the flat prairie, people calculated distances by measuring the circumference of one wagon wheel and counting the number of times the wheel turned. Since Flora's land had both bush and creek, it was impossible to drive or ride or even walk in a straight line. She had hunted for those two missing pegs for days before pacing out the distance as best she could, driving stakes into the ground, and topping each one with a buffalo skull that gleamed like ivory in the long grass.

"Apparently you are mistaken." Mr. Payne was plainly enjoying himself.

"What size is this road allowance?" Flora asked, dreading his answer.

"Sixty-six feet wide." He was still grinning as he rolled up his ball of twine. "You have five acres in crop, but only four of them belong to you. You made the mistake of cultivating the government's property. That strip along the south side amounts to exactly one acre."

Flora was speechless. Twenty per cent of her precious field!

"How many bushels to the acre did you get, Miss Craigie?"

"Thirty-five." She bit her lip, almost wishing she had lied.

"Since I'm a generous man, I'll allow you to cultivate the extra acre next spring—if you're still ignorant enough to be here. In the meantime, that's thirty-five bushels you owe the government, or thirty-five dollars."

Flora saw her extra income dissolve like the melting snow. "I don't have that much cash, not until the grain is sold," she whispered.

"I'll collect it the next time I'm in the neighbourhood." He raised his bowler and made a mocking bow. "On behalf of the Dominion of Canada, I thank you for your generous donation."

CHAPTER TWENTY-TWO

To everyone's relief, the sixth of October dawned bright and clear. The glorious sunrise blossomed like a bouquet of blood-red flowers as Flora and the Penroses packed the wagon with patchwork quilts, picnic lunches, jugs of water, and oats for the horses. At the last minute, Nellie ran into the cabin and fetched Jewel's rag doll, Lolly—a handkerchief with a knot tied at one end for a head, and buttons for eyes.

The homesteaders were heading to the annual fall fair in Toddsville.

In honour of the occasion, the girls wore their best cotton dresses and pinafores. Nellie's straight brown hair was braided so tightly that her eyebrows were raised. Mrs. Penrose sported a straw hat trimmed with her own crocheted lace, and Flora had abandoned her breeks in favour of her grey skirt. By this time, it felt unnatural to have something swishing around her ankles. Her pink shirtwaist was patched, but presentable. To complete their ensembles, they carried parasols loaned by Wren.

Flora had deliberated whether to attend the fair. After paying off her debt to the government, she didn't have an extra cent—but she was longing to visit the town for reasons she dared not confess. It had been months since Nurse

Godwin's warning. She concluded that either Hector was searching south of the border, or he had given up altogether. She told herself that she couldn't hide until the crack of doom.

Still, she felt a little apprehensive as they approached the fairgrounds. Wagons and buggies rolled in from every direction. The population was growing rapidly, and new settlers arrived every day. Flora consoled herself that nobody would notice her in this throng. The women found a spot in the shade and unhitched the horses before hurrying toward the grounds, feeling quite elegant as they unfurled their parasols. Reasoning that the sunshade would provide enough concealment, Flora left her face uncovered. The children were fairly dancing with excitement.

The crowd represented a hodgepodge of settler diversity. Here were two rough-looking bachelors, there a group of ladies in gloves and picture hats. Families abounded, some with nine or ten children. Even the shabbiest of them wore washed and mended shirts and breeches, flowered frocks with embroidered collars. Elderly men sat in the shade, smoking hand-rolled cigarettes and complaining about the government. Teenage girls linked arms, giggling and whispering. Flora overheard snatches of conversation in foreign tongues—she recognised German and French, but the others were unfamiliar.

While the three children went off to explore, Flora and Mrs. Penrose walked into a canvas tent containing field and garden exhibits. The smell inside was a mixture of sweet peas and onions and Sunday clothes washed with lye soap. They admired the floral arrangements first—some of them four feet high, stalks of purple and red gladiolas, intricate dahlia blossoms as large as dinner plates—before moving on to the vegetables, commenting that their own potatoes and carrots were just as fine. The heavyweight championships had gone to a fourteen-pound turnip and a seventeen-pound cabbage. And the glorious display of grain! These were handpicked and bound sheaves of wheat, oats, and barley. Flora was filled with the desire to create a wheat sheaf every bit as flawless.

A long table held homemade bread, butter, cheese, baking, and a row of jams and jellies like a necklace of brilliant gems. "That strawberry pie should never have won first prize," Mrs. Penrose whispered. "The fruit is already soaking through the pastry." There were rich, syrupy wines made from chokecherries and dandelions and black currants.

Other tables were laden with handcrafts—intricate crocheted tablecloths, colourful scrap quilts with stitches as delicate as pencil points, knitted baby blankets, and hooked rugs bearing images of animals and wildflowers. The men had also been busy during the winter months, producing tooled leather harnesses and wooden checkerboards and birdhouses.

When they had admired and criticized to their satisfaction, the women wandered outside to the show ring, where Jack was watching the local farmers trotting out their finest cattle—russet Shorthorns and white-faced Herefords and black Aberdeen Angus breeds, their tails brushed and horns polished.

Flora peeped from beneath her parasol, scanning the crowd. "I don't recognize anyone."

"How could we, since we never go anywhere?" Mrs. Penrose said. "Wait, there's Mr. Sanderson! That must be his wife with him."

"And there's Jessie McDonald!" Flora said, spotting their neighbour in the distance, wearing her usual buckskin breeches.

As they approached the poultry tent, the Chicken Ladies emerged, Wren carrying a fluffy Buff Orpington inside a cage. A red rosette reading "First Prize" was pinned on Wren's ruffled blouse.

"Hello, my dear friends! Isn't this a wonderful day! My darling Beatrice swept the field!"

As if the hen understood, she gave a victorious squawk, and everyone laughed.

"I must get this little girl home—she isn't used to so much excitement!" Wren said. She and Miss Edgar hurried off to their buggy.

After eating their picnic lunch on a quilt in the shade, the group tried to watch the baseball tournament, but found the rules confusing. What was a foul ball, anyway? More entertaining were the children's events: three-legged races, egg-and-spoon races, sack races, and simple foot races.

"Nellie, why don't you enter the foot race?" her mother suggested. "You're so quick, and the prize is one whole dollar." It took some coaxing, but Nellie lined up with seven other girls, all taller than her. Only Nellie was barefoot. She had outgrown her old boots, and Jack's were too big. Mrs. Penrose was waiting until winter before buying her a new pair. Nellie's cheeks were flushed under her deeply tanned skin, and her little jaw was set with determination.

The local blacksmith stood to one side, holding a whistle. "Take your marks!" He raised the whistle to his lips and blew.

The girls darted forward, their calf-length skirts billowing in the breeze. Nellie was in third place when they rounded the halfway point.

"Run! Nellie, run!" Mrs. Penrose, Jack, and Flora screamed their loudest.

Even Jewel shouted, "Go, go, go!"

Nellie's legs pumped so fast that her feet were invisible in the dust, her face contorted with effort. At the last second, her dirty bare toes crossed the finish line inches before the next girl's shoe.

"We have a winner!" The blacksmith shook Nellie's hand and presented her with four shiny quarters.

She couldn't stop grinning as she skipped over to her family, waving her fist in the air.

"Well done, Nellie!" In the way of all mothers, Mrs. Penrose beamed as if she had won the race herself. "How will you spend your money?"

"Follow me!" Nellie led the way to a booth made of four posts with a roof of branches for shade, where several women scooped homemade ice cream out of a wooden barrel lined with ice. The three children each received a five-cent bowl.

"Jewel has never tasted ice cream," Mrs. Penrose said. She held out the spoon and everyone laughed at Jewel's face when the smooth, cold substance touched her tongue. "More!" She grabbed the spoon and began to feed herself enthusiastically.

"Here, Mum." Nellie gave her mother the remaining coins. "You have the rest."

Mrs. Penrose looked reluctant, but she took the money. "I'll pay you back, my love, that's a promise."

There was a flurry of activity now, as the crowd moved to the field to watch the equestrian events. Every prairie inhabitant owned horses, and many of them vied for the honour of having the strongest, the fastest, or the best trained animals.

In the individual event, each rider took his horse around the track at a walk, a trot, and a gallop. The audience was keenly interested in the results, and voices rose as everyone expressed a firmly held opinion. The autumn air was thick with the smell of horseflesh, and flies covered the piles of manure. Two boys gathered them up with a wooden wheelbarrow and a shovel.

The ladies' driving competition followed. Each of the five entrants drove a fancy, polished, two-wheeled carriage drawn by a single horse, similar to the rigs Flora had seen on Sunday drives in Aberdeen. As they trotted around the track, the judge stood at one side and made notes on the skill of the drivers, the obedience of the horses, and the overall appearance of their elegant equipages. Flora noted that this event was dominated by the English ladies, since the homesteaders had little time or money to spare on such follies.

Wearing a black linen suit and red leather driving gloves, the winner sat on the bench of a black carriage lined with red satin, driving a high-stepping black Hackney horse, his mane and tail braided with matching red ribbons. As she made her victory lap around the track, Flora recognised her.

It was Alix Westhead.

The carriage swept past them, the driver nodding regally to the crowd.

When she noticed Flora, her smile changed to a scowl and she snapped her whip at the horse, looking as if she would prefer to lay into Flora instead. Having taken the bold step of leaving off her veil, Flora wished again that she weren't so tall. She bent her knees beneath her skirt and lowered the parasol over her face.

It was time for the main event, the Indian pony races. They weren't allowed to compete with the English thoroughbreds. Flora suspected it was because the British feared humiliation if their expensive horses lost.

A large group of Indians now came from their tipi camp at the far end of the grounds to watch. Until now they had kept to themselves, visiting around their own campfires. Both men and women wore braids, but the women's heads were covered with kerchiefs, shawls or blankets. As they ringed the track there was a murmur in the crowd, a noticeable drawing back among some of the well-dressed whites.

Ten Indian men mounted their ponies. When the whistle blew, they thundered down the field in a cloud of suffocating dust, braids streaming behind them. A few riders let out fierce howls. It was a stirring sight, and Flora imagined how fearsome they must have appeared when advancing into battle.

When it was time for the women's races, Miss McDonald on Tipiskow lined up with nine other riders. At the sound of the whistle, the horses lengthened their bodies and shot forward as if launched from a cannon. Flora and Mrs. Penrose cheered loudly as their neighbour flew past, and she darted a quick sideways look at them.

Miss McDonald won easily. After dismounting to accept her five dollars, she leaped onto her horse from a standing position. She pulled on his reins, and he stood on his hind legs and danced in a circle, then dropped to four hooves and bent his front legs, taking a bow. There was wild applause from this crowd of horse-lovers.

The last race was for the Indian boys, who set off like a flock of startled birds. They were nearly around the track when one pony stumbled and went down. He pitched onto his head, tumbling and rolling in the dirt, while his young rider jumped clear.

The pony lay on one side, screaming with pain, his front leg bent at an awkward angle. Several people in the crowd covered their ears, but the Indian women hurried onto the track. One of them pulled a long knife out of her belt, bent over the horse, and cut its throat. So skillful was she that the horse's scream stopped instantly. A sheet of blood gushed from the wound and soaked into the dust.

There was a collective gasp from the crowd. Several women cried out. One of them swooned, falling sideways into her husband's arms, while a young mother grabbed her children's hands and hurried away. Others watched in horrified fascination.

The Indian women set to work with their knives, first skinning the horse and then carving it into pieces, leaving the entrails in a steaming pile in the dirt. Each woman wrapped a hunk of raw horsemeat in a blanket and set off for the tipi village with her bloody burden.

"How nauseating!" She heard a familiar voice behind her. "Those savages should never have been allowed to participate." Flora turned to see Mrs. Westhead.

"I heard this country was uncivilised, but I never bargained for this," said the woman beside her in an English accent. "I want to pack my bags and leave on the next train."

"Why don't you?" Flora was startled to hear Miss McDonald. She had come up behind them on moccasin feet. "These people are starving. I suppose you would rather they buried that horse instead of feeding their hungry children."

The ladies hurried away, Mrs. Westhead holding a dainty handkerchief over her nose as if she smelled something bad.

Miss McDonald gave Flora a challenging glare and turned away, head held high. "Miss McDonald, wait!" Flora touched her arm.

"What do you want?"

"I'm glad you gave those women a good scaulding. They deserved it."

The other woman didn't reply, but a smile twisted her lips as she walked away.

By sunset, many families were packing up. There was a dance at the community hall, but unaccustomed to driving the trail at night, the ladies were anxious to get home. The two older children ran ahead to hitch up the team. Jewel was already asleep in her mother's arms.

As the women threaded their way between the wagons in the growing darkness, they encountered a group of men passing a bottle from hand to hand.

A couple of them stared, and one of them whistled. "You those gals from Ladyville? Where are you going in such a hurry? Aren't you coming to the dance?"

"Don't answer them," Mrs. Penrose whispered, and the women hastened their pace.

Flora heard footsteps behind her, and felt a heavy arm go around her waist.

"Come on, little lady, give us a goodbye kiss!"

She tried to shrug the man off, but his grip tightened. His breath stank of liquor and tobacco. She wanted to strike him with her furled parasol, but she couldn't free her arm. Although she twisted and turned, he managed to slide his wet lips along the side of her bare neck. The sensation was revolting.

"Leave her alone!" someone shouted.

Flora turned and her heart leaped as she saw a pair of broad shoulders against the flaming scarlet sky. She had been looking for those shoulders all day.

Dr. Farraday rushed toward them, grabbed the man's arm, spun him around, and punched him in the jaw. Cursing, the man sprawled in the dirt before scrambling to his feet and lurching off.

"Are you all right, Miss Craigie?" The doctor gripped Flora's arm.

"I'm fine," Flora said weakly, as she scrubbed her neck with her handkerchief.

Her pulse was racing. She wasn't sure if it was because of that revolting man, or the doctor's presence.

"You ladies shouldn't be out here by yourselves after dark!"

"We were just leaving," Mrs. Penrose said. "Thank goodness you came along when you did!"

The doctor was still holding Flora's arm. "I would have been here sooner but I had a case south of town. I hurried back because I know there'll be injuries later, once the drinking and the fisticuffs start. Besides, I was hoping to see you. All of you," he added.

He helped Mrs. Penrose climb into the wagon before taking Flora's hand in his. She allowed him to assist her, just to feel the warmth of his grasp. It seemed even stronger in the thick dusk.

"Aside from that unpleasant encounter, I hope you had an enjoyable day," he said.

"We certainly did, Doctor," Mrs. Penrose replied. "Ladyville did itself proud! Nellie won a foot race, Miss McDonald won a pony race, and Miss Greenwood won first prize for her hen Beatrice!"

"Excellent! And you, Miss Craigie? Did you have a good time?"

"Oh yes," she said, trying to maintain a tone of civilised politeness despite the heat radiating up her arm from their clasped hands. "I was quite dazzled by the bright lights. Now I maun put my shoulder to the wheel once again."

She could barely detect his features in the dusk, but his cheek was so close that she could smell his scent, a faint fragrance of soap and sweat and something else that was him alone. After what seemed a long time, she extricated her hand.

As the wagon rolled away, she looked back. From the nearby tipi village came the faint sound of drums and chanting voices, a haunting sound that stirred Flora to the depths of her soul. Dr. Farraday stood in the same place, his figure outlined in the fading twilight, his hand raised in farewell.

CHAPTER TWENTY-THREE

Y ou're still here."

Flora was forking hay into Felicity's stall when she saw Jessie McDonald in the doorway.

"Yes, still here and planning to stay." Flora jammed her pitchfork into the haystack as if she were nailing herself to the mast.

"Huh." Miss McDonald led her mustang into the barn and unbuckled his saddle. She hoisted it off his back and plunked it down on a pile of scrap lumber. It was a western saddle, polished and gleaming, with a tooled floral pattern and a chased silver saddle horn.

"This is for you. Pay me back when you can."

Flora was astonished by this generous gesture. "It's a braw saddle, Miss McDonald, but I already have one."

"That useless waste of leather!" She gestured toward the English sidesaddle, hanging on the stall. "You can't ride on that thing! It isn't fair to you, or your poor horse!"

Flora dared not refuse. She stared at the saddle, wondering if she could possibly ride with her legs spread. It seemed so indecent. However, since arriving in Canada she had done a lot of things that would be considered unlady-like.

"I can't thank you enough. Won't you come inside and have tea with me?"

Miss McDonald stroked her horse's neck while she considered. She gave a curt nod before following Flora into her shack. Perhaps this reserved neighbour was finally prepared to let down her guard, Flora thought.

While they waited for the kettle to boil, the newcomer walked around the cabin. She picked up the book lying on the pillow and read the title aloud. *Call of the Wild* by Jack London. After they sat down, Flora took the plunge.

"Miss McDonald, do you have Scottish roots? Yours is a common surname in my own country, as I'm sure you know."

The other woman nodded. "Angus McDonald was my father's father. He came from the Orkneys to work as a middleman for the Hudson's Bay Company. That's the man who sits in the middle of the canoe. He was a good man, married my kokum, my Cree grandmother, in church. She taught him everything—how to hunt and trap, what plants to eat, good medicine. For a joke, some people call us 'improved Scots' because the Indian blood is such an asset."

Miss McDonald set down her cup and fixed Flora with her piercing grey eyes. "There's nothing wrong with my name, but I don't like being called Miss. You can call me Jessie."

"Thank you, Jessie, and I hope you will call me Flora."

The two young women smiled rather self-consciously at each other and sipped their tea. Jessie spoke first. "Was your father a farmer back in Scotland?"

"No, he was a chemist, what the natives might call a medicine man. My mother's parents farmed, though, so maybe it's in my blood. They had a wee croft in the Highlands, about five or six acres. They grew vegetables, had a few pigs and a cow."

"Did you spend much time with them growing up?"

"None at all. My grandparents were forced off their farm before I was born, although my family had lived there for generations. They were evicted, along with thousands of other people, because the English landlords wanted to use the land for grazing sheep."

"Those English devils, with their hunger for other people's land!" Jessie's eyes flashed with anger. "Maybe our families do have something in common after all."

There was another brief silence while they sipped their tea, and Jessie sat frowning as if she were angered at Flora's story.

"Jessie, may I ask another question? Where did you attend school?"

"My father taught me to read and write at home," she replied. "When I was eleven, my parents sent me to a residential school. Unlike the Indians, Half-Breeds weren't forced to send their children away to school, but some of them wanted their children to enroll so they could get a good education. I was rebellious, and they thought the rules would be good for me."

She tossed her head. "I did get an education, but not the kind they meant. The priests wanted to beat the Indian out of us. They claimed that killing the Indian in the child was the Lord's work."

Flora gasped, aware that the Bible said no such thing. The other woman ignored her and continued to speak, as if she had suppressed her story too long and was determined to share it with Flora.

"There was one priest—he tried to touch me, but I threatened to steal a knife from the kitchen and stab him in his sleep. I wasn't one of those timid little rabbits that did whatever they were told. My mother wanted the devil taken out of me, but that's what saved me in the end."

"What happened then?"

"I was beaten more than once, but he never laid a finger on me again. I came home at Christmas and told my parents I would never go back."

"That's appalling!" Flora was ashamed of her own ignorance, and she made a silent vow to become better informed. "You've had no other formal education?"

"No. I taught myself by reading books. My brothers never went to school, either."

"How many brothers do you have?"

"Two brothers, both older. They help me out now and then. They built my cabin for me. My mother lives with them, since my father died. They're up in Lac Ste. Anne, sixty miles north of Edmonton."

"Don't you miss your family?"

"I do, but I'd rather live alone. Two different men came to my father and wanted to marry me, but both times I refused. No man will break me to harness."

She tossed her head again. "My father called me as pigheaded as a grizzly, but that's why he left me his land. He was worried about what would happen to me without a husband."

Flora smiled. Fathers were the same the world over. "Did your brothers mind?"

"No. They're hunters and trappers. They would have sold the land for a few dollars. It isn't worth much to anyone but me."

The sky was the same colour as the wet stones on the beach at Dornoch. The icy wind whipping the last few November leaves from the trees was a harbinger of things to come, none of them good. Flora was stacking firewood around her shack to help keep out the cold when Samuel Farraday rode into the yard.

Dismayed at her own reaction to the sight of him, Flora dropped a stick of wood on her foot. She was determined to extinguish this dangerous feeling, stamp it out like a smouldering spark before it set the whole prairie on fire. Berating herself for a fool, she smoothed her hair and went to greet him. The doctor dismounted and pulled off his hat. His hair was longer and shaggier than ever.

"Dr. Farraday! How nice of you to call." Her voice was a little breathless.

"Good morning, Miss Craigie. I'm here to ask you for a favour."

"Of course. Let's go inside."

Flora hung the doctor's coat on the nail behind the door before putting on the kettle. "Sit down and tell me how I can help." She took the other chair and gave him her full attention. Ruefully, she realised that wasn't difficult.

"Ten days ago, I assisted a young woman named Daphne Dawson to give birth. I don't know what kind of abuse she's taken from her husband, Murdo, but she has bruises on her arms and legs. I asked her about them while he was outside. She became fearful and refused to answer, but she might confide in another woman. If she wants to leave him, I can help."

Flora forced her expression to remain impassive. The doctor would never suspect that she understood the problem only too well.

"What makes you think I'm the best person for this?"

"Mrs. Penrose has her own children to care for. Miss Edgar may be a trifle too stern, and Miss Greenwood the opposite. I believe you have the perfect combination of compassion and strength that's called for in this situation."

"I appreciate your trust, Dr. Farraday. I'm not sure she'll listen to me, but I'll try."

The doctor waited outside while Flora changed into her riding outfit. She had cut her brown woollen skirt down the centre and hemmed the edges, creating a divided garment that allowed her to ride astride. The ability to grip the horse between her knees, the improved balance and control, was worth more than anyone's opinion of her shamelessness. Even so, she felt bashful when she emerged from the shack and felt the doctor's eyes on her. He followed her to the barn and helped her saddle the horse. Flora swung herself onto Felicity's back, conscious of the muscular horsepower between her legs.

The route to the Dawsons intersected the Buffalo Lake Trail and ran five miles north. The horses couldn't move faster than a trot because the rutted trail was so rough, having frozen and thawed and frozen again. As they rode along single file, Felicity following Pal's snowy tail like a beacon, Flora reflected on the doctor's attitude. He was clearly sympathetic toward Mrs. Dawson's plight. How would he feel about Flora if he knew her terrible secret? She wasn't aware of any religion, any country, that did not consider a wife's desertion of her husband as an unforgiveable sin, if not an outright crime. Yet apparently the doctor didn't agree.

As they rode into the Dawsons' yard, Flora felt nothing but pity when she saw their humble dwelling, something called a dugout, excavated into the side of a hill. Three sides were buried and only the front wall was made of logs, relieved by a single window. A man flung open the door and stepped outside. He was handsome, with a beefy frame and a strong jaw, and Flora saw that he would be attractive to women. However, there was something brutish in his small eyes. He glared at them warily while the doctor explained that he wanted to check on the new mother and baby.

"The missus is fine. She don't need nothing. I hope you aren't going to charge me for a visit."

"Not at all. I was in the neighbourhood." The other man assumed a suspicious scowl, understandably, since nobody else lived around for miles. "This is Miss Craigie. She's acting as my nurse today. Would you mind if we examine the little girl?"

The man gave a single nod and gestured toward the door.

The dugout was dark and dismal, although the dirt floor had been swept. Here were the usual furnishings—bed, table covered with oilcloth, two chairs, and cookstove. The baby was lying on the floor inside a wooden packing crate. A young woman stood in the corner, almost invisible in the gloom. She was small and slender, no more than a teenager herself. She looked at her husband and he nodded permission before she spoke.

"Hello, Doctor."

Even in this murky light it was impossible not to see the livid bruise covering the right side of her face. But the doctor pretended not to notice anything out of the ordinary and bent over the baby.

"She looks well! You've been taking good care of Miss Caroline, I can tell!"

Flora was struck by the tender way he lifted the baby and cradled her in his arms.

"There's nothing wrong with the brat's lungs, anyway," the man said. "She screams her head off day and night." He laughed, but his wife cast a frightened glance at him.

The doctor unwrapped the baby and examined her. "Her cord has fallen off, and the stump is healing nicely. You have a fine, healthy daughter here, Mr. Dawson."

The man lifted the stove lid and spat a gob of tobacco juice into the fire. "I don't need a girl! I need a strapping boy to help me with this place. This one is no use; just another mouth to feed!" He jerked his thumb toward his wife, and Flora wasn't sure whether he was referring to her or the child. The young woman twisted her lips into an affected smile, as if he were joking, but stopped when her husband glared at her.

The doctor set the baby gently in her box before addressing her father. "I believe my horse has a stone in his shoe. Would you mind giving me your opinion, Mr. Dawson?"

"I suppose," the man said disagreeably.

"Thank you kindly. Miss Craigie, you may wait here."

When the door closed behind the two men, the woman's face relaxed. She was quite pretty despite her bruise, once the strain and fear left her features.

"Shall I make tea?" she asked.

"No, thank you." Flora had no time to waste on pleasantries. "Ach, I'm going to come straight to the point. The doctor told me he observed bruises on your body, and he's concerned for your safety."

The woman's eyes darted to the door. She didn't speak.

"Please, won't you consider leaving him? Do you have somewhere to go?"

The woman whispered, as though her husband might hear her from the yard. "I want to leave, Miss Craigie, and go home to my parents. They live in Winnipeg. It isn't only me, it's Caroline. Last night he lost his temper and shook her. When I tried to stop him, he hit me." She raised her hand to her cheek. "I'm afraid he might kill us both."

Flora's heart went out to her. "If you can make it into Toddsville, the doctor will drive you and the baby to the station in Lacombe."

The woman's expression was both hopeful and terrified. "It's too far to walk, but maybe I can steal the horse while he's asleep."

"Would he follow you as far as Winnipeg?" Flora asked, thinking of Hector.

"He wouldn't dare show up there, Miss Craigie. I have three brothers who would kill him if they found out what he was doing to me."

Heavy footsteps were heard, and the door banged open. Mr. Dawson looked at his wife, who was a picture of guilt, and his face darkened. That look was all too familiar. Flora had seen the same coldness and rage in Hector's eyes.

"Doctor, I'm afraid we're going to be late for our next call," Flora said.

"Yes, of course." They made their farewells. Flora held out her hand to Mr. Dawson, trying not to flinch, and then took his wife's hand and gave it a meaningful squeeze. She saw tears in the young woman's eyes and hoped she would be able to keep her secret.

Three nights later, Flora was preparing to extinguish her lamp when she heard a knock, so faint that she wasn't sure if it was the wind. She peeked out her front window and saw a shrouded figure slumped against her door, clutching a blanket-wrapped bundle.

When she opened it, someone staggered and fell into the room. In the dim light, Flora barely recognised Daphne Dawson. Her face was swollen and black with bruises.

"I couldn't wait another day, Miss Craigie."

"You poor wee thing! Here, give me the bairn!" Flora took the bundle into her arms, and the infant looked at her with the same trusting gaze as her mother.

"I hope you don't mind." Mrs. Dawson's voice broke. "Toddsville was too far to walk, and I had nowhere else to go."

Flora's heart contracted with compassion for the poor woman. Hector had punched her only once, and that was a blow she would never forget, one that still gave her nightmares. How would it feel to be struck repeatedly by someone so much stronger than yourself?

Holding the baby, she helped her mother limp across the room to the cot. Mrs. Dawson clung to her as though she had no strength left in her legs and collapsed with a hiss of indrawn breath.

"How did you get away?" Flora asked.

"He took the horse this morning and went hunting. The minute he was out of sight, I wrapped up Caroline and started to walk."

"How did you find me?"

"I reckon everyone around here knows about Ladyville, Miss Craigie, but it took me a long time because I lost the trail twice. Good thing there's a full moon."

"And your husband? Where has he gone?"

"He calls it hunting slow elk, but that's his idea of a joke. He's gone to rustle some poor rancher's cow. He'll come looking for me when gets home."

Flora's mind worked frantically. Beau was away for the night. She could hitch up the team and drive to Lacombe herself, but she was reluctant to travel over that muskeg trail in the dark. It would be a disaster if they got stuck and Dawson found them. She must wait until first light and drive the hapless woman to Toddsville, where the doctor could protect her.

The fire was hot, so she warmed her leftovers—baked beans and mashed potatoes. Mrs. Dawson's lips were so cracked and split that she could barely chew. Flora helped mother and bairn into bed before lying down on the floor wrapped in her buffalo robe.

She tried to sleep but it was impossible. In the still of the prairie night, sound travelled a great distance. The howling of coyotes, the whisper of the wind in the trees, the stamping of Felicity's hooves in the barn—all were magnified in the stillness. She heard Mrs. Dawson moaning in pain. Once the baby whimpered, but her mother nursed her and she went straight back to sleep.

Flora had fallen into a fitful doze when she heard hoofbeats. She rose and hurried to the window. In the bright moonlight she recognised the rider. It was Murdo Dawson.

His wife peeked around Flora and gave a horrified exclamation before clapping her hands over her injured mouth. Flora grabbed a chair and propped it under the latch, although it wasn't much of a barrier if anyone really wanted to come inside. The door had never been locked. She wished Taffy would appear, but he was probably off chasing rabbits.

Dawson dismounted and tied the reins to a nearby branch. He marched up to the shack and pounded on the door with both fists.

"You got my wife in there?"

Flora's only hope was to persuade him that he was in the wrong place. "Nay, your wife isna here!" she called out, trying to sound convincing.

"You're lying! Send her out or you'll be sorry!"

Perhaps she could frighten him away. Flora grabbed the loaded Winchester standing against the wall and yanked open the window a few inches. She stuck the barrel through the gap and fired a single shot toward the moon.

In the confines of the shack, the explosion was deafening. His horse snorted and reared, spooked by the noise, and Felicity gave a frightened whinny from the barn. "I told you, she's not here!" Flora shouted. "Go away and leave me alone!"

She peeked out from behind her flowered curtain. Would he believe her? He stood motionless, as if he were thinking about what to do next. The moon overhead was a glowing white sphere, and his figure cast a long and menacing shadow. There was a hush while she held her breath and motioned Mrs. Dawson to be quiet.

The silence was shattered by the baby's piercing cry. Her mother snatched her off the bed and muffled her tiny mouth against her breast.

"I hear that squalling brat!" Dawson screamed with rage, stamping the ground like his frightened horse. "Either you open that door, or I'll blast it open!"

Fuelled by a vivid memory of Hector, Flora's own fury rose to meet his, the blood pounding in her temples. The brute must be off his head if he believed she would deliver a helpless woman and child to him. "Gang awa, you scabby bag of shite, and leave us be!"

He headed for his horse. For a moment she thought he might leave. Instead, he reached for the leather scabbard hanging from his saddle, unsnapped the cover, and pulled out a shotgun.

There was nowhere to hide. "Get down!" she hissed, pointing to the cot. Mrs. Dawson fell to the floor and wriggled underneath, shielding the babe with her body.

Flora squatted below the window, her back against the wall. She heard Dawson break open the shotgun, load the cartridges, and slam it closed again. She covered her ears, bracing herself for the blast that would tear the door into splinters.

Instead, there was another sound, as loud as thunder in the hushed night. It was a horse, approaching at a full gallop. Flora raised her eyes above the sill.

Into the moonlit clearing rode Jessie McDonald on Tipiskow, her hair loose and streaming. She let out a terrific yell and dragged the mustang to a halt so that his back hooves skidded in the dirt. She raised her arm over her head like an avenging angel. A bullwhip sailed through the air with a mighty crack and wrapped itself around Dawson's right arm. He dropped the shotgun and grabbed the whip with his left hand in a vain attempt to extricate himself.

Jessie backed her horse away. The man fell and was dragged several yards before he managed to loosen the whip. He clambered to his feet while she drew her arm back again. This time, he took the full brunt of the lash across his left cheek. He clutched his face with both hands, screaming in pain. Blood spurted between his fingers. He ran for his horse and had one foot in the stirrup before the whip struck again, wrapping itself around his standing leg. He dropped to the ground, scrabbling with his feet and hands like a crab, blinded by his own blood.

His assailant uttered her terrible yell again and shouted something in Cree. In response, the man's horse reared and ripped itself away from the tree. It left at a full gallop, the broken branch hanging from the reins. Dawson set off after it, staggering and limping.

Flora threw open the door. "Jessie, thank God in heaven you came!"

"I heard your shot," she said.

"You saved our lives!"

"What did that man want?"

"He wanted his wife. She ran away from him and came here."

"Bastard!" She spat on the ground. "Next time, shoot to kill." She wheeled her mustang and thundered off into the night.

CHAPTER TWENTY-FOUR

Flora lowered herself into the round tin tub, sighing with pleasure. She rarely had more than a daily wash, since it took several hours to melt the snow and heat enough water for a bath. After soaking for a few blessed moments, she shaved several tendrils from a bar of yellow soap, worked it into her scalp until it formed a lather, and rinsed her hair with three jugs of warm water. By the time she cleaned her fingernails with the paring knife, the water in the tub had cooled. She rubbed herself dry, and then washed the floor with the bath water before tossing it outside in a sparkling arc that froze when it hit the ground.

It was Christmas Day, and everyone in Ladyville was invited to the yellow house for dinner. Fortunately, the skies were clear. The winter sunshine made a pale square on the floor through her front window. It was cold, but not unbearable: the red mercury line in the thermometer outside her door showed minus eighteen degrees Fahrenheit.

Flora brushed her hair, which shimmered like dark fire in the dim sunlight, and wound it into a loose chignon before dressing in her one good outfit, her silk blouse and tweed suit. Having purchased this outfit for her marriage ceremony, she would have dearly loved to consign it to the flames. However, she couldn't afford to be sentimental.

She pinned her only piece of jewellery at her throat, a silver Celtic brooch. She pulled on her thick socks and leather boots, and topped everything with her heavy coat and woollen muffler. Tying her high-heeled shoes together with their own laces and slinging them over her shoulder, she wrapped her dessert offering in a towel and set out.

When she knocked at the door, festively adorned with a wreath of spruce boughs, she heard Wren call, "Come in! Come in! Merry Christmas!"

Flora stepped inside and shut the door. The Penroses were already there, and she stopped short at the sight. "Doesn't everyone look bonnie!"

Nellie and Jewel wore matching indigo dresses, their Peter Pan collars edged with crocheted lace. Mrs. Penrose was transformed in her indigo gown with a square neck that showed off her fine bosom. A gold locket hung around her throat, and for once her fair hair was smooth and shining. All three dresses had been cut from the bolt of wool that Flora had purchased at the general store. Jack was smart in a checked shirt and a black tie.

Miss Edgar was attired in her usual severe skirt and white blouse, although she had added a pair of pearl drop earrings, and Wren was somewhat over-dressed in a gown of bronze taffeta with puffed sleeves. Seated on a kitchen chair was Beau, wearing a red satin shirt. His hair was parted in the centre and slicked down with pomade that Flora could smell even from this distance. Although he had turned seventeen years old in August, he appeared even younger without his hat.

"I brought my special dessert, as I promised," Flora said. She set the towel-wrapped enamel basin on a low table before hanging up her coat and changing into her shoes. "I'll pop this into the kitchen." Holding the dish in both hands, she stepped through the arched doorway to find a tall man standing with his back to her.

"Dr. Farraday! I didn't expect to find you here!" Flora was embarrassed by the delight in her own voice.

"The ladies sent Beau to invite me for dinner. A bachelor never refuses a good meal, you know." He wore his usual charcoal suit and white shirt with his blue tie. Flora wondered if he owned any other clothes.

She set her dish on the counter and tried to regain her dignity. "What a delicious smell," she said. A rich odour filled the air, accompanied by a sizzling sound.

"Yes, isn't it? Miss Greenwood couldn't bear to kill any of her darling hens, so she ordered a turkey."

Flora laughed as if he had said something clever.

The doctor stepped aside, allowing her to enter the living room first, and Flora noticed the spruce in the far corner. "Ach, that's a braw tree!"

Wren nodded with enthusiasm. "Beau found it, Miss Craigie. Isn't it splendid?" It was indeed a luxurious tree with thick, evenly spaced branches. These were decorated with dried cranberries, paper snowflakes, gingerbread men, and scraps of colourful yarn. On the floor underneath were several packages wrapped in brown paper and tied with red ribbon.

A knock sounded. "Another guest!" Wren said. She ran to open the door, and a stranger entered. "Howdy, folks! Merry Christmas!"

If it hadn't been for his voice, no one would have recognised Sourdough. He had shaved off his wild, curling beard to reveal a firm, square jaw with a cleft so deep it could have hidden a raisin. Everyone stared incredulously except Jewel, who buried her face in her mother's lap.

Sourdough stepped forward, his size making the room shrink, and set a violin case on the floor before shrugging off his rawhide coat. His clothes were worn and his red plaid shirt was missing the top button, but at least they were clean, thanks to Mrs. Penrose. A pair of red suspenders held up his woollen trousers.

Another knock sounded, and all heads turned. Who could it be? Flora didn't think the reclusive Chicken Ladies had any other friends. Wren opened the door, and everyone goggled to see Jessie McDonald.

"Miss McDonald! I'm so glad you came!" Wren took her parka and hung it on a hook. Instead of her usual leggings, she wore a black skirt and a white blouse, a woven red sash around her waist. She had arrived on snowshoes— Flora had once seen her skimming across the field on these odd devices that looked like tennis racquets—and she now stacked them against the wall before exchanging her boots for a pair of beaded moccasins. Her braid was tied with a buckskin thong.

"Merry Christmas, everybody." Miss McDonald sat down and stared around with a challenging air, as if daring anyone to comment on her appearance. The others immediately began to talk about the weather.

Wren and Miss Edgar retired to the kitchen to serve dinner. The table, extended with planks and covered with sheets, was set for ten. The Penroses had brought three chairs with them, and Beau was sent to fetch both chairs from Flora's shack. The children sat on wooden crates, while Jewel perched on her mother's lap.

When they were seated, the diners bent their heads and Wren said grace: "Thank you, Lord, for the food before us, for all the beauty and bounty of the earth; for the comfort and joy of life, for our homes, for our friends, for our life in this new country, and for the goodwill of all people. Amen."

Everyone repeated "Amen" with great feeling.

Then the feast began. For eleven people who ate sparingly from necessity, this was the best gift any of them could have received. Wren had outdone herself, preparing roast turkey with bread stuffing, mashed potatoes with gravy, high-bush cranberry jelly, and stovetop turnips sprinkled with brown sugar. There were side dishes of pickled beets and devilled eggs from the Buffs, and fresh white rolls. When everyone had eaten a second helping—in Sourdough's case, a third helping—Wren announced, "We aren't finished yet. Miss Craigie has made us a delightful treat. What do you call it?"

"Cranachan," Flora answered, rising from her chair. "Let me help you serve."

Flora's special Scottish dessert was a trifle, traditionally made with whipped cream, ripe raspberries, and oatmeal soaked in whisky. She had used wild strawberries, picked in the summer and preserved with a little sugar. As she walked to the counter, she winked at Beau. It was he who had brought Flora the whisky, and she hadn't asked from where.

Everyone pronounced it delicious and asked for seconds. The children were allowed only a taste because of the alcohol, but Wren produced three striped candy canes for their dessert instead.

The satisfied guests trooped back to the living room and sank into their chairs. Miss Edgar opened the china cabinet and brought out two bottles of her homemade dandelion wine. The men accepted a glass with alacrity. Mrs. Penrose and Miss McDonald also nodded in agreement.

Flora had never tasted wine, but she knew from Mrs. Galt and her friends that it was accepted among upper-class women. Feeling quite daring, she agreed to try it. "Just a wee dram, mind," she said.

After the first generous glass, which tasted pleasantly warm and earthy, the party became noticeably relaxed. Sourdough sprawled in Miss Edgar's armchair, the only one big enough to hold his oversized body. Flora noticed his eyes resting on Mrs. Penrose.

"Would you care for another drink, Mr. Buckhorn?" Miss Edgar asked.

"Don't mind if I do!" He held out his glass for a refill.

"Oh, surely we've known each other long enough that we can drop the formality and call each other by our first names!" Wren said. "Does everyone agree?" There was a chorus of yesses.

Samuel Farraday, who had loosened his tie, was in high spirits although he had barely touched his wine. He entertained the children by showing them how he could draw his handkerchief out of his pocket with a crack like a whiplash. "It's a modest achievement, but when I was twelve years old I spent one entire summer mastering it," he said.

Wren clapped her hands. "Let's play charades!" Her face was glowing, and Flora suspected that she missed the society of others. Everyone enjoyed themselves hugely, especially when Sourdough tried to act out "Dance of the Sugar Plum Fairies." Even Jessie McDonald laughed aloud, a sound nobody had heard before.

"Time to open the presents!" Wren called out. Although she had told the guests not to bring anything but themselves, she had a gift for everyone. For Samuel and Flora, books. Hers was *The House of Mirth* by Edith Wharton, and his was *The Seats of the Mighty* by Gilbert Parker. For Peggy Penrose, a cake of perfumed soap. For Sourdough, a pouch of pipe tobacco. Beau received a brilliant yellow scarf that he immediately knotted around his neck. For Jack, a harmonica. For Nellie, a book titled *The Little Princess* by Frances Hodgson Burnett, and for Jewel, a rubber ball. As each gift was opened, everyone exclaimed with appreciation.

Perhaps the most thoughtful gift was for Jessie: a framed watercolour of Tipiskow, signed by the artist herself, Henrietta Greenwood. Jessie stared at it for the longest time before giving Wren one of her rare smiles.

Jessie then went to her leather pouch, where she drew out three items for the children. Jack's face lit up when she gave him a wicked-looking hunting knife in a beaded leather sheath. And for the girls, two exquisite dolls made from tanned hide, soft and white and pliable. Each wore a red calico dress trimmed with rabbit fur. They had tiny black braids made of horsehair, and black beads for eyes. Their hands were fashioned from animal teeth, chipped on the edges to resemble fingers.

Flora had thought Nellie was too old for dolls, but she clutched it to her chest with a cry of rapture, while Jewel covered her doll's face with kisses.

"Jessie, wherever did you find those?" Wren asked.

"I made them," she said. Without being prompted, Nellie went over to Jessie and thanked her shyly before returning to sit on the floor and examine her doll's clothing.

Now there was a general call for music. Sourdough pulled out his violin and began with a melody that everyone recognised: "My Darling Clementine." Flora sang in harmony with the others, enjoying their mingled voices. She hadn't realised how much she missed her church choir. Sourdough had a deep bass and Beau had a musical tenor. Miss Edgar—it would be impossible to call her anything else, Flora decided—sang slightly off tune, but it was lost in the overall effect. The doctor was seated next to her, and she was very conscious of his mellow baritone.

"You have a lovely voice," he said. "Won't you give us a solo?"

She protested, but the others joined in, "Yes, Flora! Do sing for us!"

Flora considered. "Do you know 'Loch Lomond'?" When Sourdough began to play, she sang her favourite song in all the world. "By yon bonnie banks and by yon bonnie braes, where the sun shines bright on Loch Lomond." The applause was enthusiastic, and Beau put two fingers in his mouth and gave a piercing whistle.

Sourdough drew the bow across his strings and broke into a rollicking jig. Jessie jumped up and began to dance, hands held at her sides, feet twinkling like beaded stars as they darted forward and backward, side to side. Everyone clapped in time to the music.

"Again, again!" Sourdough broke into another merry tune, and this time Jessie reached out to Nellie. The little girl took her hands and tried to follow her steps. While they were jigging, Jewel jumped and twirled around the room, staggering and falling and making everyone laugh.

After Jessie collapsed into her chair, Sourdough played a few slower melodies. Together the group sang "My Wild Irish Rose" and "Can I Take You Home Again, Kathleen?" Even Jack and Nellie knew most of the words.

When Sourdough began playing a Strauss waltz, the doctor rose to his feet and extended his hand to Wren. Together the two of them revolved gracefully around the room. Flora was glad she had a reason to stare at him. He then invited Miss Edgar, who shook her head, and Jessie, who also declined.

He turned to Flora. "Will you do me the honour, Flora?" He pronounced her first name for the first time as if it were a rare and precious flower. She had never learned to dance, since the kirk forbade it. However, that was another time and another place.

She stood, and the doctor's hand went around her waist while his other hand clasped hers. She wondered if he could feel her heart throbbing through her palm. The doctor proved to be a natural leader and she followed him easily. It seemed as if they had waltzed a hundred times before. When the music stopped, the doctor bowed before releasing her hand.

By midnight, everyone had stayed up three hours past their usual bedtime. Jewel was asleep on a blanket in the corner, clutching her new doll to her chest, and Nellie's eyelids were drooping.

"One last tune," said Sourdough. "Let's bring in the new year early with a ballad from Flora's countryman, Robbie Burns himself." As the gold clock chimed twelve times, he began the sweet, melancholy strains of "Auld Lang Syne."

Everyone stood in a circle with crossed arms, holding hands with the person on either side, and sang together. Flora stood between Beau and Samuel, unconsciously leaning into the solid muscle of the doctor's shoulder as they sang the familiar words: "We'll take a cup of kindness yet, for auld lang syne."

They made their goodbyes and went out into the freezing night. Sourdough insisted on seeing the Penrose family home, and the doctor, who had been offered a bed in Beau's cabin for the night, offered to walk with Flora. The dark sky was pinned with millions of glittering stars, and Flora didn't even feel the cold.

CHAPTER TWENTY-FIVE

After the new year, Ladyville drew itself into a ball and settled down for the long, dark season. Flora wasn't as apprehensive this year, having been blooded in battle during that first ghastly winter. Besides, she was no longer a stranger in a strange land. Everything she touched had the comfort of familiarity. She recognised each turnip as she sliced it up. When she tossed a log on the fire, she recalled the dead tree dragged from the bush. When she baked her weekly bread, she fed both body and soul with the grain she had planted with her own two hands.

Seated at the table, Flora stretched out her fingers and examined them. They were far from beautiful, despite the frequent applications of bear grease that Jessie shared with the other women. Flora smeared it on liberally each night before bed, but that didn't disguise the angry burn on her knuckle from the stove, a splinter that was working its way out of her thumb, or the nasty rope graze across one palm she had suffered when Felicity shied at her own shadow. Yet she admired her hands all the same, because they bore the wounds of war.

She went back to sorting her seeds.

"The miller said you'd better watch out for wild oats," Beau had informed her. After selling her grain in Lacombe, he had taken one bushel of wheat to the mill and brought back two twenty-pound sacks of flour for her personal use. One was white, milled from the inner part of the kernel; the other was coarse and speckled, ground from the whole grain. The rest of her seed wheat was stored in the Penrose barn until spring.

Flora had agonised all summer over the noxious wild oats sprouting in her field, easy to spot because their heads were taller and shaggier than those of the wheat. She yanked out as many as she could reach, but dared not walk into the crop for fear of crushing the plants. She hated the idea of the oats contaminating her field next spring, watching them spread like a biblical plague, sucking the health and strength out of her wheat.

She decided to do something about it. Each morning when the feeble winter sun struck her front window, she filled her enamel basin with seed wheat from a sack in the corner, and dumped it onto a clean sheet covering the kitchen table. Using a table knife, she separated the hated wild oats from the wheat kernels. The oat seeds were larger, sharp and spiky, with a point at one end. She fancied that the wheat kernels had smiling little faces, while the wild oats were tiny beasts, baring their teeth. She found it immensely satisfying to find and destroy them. Every time she filled an enamel mug with the creatures, she tossed it into the flames and watched them burn.

With no sound but the crackle of the fire and the muffled silence of the white world outside, Flora was alone with her thoughts. To her surprise, she found them largely gratifying.

Last year, she had feared that Hector would find her. That threat had receded like a distant thundercloud drifting away in another direction. If he and his bloodhound Holmes hadn't tracked her down after nineteen months, chances are they never would.

Last year, she had worried that she was too weak physically to do the necessary work. Since then she had gained so much strength and endurance that she was now as hardy as most men. Well, maybe not Sourdough, but certainly Beau.

Last year, she had been frantic with anxiety about her first crop, but she had planted it, scythed it, and threshed it, and the results were spread out before her eyes. She had sold her grain in Lacombe—mercifully, Alix Westhead's influence didn't reach that far—and she had made enough cash to last for one more year.

In truth, Flora had underrated herself. That wasn't so astonishing, since she had proven to be such a dismal judge of character. She had been dead wrong about Hector—although she could hardly have known his true nature, since he was such a skilled manipulator. She felt sorrowful as she remembered all the innocent Scots he had convinced to buy phantom farms.

But she was prepared to admit her own culpability. Her desire for a home had blinded her to the warning signs. She upbraided herself when she remembered how easily she had been lured by the promise of a stone house in Vancouver. She had paid the price for her greed by ending up in a mere shack, no better than the ones she had scorned from the train.

Aside from Hector, she had been gravely mistaken about other people, as well. Take Sourdough Buckhorn. The farmer she had once believed was their enemy had revealed a heart of purest gold, and Flora had not recognised it. Despite her unworldliness, Peggy Penrose divined his decency long before it became apparent to Flora.

Her lack of appreciation for children had ceased to exist. Jack was a wonderful support to his mother, and Nellie such a clever little thing. Jewel was nothing but an angel from heaven. Just last week, when she entered the Penrose cabin, the little girl had held out her arms and called, "Fora!" Fora!" Flora had picked Jewel up and kissed her soft cheeks and cooed like the most besotted mother, feeling a sharp pang of regret. If things had been different, she might have had babies of her own. To be sure, Hector would have made a deplorable father, a man who kicked dogs and struck women in the face.

The Chicken Ladies had revealed themselves to be everything desirable in neighbours, sharing their food and their books and most importantly, their sympathy. Jessie McDonald, whom Flora had once considered uncivilised, had ridden for the doctor and saved her from that daft Mr. Dawson. Jessie was both accomplished and fearless, a woman to be reckoned with.

Peggy Penrose's strength of character was the greatest eye-opener. Flora remembered the funny little woman she had met in Red Deer, the one with the working-class accent. The one who slurped her tea and believed in pixies. Last week a fox had gotten into the barn, no doubt seeking to devour Mr. Grey and her kittens, who kept warm by sleeping on Blossom's back. When Peggy heard the cow bawling, she ran outside in her nightgown and struck the fox over the head with the back end of the axe blade—and the next day, she skinned it herself and sold the hide to Jessie. No man could have done more.

Last year, Flora had been reluctant to associate with these women she had wrongfully assumed were weak. She burned with shame at her own ignorance. The residents of Ladyville were the strongest people she had ever met—male or female.

TODDSVILLE FREE PRESS
March 1, 1907

RAILWAY COMING TO TODDSVILLE!

What rejoicing was heard in our fair community this week when it was announced that the long-awaited Canadian Pacific Railway's spur line will be built from Lacombe to Toddsville!

The happy news arrived in the form of a telegraph issued at

CPR's head office in Montreal by Chairman William Van Horne, stating, "This aligns with our intention to construct branch lines leading from the main Calgary–Edmonton route both east and west, radiating like rays from the sun, continuing our grand plan to link all Canadians by rail."

Thankfully, Toddsville beat out stiff competition from communities to the north and south. There isn't a man among us who has not experienced the inconvenience of being cut off when the Buffalo Lake Trail is closed due to inclement weather or flooding.

Bill Spurrel, owner of the Imperial Hotel, is planning an immediate expansion, since the station will draw more travellers to the region. General store proprietor Robert Sanderson said he will not have to relocate his business, as previously feared. Our own doctor, Samuel Farraday, pointed out the greater benefit to our citizens. "The railway means the difference between life and death for many of our number, particularly women who are experiencing difficulties with pregnancy or childbirth."

Details have yet to be announced, but it is hoped the first spike might go down this fall.

By late March, the snow was still piled high around Flora's shack, but the indigo twilight lingered each evening as if the sun were reluctant to depart. She had disposed of her wild oats and begun to study her seed catalogues. She was eager to plant a new variety of potatoes with the delightful name of Wee McGregors. Wren told her that it was time to plant potatoes when the air was warm enough to stand naked beside the patch, and she was counting the days until that happy hour.

One afternoon Beau knocked and asked Flora to visit the ladies on a matter of utmost importance. She washed her hands and tidied her hair, although she didn't change her clothes—by now, the ladies were accustomed to seeing her in breeks—and hurried to their house. As she walked down the snowy drive-way lined with maples, she was struck once again with what a lovely home the Chicken Ladies had created. The buttercup-yellow house exuded comfort and warmth. Even the smoke drifting lazily from the brick chimney seemed to spell the word "home" in the sky. The lace curtains waved hello as she climbed the verandah steps, and the stained glass window winked at her.

Wren answered the door. Uncharacteristically, she wasn't smiling. Miss Edgar rose from her chair, a copy of the *Toronto Star* in one hand. "Flora, please take a seat."

She shed her outdoor things and sat down. "What is it, Miss Edgar?"

"We want to share with you something we found in today's newspaper—actually, it's two weeks old, but Beau just brought it from town." With fore-boding, Flora braced herself. Surely Mrs. Westhead would not be writing to the *Toronto Star*.

Miss Edgar studied Flora over the top of her reading glasses. "Perhaps I'd better let you read it yourself." She passed her the newspaper, folded open to the correct page.

Flora read it. Time seemed to stop, although she could hear the clock still ticking on the shelf. She didn't dare raise her eyes from the page. She read it again, and then a third time, wishing she were somehow mistaken and the words might change.

MISSING PERSON

Mrs. Flora May Mackle was last seen on May 1, 1905, before leaving the Pacific Express passenger train somewhere between

Calgary and Revelstoke. She is twenty-five years old with auburn hair and a fair complexion, five feet ten inches tall with a good figure. She has a pronounced Scottish accent. Anyone with information leading to her whereabouts is requested to write to Hector Mackle, in care of the CPR Head Office, Montreal, PQ. Reward of $100.

Miss Edgar spoke first. "We thought it was quite a coincidence, this missing person having such a similar name and physical description."

Flora tried to fabricate some story that would satisfy the ladies, but she quickly concluded that this would be not only futile, but grossly unfair. She would have to trust them.

"It's so similar because I am she." She nearly choked on the words. "I am Flora Mackle."

There was a hush before Miss Edgar replied. "We don't need to know the particulars, Flora. We just wanted to inform you that someone is most keen to learn your whereabouts."

Flora forced herself to raise her head and meet Miss Edgar's steady gaze. "You don't hate me?"

Both ladies exclaimed at once. "Flora! Don't be silly! I think we understand your character by now!" Wren said.

"Thank you." Tears of relief came into Flora's eyes, and the burden she had felt for so long lifted slightly. "You've been verra kind to me, and I've always felt badly about deceiving you, and Peggy, too. I will tell you the truth."

"You must have had your reasons." Miss Edgar's tone was not unkind.

Flora sat up straight in her chair, squeezing her hands together in her lap. "I was married to Hector Mackle for a short time," she began. "That is, I'm still married to him, but I knew him for only four weeks."

When she had finished her sad little tale, both ladies looked shocked.

"Men are such beasts!" Wren burst out. "If it weren't for the likes of Mr. Buckhorn and the good doctor, I would renounce them utterly!"

Miss Edgar's voice was reassuring. "It is significant, Flora, that your husband—if indeed we can call him that, rather, let's just say the man in question—is asking that people write to him in Montreal. I suspect he doesn't have any idea where you are, or even whether you are still in the country."

She sat for a moment, drumming her fingers on the arm of her chair. "One hundred dollars is a tempting sum. Fortunately for you, few people in western Canada read the *Toronto Star*, although it is the largest newspaper in the country. In fact, I'm the only subscriber in this region. The postmaster himself told me so. May I ask, Flora, who else knows your past?"

"One other person, and I have every confidence in her discretion."

"Since yours was a marriage in name only, there's always the possibility of a legal annulment. But the fact that you lied to the authorities about your marital status would put your homestead in jeopardy. It's a difficult situation."

Miss Edgar was clearly thinking aloud, and Wren gazed at her as if she could produce a magical solution. Finally, the older woman spoke again.

"I believe that you're safe for the time being. Wren and I will do what we can to protect you. We're fully aware of the consequences, should his search be successful. That would be a grave injustice."

Flora felt too emotional to answer. She had shared her secret, and the Chicken Ladies had responded with understanding and forgiveness. Nevertheless, the newspaper advertisement was a stunning blow. She remained slumped in her chair, her limbs leaden with despair. She had been living in a fool's paradise, hoping that Hector had abandoned the chase. More than that, she had cherished a notion—one that she was reluctant to admit even to herself—that he might have departed for a better world, or at least another world.

Instead, he was very much alive. And she knew now that he would never give up searching for her until one of them was dead.

CHAPTER TWENTY-SIX

Again, the miracle called spring arrived. A mighty paintbrush swept over the stark black-and-white landscape and covered it with a green water-colour wash. As the world returned to life, so did Flora's senses. Her eyes were dazzled by every startling new tint, the vital scent of wet earth filled her nostrils, and even her fried potatoes and onions tasted more succulent when eaten out-doors.

She heard the children shouting and laughing at the Penrose place, and understood exactly how they felt. She sprinted to the barn on legs stiff with dis-use, simply for the thrill of running. Taffy barked wildly at the throngs of geese flying north. Blossom, bred last fall by a neighbour's bull, bore twin spindly-legged calves named Daisy and Dandelion. The Buffs brought forth a flock of downy chicks.

One morning Flora checked her calendar to find it was May 9, 1907. Two years ago today, she had filed her claim. She checked again, because it was so easy to become confused when governed only by the rising and setting of the sun.

Once she had even lost a day. She visited the Penroses to fetch her butter and milk, thinking it was Saturday—and found the family dressed in clean clothes, sitting around the table while their mother read aloud from the Song of Solomon, "'For, lo, the winter is past; the rain is over and gone; the flowers appear on the earth; the time of the singing of birds is come, and the voice of the turtle-dove is heard in our land.'"

Flora herself had stopped observing the Sabbath—abandoning her husband was such a grave sin that she felt God and the kirk could never forgive her. She had often heard the Bible verse: "Whither thou goest, I will go; whither thou leadest, I will follow," recited during church weddings, had seen it engraved on tombstones. Yet she had decided not to follow Hector, no matter where he was going.

She had pondered her decision numerous times. Would it have been more honourable to allow Hector to kill her, in order that her soul reach Paradise unblemished? Flora thought not. Nonetheless, she still felt the odd stab of guilt.

Today was a special day, though. One might call it New Year's Day, the beginning of the final twelve months of her challenge. Flora felt the need to celebrate, so she added two heaping tablespoons of brown sugar to her porridge. After sweeping and airing the shack, she turned Felicity loose to paw through the remaining skiffs of snow in search of fresh grass. She pulled on her work gloves and started clearing the dead vegetation away from the garden. She was deciding whether to start a batch of vegetable chowder for supper when she saw someone riding down the hill. She recognised the doctor while he was still a distant figure—so tall in the saddle, his shoulders so broad. She dashed inside and had just time enough to wash her hands and tidy her hair when his knock sounded.

"Samuel! How grand to see you." This was no exaggeration. People did not pay social calls in winter, and Flora had seen him only twice since Christmas.

The first time he had come to tell her that he had received a thank-you letter from Daphne Dawson, who was safely in the arms of her family in Winnipeg and wanted to pass along her gratitude to Flora. Her husband had surrendered his claim and moved away to the West Coast after receiving an unwelcome visit from Daphne's brothers.

The second time the doctor dropped in to check on everyone's health. At least, that was what he claimed.

On both occasions Flora had been courteous but distant, trying to crush her feelings under her own booted heel. It wasn't only a sense of animal magnetism that she felt toward him. She was attracted to everything about the man: his decency, his sense of humour, his dedication to his work. The views they held in common about the West, about the world.

Flora knew she was staring but couldn't help herself. The doctor stared right back. She tore her eyes away from his and stepped aside. "Won't you come in?"

"I was hoping that you would come out," he said.

Flora had forgotten what a nice voice he had. She could listen to his accent all day. But she wasn't sure what he was asking. "Are you visiting a patient?"

"Believe it or not, I have a free day. No babies are due, the farmers are busy with their spring work, and I'm counting on the fates to allow me a breathing spell. Would you care to go for a ride?"

Flora hesitated. For the first time, she truly understood the meaning of the term "playing with fire." She wanted to put her hand into the flames more than she had ever wanted anything in her life, even though she was aware that it could only result in grave injury.

"I would love to, Dr. Farraday," she said.

His face broke into a smile. "Excuse me, Flora. I'm not laughing at you, I promise. I can't help smiling every time you say my name."

He waited outside while Flora changed into her riding skirt and donned her blue-striped shirtwaist, happy she had done her washing two days earlier. She pulled on her tweed coat since the air was still cool, pinned her felt hat over her unruly hair, and hurried outside to saddle Felicity. The horse tossed her head and stamped with anticipation, sensing a good gallop ahead. She was shaggy after the long winter, her hair grown thick to keep out the cold. She and Pal whickered at each other in greeting.

"Where are we going?" Flora asked as they trotted away from the shack.

"I thought we would ride toward the Red Deer River. There are marvellous views from the hills above. Shall we let the horses out a little?"

"Oh yes!" said Flora, pressing her knees into Felicity's flanks. The two horses simultaneously broke into a gallop as if they had sprouted wings, like the mythical Pegasus. Flora felt the blood rushing through her veins, the power of the horse between her legs, and it was all she could do to resist uttering a cowboy yell.

After a couple of miles, the horses slowed to a trot, and then to a walk. Flora and the doctor exchanged satisfied grins. His eyes were bright and his cheeks scarlet, and Flora knew she looked the same. He removed his hat and tied it to his saddle horn. The breeze lifted his thick hair.

There was so much beauty around them that Flora wanted to gather it in her arms. The prairie grass swelled and dipped under the cloudless sky. The first clumps of shy crocus blossoms peeped out of their frosty beds, and the liquid notes of the yellow-breasted meadowlark praised the heavens.

They stopped to fill their canteens and let the horses drink at a spring-fed slough. The doctor pointed out the buffalo run, radiating outward like spokes in a wheel, worn deep in the sod where the animals had walked in single file. Nearby was a granite boulder the size of Flora's shack, deposited by some melting glacier, where they had stopped to rub their humps, polishing the stone until it shone.

"Not long ago, four million buffalo roamed these plains," he said. Flora imagined she could glimpse their ghostly forms on the path, silent spectres of a vanished race.

They spent a magical hour before emerging on a ridge that overlooked the Red Deer River, wending its silvery way through the wilderness. Below them lay a vista of unparalleled splendour. The grassy parkland stretched away for miles, varied with bluffs of poplar and willow, studded by small glittering ponds. The creeks tumbled down to the river like green serpents, lined with the deeper colours of the spruce and pine fringing their banks. The river itself could be followed with the naked eye until it was lost at the foot of the great Rocky Mountains, hazy and lilac on the western horizon.

Flora and Samuel sat side by side on horseback, knees almost touching, while they marvelled at the view.

He turned to her with a smile. "Are you hungry?"

"Ach, where's my heid!" Flora exclaimed. "I didn't bring anything to eat!" Aware that it was woman's duty to feed the male species, she was mortified for forgetting to throw so much as a few scones into her saddlebag.

"I didn't expect you to. I have enough provisions for both of us."

Although Flora had vaulted off Felicity's back hundreds of times, she allowed the doctor to help her dismount, just for the pleasure of it. He took a red-and-black trading blanket from behind his saddle and unrolled it on the grass.

Flora sank down, feet tucked beneath her, and watched as he opened his saddlebag to reveal its appetising contents: a roast chicken, a loaf of new bread, a pat of butter, four hard-boiled eggs, salt and pepper in a piece of twisted paper, and a generous chunk of cheddar cheese.

"Please, help yourself," he said, lowering himself to the blanket.

Flora tried to nibble daintily, but she was too hungry. "Wherever did you get all this food?" she asked, imagining a grateful patient.

"I made it myself," he said. "I even baked the bread."

"You can cook?" Flora was incredulous. She had never met a man who was at home in the kitchen. Her own father could barely boil the kettle.

"My mother has three sons, and she taught us how to make a few simple meals. I've often been grateful for it. I quite enjoy cooking, although I don't usually have the time." There was so much she didn't know about this man, Flora reflected, so much she wanted to know. And never would.

When they finished, Samuel gathered dry twigs and lit a fire. From his other saddlebag, he brought out an enamel kettle, filled it with fresh water from his canteen, and added a packet of loose tea. Soon it was hissing merrily on the flames.

"I couldn't carry fresh cream, so I brought the tin cow instead." He produced a can of evaporated milk and poured it into two enamel mugs. *We both take cream in our tea*, Flora thought romantically, *something else we have in common*—and then chided herself for her own absurdity.

"And now for dessert!" He reached into his coat pocket and pulled out a package wrapped in tissue paper, which he opened to reveal two bars of Hershey's Milk Chocolate.

"I haven't tasted chocolate since I arrived!" Flora exclaimed.

"It's my secret vice," the doctor said. "Sandy Sanderson keeps me supplied."

Flora allowed the chocolate to melt on her tongue, closing her eyes in ecstasy. She opened them again to find him watching her. He quickly averted his gaze.

After putting away the remains of their picnic, they sat together on the blanket, sipping their second cup of strong creamy tea. The smoke from the fire drifted lazily across the river valley and mingled with the vanilla scent of the white blossoms bursting forth on a bank of saskatoon shrubs. A few deer poked their heads from a stand of spruce trees and bounded away, sailing over the earth as gracefully as butterflies. A mountain bluebird flitted past like a jewel in flight, singing "Puritee, puritee!"

The doctor set down his empty mug and smothered a yawn. "Would you mind if I took a quick nap?" he asked. "I had a late night." Minutes later, he was sound asleep.

Flora watched him greedily, able to stare as much as she wanted. He had shaven that morning, but a faint shadow covered his jaw. His eyebrows were well marked, his eyelashes long and thick. There were shadows under his eyes—Flora wondered how late he had stayed awake roasting the chicken and baking the bread. She clasped her hands around her knees, resisting the impulse to wind a curl of his dark hair around her finger.

Twenty minutes later, the doctor's eyes flew open and rested on Flora. There was the briefest hesitation before he sat up and put his arm around her.

So this is how it feels when women in novels say they were powerless to resist, Flora thought. She raised her face and he kissed her. A wave of heat travelled from her mouth as if poured into it like a warm waterfall, through her body and down to her toes. Flora was glad she was seated, because otherwise she would have fallen. The kiss lasted a long time, although not long enough. They sat quietly for a few moments, Flora leaning against his shoulder. Her heart was pounding so hard that the stripes on her bodice leaped up and down.

The doctor rose to his knees. "Flora, I earn six hundred dollars a year. That isn't a lot, but it's enough to support two people. Being a doctor's wife isn't much of a life because I'm away so often, sometimes for days at a time. If I didn't have every confidence in your ability to care for yourself, I wouldn't dream of asking you to marry me. But you're different. You have what it takes to survive out here."

Flora was reluctant to interrupt what sounded like a rehearsed speech. She turned her head and stared blindly toward the river valley below.

The doctor's voice changed. "Flora, I'm awfully in love with you. I want to spend the rest of my life trying to make you happy. Everything I own is yours, body and soul. I know you want to earn your homestead, and I love you for it. Even if we can't announce our engagement yet, won't you make me the happiest man in the world by saying yes?"

His words were so sincere that she didn't doubt them for an instant. Flora felt a rush of scorching shame. She should have prevented the relationship from progressing this far. She had led him on, as her mother would have said. Now, because of her own weakness, she was going to murder his hopes as well as her own.

She didn't answer immediately, wanting to savour the joy of being loved for a few fleeting seconds before pushing it away forever. A hush fell over the landscape, and even the birds seemed to stop their evening chatter. Flora kept her eyes on the river valley, not wanting to see his reaction. "Samuel, I'm honoured by your proposal, more than words can express. Any woman would be. But I must refuse."

The doctor let out his breath in a rush, as if he had been holding it. "Is it possible that your feelings might change in time?"

Her jaw was stiff, her mouth trying to clamp down on the words she didn't want to utter. Finally, she managed to speak. "I can only say that I am better fitted to travel this world alone."

This little speech sounded both pompous and ridiculous, and she knew that he deserved a better answer. Perhaps she should tell him that she didn't care for him and never would. But lying wasn't in her nature, and she refused to lie to him now.

Flora turned and saw from his expression that the cut went deep. She felt it slicing into her own heart. Nothing she had ever experienced hurt so much. After a short silence laden with misery on both sides, the doctor swallowed hard. "It's getting late. Shall we go?"

They made sure the fire was extinguished and mounted their horses. The ride home seemed to take forever. Neither of them had spoken a single word as they rode up to her shack.

Flora dismounted before he could touch her. "It's verra late, and you have a long ride ahead," she said. "Thank you for this wonderful day, Dr. Farraday. I'll never forget it."

The doctor took off his hat. "Flora, if you ever need anything—I'll always be here for you. Nothing that happened today changes that."

As Samuel rode away, the pale sky shone with tints of aquamarine, shell pink, and palest blue, fading to deep purple in the distance. For once, Flora was unaware of the beauty of her surroundings. She watched until his horse disappeared over the crest of the hill, heedless of the hot tears sliding down her cheeks.

CHAPTER TWENTY-SEVEN

The June sunshine stroked their backs like warm, caressing hands as Flora helped Peggy pin a row of shirts and overalls on the clothesline. A restless breeze from the creek turned over the poplar leaves, bright green on one side and dull green on the other. The wet clothing snapped and stiffened its arms and legs as if struggling to escape.

Flora recognised two of Sourdough's massive plaid shirts, neatly mended with all the buttons in place. "You've certainly smartened up old Sourdough," she said. "You would never recognise him now, with his hair trimmed and his clothes spotless."

Peggy smiled around the clothespin clamped in her teeth. "He was always a diamond in the rough, just needed a bit of polishing."

The breeze freshened and the wheat in the nearby field swayed like a drapery of green and gold shot silk. The two women turned as one to gloat over it. "It makes me nervous to talk about the harvest, in case we jinx ourselves," Flora said. "But Peggy, look at it! Did you ever see anything so bonnie?"

Even amid her misery, the sight of her bumper crop lightened Flora's spirits. The piercing agony she had felt after refusing the doctor had moderated to a grinding ache, and occasionally—only occasionally—she was able to forget her pain for a few brief moments. Over and over she relived her ecstasy at hearing his declaration of love, and her despair at being unable to share the depths of her own heart. How she rued the day she had married Hector Mackle. Yet if she hadn't, she wouldn't be here, building a new and better life for herself.

The homestead was her strength and her salvation, and she flung herself into her labour with renewed devotion. "We work all the hours that God sends," as Peggy said, and it was true that Flora was never idle for a waking moment. Only after she lay down her head at night did the hot tears soak her pillow. If she were fortunate, sheer exhaustion brought a few hours of blessed relief.

They had hung up the last woollen sock when they saw a rider cantering down the hill. He shouted halloo and waved his cap.

"Why, it's Mr. Cook!" Flora said.

He bowed to the women before dismounting and whacking the dust off his pants.

"Mr. Cook, this is an unexpected pleasure!" Peggy said.

Their champion hadn't changed in the two years since they had met, except that his elfin face was more weather-beaten, his skin browner and his teeth whiter by comparison. His hair still resembled the bristles on the brush that Flora used to groom Felicity.

"Morning, ladies! I hope you're both in the pink."

"What brings you out here, Mr. Cook?" Flora asked. "Are you scouting for land?"

"Not this time. I come on a serious matter. I wonder if we might have a word inside your house, Mrs. Penrose—and a fine house it is, too."

His eyes roved around at the neat yard, the washing on the line, the healthy pile of firewood. Blossom grazed in the shade beside the barn, wearing a wreath of dandelions that the girls had hung around her neck. Nearby, Petal kept watch over her baby sisters. Mr. Grey walked sedately across the yard while two kittens chased her upright tail. Taffy dozed in his doghouse, which bore a crudely lettered sign: THE HOUSE THAT JACK BUILT. Shouts of laughter were heard from the creek. Sourdough had fashioned a swing from an oval horse collar and the children were swooping out over their favourite swimming hole and plunging into the water below.

Mr. Cook had such a naturally cheerful face that it was almost shocking to see his woebegone expression. "You ladies have worked like Old Scratch and made a dandy job of it, too. That makes what I got to tell you all the more burdensome."

After they were seated and their guest had refused tea, he leaned forward, elbows on his knees. "Ladies, I chose this very spot so you would have female companions. Now I'm thinking I made a bad mistake."

"Why would you say that, Mr. Cook?" Peggy asked. "Our neighbours have been most helpful."

He shook his spiky head. "It isn't the who, Mrs. Penrose, it's the where."

"But this is a choice piece of land. We're ever so grateful to you for bringing us here."

Mr. Cook twirled his cap in his hands. "I better make a clean breast of it. Right from the get-go, I heard Sterling Payne was a burr under your saddle. I thought it was because he has an aversion to women, especially the independent sort. He never guessed that you'd last through the first winter. To be honest, I had a few doubts myself. But you didn't leave after the first, nor the second neither."

Peggy beamed, but Flora was too apprehensive to smile.

"Then he thought if he put the boots to you, threatened you with all kinds of rules and regulations, that you'd throw in the towel. I heard that he charged you for the wheat you planted on the road allowance, Miss Craigie. That was a damned shame, pardon my French."

"It was a serious setback, Mr. Cook, but I managed to overcome it."

"You surely did. You ladies have set a shining example to the newcomers around these parts, even spurring on the men. I figured there must be something more behind Payne's cockamamie grudge. I kept my ear to the old sod, heard some gossip, asked some questions. It all makes sense now."

Flora had once observed an ominous thunderstorm in which sheets of lightning flashed from one side of the horizon to the other as if the gods were battling for dominance. The air had been so charged that the hair on her scalp rose as she dashed toward her shack. Now she felt that same crackle in the air, that sense of impending doom. "Please, Mr. Cook, don't keep us in suspense."

"You know who Frank Oliver is, that big wheeze up in Edmonton. Well, the homestead inspector is his pet hunting dog, comes to heel whenever he whistles. The story I heard is that Payne, that scrawny lickspittle, was told to get you ladies off your land because Oliver wants to buy it himself. He'll use a fake name to cover his tracks."

"Frank Oliver!" Peggy exclaimed. "Why would the minister want our farms when there's so much empty land to the north and south?"

"Because your property is going to be worth a Red River cartload of money. The CPR always puts a station halfway between two towns, and this is the midpoint between Lacombe and Toddsville, practically right where I'm sitting." He stabbed his forefinger on the table for emphasis. "First comes the station, then a hotel, a store, a post office and what-have-you, and before you can say knife there'll be a new town here."

"The government can't just cancel our claims without cause!" Peggy's eyes were wide and fearful. "What about our contract?"

"It won't be the first time Oliver has pulled this swindle. The land speculators around here are as thick as mosquitoes on a slough. They buy empty land, carve it into lots, and sell it to merchants. Most of those plans are pie in the sky, they even come with fake maps. But a few of them are real. Oliver has a lot of irons in the fire, and he knows where the next big thing is going to happen."

"Doesn't the railway company have anything to say about it?"

"Van Horne hates land speculators like poison, but he's helpless as a baby in a blizzard to stop it. He'd be madder than a nest full of hornets if he knew what Oliver was up to, because the two men are sworn enemies, ever since Van Horne decided to run the transcontinental railway through Calgary instead of Edmonton. Oliver's newspaper almost went belly up when that happened."

Flora closed her eyes. Maybe if she couldn't see his mouth, she wouldn't hear his words.

"It's supposed to be top secret, but Payne's already asking businessmen in Toddsville, all hush-hush like, if they want to buy land at the new town site. Bill Spurrel, who owns the Imperial Hotel, earmarked the quarter right next to the station for another hotel and tavern. Payne promised to sell it to him as soon as it's vacant. That would be your home quarter, Miss Craigie."

Flora felt the shaft of lightning strike her body and flow through her veins. She looked down at her hands, half expecting to see that her skin had turned black.

Peggy was crying now. "What can we do?"

"Not much, I'm sorry to say. It ain't just you two ladies—they're going to take away the land belonging to the Half-Breed gal and the Yankee pards as well. The scuttlebutt is that Oliver wants to get rid of Ladyville altogether, and this is a perfect way to do it. He can kill two birds with one stone. In this case, five birds."

Mr. Cook rubbed his mouth with one hand, as if he wanted to erase what he had told them. "I'm not acquainted with your neighbours, so I'll let you give them the sad tidings."

He rose and jammed his cap onto his stubbled head. "I imagine they'll pay the others a little cash, since they own title, but I wouldn't hold out much hope for getting any return on your investment out here. I'm real sorry, ladies. No point throwing good money after bad. You might want to cut your losses and get out now."

CHAPTER TWENTY-EIGHT

July 1, 1907

Miss Flora May Craigie
General Delivery
Toddsville, Alberta

Dear Miss Craigie:

You are hereby given notice that your Application for Homestead
Patent dated May 9, 1905, and registered in your name will be
cancelled and the property will revert to the Dominion of Canada.
You are required to vacate the premises on or before September 1,
1907.

Signed:

Sterling J. Payne

Homestead Inspector

Dominion of Canada

July 1, 1907

Mrs. Alwyn Penrose
General Delivery
Toddsville, Alberta

Dear Mrs. Penrose:

You are hereby given notice that your Application for Homestead
Patent dated May 9, 1905, and registered in your name will be
cancelled and the property will revert to the Dominion of Canada.
You are required to vacate the premises on or before September 1,
1907.

Signed:

Sterling J. Payne

Homestead Inspector
Dominion of Canada

July 1, 1907

Miss Roberta Elizabeth Edgar
General Delivery
Toddsville, Alberta

Dear Miss Edgar:

You are hereby given notice that the property registered in your
name is being expropriated by the Dominion of Canada under the
Expropriation Act. Financial compensation will be granted equal to

the amount of your original purchase. You are required to vacate the premises on or before September 1, 1907.

Signed:

Sterling J. Payne

Homestead Inspector

Dominion of Canada

July 1, 1907

Miss Jessica Jane McDonald

General Delivery

Toddsville, Alberta

Dear Miss McDonald:

You are hereby given notice that the land registered in your name is being expropriated by the Dominion of Canada. You may apply in writing to the Ministry of Indian Affairs, care of Superintendent-General Frank Oliver, for financial compensation. You are required to vacate the premises on or before September 1, 1907.

Signed:

Sterling J. Payne

Homestead Inspector

Dominion of Canada

BOOK
FOUR

CHAPTER TWENTY-NINE

Flora lay rigidly in her cot, eyes staring into the midnight summer dusk that filled her shack, watching the memories emerge from the shadows like reluctant ghosts.

The story her mother had related so often returned to her with new meaning. Isobel had been six years old when soldiers arrived at her father's cottage and ordered the family outside. One held them at gunpoint while others scattered the coals from their peat fire until the thatched roof flared. The Mackays were forced to watch in anguish as their home and all it contained went up in flames. Isobel remembered every detail to the day of her death.

Flora had listened to this tragic tale with pity, but never before had she felt pure outrage. Now the cruel injury done to her family struck her afresh. It was about to happen again. To her. If she refused to abandon her farm, red-coated Royal North-West Mounted Police officers would seize her possessions, padlock her door, and leave her homeless.

She ground her teeth, remembering her grief at losing the comfortable stone dwelling in Dornoch, the only home she had ever known. Then her disastrous attempt to secure a house through marriage, a house that had proven as ephemeral as the marriage itself. And finally, her last and best chance, seemingly granted by the moving finger of fate—an opportunity to earn her own wee hoose with the sweat of her brow.

All in vain.

Unlike her excitable mother, Flora was slow to the boil. But her boiling point had finally been reached. She could feel her blood bubbling and fizzing and throbbing in her veins. Clasping her hands, she swore on the bones of her mother and every ancestor she possessed that history would not be repeated.

After a sleepless night, Flora ate her breakfast with icy deliberation. She braided her hair tightly before dressing in her silk blouse and tweed skirt. She pinned her Celtic brooch on her tartan shawl with as much ceremony as any Highland chieftain ever donned his plaid. Then she set off for the yellow house, her scuffed work boots rising to her knees with each step, her arms swinging to shoulder height.

Flora was deaf to the music of the summer morn—the liquid murmur of the creek, the chirping of the orioles, the whirring of grasshoppers in the long grass. Instead, her ears rang with the soul-stirring skirl of the bagpipes, rallying the spirits of her clansmen and summoning them to war. *This must be how it feels to go into battle*, she thought; *the steely calm, the concentration of will*. She recalled the legendary Battle of Culloden, when two thousand brave Highlanders were shot and stabbed and bludgeoned to death by British redcoats in forty horrific minutes.

But not without putting up one hell of a fight, by God.

When she pounded her fist on the door, Miss Edgar opened it. "Flora, please come in. Everyone else is here."

Peggy was sitting bolt upright, her untidy hair falling around her face. Wren was in her usual rocker, quietly weeping, while Jessie stood motionless against the wall beside the door.

Flora was too agitated to sit down. She stood while Miss Edgar seated herself in her plush armchair and spoke with her natural air of authority.

"As you know, Wren and I took the train to Calgary to meet with our lawyer and determine whether we have any legal grounds for challenging this expropriation. We arrived home late last night."

She paused, as if unwilling to continue. "His advice was discouraging. Apparently, our situation is not without precedent. A widow in Manitoba was forced off her homestead because the government wished to build the town of Virden. Later it was found that the local member of Parliament owned the surrounding property and sold it for a ridiculous profit when the new town site was established."

"So even the law is not on our side?" Peggy asked.

"Unfortunately, we have no legal recourse. And that means we are out of options." Miss Edgar's expression was sorrowful. "I speak for both of us when I tell you how much we have enjoyed your company during the past two years. It will be difficult to part ways, but in the words of Longfellow, it's time to fold our tents and silently steal away."

The words had barely left her mouth when Flora stamped her boot on the braided rug. "Miss Edgar, I'm not prepared to fold up my tent! We may not have any friends in government—ach, we may not even have the vote—but that doesn't mean we have no voice! I say we refuse to be silenced!"

All eyes were upon her. "How do you propose we do that, Flora?" Miss Edgar asked.

"We must draw attention to our plight! Tell everyone about Payne's harassment, create bad publicity for the federal government and the Liberal party and that swine Frank Oliver! The suffragettes in England are smashing windows and starting fires, for the love of God! Christabel Pankhurst spit in a policeman's face! They aren't afraid to fight for their rights!"

Flora stared into each woman's eyes as if she could hypnotise them into agreement. "That poor widow in Manitoba was alone against the government, but there are five of us. Five women can cause a huge stramach!"

Jessie stepped forward and stood beside her. "They sure as hell won't steal my property without a struggle! Do you know how long it took my father to receive title to his land? Nine years! I was just a child when the government kicked the Half-Breeds off their farms in Red River so they could be occupied by white settlers! And all they gave him in return was a piece of paper!"

Miss Edgar's voice was compassionate. "Jessie, we are sadly ignorant of these matters. Perhaps you would be kind enough to explain."

"The government promised him land somewhere else, and they gave him a scrip coupon to claim his title. Every time he presented it, they demanded another form, another oath, another approval from Ottawa."

Her expression was fierce, and she gripped the hunting knife at her belt. "It was all for show. The government never wanted us to own land. Even the Indians have more rights than we do—at least they were granted reserves! My people sold their coupons to white scrip sharks for a few dollars, or a bottle of whisky. They were forced to leave everything behind in Manitoba and drift across western Canada, searching for new homes. Some of them ended up living on road allowances. When Louis Riel tried to defend our rights, he was hung for it!"

Jessie's grey eyes flashed silver, like the sunlight on her knife blade. "My father was famous for his patience. He could lie in the snow for hours, as motionless as a stone, waiting for an elk herd to appear. So he agreed to every request, every obstacle. After nine years, he finished the last step and was told to apply for his title. And they still tried to make it as difficult as possible. They sent him to the lands office in Battleford, three hundred miles away from our home in Lac Ste. Anne!"

Jessie rarely showed her emotions, but now her voice shook. "It took him weeks to travel to Battleford with his dogsled in the dead of winter, and he came down with pneumonia on the way home. He died with the title in his hand."

She raised her right fist as though she were clutching an invisible title. "And this is what they gave him! This piece of worthless land, nothing but bush and rocks. But it's mine now, and no white devils will take it away from me!"

Her listeners were silent, but their sympathy was so profound that it filled the room.

Flora reached out and gripped the other woman's hand. They did indeed have something in common, aside from their shared Scottish blood. "Jessie and I are agreed. What say the rest of you?"

Wren's voice quivered. "I know it's profoundly unfair, but I'm afraid we can't win this fight. Frank Oliver has too much power. We'll drive ourselves to distraction, and for nothing! I think we should leave now." She bowed her head, refusing to meet their eyes.

There was another pause before Miss Edgar spoke again. "Wren and I had a similar battle in Boston, over a different issue—although perhaps not so different, after all. It caused us a great deal of distress and Wren was bedridden for weeks. That's when we decided to move to a remote place where we wouldn't be victimised by some misguided sense of morality. However, it appears there is no such escape."

She turned to Wren and said in a gentler tone, "My dear, any action we take, whether we go quietly or stay and fight, comes at a personal cost. We must determine which is the greater sacrifice."

Wren looked at her friend with swollen eyes, twisting her damp handkerchief. "I'll do whatever you think is best, Robbie."

The room fell silent again, waiting for Miss Edgar's decision. She drummed her fingers against the arm of her chair while she considered.

"I expect it's a losing battle, but everything in me rises up against oppression," she said finally. "Perhaps it's the spirit of my American forefathers. You aren't the only ones who were mistreated by a colonial government. It is gall and wormwood that we can be cancelled this way, as if we never existed. They offered us the same amount we paid for the farm, with no allowance for the house and all the other improvements we've made."

Her eyes travelled around the room. "Our home will be occupied, no doubt, by some crony of Oliver's. And for no other reason than our gender."

She seemed to be gaining strength from her own words. "Perhaps we can do something. We are not without our supporters. Peggy, you have friends among the local bachelors, and Dr. Farraday is an influential member of the community. I'm confident he'll take our side." She shot a quick glance in Flora's direction.

"Well, I don't have any friends around here," Jessie broke in. "You must be dreaming if you think anybody is going to defend my rights. At least your skin is white."

"Perhaps," said Miss Edgar, "but you will notice that the colour of our skin in this case is far less important than the—shall we say, the physical attributes of manhood."

"You mean we don't have any balls!" Jessie retorted. Wren shrank back in her chair, and even Miss Edgar looked slightly shocked.

"Precisely," she said, after a moment. "However, there's an old saying: 'Bare is the back without brother behind it.' In this case, we can substitute sister for brother. Jessie, I believe we are sisters under the skin, no matter what colour. And you cannot say that you are without friends. There are four of them in this room."

Flora sensed the tide was turning. "Miss Edgar, does that mean you and Wren are willing to help us fight those . . . those bastards?" She had never uttered the word before in her life.

Miss Edgar glanced at Wren again before answering. "Our powers are limited, but we must do whatever we can."

Peggy hadn't spoken. The others watched as she rose from her chair and stood erect, a small but determined figure. "When I first came here, all I wanted was a farm for Jack. He had the most to lose by staying in Wales. I knew if we could stick it out until his eighteenth birthday, he would take care of me and the girls. But now, thanks to you ladies, I have a different attitude."

She lifted her chin, as if trying to grow taller.

"Why shouldn't my girls have the same rights as my boy? Why shouldn't they have the right to homestead if they want? Why shouldn't they have the vote? Why shouldn't they run for prime minister someday?" Her voice was growing stronger, her chest heaving.

"I don't expect we can win, but I want to show the children that some things are worth fighting for. So yes, I say let's give them everything we've got with both barrels!"

"Hurrah!" Flora jumped into the centre of the room. "There's an expression in my country, firing the heather—that means causing a mighty uproar!" She raised her right fist over her head as if she were clutching an invisible claymore.

"My friends, it's time to fire the heather!"

CHAPTER THIRTY

MISS EDGAR

Miss Edgar struck a wooden match on the sole of her shoe and lit her cigarette. Wren didn't allow her to smoke in the house, except for this single indulgence that she savoured each night before stoking the fire and going to bed.

Usually she read a novel while sipping her whisky nightcap, but tonight she sat thinking. She knew that Wren's nerves weren't up to a lengthy battle. One could only hope that the matter would be resolved quickly, one way or another.

She exhaled a mouthful of smoke in three perfect rings, reflecting on how much they had already suffered from the fetters of civilization. The two women had been perfectly happy in Boston until one of their students, an imperious wench named Penelope who bullied the younger girls, started a rumour that there was more to the friendship between Miss Greenwood and Miss Edgar than met the eye. The girls began to whisper among themselves. It was all over when one of them burst into Miss Edgar's room and found Wren sitting on the bed cross-legged, in her stocking feet. The women were only chatting, but the story went round that they were engaged in something unnatural.

A week later they were summoned to the headmaster's office and dismissed. "Several parents have threatened to withdraw their daughters," he said. "I'm sorry to lose you, but you've given me no choice."

Miss Edgar and Wren bade farewell to their brightest girls, the ones who cried and begged them to stay in touch, and decamped for a boardinghouse while they decided where to move next. Boston had lost its appeal.

Wren sank into such a depression that she could barely get out of bed. But it was she who spied the newspaper advertisement for a farm in Alberta. Miss Edgar pointed out that the Canadian climate was positively glacial, but on reflection they decided they could bear it. Boston wasn't exactly the tropics, either.

The next day they went to the public library and studied a map of Canada. What convinced them was the distance from everything they had known. The country was nearly uninhabited, and the price so reasonable that they could afford to build a new house. Wren had some romantic notion of raising chickens, and Miss Edgar just wanted to make her happy.

How ironic that trouble should follow them here. Yet this time, they were not alone in their plight. They had to fight this injustice, not only for themselves, but for their friends—and all the other women who would come after them.

Miss Edgar stubbed out her cigarette so viciously that the sparks flew onto the rug.

It was time to fire the heather.

WREN

Wren lay awake, her fingers pleating and unpleating the lace frill around the neck of her nightgown. She knew she wouldn't sleep until Robbie came upstairs.

A public fight was the last thing she wanted. Avoiding conflict was the motivation for leaving their birthplace and moving to a foreign country where they would not be judged. And the first year had been so wonderful. How they had enjoyed planning and building their house, down to the last detail. And the hens! Wren's hands ceased their restless moving and she smiled, imagining their warm feathered bodies asleep on their perches in the coop. She wished she could join them.

But now it appeared that a fox had entered the henhouse, a predator named Frank Oliver. And he was about to tear into pieces everything they had worked for. Wren didn't hate anybody, but if she did, she felt sure that it would be Mr. Oliver. She shivered under the double wedding ring quilt, the one she had sewn so lovingly when they moved into their new home.

Men were such rapacious creatures. They swore and drank and mistreated their animals and started wars. How much better off the world would be if there were no men. Or at least, if the rules of gender were reversed and they were subordinate to women. If only women had the vote, and men did not! She pictured a peaceful planet where women lived together in harmony and men did their bidding.

In all fairness, though, women could be nasty creatures. That girl Penelope was one of them. And Mrs. Westhead was a formidable enemy. Wren moaned aloud when she recalled the toll that their previous ordeal had taken on her health. She dreaded having to go through that again—hearing the evil names that people muttered, seeing the sideways looks.

She just hoped that she could survive, for the sake of her friends. Especially her beloved Robbie. Firing the heather sounded wonderful in theory, but Wren expected more smoke than fire.

PEGGY

Peggy opened the oven quietly and placed a bowl of bread dough inside to rise overnight. The children were asleep. In her nightly ritual, she walked over to their beds and admired each of them in turn.

Jewel resembled a pink-and-gold gem in her hammock. How Peggy wished that her father could see her. He had never laid eyes on this little angel with shining curls, so similar to his own. She had her father's temperament, too. Alwyn was the kind of man who accepted his fate and made the best of it. It was Peggy who railed against their lot in life, she who had always wanted to leave Wales.

Jack looked younger asleep. Peggy's chest swelled with love and pride as she admired his face, showing the outlines of the man he would become. In many ways he was already doing a man's work. Yet whenever she felt sorry for him, she remembered that if they had remained in Wales, he would be setting off for the pit every morning. Here he had fresh air, clean water, and the wilderness he embraced as if born into it.

Nellie had finally lost her look of sadness and strain. Of all the children, she missed her father the most. Perhaps Peggy was too hard on her, giving her chores beyond her years, but she always rose to the occasion. She straightened Nellie's blanket and found her deerskin doll tucked inside. Peggy bent and kissed her forehead. "My calon bach," she whispered. "My little heart."

What would happen to them if they were forced off the farm? Could she raise enough money to return to Wales? Her sister would take them in, but it would be a tight squeeze with two families sharing one cottage. And Jack would have no other option but to work in the mine.

Peggy blinked away her tears, determined not to weep. It was a hard world for a woman alone, and nobody knew that better than the residents of Ladyville. But the other women had only themselves to worry about. She had these three beautiful souls. She was ready to fight for them, to the death if needs must. What was that phrase that Miss Craigie had used—firing the heather?

Peggy's heather was fired.

JESSIE

Jessie sat before the stove, pushing her needle through a piece of harness, far too angry to sleep. She imagined the various ways she might kill Frank Oliver. Gut him with her hunting knife. Blow a hole in his chest with her rifle. Or maybe just whip him until he crawled on his belly and begged for mercy.

In truth, while Jessie found some relief in her fantasies, she had never killed anyone and never would. She could understand, though, how those deprived of their rightful inheritance would take up arms. Her father was far too law-abiding to consider violence. Just as well, or he might have died at the Battle of Batoche in Saskatchewan, when the Half-Breeds made one last desperate stand against the British troops, firing nails and forks when they ran out of bullets. Unfortunately, the cannons that General Middleton's troops shipped west on the new railway were too much for them.

Jessie had promised herself that she would never make the same mistake as her father, believing that he dealt with honourable men. He had presented his land scrip coupon with every confidence that Queen Victoria's government would make things right. Over the years, Jessie had watched his faith dry up like a lump of buffalo dung. She was relieved that he wasn't alive to see what was happening.

Why had she walked into the same trap as her father? She had been stupid to believe that the government couldn't take her land away. She didn't even have Treaty Rights, although her mother's family said those weren't worth the paper they were written on. Oliver was already carving up reserves in Alberta, awarding chunks of treaty land to his wealthy friends.

Jessie jabbed her needle through the leather strap so viciously that it pierced her finger. She sucked the blood from her hand. It was strange that her allies were other women, and white women at that. She had always pictured them as weak and lazy creatures who wouldn't survive the first winter. More surprisingly, they treated her as an equal.

Jessie had always drawn her strength from the spirits of her Cree ancestors. Now she thought her courage might have an additional source. Perhaps it was the call of the Scottish blood she shared with Flora. Perhaps her own white forefathers had been Highland warriors.

And she relished the prospect of firing the heather. She envisioned a massive prairie fire, sweeping over the land and scorching everything in its path.

Jessie vowed to start one almighty inferno.

CHAPTER THIRTY-ONE

TODDSVILLE FREE PRESS

July 10, 1906

MINISTER TO VISIT TODDSVILLE

Mr. Frank Oliver, our esteemed federal Minister of the Interior and superintendent-general of Indian Affairs, will make a weeklong visit to Quarter Circle One Ranch, owned by Charles Westhead and his wife, Alix, to hunt for antelope. The honourable gentleman vows there is no better game to be found in Alberta, and this editor is inclined to agree. The residents of Toddsville and area wish him good luck and straight shooting.

CHAPTER THIRTY-TWO

Flora halted the horse at the end of a long, gravelled driveway and sat in the buggy belonging to the Chicken Ladies, marshalling her courage. Before her was a two-storey shingled house with several wings, much like the one where she had been a servant for six long years. Even now, her first instinct was to slink around to the back entrance.

The Westheads had spared no expense in re-creating an English manor house, which looked as incongruous as a palace on the prairie. Decorative beams painted dark green crisscrossed the exterior, adorned with clinging vines, and two brick chimneys protruded from the roof. The lawns were pristine, every blade of prairie wool replaced with manicured grass and geometrically precise flower beds. Apparently, Mrs. Westhead fancied herself a horticulturist.

Flora exhaled deeply as she attempted to shake off her neshness. She was nobody's servant, but an independent woman with means of her own—and today, she was confident that she looked like one. The ladies had agreed she should dress to impress the noted politician.

The August weather was too hot for her good tweed suit, but Flora had cleaned and pressed her grey skirt, using the flat irons at the yellow house. Wren produced a white blouse with a lace bib front. Miss Edgar lent her the pearl earrings she had worn at Christmas. Wren trimmed a broad-brimmed straw cartwheel hat with a black velvet band and a cluster of artificial pink roses, and Beau polished her high-heeled shoes with saddle soap. Nellie, who was learning to embroider, gave her a lace-trimmed handkerchief with a rather shaky daffodil, the national flower of Wales, stitched in one corner for good luck. This was tucked into Flora's sleeve. A pair of Miss Edgar's fawn-coloured kid leather gloves, buttoned at the wrist, covered her work-roughened hands.

Pulling out a small mirror that Wren had loaned her, Flora tidied her hair. Although she had left Ladyville at dawn, she was too tense to feel weary. Her eyes were bright with nervous anticipation.

It was time to meet the enemy.

She drove down the lane, hitched her horse to the wrought-iron post outside the front door, mounted the steps, adjusted her hat one last time, and rapped sharply with the brass knocker. A long-faced woman answered the door, wearing something that resembled a maid's uniform. A clean white pinafore was tied over her printed cotton dress, but her white cap was crooked and her thick bangs hung over her eyebrows, adding to her horsey appearance. Flora's former employer, Mrs. Galt, would not have approved.

"Good afternoon. Is your mistress at home?"

The woman let out a snort. "God forbid I should disturb her ladyship while she's having her rest. I'm not allowed to wake her until four o'clock, when I fix her hair and help her dress for dinner—as if she can't dress herself, like the rest of us. It's *Maisie, do this*; *Maisie, do that*—from morning until night."

Flora was taken aback by the woman's familiarity. This must be the maid that Mrs. Westhead complained about in Dr. Farraday's office. If this was how servants in Canada spoke about their employers, perhaps Mrs. Westhead had some grounds for grievance. "You don't need to wake her," she said in a firm voice. "I'm here to see Mr. Oliver."

"Does he know you're coming?"

"No, but I'm hoping he can spare a few moments. My name is Miss Flora Craigie."

The woman hesitated and looked behind her before opening the door. Flora followed her into a carpeted entrance with a wide staircase, lined with several closed doors. On one side of the hall was a carved mahogany table bearing a brass candelabra and a Chinese porcelain bowl filled with yellow and orange zinnias. The maid clumped down the hall on shoes that looked as if they pinched, opened the door on the right, and ushered Flora into the parlour. She didn't invite her to be seated. "Stay here."

Flora felt the weight of old-world opulence settle on her shoulders. Her shack could have fit inside the parlour with room to spare. The walls were covered with figured blue and green wallpaper. An English hunting scene hung above the stone fireplace, and a screen embroidered with peacocks stood in the hearth. A stag's head sporting an impressive set of antlers hung on the opposite wall. His glass eyes stared accusingly at Flora.

Hearing footsteps, she whirled to face the door. A man entered, carrying a tennis racket. His annoyed expression vanished when he saw Flora. "How do you do, Miss Craigie?" She registered the admiration in his eyes and was thankful that she had taken pains with her costume.

Frank Oliver was a slender man of average height, wearing cream-coloured flannel pants and a pinstriped shirt with the sleeves rolled up to his elbows. His most marked feature was a bushy white moustache that covered his lips and protruded at least four inches into space from each side of his narrow jaw. This vanity alone would have turned him into a caricature, were it not for his hawk's eyes. They studied Flora as if she were a prairie fieldmouse worth devouring.

She nodded to him. "Thank you for seeing me, Mr. Oliver."

"Not at all. It's a pleasure to meet such a charming young lady." He gestured to a chair. "Won't you sit down?"

Flora perched on the edge of a green velvet armchair, while Oliver set down his racquet and lowered himself to the leather sofa opposite her. He spread his skinny legs wide and stretched one arm along the back of the couch, the picture of casual relaxation. "What can I do for my elegant visitor? Are you here to tell me of your need for a public library? I've already heard from Mrs. Parlby on that score."

Flora took the plunge. "No, Mr. Oliver. I'm here to speak with you about the government's plan to expropriate four farms east of town."

His bushy eyebrows drew together and became one. "You astonish me, Miss Craigie. What possible interest could you have in those farms?"

"I've been living there for more than two years. My Homestead Application is in process."

Oliver sat up straight and scrutinised her. "So you're one of those farmers from Ladyville. I must say, I didn't expect you to be so refined. What possessed a young woman like yourself to undertake such a Herculean task?"

Flora ignored the veiled insult. "Mr. Oliver, I'm well on my way to proving up my homestead. I'm begging you not to expropriate our land. It would create a terrible hardship for all the owners. I'm confident that a man of your intellect must sympathise with our situation."

The women had discussed at great length how to approach Oliver. They had conceived a number of suggestions that ranged from holding him hostage in the barn, to extracting his fingernails one by one. Jessie proposed shaving off his precious whiskers and leaving him as hairless as a pig. Ultimately, they had decided that their best hope was to flatter him.

Oliver was already shaking his head, a smirk barely visible under his bloated moustache. "Miss Craigie, allow me to enlighten you. Homesteading was never meant for the weaker sex. If you want to farm, you must marry a farmer. It's as simple as that."

He rose from the sofa, and Flora had no choice but to stand as well. Oliver was smiling in a way that was slightly predatory. "I have only to look at you to understand you are not suited to the life of a farmer."

Flora wondered if she had made a mistake dressing like a lady, rather than galloping up to the front door in her breeches. She forced herself to smile back. "Appearances can be deceiving, Mr. Oliver. I promise you that I am just as capable as any man in Alberta."

"Fine words, Miss Craigie, but they won't change my mind. Even if you could manage the work, which I doubt, it is the man's business to lead, and the woman's to follow. With your obvious attributes, you could provide some fortunate fellow with a desirable companion. There's a reason that you ladies are called angels of the hearth."

He gave a courtly bow. "Allow me to escort you to your mode of transport." He extended his elbow, and Flora reluctantly took it. Compared with her own muscular biceps, his upper arm felt scrawny under her hand. She thought with contempt that he was unfit to do the physical labour that she performed every day. The only manure he shovelled came from his mouth.

As they walked down the hall, Flora bent her knees beneath her skirt so she wouldn't tower over him, wracking her brains for another argument. "Mr. Oliver, you're such a popular politician that you must be most responsive to the wishes of your constituents." She wondered if she were laying it on too thick, but gambled on the size of his ego.

"Indeed, I hope that I am."

"If my friends and I were to demonstrate that we have the support of your voters, would that influence your decision?"

"You're wasting your time and my own, Miss Craigie." He chuckled tolerantly, as if humoring a child. "Why would any man want to change the laws that were so clearly established for the common good?" He opened the door.

"If you were to see evidence to the contrary, would you review our case?" Flora held her breath.

"You're certainly persistent, Miss Craigie. I admire a woman with spirit, however misdirected. If you show me that the local voters support your objective, I may, and I emphasise the word *may*, reconsider. Now, good day to you, dear lady."

Flora thanked him graciously and took her departure. As her buggy rolled down the driveway, she thought the meeting had been a qualified success. Although she had arrived unannounced, Mr. Oliver had listened to her request. He had treated her with respect. He hadn't made any promises, but he hadn't refused her outright. She understood why he was such a popular politician. Now all that remained was to convince his electorate.

When she reached for Nellie's handkerchief to mop her damp forehead, she found it was no longer inside her sleeve. She must have dropped it. Knowing how many hours Nellie had laboured over that handkerchief, Flora couldn't bear to leave it behind. She pulled on the reins and turned the buggy around.

As she mounted the front steps, she saw that Oliver had left the door standing ajar. She spied her handkerchief lying on the floor beside the hall table. Rather than ring the bell again, she stepped inside. She was bending down to pick it up when she heard masculine voices from behind the door on her left. It was open a few inches and their words were perfectly audible.

"Who was that girl?" asked someone with a plummy British accent, followed by the clink of a bottle against a glass.

"Her name is Craigie, one of the women homesteaders over at Ladyville," Oliver's voice replied.

"What did she want?"

"You know their claims are going to be cancelled, Charles. She wants me to reconsider."

"What did you tell her?"

Flora froze while she waited for Oliver's response.

"I told her I would think about it, if she generated enough voter support.

But she doesn't have a hope. Nobody will listen to them—a serving girl, a Welsh widow, a couple of Yanks, and a Half-Breed. I jollied her along because she's such a juicy little tart, with that mane of red hair. Some man will be lucky to get a piece of that."

Flora gasped and clapped one hand over her mouth while both men sniggered—there was no other word for it. They sounded like a couple of vulgar schoolboys.

Then Oliver spoke again. "She should move to Edmonton. She could make a lot more money lying on her back with her legs spread than trying to farm, the stupid bitch. I know just the place for her—Big Nelly's whorehouse. I'd be one of her best customers."

The floor tilted under Flora's feet as if she were still on board the ship, and she sank to her knees on the Persian rug. Never in her life had she heard a woman spoken about in those terms, least of all herself. She grabbed the newel post for support. As she pulled herself upright, she saw a woman standing on the third step from the bottom, motionless.

It was Alix Westhead.

It was obvious from her stunned expression that Mrs. Westhead had over-heard the same conversation. Her eyes were so wide that the white showed around her irises. Her mint-green dress was cut rather low in the bodice, and her face and throat were suffused with a blotchy red colour.

They locked eyes. Flora saw a complicated set of emotions cross the other woman's face: the same shock that she was experiencing, followed by rage, then mortification. As she stared down at Flora wordlessly, the gold locket jumping up and down on her chest, Flora could have sworn her expression softened. But before the other woman could speak, Flora snatched up her handkerchief and fled.

The doctor was the first to sign their petition, his signature as large and bold as he could make it: *Samuel Tait Farraday.*

"Our dear doctor takes the petition on his rounds. He tacked a copy on his office door, and another one at the post office," Miss Edgar said. "He explains to every homesteader that if the government can take away our farms, then it could happen to them."

Peggy also did her utmost. She talked to the Hedley boys, and they said it would be a darned shame if she lost her farm, and who would do their laundry then? They signed the petition. She told her story to Mr. Dunne, who immediately proposed again. Despite her refusal, he also signed.

A few tendrils of smoke appeared amid the heather. As the news spread, area residents became engaged in the debate, eager to see who was taking sides. "We have thirty-seven names," Peggy said after the first week.

Beau was courting a pretty teenager named Etta who worked at the newspaper office. She told her girlfriends, who were young enough to feel hopeful about women's rights, and they talked to their mothers. Another twelve names were added, all of them female. Flora appreciated their help but was painfully conscious of the need for men's signatures, since the women were so easily dismissed.

After Beau delivered a load of Wren's eggs to the general store in Lacombe, the owner, Caroline Day, displayed the petition on her front counter and encouraged her customers to sign. The following week, Beau met Mr. Cook on the trail. The land locater took a copy and nailed it up at the Red Deer livery stable. When Nurse Godwin spotted the petition, she requested a copy so she could distribute it to the staff and patients at the hospital.

Even Jessie proudly produced six signatures from local ranchers who didn't want to lose her services as a horse trainer.

Flora was at a loss, since she knew so few people outside Ladyville. Instead, she fired off a flurry of anonymous letters to the newspapers in Lacombe, Red

Deer, and Edmonton. She was pleased when one of her compositions, signed "Prairie Rose," was published in the *Edmonton Bulletin*, owned by the hated Frank Oliver himself.

"Mrs. Parlby is doing an excellent job gathering signatures in her social circle, and even a few from their husbands," Miss Edgar told Flora. "She said Alix Westhead refused to sign, but you'll notice she hasn't written another letter to the newspaper, either. Mrs. Parlby said she used to praise Frank Oliver constantly and now she never mentions him. She seems to have gone off him, for some reason."

Flora didn't respond. She hadn't been able to bring herself to tell the ladies what she overheard at the Westhead ranch, partly because she was embarrassed to admit that she had been eavesdropping, but mostly because she could not wrap her tongue around those hateful words. She felt unclean just thinking about them.

"The letters are coming thick and fast now," Miss Edgar said, handing the *Toddsville Free Press* to Flora, dated August 10, 1907.

Dear Editor:

About the ladies at Ladyville. They didn't even know how to harness a team when they got here, but they caught on quick. They have put their hand to the plow and worked as hard as any man. Let them keep their land. Fair is fair.

Percy Quentin Buckhorn

"How wonderful!" said Flora. "Everybody knows Sourdough, and if he's on our side, that must count for something!"

Miss Edgar chuckled. "That letter was a greater effort than you might think. He asked me to write it for him, claiming that his eyesight was too poor to make out the words. When I gave it to him to sign, he said, 'I need a scrap of paper to practise on. It's been so long since I signed my name, I reckon I forgot how.' He laboured away and managed to create a legible signature that was good enough for the newspaper."

"Dear old Sourdough!" Flora said.

"Not only that, but he's carrying a tattered copy of the petition around in his overalls and persuading his cronies to sign. Says he won't haul hay for them unless they do."

"Is it possible we might reach one hundred signatures?" Flora hardly dared to hope.

"I'm not sure. Beau says public opinion is divided. Keep reading."

Dear Editor:

It saddens me to think that a woman should be reduced to perform the same toil as a man, losing all her feminine grace and charm. I can scarcely believe that any girl except one without her intellectual faculties would choose such a life—unless she is a complete failure as a woman in every other aspect.

"A Real Lady"

Dear Editor:

I am acquainted with Mrs. Margaret Penrose, a woman of indomitable courage who is homesteading west of town. Despite losing her husband in a tragic mining accident, she is determined to provide a future for her three fatherless children. Mrs. Penrose is a God-fearing woman who is raising her family in the Christian faith. Although unable to attend church on a regular basis, she observes the Sabbath and makes a friend of her Bible. She is a most desirable asset to our community.

As it says in Isaiah 1:17, "Learn to do right; seek justice. Defend the oppressed. Take up the cause of the fatherless; plead the case of the widow." I speak for many members of my congregation who are in sympathy with Widow Penrose, along with the other good ladies of Ladyville.

Reverend Crawford Crawley

Dear Editor:

In the words of Rudyard Kipling: "God gave all man the earth to love, but since our hearts are small; ordained that one small spot should be beloved over all." Let the ladies have their small spot on God's creation, same as the men.

Mrs. Elaine Meehan

Dear Editor:

Women don't have the muscle that's needed to get this country up and running. A strong man has his hands full, so how can we expect the fair sex to make a go of things? Even if they hire someone to do the work, they'll be on the first train out of Lacombe as soon as they have their title in their pockets. The Homestead Act wasn't created for that purpose. We don't want any pioneers in petticoats here.

Archibald Delaney

Dear Editor:

If the government can expropriate homesteads and even titled farms, why do we have laws in the first place? Do those robber barons in Parliament think they can give away land with one hand and take it back with the other? A man's home is his castle. That goes for women, too.

William Haynes

Dear Editor:

I'm against allowing the Indians to own good agricultural land. They waste it, they don't know what to do with it. You can't make farmers out of them. They should have been sent into the mountains rather than settled on reserves where they can come into town and mingle with their betters.

Richard Stone

Dear Editor:

I have been trading with the local natives for years, and I can tell you they make fine neighbours. I have never seen people more hospitable. If they have plenty, they share willingly with the less fortunate, Indian or white man. They have bailed me out of many a tight spot.

If the government saw fit to give that Half-Breed girl a chunk of land, then let her have it. It is nobody's business what she uses it for. Also, she's a fine horsewoman and gentled a wild stallion that I couldn't do nothing with.

Axel Burrows

CHAPTER THIRTY-THREE

RED DEER NEWS

August 16, 1907

OLIVER TO MEET WITH RED DEER AND
AREA CONSTITUENTS

Frank Oliver, the federal Minister of the Interior and superintendent-general of Indian Affairs, will attend a public meeting at the Alexandra Hotel in Red Deer on Friday, August 23, 1907. The honourable minister will outline his vision for our new province and entertain questions from constituents. Sponsored by the Red Deer Agricultural Society, the meeting begins at 7 p.m. sharp.

CHAPTER THIRTY-FOUR

As they mounted the front steps of the Alexandra Hotel, Flora recalled her first and only visit to Red Deer. Her overwhelming emotion then had been terror that Hector would find her. Now that nightmare—although she occasionally woke in a panic, clawing at the invisible hands around her throat—was dwarfed by an even greater one: the loss of her home.

Seven days remained. The residents of Ladyville were aware that this public meeting in Red Deer was the only opportunity to present their petition to Oliver in person. They had travelled together in a motley procession, Beau and the Chicken Ladies in their buggy, Flora and the Penroses driving their team and wagon, and Jessie on horseback.

Flora attempted to be fatalistic. Although they had done their utmost, she knew the public was as fickle as a stormy summer sky. The harvest was imminent, and within days everyone would be necessarily occupied with their crops. The Chicken Ladies didn't appear confident, either. Wren had started to pack her books and her dishes, and Miss Edgar hadn't discouraged her.

Even prairie fires burned out without enough fuel.

Wooden chairs filled the meeting hall, and the Ladyville residents seated themselves in the third row. Nellie and Jewel gazed around in wonder. The others might have admired their surroundings, too, had they been less anxious. Harold Snell, the local jeweller who had purchased Flora's pearl, had been married here two days earlier, and the hall was still decorated with Chinese lanterns and strings of red, white, and blue bunting. A Union Jack and a framed photograph of King Edward VII hung above the wooden stage, where a table and three chairs had been arranged.

"See who's here." Flora nudged Miss Edgar.

The women watched as Alix Westhead, wearing a rose-coloured gown and matching hat with an ostrich feather, swept past them and seated herself in the first row between two men. Miss Edgar whispered the name of the man on the left, who had notebook and pencil in hand: John Carswell, editor of the *Red Deer News*. The man on Mrs. Westhead's right needed no introduction: it was Sterling Payne. He turned to observe the crowd, and when his eyes fell upon their group in the third row, his thin lips curled under his thin moustache.

People continued to pour in. The smell of the outdoors came with them—fresh air, muddy boots, ripening grain from the nearby fields, and now and then a whiff of the stable. The hubbub grew as farmers and townspeople greeted each other. After the hall was filled, men offered their chairs to women before going to stand against the walls. Flora spotted the doctor among them and was annoyed at her leaping pulse. Over the weeks she had repeatedly wrung her own heart like a dishrag, hoping to squeeze out every drop of sentimentality. She studied the toes of her worn shoes and tried to calm her nerves.

At seven o'clock precisely, three men stepped onto the stage—Red Deer mayor Hally Gaetz; agricultural society president Henry Jamieson; and Frank Oliver himself, his white moustache looking more than ever like a small, bushy animal.

"I wonder how he eats soup through that thing," whispered a voice behind Flora.

Following an unctuous welcome from the mayor, two shy little girls presented Oliver with a bouquet of coral chrysanthemums. He thanked them and set it on the table. There was general applause, although Flora noticed that some people weren't clapping. The Liberals had squeaked to victory in Alberta's first election, and not everyone was happy with the way the federal government was taxing their new province.

Oliver began to speak. "Ladies and gentlemen, we are on the dawn of a new civilisation, one that will bring peace and prosperity to this region for the next hundred years. My good friends in the agricultural society will agree with me that there is no greater service to mankind than the production of grain. We grow the best wheat in the world! Yesterday Red Deer was a dot on the map, today it's a boomtown with fifteen hundred souls. And it is the homesteaders, the good, honest, hardworking men from Britain and the United States—and yes, even countries like Germany and Russia—who will make Alberta the greatest province in Canada. Gentlemen, I welcome your questions."

It was now or never. As if her head was pulled by an invisible string, Flora turned and caught the doctor's eye. He gave her an encouraging nod. She rose on trembling legs. "Mr. Mayor!" Her voice was high and thin in the great hall. He glanced in her direction, trying to see where the sound was coming from. Flora raised her hand. "I have a question."

"Come up here, madam, so we can all hear you."

Flora climbed the steps and faced the room, her knees bent and her shoulders hunched. She had never spoken before a crowd. "Good evening. My name is Flora Craigie."

"Speak up!" a couple of people yelled.

Flora swallowed, trying to get moisture into her dry mouth. She estimated the crowd at two hundred people, and suddenly the room seemed full of enemies. Mrs. Westhead avoided her eye, staring over her head at the king's photograph. The newspaper editor watched with his pencil poised. When Flora's gaze lighted on Sterling Payne, he sneered. A surge of anger gave her new courage. She straightened, raising herself to her full height.

"Ladies and gentlemen." This time she used her most carrying voice. "I am standing here before you on behalf of myself and four other farmers who will lose their land if the Dominion of Canada takes it away. My friends and neighbours, Miss Greenwood and Miss Edgar, own their title outright. They built a beautiful home and established a successful business selling eggs. You may have enjoyed the fruits of their labours."

There was a scrape of chairs as everyone craned their necks to catch a glimpse of them.

"My friend and neighbour Miss Jessie McDonald is also the legal owner of her property. Scrip was granted to her family when their land in Manitoba was confiscated by the government. I know some of you have had your own battles with bureaucracy."

She paused while a smattering of laughter went round the room. "Their struggle lasted nine years, longer than many of you have lived in this country. And now that same government wants to take her land away again."

Heads turned to scrutinise Jessie, who had abandoned her buckskins for a neat skirt and blouse. She gazed back at them, unsmiling.

"Lastly, my friend and neighbour Mrs. Margaret Penrose and I filed our claims here in Red Deer two years and four months ago. We have houses and barns, we have fifteen acres in crop, and by next spring we will have done everything the government asked of us, and more."

Flora had everyone's full attention. She braced herself for the coming battle, and for one brief moment she could have sworn she heard the faint skirl of the pipes. She took another deep breath.

"Since we arrived, the male homesteaders of our acquaintance have received two annual visits from the homestead inspector, Mr. Sterling Payne, seated in the front row." She pointed to him. He wasn't sneering now. His normally pale face was flushed with what appeared to be rage.

Flora's voice rose. "During the same period, I have received seventeen visits from Mr. Payne, and Mrs. Penrose has received twelve. He has reviewed our paperwork numerous times and searched every inch of our property for mysterious unidentified gentlemen. He even conducted a thorough inspection of my toilet hole!"

The room erupted in laughter. Flora sensed the mood swinging in her favour. Nobody liked government officials, even at the best of times. She waited for the noise to die down before continuing. "Mr. Payne has threatened us. He has insulted us. He has questioned not only our motives, but our morals!"

The crowd murmured, and a female voice called out, "Shame, shame!"

In her right hand, Flora held a sheaf of papers that constituted their petition. It was a grubby lot, stained with food and scorch marks, but neatly rolled and tied with a black velvet ribbon. She stepped toward the minister, whose mouth was fixed in a hard line below his moustache.

"Mr. Oliver, we have earned the right to remain on our land. This petition carries six hundred and ten signatures from those supporting our cause. Considering that eleven hundred votes were cast here in the last election, this represents a substantial number of your constituents." Flora didn't mention how many of those signatures were from women.

She held out the sheaf, and after a noticeable hesitation, he took it. Flora turned to the crowd again and spoke in ringing tones, "I ask you here and now before this crowd, Mr. Oliver, will you revoke this terrible injustice? Will you cancel the expropriation notices on our farms and leave us in peace?"

The applause was warmer than Flora had expected. The newspaper editor scribbled furiously. One person was still clapping after everyone else had stopped. Flora glanced toward the sound and saw Dr. Farraday beating his palms together.

Without looking at the roll of paper, Oliver set it on the table. "Miss Craig, is it? Thank you for that little speech. Please take your seat and I'll explain."

She was forced to return to her chair, the hot blood pounding in her face.

Miss Edgar patted her on the knee and whispered, "Well done, Flora."

Oliver stood to address the crowd. "Friends, you are aware that every man jack in the province is clamouring for the steel. The Canadian Pacific Railway has chosen the best possible route between Lacombe and Toddsville. A station will be built at the halfway point, the logical place for a new town site, and this requires the acquisition of four farms. Two occupants have no legal claim on this land, and the other two will receive appropriate financial compensation. Now, perhaps we can move on to more important matters."

The women of Ladyville exchanged looks of misery. So their efforts had come to nought. They had reached the end of the line, and with it, the brutal destruction of all their dreams. Flora swallowed hard, desperate not to cry.

The noise level in the room swelled as the crowd began to grumble and mutter. Before the mayor could call for order, a thin woman in a patched dress with a muddy hem rose to her feet. "I got something to say to you, Mr. Oliver. I bin working my fingers to the bone for my brother since I come out four years ago. He got title, and I got nothing. It ain't fair, that's all. It just ain't fair." She sat down again and glared at the minister.

The woman behind her was nodding as she stood up. "Any woman who rises at four, feeds the animals, and gets breakfast for six children while her husband is lying abed can farm as well as any soul in this room!" The man on her left, presumably her husband, kept his eyes on the floor.

Another man, easily identified as a farmer by his horse clipper haircut and snowy forehead above his tanned face, rose to his feet. "James Raeburn is my name. I don't hold with women farmers. It's no great loss if these ladies lose their land. Likely they'll just get married anyway!"

Before he had taken his seat, the woman beside him was standing. "I'm

Gertrude Raeburn, Mrs. James Raeburn!" She glared at her husband. "There's no reason to think these ladies won't stick. A widow with five kiddies south of Lacombe proved up and bought another two quarters besides. She's been running that place for eight years now!"

The muttering began again, accompanied by much nodding and shaking of heads. Despite her disappointment, Flora was glad she had given voice to the cruel injustice shared by all these women. She was scanning the room, trying to get a sense of the audience's mood, when she caught sight of a latecomer entering through the rear door.

He was an enormous figure, nearly as wide as he was tall, wearing an expensive three-piece herringbone suit that had such a flattering cut it must have been tailored to his measurements. With his neatly trimmed brown moustache and short beard, he resembled the photograph of the king. He certainly had the same keen eyes and commanding air.

He moved to stand against the back wall as a little man with a monocle took the floor. "If you look south of the border, you'll understand why letting women homestead is a mistake," he called out in an English accent. "In Montana, single women take up one out of five homesteads! These women will sell their farms and move on, and meanwhile, every man in need of a wife is left high and dry!"

There was a murmur of response in the crowd. A woman in a feathered hat was waving her hand. "Mr. Oliver, my niece went down to Montana to claim a homestead, and she proved up six months ago! She's as happy as a clam in the land of Uncle Sam. Why is our country so backward that we push our own Canadian girls behind the door?"

The minister's expression was grim. He shot the mayor a meaningful look, but the mayor showed no sign of intervening.

A burly man with ginger whiskers was already on his feet. "This isn't about farming! This here is about women getting franchised. First you let them farm and before you know it, they'll demand the vote! If that happens, I'll be on the next boat to China!" He sat down as several men started clapping, and one yelled, "Hear, hear!"

A boyish young man in suspenders stood up next. "What's wrong with them having the vote? My wife always done her share, and the way I see it, if we have her vote as well as mine, that's all to the good! We need a voice in Ottawa if we're going to kill the monopoly of the railways and the grain companies. Think about it, boys! If our wives had the vote, we could really put the thumbscrews to those gangsters back east!" Enthusiastic applause followed, and several people darted black looks at Oliver.

"Only if she votes the same way you do!" a woman called, and laughter broke out at the nonsensical notion of a wife voting differently than her husband.

A middle-aged man pushed back his chair in the front row and faced the crowd. "I'm Frederick Krause, the owner of this hotel," he said with an air of self-importance. "Some of the good ladies in our community are members of the Women's Christian Temperance Union. If they have their way, I'll have to close my tavern and there'll be no place to wet your whistles. That's where women's rights will lead if you're not careful!"

He was answered by a grey-haired woman in a blue coat, who practically vaulted to her feet. Pinned to her chest was a white ribbon tied in a bow, indicating her membership in the temperance union, pledged to rid the world of the curse of alcoholism. "And a good thing, too!" she called. "Our new province must embrace sobriety! Too many husbands and fathers spend their money on the devil drink, instead of staying at home with their families where they belong!"

Jeers and catcalls came from male voices. "No wonder they call it 'Women Continually Torment Us!'" one called out, to scattered laughter.

The mayor shouted over the unruly crowd. "The question put to Mr. Oliver was whether these ladies should be allowed to keep their farms. This isn't about whether they deserve the vote, or whether to bring in prohibition!"

"But that is the point!" one man shouted. "You give them an inch and they take a mile! Pretty soon they'll be running the whole dang shebang!"

The room erupted in noisy conversation once again, and this time the mayor raised both hands and motioned for silence. "Does anyone else wish to speak to Miss Craigie's question?"

At the back of the hall, a tall woman stood. She wore a simple navy suit and a black cartwheel hat. "I do, Mr. Mayor, most emphatically," she said. "My name is Irene Parlby. I came out from England nine years ago to visit my friend, Mrs. Westhead, and I never went home again. My husband Walter and I own Dartmoor Ranch, near Buffalo Lake."

The mayor nodded respectfully. "Mrs. Parlby, as one of our earliest pioneers, your opinion is most welcome. Please, take the stage so everyone can hear you."

The woman mounted the steps and surveyed the crowd.

"I was recently elected president of the new Women's Country Club in our community, an organisation formed for the benefit of all. We support mothers with young children, we raise funds for medical and school supplies, and we are trying to establish a public library."

Several people clapped, and one woman yelled, "Bravo!"

"Our members have discussed this issue at length, without coming to any unanimous agreement. Personally, I hold the opinion, the fixed opinion, that these women should keep their farms. The issue of land ownership goes straight to the heart of women's rights. I believe that if it were five men asking for your support, Mr. Oliver, there would be no hesitation on your part. I would invite those who agree with me to stand and raise your hands."

The residents of Ladyville leaped to their feet, hands reaching for the ceiling. Several women wearing white ribbons stood and glared at the minister challengingly. Dr. Farraday and Beau, along with a handful of other men, stepped forward from the wall with their hands raised. Flora was pleased to see Sourdough among them, looking respectable in clean overalls. He nodded and smiled at the children, and Jewel gave a happy crow of recognition and waved at him.

The boyish young man assisted his pregnant wife to her feet. When the woman beside them tried to rise, her husband pulled at her skirt. She slapped his hand away and stood up. Flora saw Nurse Godwin standing near the back, with a shawl thrown over her white pinafore. She must have come straight from the hospital.

Mrs. Parlby's calm gaze travelled around the room while she waited for those undecided to make up their minds. An elderly woman stood up with difficulty, leaning on her cane. Two teenaged girls rose, giggling self-consciously. A young woman with a baby in her arms stood, then glared down at her husband until he joined her. Two teenaged boys took their mother's arms, and the three stood together. The bearded stranger at the back didn't move, but his eyes scanned the room with a keen expression.

As each person stood, Flora felt more optimistic. Surely this open show of support from complete strangers, many of them men, must have some influence on the minister. But her hopes were dashed when she looked at the stage. Oliver wasn't even watching the crowd. He pointedly took out his pocket watch and checked the time.

Mrs. Parlby's eyes searched the room, her lips moving. "I count forty-six good citizens who support these ladies in their quest. Thank you, my friends, for demonstrating the courage of your convictions."

Everyone resumed their seats and gazed expectantly toward the stage. Flora and Miss Edgar gripped hands under their skirts. Peggy hugged Jewel so hard that she let out a squeal.

The mayor addressed the minister. "Bearing in mind what we have just heard, I will ask Mr. Oliver if he is prepared to give the young lady a different answer to her question."

"Get on with it, Oliver!" somebody yelled. "My cow needs milking!"

The minister stepped to the front of the stage. His genial attitude had vanished and his eyes were as hard as black stones in his white face. "My decision is final. If you will excuse me, I have an early train in the morning. I must bid you all good evening."

The room erupted in a medley of cheers and boos. The women of Ladyville turned to each other in despair. Jessie's expression was fierce, and the ready tears flowed from Wren's eyes. Jewel began to whimper in sympathy. All at once, Flora felt the impending separation of her dearest friends more keenly than the loss of her farm.

"Mr. Mayor, one moment, if you please!" A voice thundered through the hall, and all heads turned as the huge man in the herringbone suit strode down the aisle. Despite his size, he bounded lightly up the steps.

When Oliver saw the man approach, his jaw fell open beneath his moustache. He sank back into his chair as if his legs wouldn't support him.

"Mr. Oliver, greetings," the big man said in his booming voice, before bowing to Mrs. Westhead in the front row. "My dear lady, what a pleasure to see you again." The plume on her hat quivered as she gave a slight nod.

The newcomer stepped to the front of the stage with such an air of authority that a hush fell over the room. He was so large that two Frank Olivers could have fit inside his waistcoat. "My name is William Van Horne. I'm the Chairman of the Canadian Pacific Railway."

There were gasps and exclamations. Flora and Miss Edgar exchanged blank looks. What on earth was Van Horne doing here? Oliver sat motionless in his chair as if he were strapped into it, awaiting death by electrocution.

"Ladies and gentlemen, I want to thank you for an instructive discussion. I congratulate you most heartily on your keen interest in public affairs." Van

Horne's resounding voice filled the hall. "However, I have something material to add to this debate. As you know, my company plans to build a branch line from Lacombe to Toddsville. It was brought to my attention two weeks ago that this would result in the expropriation of four farms, and the land would be sold for a new town site."

How had he heard about them? Surely a man of his stature must be preoccupied with more important matters. Miss Edgar squeezed Flora's hand so hard that it hurt.

"I must inform you that the bane of my profession is land speculation. It is a disease in this country, a scourge that needs to be eradicated." He inclined his head toward Oliver. "I'm sure my colleague, the honourable minister, will agree." He emphasised the word *honourable*.

Oliver seemed to shrink in his chair. He didn't speak, but finally remembered to close his mouth.

"I am so opposed to land speculation that I will dismiss any employee who reveals information leading to this nefarious practice. I have issued a bulletin to this effect." Van Horne pulled a piece of paper from his pocket and read aloud, "'The permanent locations of railway stations will be made with reference to the interests and convenience of the public and of the company, and without regard to any private interests whatever.' Signed by myself, W. C. Van Horne, Chairman of the Board, Canadian Pacific Railway."

He folded the paper and tucked it away in his massive waistcoat. "Since the original route will result in unnecessary hardship for these owners, I have decided to change it. We'll build our new station halfway between Lacombe and Toddsville as planned, but three miles farther north, on land that has yet to be claimed or settled. Construction will begin immediately after the harvest is completed."

The room erupted in pandemonium. People leaped to their feet, clapping and cheering. Four men's hats and one woman's sunbonnet were tossed into the air. Mrs. Parlby shook hands with friends on each side of her. The white ribbon brigade embraced, and several of them headed for the third row, eager to salute Flora and her friends.

"Is it true?" Wren asked in a faint voice. "Are we really and truly safe?" This time it was the implacable Miss Edgar who was sobbing. The Penroses hugged each other in a group, jumping up and down. They reached out and drew Jessie into their fold. Flora couldn't resist looking at the doctor, who raised his clasped hands into the air.

She wanted to thank Van Horne, embrace him, throw herself at his feet in gratitude, but the great man was already surrounded by a crowd. Oliver had silently folded his tent and slipped away. The sheaf of signatures they had worked so hard to gather was abandoned on the table, beside the bouquet of wilted chrysanthemums.

Sterling Payne leaped to his feet, jammed his bowler on his head, and strode down the aisle. As he passed them, his thin lips curled into a snarl.

"One more thing!" Van Horne's boisterous voice filled the room. He raised his enormous left hand, which was gripping an unlit cigar. The crowd hushed.

"We'll dedicate our new station in Toddsville to the first white woman in the area, and by extension that means renaming the village itself. From now on, this thriving young community, the flower of our new nation, will be known as Alix, Alberta! Long may she blossom!"

Alix Westhead stood and turned toward the room. She was erect as usual, shoulders squared, chin held high. Her gaze fell upon the five women.

There was a tiny smile on her face.

CHAPTER THIRTY-FIVE

Flora woke from the first deep slumber she had enjoyed in weeks to hear Taffy barking at the top of his little lungs. He often barked at night, but usually the sound echoed faintly in the distance as he warned off coyotes venturing too near his territory. She rolled over and tried to go back to sleep.

The noise grew louder. For such a small dog, he had a robust bark. It sounded as if he were just across the creek, defending his own property. Was there trouble at the Penrose place? Flora rose and went to the creek-side window. The moon was full, casting a light across the landscape, but she could see nothing amiss. She stepped over to her front window. The pale glow illuminated the ghostly prairie, and she saw three dark figures on horseback coming down the hill at a slow walk. It was a calm night, and by opening the door a crack she could hear their hoofbeats, as quiet as the rustle of leaves.

Flora watched them approach with a sense of unease. The trail past her property leading south was growing busier as more land in the area was settled, but people didn't usually travel at night unless there was some emergency. These riders were moving as if they had all the time in the world—or they didn't want anyone to hear them.

She strained her eyes, wondering why she could not make out their features. As they came closer, Flora received a shock that ran from her scalp to her toes. All three riders were wearing hoods with holes cut out for their eyes, looking like a trio of medieval executioners. At the bottom of the hill, they wheeled toward her shack.

They were coming for her.

Flora shrank back against the wall, her heart roaring. There was nowhere to hide, and they would see her in the bright moonlight if she tried to run away. There was no time to dress, but she threw her shawl over her pyjamas, clutched it around her throat, and waited breathlessly until she heard the jingle of spurs outside.

A moment of silence, and then a man shouted, "We don't want no landgrabbers here!" followed by a thud as something struck the side of the shack.

So that was their game. These ghoulish devils had heard about her success in Red Deer and they were trying to intimidate her. If she didn't react, maybe they would blow off steam like an overheated threshing machine and go away.

The sound of hoofbeats circled the shack. Flora was huddled below the front windowsill when a rock flew through the glass, which exploded into shards. It was the same window she had replaced after the hailstorm with great difficulty and expense. How dare they damage her property? Perhaps a warning shot might scare them off. It had almost worked with that horrible Murdo Dawson. How Flora wished that Jessie would appear again like Joan of Arc with a bullwhip in her hand! But she was away in Lacombe, selling two of her colts.

Flora snatched up her rifle and cocked it before she remembered that it was unloaded. Last week she had emptied her gun at a fox that was hanging around Ladyville in hopes of making off with one of the Buffs. With all the anxiety and anticipation of the public meeting, she had forgotten to load it again.

She reached for the box of shells sitting on the shelf above her bed. In her haste, the box fell to the floor and the shells rolled in every direction. She knelt and drove a splinter of glass into her kneecap while feeling for them in the darkness. To her relief, her hand found one shell and then another. She fumbled them into the chambers.

Thrusting the barrel through the broken window, she saw one masked rider seated on a pinto and aimed high over his head, toward the moon. The crack of the rifle was thunderous in the still night. Taffy's barking was much closer now.

A second rider, short and stocky in the saddle, came around the corner and shouted, "Get the hell out of here and go back where you came from!" Flora dodged when she saw him hurl another rock. It flew through the shattered window, hitting the shelf over the stove and knocking her enamel dishes and copper pot onto the floor with a terrific clatter. If she hadn't ducked, the rock would have struck her, possibly even struck her dead.

Flora was seriously alarmed. This was more than simple harassment. They seemed intent on causing actual harm. She crouched under the table, wondering how to defend herself, when she heard the third man yell in a high, shrill tone. "Burn her out, boys!"

Flora would have known that voice anywhere. A feeling of sick dread swept over her.

Heedless of the glass splinters littering the floor, she leaped to the creekside window and saw him heading toward her crop. He rode his horse over the fireguard that Sourdough had plowed around her field and dismounted, his outline sharp in the brilliant moonlight. He went down on one knee, clutched a handful of ripe grain, struck a match on the sole of his boot, and set it alight. The stalks flared and began to burn.

"No!" Flora screamed in panic.

The man ran a few steps and started a second fire.

Flora smashed her unbroken window with the butt of her rifle and fired another shot. This time she aimed right above the man's head. He must have heard the bullet whiz past, because he flinched and glanced behind him, but continued his grim task. All along the edge of the field a row of flames leaped up to the night sky.

Having used both bullets, Flora dropped to her knees and scrambled for more. She found one but dropped it. Maddeningly, it rolled under the bed out of reach. She heard the roar of fire, jumped to her feet, and ran to the window to see what was happening.

The first rider, whose pinto was prancing and pawing the ground, drew something from his saddlebag. He struck a match on his saddle horn and ignited what looked like a log. It burst into flames so suddenly that it must have been soaked in kerosene. He flung it toward her shack.

Flora heard the whoosh of the torch and the thump on the wooden roof as it landed. She screamed, but her voice was muffled by the crackle of flames above. Tendrils of smoke began to seep from the cracks in the stovetop. There was a yell from outside. "Come on out, missy, or you'll be burned alive!"

She ran to the creek-side window again in time to see the stocky man jump off his horse. He pulled another torch from his saddlebag, ignited it, and hurled it toward the barn. It flew end over end, landed harmlessly on the sod roof, rolled off the edge, and fell into a pile of hay stacked against the outer wall. The dried grass flared up instantly and the log wall began to burn.

From the barn came a high-pitched whinny. Felicity was trapped in her stall.

Flora burst out of her shack into the fresh air, coughing and gagging. She could hear her horse's panicked cries. Ignoring the three men, she pulled her shawl over her mouth and nose and ran into the burning barn. Felicity's hooves were thumping and crashing against the rickety gate that barred the opening to her stall. Flora lifted the leather thong that held the gate shut, and the horse's terrified eyes flashed white through the smoke as she dashed past and galloped away into the night.

As Flora ran from the barn, a small furry body flew past her. Taffy tackled the stocky man, knocking him to the ground. The amiable collie had become a wild animal, biting and tearing at the man's leg. His victim tried to fend off the dog by punching it in the head.

"Get this beast off me!" he yelled at his friends.

The first man rode his pinto toward Taffy and pulled his rifle from the scabbard beside the saddle. Flora was afraid he might shoot, but instead he struck at Taffy with his rifle butt until the dog backed off, still snarling and snapping.

The sound of a woman screaming and a baby crying added to the commotion. The Penroses were on their way.

"Come on, boys, let's hightail it!" The man on the pinto wheeled and galloped toward the hill, followed by his stocky companion.

The third rider mounted his horse and followed them. Before leaving the yard, he drew to a halt and turned in the saddle for one lingering look at the blaze.

Flames shot from the windows of the shack as if they were trying to escape. Flora ran toward the door, but the searing heat drove her back. In a matter of minutes her home had become an inferno.

Her crop! She must save her crop! Flora snatched a burlap sack from the ground beside the root cellar and flew to the creek to soak it. There she met Peggy and Jack, leaping across the stones, already armed with wet sacks and shovels.

Without exchanging a word, all three hurtled toward the burning field. Flora ran so fast she hardly felt the smouldering cinders beneath her bare feet. She tore off her shawl and tossed it aside.

Although the flames sprang up higher than their heads, they attacked the blazing field with their sacks. The fire was a wild, freakish spirit bent on destruction, a thing that defied their efforts and poured over the dry field like a flood. Flora fancied she could hear the grain screaming for help as it burned to death.

Through the smoke she saw Beau running ahead of the Chicken Ladies, who were dressed in silk wrappers and rubber boots. Beau went to work beside the Penroses, while Wren began to beat the flames with a broom. Miss Edgar filled her bucket from the creek and tossed the water into the conflagration, but it vanished with no perceptible decrease in the fire. Flying embers dotted the night air in a blizzard of orange snowflakes.

"It's too late to save the crop!" Beau yelled. "We have to stop the fire before it hits the bush!" The blaze had already leaped the fireguard and ignited the long grass on the far side of Flora's wheat field. If it reached the trees, it would speed through the dry underbrush like a freight train and consume Jessie's cabin.

Flora remembered the horses trapped in their corral. Beau was the strongest runner. She shouted at him above the roar. "Jessie's horses!"

He nodded and sprinted toward the trees. Ten minutes later, five wild ponies, snorting with terror, galloped out of the bush, jumped the creek, and vanished.

With renewed desperation, the firefighters attacked the line of flame, which was dancing, rising up, and bowing down under their sacks and shovels. Back and forth, they ran to the creek to douse their smouldering sacks. Taffy charged the flames, barking as if he could scare them into submission. Gradually, the line of fire became shorter, eating itself to death in the charred earth as if chewing off its own limbs. Her face and body pouring with sweat, Flora stopped to catch her breath.

Then a sudden breeze gusted from the south. With new life, the fire turned on the wind and rushed over the grass toward them. The flames surged up again like mad demons, faster than a horse could run.

"Into the creek!" Flora heard someone scream—she thought it was Miss Edgar—and they flung themselves into the water, stained blood-red with the light of the fire. It raged after them, reaching the water's edge with a hissing fury, throwing fistfuls of sparks into their faces. Flora smelled burning hair and felt something hot strike her cheek. Everyone ducked below the surface to avoid the flying embers.

When Flora raised her head to take another breath of sizzling air, she saw Miss Edgar and Wren clinging to each other in the flickering light. Beside them, Peggy clutched her son's shoulders as they ducked and surfaced—one, two, three times.

When they raised their heads for the fourth time, they witnessed the fire's final demise. It burned itself out at the water's edge with a sibilant sound and a final explosion of sparks, as if enraged at its own failure.

The weary group stood panting and gasping in the water for a few minutes, too exhausted to move, before dragging themselves up the bank on the far side. Nellie appeared like a little white ghost in her nightgown and helped them to extinguish several small blazes, started by embers floating across the water. They could hear Jewel howling in her hammock.

When the last glowing spot was dead, Peggy and Nellie hurried back to their cabin to comfort Jewel, while Beau and Jack crossed the creek to scour the scorched earth and ensure that no deadly coals were lurking.

"Flora, you must come home with us." Miss Edgar put her arm around Flora's waist. It was only when she took a step that she realised how badly her feet were burned. The pain in her soles was agonising. "Wren, take her other side."

Together they half dragged, half carried Flora back to the yellow house. When they went inside and Miss Edgar lit the lamp, Flora felt an impulse to laugh that bordered on hysteria. The two ladies—one tall and one short—resembled blackened scarecrows, their eyelashes singed around their white eyes. She knew she must look the same.

Miss Edgar went straight to the china cabinet and poured three full glasses of brandy. After they gulped back their drinks wordlessly, she asked, "Flora, who did this?"

Through a throat stiff with smoke, she croaked, "Sterling Payne."

CHAPTER THIRTY-SIX

T his will help," Jessie said. Flora sat on the verandah while her friend knelt at her damaged feet. It was a lovely morning. Sunshine poured out of the sky like amber liquid from an azure cup, and the Manitoba maples lining the drive wore a bronze blush. Only the lingering smell of smoke cast a pall over the landscape.

Jessie held a honeycomb, salvaged from a stump she had found near her cabin. She dipped her fingers into the oozing honey and spread a thick layer on Flora's blisters. Such was her trust in Jessie's traditional knowledge that Flora uttered no protest.

"Ecclesiastes. The Lord hath created medicines out of the earth and he that is wise will not abhor them," Peggy murmured from the other rocking chair, her fair hair frizzed around her face like a burnt halo.

Flora had spent the previous two days in bed, exhausted and sick at heart. She still couldn't stand on her injured feet without assistance. This morning Wren had risen early and heated several buckets of water. She helped Flora downstairs and into her tin tub, bathing her with scented soap and tactful sympathy, washing the smoke and cinders out of her hair. Flora felt marginally better once she was dressed in Miss Edgar's twill skirt and Wren's blue-sprigged blouse.

Wren also scrubbed her flannel pyjamas, although these were so peppered with burn holes that they could serve no useful purpose other than providing patches for a quilt. Nellie found Flora's tartan shawl on the bank of the creek, reeking of smoke but with only two tiny spark holes. Wren washed and darned it, and it was flapping on the clothesline. Her Celtic brooch had been caught in the shawl's folds. Beau had polished it until it shone like one of Mrs. Galt's teaspoons, and Flora had pinned it at her throat for comfort.

As Jessie wrapped strips of cotton around her feet, Flora felt some relief from the burning sensation that had kept her tossing restlessly in Miss Edgar's bed while the older woman slept on the floor beside her.

Much worse than the pain in her feet was the agony in her breast. She had won the battle but lost the war. The Homestead Act made no exception for illness, pests, drought, flood, famine, or fire. She could never prove up now, not without a house or a barn. Although she had broken thirty acres and seeded fifteen, her crop was in ashes. She had no money, and no source of income.

"Jessie, will you please take me home?" There was a catch in Flora's voice as she uttered the words. It was no longer her home, never would be again. "I need to see it for myself."

With her usual economy of motion, the other woman turned and whistled. Tipiskow appeared at a trot, and Jessie helped Flora down the steps and hoisted her onto the horse's bare back. She led him along the trail until they reached Flora's homestead.

Before them was a scene of utter desolation. Nothing remained of the shack but a pile of charcoal and ashes. A few feathery wisps swirled into the air, caught by a passing breeze, while sunlight flashed on fragments of glass. The cookstove perched at a tilt, burned and cracked beyond repair. A couple of utensils lay amid the wreckage, but everything else had vanished.

Flora's gaze travelled with slow deliberation around the yard. Another large heap of cinders lay where the barn had stood. Lying in the debris were the metal tines of a pitchfork and a blackened tin bucket. Thankfully Felicity had escaped unhurt. That very morning she had arrived at the yellow house, stamping and whickering. She quieted when Wren opened the front door to show her that Flora was seated inside, then followed Beau to the roomy barn beside the yellow house for a rubdown and a feed of oats.

With an effort, Flora forced her eyes toward the field where her wheat children had once danced in the breeze and waved their golden heads. It was a flat black desert. Nothing remained but a thick layer of charcoal, a veritable graveyard of all her hopes.

Flora wasn't much of a crier, but without warning, her chest constricted. She made a harsh sound and began to weep with great, heaving sobs. She remembered picking out the wild oat seeds by hand, singing to the grain, cutting and stooking and winnowing. She remembered the good nutty crunch of her own whole wheat bread. All turned to dust and ashes.

Whatever would she do now? She knew the Chicken Ladies would be as generous as their purses allowed. She could borrow enough money for a one-way train ticket. Yet where would she find another refuge? She was protected here, surrounded by friends, safe from the spectre of Hector. She would have to write to Nurse Godwin and explain that her benefactor had been wrong. She didn't belong to that gallant company who sails against the tide after all. Flora buried her face in the mustang's mane and keened like a babe.

Finally she raised her head and reminded herself that she hadn't failed, not really. In her misery, Flora remembered Sterling Payne's silhouette as he fired her crop. He had been her nemesis from their first meeting at the general store, and his dislike had deepened to hatred when she had refused his so-called special arrangement. He had taken his revenge and would escape unpunished. The ladies had agreed that without proof, nobody would believe

Flora's word over his. Besides, the last thing that Flora wanted was a visit from the local Mounties.

"Do you want me to go after him?" Jessie had asked.

Although the idea of a bullwhip wrapping itself around Payne's scrawny frame was tempting, Flora shook her head. "There's no point in seeking more trouble."

Jessie had spat on the ground. "The white man always wins," she said. Now she reached into her pocket and passed over a clean handkerchief. Flora blotted her eyes, trying to compose herself.

"Someone's coming," Jessie said, gazing toward the eastern horizon. Flora couldn't see anything, but her friend had the senses of a fox. They watched until a wisp of dust appeared behind the hill.

The silhouette of a tall, bulky wagon emerged against the morning sky, drawn by a team of four heavy horses. It began to descend the hill, and another wagon took shape behind it. That one, too, was carrying a heavy load.

As the wagons slowly creaked down the hill, a buggy appeared behind them, drawn by a single horse. That was followed by a couple of riders on horseback. A third wagon took shape, then a fourth. Another pair of buggies. A two-horse team came over the hill, pulling a hayrack. Several women were seated on bales of hay piled on the flat deck, while boys and girls sat around the sides, swinging their feet.

"Where can they be going?" Flora asked.

Jessie didn't answer.

The wagons and buggies and riders continued to file down the hill in a stately procession. The Chicken Ladies appeared to see what was happening. The Penroses skipped across the creek, Jack carrying Jewel on his back.

"Who are those people, Ma?" Nellie asked.

"I don't have the foggiest," Peggy replied.

The first wagon reached the bottom of the hill and turned left. "They must be heading south," Beau said, but the driver pulled on the reins and drove into Flora's yard. He shouted at the team and brought the wagon to a halt. It was piled high with lumber.

The driver jumped from his seat and took off his hat. "Are you Miss Craigie? Where do you want your new shack? Right next to the old one?'

Flora's mouth fell open. "There must be some mistake. I didn't order any lumber. I hope you haven't come all this way for nothing, because I can't pay you."

The man grinned. "You don't need any money, Miss Craigie. When a settler gets burned out, everybody in the district pitches in to build a new house and barn for him—or her, although we've never had a her before. It's called 'a raising bee.'"

Flora looked at the parade streaming down the hill while she struggled to comprehend his words. "What, you mean—in return for nothing?"

"Yes, ma'am. If you stick around, you can repay the favour next time another poor soul loses his home. Two years ago, Mick McClarty knocked his pipe out on the top rail of his corral and practically burned down the whole territory, but everyone came out to build him a new barn—even though it was his own dang fault." He scratched his forehead as he looked around the yard. "What happened here, anyway?"

Flora avoided his eye by gazing at the charred remains. "It must have been a lightning strike."

"Is that so," he said, looking doubtful. "Well, those freak thunderstorms can be pretty unpredictable." He shouted at the man driving the wagon behind him. "Let's unload over here."

Buggies and riders began to enter the yard, tying up their horses and unpacking supplies, assisted by Jack and Beau. Following a hasty confab, the Penroses hurried home to dig up some new potatoes, and the Chicken Ladies went to gather their eggs. Food would be required, and plenty of it.

Flora was so stunned by this hive of activity that she didn't notice the rider cantering up beside her. It was Samuel Farraday.

He reached out and covered her hand where it gripped Tipiskow's mane. "Flora, I'm terribly sorry about the loss of your home and your crop, but so thankful you weren't harmed." His green eyes met her swollen red ones, which filled again at the sound of his voice.

Jessie was still standing beside the horse's head. "Her feet," was all she said.

The doctor looked down at the cloth strips soaked with honey. "Do you mind if I examine them?" Jessie led Tipiskow to the creek bank, followed by the doctor. He dismounted and took a blanket from behind his saddlebag.

"I'll see to your horse," Jessie said, and she led the palomino away. The doctor spread the blanket on the thick grass before lifting Flora from the black mustang's back. As his hands went around her waist, Flora's legs trembled, and she couldn't have stood even if her feet were uninjured. She put her arms around his neck, and he lowered her to the blanket before kneeling before her and removing the bandages.

"That must have hurt." He touched her feet tenderly, lifting each one to examine her blisters. The contact sent shock waves up her legs in a blend of pain and pleasure. He took his time wrapping them again, and his hand lingered on her bare ankle.

"I could give you some salve, but Jessie's treatment is probably just as effective. The honey will absorb the fluid from the blisters and keep the wounds moist while they heal. Are your friends taking good care of you?"

"Yes, Miss Edgar and Miss Greenwood have offered to let me stay with them until I can walk."

"I want to visit you again, make sure those blisters don't become infected." A flush covered his strong brown neck. "I can't stay and help, unfortunately. One of my patients, a little girl, has pneumonia and I must drive her into Lacombe. I came only because I wanted to see with my own eyes that you were all right." His voice was thick with emotion. "Flora, you might have been killed!"

"Dinna fash about me, Dr. Farraday. I'll be fine." Flora tried to sound as if she meant it, although she really wanted to fling herself into his arms, weeping. For a few moments, neither of them moved or spoke. A burst of laughter came from the yard, as if mocking their misery. When the doctor finally took his leave, Flora couldn't even trust herself to say goodbye. Her eyes never left his figure until he disappeared over the hill.

All that day Flora sat on the grass and watched everyone else at work. Jessie appointed herself to care for the horses, unsaddling and unhitching them, bringing them to the creek to drink, and tethering them in the shade.

Beau and Jack picked through the ruins in an effort to locate anything salvageable. Jack came running up to Flora with two sooty dimes, as pleased as if he had found pirate treasure. After they finished, the boys dug shallow holes and scraped into them the remnants of Flora's shack and barn and outhouse.

It was while they were raking the area flat that Beau gave a shout. He had discovered Flora's root cellar. The wooden cover was intact, buried under the ashes. He pried it open and climbed down the ladder, then emerged with his fist raised in triumph. Flora had harvested and stored her vegetables a week ago. She waved back, comforted by this small victory until she remembered a greater one—her cash, buried inside the cellar's earthen wall. She wasn't insolvent after all. She wept again, this time with relief.

The womenfolk used boards and sawhorses to set up tables before bringing out loaves of bread, roasts of beef, hams, jars of pickled beets, wheels of cheese, pies, cakes, and jugs of lemonade. Peggy and the Chicken Ladies returned with their own contributions, and helped to unpack the baskets of food.

One woman started a fire. Flora shrank back on her blanket when she saw the flames and smelled the smoke, but soon an enamel coffee pot was sending its fragrance through the late summer air. Tea was passed around in cups whose handles were tied with coloured yarn to mark their owners.

Meanwhile, both the shack and the barn were taking shape. A couple of experienced carpenters were appointed foremen, and everyone leaped to do their bidding. The older boys carried the lumber and tools, and the big girls minded the little ones. Children paddled in the creek, shrieking with joy as if this were an unplanned holiday. In fact, there was a festive air about the place, everyone enjoying the novelty of being together. Several old ladies had come along for the ride, and they sat in the shade, knitting and chatting.

Two members of the Country Women's Club approached Flora, each carrying a bulging flour sack. These were stuffed with articles of clothing, whatever could be spared—dresses and nightgowns and even several pairs of knickers. Flora accepted them with tearful gratitude.

Jewel toddled up and handed her a bouquet of weeds she had picked herself. "Here, Fora, for you." Flora hugged her and cried again.

Although she knew from previous experience how quickly her first shack had gone up, she was surprised at the speed with which the volunteers worked. By mid-afternoon the last roof shingle was nailed in place, and two men were installing a set of shelves and knocking together a table and a pair of chairs. It resembled her old shack, right down to the placement of the windows and door. Two boys with shovels filled in the old toilet hole and dug another, while a grizzled old farmer built a new one-holer.

It was the barn that saw the greatest improvement. The men constructed a structure twice the size of the former one, with a stall for Felicity, a hayloft above, and a separate room to be used as a granary. The roof was made of solid lumber rather than sod, finished with shingles to match the shack.

Flora was so astonished by this mass effort, so humbled by their sacrifice, that she could barely speak. She sat on her blanket and counted thirty-two men and twenty women, plus an unidentified number of children who darted here and there.

Some of the volunteers she recognised. Maisie Bell was mashing potatoes and ordering the younger girls around, talking incessantly. Flora wondered if she was gossiping about her employer, whether Mrs. Westhead knew that she had entered the enemy camp. Royal Dunne loitered near the women, no doubt checking out potential wives, making himself useful by carrying buckets of water and stoking the fire.

Mr. Sanderson approached her, twisting his hat in his hands. "Just run up everything you need at the store, Miss Craigie. I was wrong to take away your credit. I'm real sorry."

James Raeburn, who had spoken against women farmers at the meeting, was on the barn roof, driving shingle nails. His wife, Gertrude, who had defended them, brought her a plate of cold ham and potato salad. It seemed everyone wanted to feed her. In an outpouring of sympathy, she was offered multiple cups of tea and pieces of cake. Filled with gratitude, Flora managed to choke down a few bites.

In the late afternoon Mr. Frederick, the newspaper editor, arrived on horseback. "I'm here to take your photograph for the *Toddsville Free Press*, ma'am, although it won't be called that much longer. As soon as I change my printing plates, it will become the *Alix Free Press*." Wanting her neighbours to receive public acknowledgement for their efforts, Flora felt she couldn't refuse. He helped her onto a chair, and she sat in front of her new shack while he positioned his camera on a tripod and took several photos.

As the setting sun washed the wooden planks of her new home with rosy light, the horses were saddled and harnessed, the tables knocked down, and the extra lumber piled inside the new barn. One by one, Flora's neighbours said goodbye. Some of them shook her hand, others stood abashed while Flora showered them with thanks, soaking so many cotton handkerchiefs that Beau had to lend her one of his fancy silk numbers.

The last man to leave was Sourdough. "Don't you worry, Flora," he said in his usual growl. "The Homestead Act says you need thirty acres in crop, but it don't say nothing about a harvest. You still got your seed wheat over at the Penrose place, and next spring I'll plant the whole thirty acres before deadline. That fire probably done you some good! It burned out the wild oats, and all them ashes make the best fertiliser."

He gave a wolfish grin. "I'll be jiggered if you don't have a bumper crop next year!"

CHAPTER THIRTY-SEVEN

A sudden squall blew up out of the west. The lightning came down in bolts like jagged teeth, and the wind howled around the yellow house with such energy that Flora and Miss Edgar couldn't hear each other without raising their voices. Every few minutes a splatter of leaves struck the windowpanes.

It was cozy inside, though, with the lamp glowing softly and the stove giving off its embracing warmth. Wren had gone upstairs to bed, and Miss Edgar was reading Darwin's *The Origin of Species* while she enjoyed her nightly cigarette.

Flora sat in one of the Morris chairs, trying to make herself useful by mending one of Wren's pretty blouses. She was still limping, but she planned to move into her new shack the next morning. Much as she enjoyed the company of the Chicken Ladies, she had been there for ten days and was reluctant to take advantage of their generosity any longer.

A particularly fierce gust of wind rattled the windows, followed by a violent hammering on the door. Flora and Miss Edgar exchanged baffled looks while she butted out her cigarette and hurriedly rose. Who would be out in this weather? Not Beau; he had celebrated his eighteenth birthday two days ago and left for Red Deer to file his claim at last. As Miss Edgar rushed across the room, there was a series of thuds that sounded as if the door were being kicked. Before she could get there, it flew open and crashed against the wall.

A man pushed past Miss Edgar, shoving her aside. He wore a long oilskin coat to his ankles and a broad-brimmed hat, dripping with water. Through the open door, Flora glimpsed his horse tied to the post, hindquarters turned into the howling wind. Miss Edgar slammed the door with difficulty against the gale.

"Gracious, what a terrible night!" she said. "You poor man! Take off your wet things and I'll fetch you a towel!" She hurried into the kitchen. The man removed his hat, revealing his bald crown. His drenched hair hung in strings over his eyes. Flora dropped her mending on the floor, and her fists closed around the arms of the chair. She knew this man.

It was Hector Mackle.

He hadn't noticed her yet, because he was shrugging off his coat and dropping it to the floor. When Miss Edgar returned and handed him a striped kitchen towel, he snatched it and began to mop his face and head. He didn't resemble the dapper gentleman that Flora had married: he was gaunt, and his skin was covered with open sores the size of silver dollars.

Only after he lowered the towel did he look around the room. Flora observed his blue eyes light up with fiendish glee as he recognised her.

"My darling wife!" he said, his voice triumphant. "How delightful to see you again!"

Flora didn't answer. She jumped to her feet and moved behind the armchair for protection, clutching the back with both hands.

Hector spoke in a gloating manner. "Did you honestly believe that I wouldn't find you? You aren't as clever as you thought you were, flaunting yourself on a public stage, spouting off in front of a newspaper reporter!"

"Mr. Mackle, I presume," Miss Edgar said, obviously grasping the situation.

"So you know my name!" Hector spoke to Miss Edgar but didn't take his eyes off Flora. "What is your part in this deception, madam? And where is your own husband?"

"I am unmarried," Miss Edgar said.

Hector gave a sarcastic laugh. "Somehow that doesn't surprise me."

The older woman lifted her chin and expanded her chest, the way Sourdough had told them to behave if threatened by a wild animal. "That is none of your business, sir, and I'll thank you not to address me in that tone."

Flora admired her attitude. Of course, Miss Edgar didn't know Hector as well as she did.

He began to pace around the room, leaving a trail of wet footprints behind him. Flora wondered if he was drunk, but he wasn't staggering. Instead, his movements were strangely jerky and uncoordinated, as though he were a puppet controlled by invisible strings. Behind his back, Miss Edgar touched her finger to her lips and tilted her head toward the staircase. Flora understood that she wanted to conceal Wren's presence. She nodded in agreement.

"Mr. Mackle, may I ask how you happened to come here?" Miss Edgar used her most dignified voice.

He answered her while opening the closet in the far corner and checking its contents. "I took the train to Lacombe, hired a horse, and followed the Buffalo Lake Trail. The Red Deer paper gave the location of my wife's homestead." He slammed the closet door. "When I came down the hill and saw your light, I assumed this was the place. What a fortunate coincidence that I was wrong."

He glanced into the kitchen to satisfy himself that it was empty before his eyes turned toward the staircase. "Does anyone else live here?"

"No." Miss Edgar's reply was swift.

"And this house belongs to you?"

"Yes, this is my house."

Her answer enraged him. "What kind of country is this, where women live in luxury and men labour like oxen?" he shouted. "I suppose you drove some poor man into his grave, and this is your reward!"

Taking a step backward, Miss Edgar changed her tactics. "Mr. Mackle, there's no need to insult me. Won't you at least sit down so we can discuss the matter?" She spoke in a conciliatory tone, gesturing toward the armchair. "I can fetch some dry clothes and make you something to eat. I don't have a spare bed, but you're welcome to sleep in the barn."

"Sleep in the barn, like one of your pigs! How generous of you!" Furiously, Hector reached out one arm and swept everything off the side table—her book, her ashtray, her reading spectacles, and her good Waterford crystal tumbler, which shattered into pieces.

The mood in the room changed abruptly. There would be no reasoning with him.

Flora glanced around for a weapon, but nothing was visible, not even a broom. She knew the Chicken Ladies owned a rifle, but Beau always took it with him when he went somewhere, to defend himself against wild animals or unfriendly strangers.

She thought longingly of her own rifle, leaning against the corner of her new shack. She briefly considered making a run for it, but she couldn't move fast or far on her injured feet. Even now, her soles were beginning to throb as she stood behind the armchair. She suppressed a whimper of despair.

Miss Edgar made one final attempt to placate Hector. "Mr. Mackle, you're soaked to the skin and you don't look at all well. Let me fetch you a drink. I have some whisky in the cabinet."

He heard the quaver in her voice, and grinned as if that gave him pleasure. "You're damned right I'm not well! The sawbones told me I only have a few weeks left. But I'm not leaving this world until I settle my score with this little slut!"

Hector leered at Flora. "Maybe you wanted to be found, my dear Mrs.

Mackle. Maybe homesteading isn't the cakewalk you thought it would be. Are you ready to come home with me and be a faithful wife, as you promised before God?"

Flora hesitated. Perhaps if she agreed to go with him, he would leave without causing any more trouble. And it was an unarguable fact that she had promised to follow him in sickness and in health.

But when she remembered how he had behaved on the train, her Scottish fighting blood rose. She wasn't that same timid girl any longer. She was as strong, as fearless as any man. She would not submit to Hector's brutality, nor would she run away and hide like a frightened jackrabbit.

"Nay, Hector, I canna do that." She glared back into his angry red eyes. "I would rather die than live with you!"

"By God, if you won't come with me, then we'll both go to hell!"

Hector lunged toward her, but Flora evaded his grasp and raced toward the door, heedless of her injured feet. She wrenched it open, a blast of icy rain blowing into the room, but Hector was close behind. He slammed it shut again.

Flora whirled to face him. He pinned her against the door with one forearm against her throat and slapped her, first on one cheek, and then the other. She was astonished by how much the blows stung. Her ears rang with the pain and shock. I mustn't cry out, she vowed, whatever he does. If Wren come downstairs, he'll murder all of us.

Through her tears, she saw Miss Edgar leap toward the stove and snatch the poker from the wood box. As Hector slapped Flora again, the older woman ran up behind him, but before she had a chance to strike, he turned and wrenched the poker away from her. Flora grabbed his arm and tried to deflect the blow, but the poker struck Miss Edgar on her temple. She crumpled to the floor.

Flora screamed then; she couldn't help it. Hector dropped the poker, grabbed her throat and began to squeeze. His fingers burned as if he had a fever. Flora couldn't draw a breath. The pain in her lungs was excruciating, and she clawed at his wrists to no avail. He seemed possessed with superhuman strength. The pressure grew behind her eyeballs until she could no longer see the room, only the face of the monster, mottled with bleeding scabs, his yellow teeth bared in the growing darkness, a string of saliva hanging from his red lips.

The nightmare was coming true after all.

As her field of vision began to shrink, she heard a shrill voice.

"Let her go!"

Over Hector's shoulder, she saw Wren on the landing in her ruffled nightgown, her hair rolled up in rags. She was pointing what looked like a toy gun.

Hector's hands released their grip. Flora took a rasping breath, drawing air into her tortured lungs, as he turned and headed toward the stairs.

"Don't come any closer, or I'll shoot!" Wren's voice sounded like the shriek of a frightened child. She was clutching the gun in both hands, but they were shaking so much Flora thought she might drop it.

Hector paid no attention to her warning. He vaulted up the stairs and grabbed for the barrel. Wren clung to it, and for a few seconds there was a brief tug of war as they teetered back and forth.

"Give it to me, you bitch!" Hector shouted, with one mighty wrench. Still hanging on to the gun, Wren lost her balance and fell against him.

There was a deafening bang. Hector tumbled down the steps and fell onto his back, with Wren sprawled across his chest. The gun flew into the air, landed on the floor, revolved several times like a spinning top, and slowed to a halt.

Nobody moved. The room was utterly silent except for the keening of the wind outside. Flora sank to the floor in a faint.

Everything was pale and blurry, as though a winter fog had stolen into the room. The shapes of the furniture seemed to shimmer. Flora wondered why she was lying on the floor. Wren was kneeling beside her, dabbing Flora's temples with a damp towel, and Miss Edgar was seated in her usual chair.

Perhaps she had been dreaming. So often she had experienced the same hideous nightmare, that Hector was trying to kill her.

Then she saw the livid bruise on Miss Edgar's temple. Flora jerked awake. "Where is he?" Her voice sounded like the croak of a crow.

There was a brief pause before Miss Edgar answered. "He's gone."

"Thank God!" The wind was still shrieking around the eaves, the rain lashing the windows. She fervently hoped that Hector would perish in the storm. "Miss Edgar, are you injured?"

Miss Edgar's voice was faint. "I'm perfectly all right, my dear. Merely a bump on the head."

Flora pulled herself into a sitting position. It was only then that she saw Hector lying at the foot of the stairs, arms and legs crookedly akimbo, sprawled in the centre of a small crimson lake. There was a ragged bullet hole over his heart, and he was clearly dead.

Flora turned toward Wren and cried out with alarm. A lurid stain covered the front of Wren's nightgown, the colour of claret. The wet cotton was plastered against her bare skin. For one dreadful moment, Flora thought she must be mortally wounded.

"Wren, are you hurt?"

Wren's face was ashen. She was still patting Flora's forehead with the towel in a mechanical fashion. Her eyes stared ahead, unblinking.

At the sound of Flora's horrified exclamation, Wren woke from her trance. She stared around wild-eyed, and then gave a piercing shriek. "He was going to kill you, Flora!" she screamed. "He was strangling you!" She threw back her head and gave way to hysterics. Flora put her arm around Wren and patted her back, averting her eyes from the gruesome corpse.

Miss Edgar, unsteady after the blow to her head, rose and took a knitted afghan from the rocking chair. She threw it over the body before tottering to the cabinet and bringing out a bottle of brandy. She knelt beside the two women, took Wren's chin in her hand, and forced her to drink straight from the bottle until Wren's sobs subsided to whimpers.

After she was calm enough, Miss Edgar and Flora removed Wren's bloody nightgown, wrapped her in a quilt, and made her lie back in her rocking chair. Within minutes, the combination of shock and strong drink caused her to fall into an exhausted slumber.

"I didn't even know she had a gun until we arrived," Miss Edgar said in a low voice. "She was so anxious about moving to the wilderness that she bought this derringer before we left Boston, and hid it in her trunk. The salesman told her it was the perfect weapon for a lady. Frankly, I'm surprised she even knew how to load it."

Miss Edgar made her way back to the cabinet and took out two of her best Coalport teacups, apparently too shaken to bother with the crystal glasses. She filled the cups to the brim with the remaining brandy and handed one to Flora. Huddled together on their chairs, they sipped their brandy and discussed in whispers what to do next.

Their first inclination was to take the buggy into Lacombe and surrender to the Mounties, explain what had happened. But the more they talked, the less probable it seemed that anyone would believe them.

"She shot an unarmed man, Flora." Miss Edgar glanced over to make sure Wren was asleep. "There would have to be an inquest. She might even go to prison."

Flora moaned, and the sound hurt her bruised vocal cords. "I'll tell them I did it. I'm the only one with a motive for murder."

"If you gave a false confession, which I strenuously oppose, Ladyville would be tainted by this sensational crime. Public opinion would turn against us, and all our hard work would be undone. Your homestead would be confiscated."

"I'll run away, change my name, lose myself in the States."

"It's doubtful that you can hide this time, Flora. And your flight would be seen as an admission of guilt. No, we must find another way."

Flora set down her empty teacup and buried her face in her hands. Her mind was blank. She hadn't understood what this meant until now, as if an unseen paintbrush had swept every thought from her head and left behind a barren white snowscape. Both women sat motionless and silent.

Flora remembered finding a rabbit in one of Jack's snares, writhing and squeaking. She had steeled herself and struck it on the head with a rock to put the poor thing out of its misery. She wished she could do the same to herself. In fact, that was the first good idea she had come up with. She looked at the dainty yet deadly little weapon lying on the floor. It had two barrels, and she wondered whether Wren had loaded more than one bullet.

Miss Edgar's eyes followed hers. "Flora, don't even contemplate such a thing!" She reached out and squeezed Flora's hand. "I have a better solution. The more I think about it, it's the only solution."

"What is it?" Flora asked in a dull voice, still eyeing the weapon. She couldn't help thinking that the situation would be resolved if she simply ceased to go on living, although her heart and soul rebelled against the notion. She didn't want to die yet. She wanted to feel the sun rise tomorrow, smell the wild roses, and admire her own waving grain. Mostly, she wanted to see Samuel's face again. Flora turned and looked at Miss Edgar, hardly daring to hope.

"That horrid creature rode out from Lacombe. Since he was up to no good, it's unlikely he told anyone where he was going. He might have headed in any direction. Besides, the prairie between here and there is wild, the trail so poorly marked, that anything might have happened to him. Remember that sewing machine salesman from Calgary who went missing last year and hasn't been seen since? He could have ridden off a cliff into the river or been eaten by wolves."

Flora closed her eyes and shook her head. "I don't understand."

"You must ride that man's horse across the field and fetch Jessie. Obviously neither she nor the Penroses heard the shot because of the storm, otherwise they would have been here."

Flora's eyes flew open. "How can she help?"

"She can dispose of the body so that it will never be found."

CHAPTER THIRTY-EIGHT

Two days later, Flora woke in her own shack. She lay still and held her breath, waiting for the familiar rush of fear and guilt. There was none. She felt only a blessed sense of release. She stretched her arms above her head and pointed her toes, filling her lungs with the scent of fresh resin. Birds twittered rapturously in the poplars outside, heralding a new morn, and the ruby dawn flooded her window as the earth turned inexorably on its axis.

The nightmare was over.

Flora had not prayed for a long time, but now she asked God that the other women would be granted the same peace of mind. Miss Edgar, with her sanguine approach to practical matters, had shown no qualms over Hector's death. And Jessie had rolled his body in the braided rug and loaded it onto his horse as though it were no more than a haunch of venison. They had agreed to keep Peggy in blissful ignorance, and they had made a solemn vow never to speak of Hector again. Nevertheless, Flora was a little concerned about Wren— soft-hearted Wren, who shed tears whenever one of the barn cats killed a mouse. Miss Edgar said she hadn't been sleeping well.

After lunch, Flora and Peggy strolled down the path leading to Jessie's cabin, happily discussing Jack's marksmanship, Nellie's journal, and Jewel's newfound attachment to Sourdough. Their progress was slow because Flora had to tread carefully, clinging to the widow's arm.

When they reached the trees, Jessie's mongrels ran toward them, wagging their tails and stretching out their necks to be petted, followed by their owner.

"I brought back your honey," Flora said, handing her a jar. "Dr. Farraday said it was a miracle cure." The doctor had visited twice, examining her feet so gently that Flora could barely keep her composure. Her injuries were healing, and he didn't need to see her again. Flora almost wished her feet had been more badly burned.

The three women stood chatting beside the scorched area that ran to the perimeter of the bush. It looked as if a flood of pitch had poured over the meadow and ended at the creek. The bare ground was dotted with rocks, twisted roots, and chunks of sod, all covered with fine black ash. The smell of soot marred the sweet autumn air. Yet amid the devastation, the charred landscape was already showing tendrils of green. "That's fireweed," Jessie said. "It's the first thing to grow after a fire. Before long, this whole area will be covered with purple flowers as high as my waist. If you grind the roots into powder, it cures all kinds of skin sores."

Peggy bent down. Flora thought she was inspecting the tender new shoots of fireweed, but she picked up a lump of dirt the size of her fist.

"What are you doing?" Jessie asked.

Without answering, Peggy turned over the lump and studied it. She spat on it and rubbed it with a fold of her apron, regardless of the ashes dirtying the front of her dress. She squatted and reached for another lump, hefting it in her hand before tossing it aside and picking up a third.

The other two women exchanged puzzled frowns. "What on earth are you looking for?" Flora asked.

Peggy didn't reply. She set off through the ashes with her head bent, as though searching for a lost coin. Every few steps, she examined another black chunk. Flora and Jessie watched as she made her way through the burned area, the hem of her dress dragging in the soot, to the far edge of the blackened meadow. Without a backward glance, she vanished into the trees.

"Peggy?" Flora called out. She was a little alarmed. After all these months of anxiety, had her friend finally become bushed? She was about to follow when Peggy emerged from the trees and hurried back to them, holding another dark lump in her dirty hands, her eyes shining. She gave a childlike skip, and the ashes rose around her in a small cloud.

"Jessie, you'll never guess what this is!" she said.

"I have no idea."

"Coal!" Peggy's eyes were shining with excitement.

"Are you sure?" Flora asked.

Peggy laughed. "If there's one thing I know, my dears, it's coal. I've breathed in coal dust, eaten it, and slept in it the better part of my life. Watch this." She placed the lump on the ground and poked around until she found a pointed rock. Bending down, she struck the lump smartly with the rock and it split cleanly into two pieces, each with a smooth side that glistened like ebony in the sunlight. "If I'm not mistaken, a seam of coal runs across the surface of Jessie's property!"

Smiling at their stunned expressions, she handed them each a piece. "Here, see for yourself."

They bent their heads over it. It was coal, all right. Flora had hauled enough buckets of coal up the stairs from the cellar to Mrs. Galt's bedroom to recognise it.

"Think of all the work we did cutting firewood," Peggy said, "and we have the world's best source of heat right here!"

"Is it worth anything?" Jessie asked.

"Jessie, the coal mines down south at Lethbridge are worth a fortune. They supply the CPR's entire rail network. If this is a producing seam, your land will become incredibly valuable!"

Jessie took the lump in her hands and turned it over as if she couldn't believe it, but Flora sensed her excitement. "I've heard about Lethbridge. The Blackfoot call it 'the place of the black rocks.' How can I find out more?"

"I know just the man!" Flora said. "I'll write to the lawyer in Red Deer, Mr. Greene. He can have the property assessed." All at once she started to laugh, and Peggy followed. After a few seconds, Jessie joined them. It was so rare to see her white teeth flashing in her tanned face that the other women laughed even harder.

"The government gave this land to your father because they thought it was worthless," Flora said, trying to collect herself. "Not only that, if the fire hadn't burned off the ground cover, we would never have found it. It might have lain here for centuries."

Flora started to laugh again. "And it's all thanks to our beloved Mr. Payne!"

CHAPTER THIRTY-NINE

Eager to repay the Chicken Ladies for their hospitality, Flora offered to gather the eggs each morning. This was no sacrifice, because she loved lifting the puffy-chested Buffs off their nests and finding the warm eggs nestled in the straw like buried treasure. She took them into the yellow house and wiped each one carefully with warm water before packing them in sawdust. Mr. Sanderson was once again taking all the eggs that Wren could provide.

This morning, Peggy joined her in the coop to collect her own eggs in exchange for her weekly delivery of milk and butter. The two women had filled their baskets and returned to the front steps when a wagon drove into the yard. Perched on the seat was a large woman with a long face.

"It's Maisie Bell!" Flora said. "You know, that gossip who works for Alix Westhead. I wonder what she wants."

Miss Bell clambered down from the wagon seat and came to the door. "Good morning, ladies," she said. "Miss Craigie, I checked your claim and saw you weren't there, so I decided to mosey on over here. Good thing I did. I got something to tell you, all of you."

"Good afternoon, Miss Bell," Flora said, dreading whatever unwelcome message the woman might be bringing from her employer. She and Peggy exchanged apprehensive looks.

They went inside and Flora introduced the Chicken Ladies. Maisie shook hands with everyone before plumping down in Wren's rocking chair without being asked, like a broody Buff Orpington. Her eyes roved around the room. "You got a nice little spread here. No wonder you weren't all atingle about giving it up."

"Thank you, Miss Bell." Miss Edgar took command, as usual. "I take it you are here on an errand for Mrs. Westhead?"

"Nope. I quit the ranch. I've had enough kowtowing to her ladyship."

Miss Edgar cocked one eyebrow. "I see. Then how can we help you?"

Maisie leaned forward in her chair with an air of importance. Her eyes fixed on the other women one by one as if she wanted to make sure they were listening. "I stopped by to tell you ladies a secret."

Miss Edgar frowned. "Miss Bell, if this is confidential, perhaps you shouldn't say anything."

Maisie chuckled. "Oh, this is too good to keep under my hat! Besides, it concerns Ladyville."

Miss Edgar set her jaw as if she were bracing herself. "Go on, then."

"Nobody knows why Van Horne showed up at that meeting in Red Deer and saved your bacon. Nobody but me, that is."

This was so unlikely that Flora thought the poor woman must be delusional, or desperate for attention. Maisie Bell seemed like the last person to have insider knowledge about the workings of the mighty Canadian Pacific Railway.

Maisie took a deep breath, looking like a cat about to relish a dish full of cream. She actually smacked her lips before she spoke, as if savouring her information. "It was all down to her ladyship, Mrs. High-and-Mighty herself."

Miss Edgar frowned. "Miss Bell, please get to the point."

"All right, then." Maisie leaned forward again with an eager look on her face. "Two years ago, her ladyship went over to England because her father was sick. I don't believe he was that sick, that was just an excuse to make a trip back home. She stayed for two months, and while she was there she swanned around, going to parties and balls. At one of those shindigs she met Van Horne, and I guess they got along like a house on fire."

Maisie certainly had everyone's attention now. She looked around again, enjoying their expressions, before she continued.

"Van Horne arranged it so they come back on the same ship together—the *Empress of Britain*, he designed that ship himself. And the two of them got friendly—very friendly, if you take my meaning. She ain't near as ladylike as she lets on."

Flora and Peggy exchanged scandalised looks. Miss Edgar raised her hand in a commanding fashion. "Miss Bell, stop. You can't possibly know this."

"Oh yes I can! I heard it straight from her own mouth!"

"She told you?" Miss Edgar shook her head. "You can appreciate, Miss Bell, that this is a difficult tale to swallow."

"She didn't exactly tell me herself, but I heard her say it. She and Mr. Westhead had a real barney one night. He was drunk and she was giving him holy hell because he didn't write a cheque for their new bull, King of the Cedars. She was always after him like that, pestering the life out of him about ranch business, why he didn't take more of an interest, how he was running the place into the ground.

"Anyway, things got heated and he called her a real bad word, I won't repeat it, and said he wished he never married her. Then she got on her high horse and sez, 'And what's more, I haven't been faithful to you!' And he sez, 'What the deuce do you mean?' And she sez, 'I had a very satisfying dalliance—that's what she called it, 'a dalliance'—'with the CPR chairman himself, Mr. William Van Horne, when we was sailing back to Canada.' And he sez, 'My God, he must have been that desperate to sleep with a cold mackerel like you.' And she sez, 'Well, at least he likes women instead of stable boys.'"

There was a horrified silence before Miss Edgar spoke, sounding angry. "Miss Bell, this is nothing but hearsay. You don't even know if it's true."

Maisie lifted her chin. "I do know it! I know it for a fact. Because three weeks before that meeting in Red Deer, she give me a letter and told me to take the buggy into Lacombe and mail it for her, and mum's the word. So while I was taking my own sweet time on the trail, I thought I might have a look-see, so I picked it open and read it, and make no mistake, she and him were an item, all right. I'll spare you the gory details since you're too respectable to hear them.

"She told him all about the big problem Ladyville was having and she said it was a crying shame and she asked him to straighten out that scoundrel Frank Oliver. She said Oliver wasn't the gentleman she thought he was. And then I sealed up the envelope and popped it in the mail and came back home, after I had a nice steak dinner and spent the night at the Metropolitan Hotel in Lacombe."

There was another stunned silence.

Flora, Wren, and Peggy swivelled their heads simultaneously toward Miss Edgar, hoping she would know what to say, while Maisie leaned back in her chair, beaming with satisfaction.

Miss Edgar took a deep breath. "Well. That is most enlightening. I sincerely hope you haven't shared this information with anyone else."

Maisie dropped her eyes to the bare wooden floor where the braided rug had once warmed the room. "I ain't told nobody else," she muttered, but it was obvious that she was lying.

Miss Edgar tried again. "For your own sake, Miss Bell, please don't mention that you tampered with Mrs. Westhead's mail. That would seriously hinder your chances of ever getting another position."

"I don't care!" Maisie said and tossed her head, which Flora thought made her look remarkably like Felicity. "I'm on my way to visit my intended, Royal Dunne. We're getting hitched next month. I'm a good cook and he's lucky to have me. I reckon I won't have to bow down to anybody ever again."

She slapped her palms on her large knees and hoisted herself out of the chair. "Well, I better be off. I have a list for Mr. Dunne, things I want him to buy before the big day. Since I was going down the Buffalo Trail anyways, I thought I would put you ladies in the know."

Wren piped up then, although her voice was fainter than usual. Even this bombshell could not affect her natural desire to play hostess. "Miss Bell, do let me give you some luncheon before you leave. You must be very hot and thirsty."

"Thank you, ma'am, that's kind of you. I don't suppose you have any saskatoon pie? That's my favourite."

CHAPTER FORTY

Flora was splitting firewood, panting with exertion and reflecting on the truth of the old homily that he who chops his own wood warms himself twice. She was imagining the blessed convenience of a coal fire when Beau came around the corner, dapper as usual in a royal purple shirt, and invited her to visit the yellow house.

Flora leaned on her axe handle to catch her breath. "I'll come when I finish this pile. Beau, I hear congratulations are in order!"

Beau's chest stuck out so far that his brass buttons nearly popped. "Yes, ma'am, I got my own homestead at last. It was a lucky break that the quarter to the west of the Chicken Ladies wasn't filed on yet. The ladies said I can keep living in their cabin until I build my own, come spring."

An hour later Flora walked up the driveway. The Manitoba maples flamed scarlet, the October sky radiated deep blue, and the yellow house mirrored the sunshine. Rows of sunflowers taller than Flora's head lined the front path. The door stood open to welcome the fresh autumn breeze, and the lace curtains fluttered merrily. This was a house built to last, Flora thought, a house to grow old in.

Yet when she called hello and stepped inside, she saw two calfskin trunks in the living room, strapped shut. The ladies were seated in their usual chairs, but they jumped to their feet when Flora entered. "What's all this?" she asked. "Are you going on a holiday?"

"There's no easy way to tell you, Flora," Miss Edgar's voice sounded sad. "We're moving back to the States, to a little town named Santa Barbara on the California coast. We have decided that Canada isn't the right place for us after all."

"Nay, surely not!" Flora exclaimed, clasping her hands to her chest. "I hope you're not going because . . . you know, because of what happened! I could never forgive myself!"

"No, Flora, it's nothing to do with you. It was your initiative that allowed us to keep the ownership of our farm in the first place. However, this country hasn't provided the refuge that we sought when we left Boston, to put it mildly. As for the climate—well, let's just say that the California weather is more conducive to raising chickens."

"Chickens and children!" Wren broke in, showing her dimples. She still had dark rings under her eyes, but looked more like her old self. "We've been discussing this for ages, and we've decided to adopt a baby boy. I've always wanted a child, and Robbie finally agreed!"

"That's wonderful, Wren. He'll be a lucky laddie with you two as parents." Flora tried to smile through the painful prospect of losing her friends.

"We'll raise him to be the type of man we admire, although admittedly those are few and far between. A man like our dear Dr. Farraday!"

"I can't say I blame you for leaving, but Ladyville won't be the same without you!" Flora bit her lower lip to stop her chin from trembling.

Miss Edgar's dark eyes were sympathetic. "We have all formed a special bond, it's true. We shall miss everyone, especially you, Flora."

Wren's eyes were filled with tears. "We already said our goodbyes to the

Penrose family. We're so fond of the children. We asked Peggy if she would allow us to pay for Nellie's education. That child should go to high school and college, too, if she wishes. I gave her my dear Buffies because I know she'll take good care of them. It will be a nice little source of income, too, since she can sell her eggs to the CPR once the new station is built."

"That's most generous, Wren. You've done so much for women in this country—both of you. You'll be sorely missed." Flora's voice was unsteady.

Miss Edgar nodded. "I believe we have created a few inroads into the old dogmatic ways of thinking. But for us, the race is run. We aren't getting any younger, you know. The great philosopher Dr. Johnson said it best: 'To be happy at home is the ultimate result of all ambition.' We came in search of a quiet life, and we're determined to find one."

Flora was too stricken to answer. As Jessie once put it, she felt as if all her hides had floated away.

Miss Edgar wasn't finished. "One more thing. Forgive me if I am speaking out of turn, Flora, but we only want your happiness. Samuel Farraday has become our friend as well as our doctor. He told us that he offered for your hand last spring, and you refused him. We expected no less of you, although that must have been difficult. If I'm not mistaken, his feelings are reciprocated."

Flora shook her head. "I'm afraid it's too late." Beau had mentioned seeing Dr. Farraday at the fall fair with a farmer's daughter named Clara Nelson. She looked pretty soft on the doctor, he said with a wink—not realising that his words were like a dirk to Flora's heart.

"I beg to differ. The doctor strikes me as a man whose affections remain constant."

Flora didn't answer, so Miss Edgar changed the subject. "We hope you'll write to us regularly and keep us apprised of the situation here. I understand the CPR is considering the name Ladyville for its new station. That would be poetic justice indeed."

"Goodbye, dear Flora. We'll never forget you." Wren enfolded her in a hug, and Flora returned her warm embrace.

"Thank you again, Wren," Flora whispered, "for everything." Wren only hugged her harder. Miss Edgar wrung her hand and wished her every success.

Her last sight of them was one tall figure and one short, standing on their verandah, waving their handkerchiefs. Flora stumbled down the lane, blinded with tears.

The threshing crew arrived this year right on time—Sourdough saw to that—and since Flora had no grain to harvest, she was helping Peggy feed the hungry horde. She finished shaping the last two loaves of bread and popped them into the oven. When they were baked, she would take them, along with the pot of beans simmering on the stove, over to the Penrose place, adding them to the mountain of food they had already prepared. Eight men would soon stagger into the yard, hot and tired and covered with wheat chaff, their eyes red and sore from the dust.

The area womenfolk competed to see who could provide the most plentiful meals, and the ladies of Ladyville were determined not to let the side down. Besides, the crew always came back first the following year to the farm with the best grub. Peggy was famous for her homemade doughnuts. "I've fried enough to form a daisy chain to heaven," she said.

The stove made the shack so hot that Flora poured herself a mug of tea and took her chair outside to sit in the shade. She heard the curious drumbeat of the steam engine across the creek, saw the men tossing sheaves into the hopper, the steam belching into the hot blue sky while a thick stream of gold poured out of the spout and into the wagon.

Flora was still mourning the loss of her own crop. However—she echoed the words of farmers throughout the centuries—there was always next year. She had heard the pattern of prairie life described as windbreak, firebreak, back-break, and heartbreak. Well, she had survived it all—especially the heartbreak.

As she sat in the sunshine admiring the sight of someone else doing the work for once, Jessie appeared. She cantered up to Flora's shack and vaulted off her horse.

"Hello, Jessie! I just boiled the kettle. Would you like some tea?"

"No thanks, Flora. I came to say goodbye."

"Where are you off to now?" Jessie's business often took her away for days at a time.

"I'm leaving these parts."

"Leaving? For how long?"

"For good."

Flora stood up so quickly that her tea slopped out of her enamel mug. "I thought you were so attached to your land!"

"It wasn't the land, Flora, it was my legal rights. That quarter is no good for horses, anyway. Mr. Greene wrote and told me he has a real nice offer from the coal company. With what they're going to pay me, I can buy anything I want."

Jessie had a faraway look on her face. "I've always dreamed about having my own horse ranch. I can build up a nice herd, breed some, break some, hire a few Indian cowboys to work for me. I know I can make a go of it. If there's one thing everybody needs, it's horses."

Flora was staggered. First the Chicken Ladies, and now Jessie! "What would your father think?"

"My father would be tickled if he knew that I put one over on the government. I'll bet my ancestors are performing a victory dance around the fire right now!"

"Oh, Jessie, I'll miss you!" She remembered how much her friend had done for them, riding for the doctor, whipping that horrible Mr. Dawson, sharing her knowledge. If Jessie hadn't spirited Hector's body away to lie in some unknown grave, Flora would probably be languishing behind bars.

"I'll miss you too." Jessie spoke with an effort. "I thought white women had no gumption, but you proved me wrong. We share a lot of common enemies, whether it's bad weather or bad horses or bad men."

"That's very true." Flora's eyes were brimming.

"I'm going to spend the winter with my people and hunt for ranch land next spring. Why don't you come for a visit? I'll show you the north country."

"I would love that!" Flora said. "I'm eager to see more of Canada. The longer I'm here, the deeper I fall in love with it. This country will have my bones."

"I'll write to you when I get home. There's no steel north of Edmonton, but I can meet you at the North Saskatchewan River with a couple of good horses."

Flora didn't want to embarrass Jessie by embracing her, so she held out her hand. To her surprise, the other woman wrapped her in a hard hug. She smelled like horses and buckskin and sweet grass and prairie wind.

Without another word, she vaulted onto Tipiskow and galloped away.

A second successful harvest was safely in the barn. The crop had "gone" to forty bushels an acre, as the locals said, and the Penroses were elated. Today Flora was going to mind darling little Jewel while Peggy drove the other children to town in the wagon to choose some yard goods for their new clothes. Over the summer they had outgrown everything they owned.

Flora skipped across the stones on feet that were completely healed. The doctor had told her the extra scar tissue on her soles would make it easier to go barefoot. The creek flowed smoothly between its banks, an undulating band of liquid cobalt that reflected the infinite sky above. The leaves fluttered like scarlet and bronze coins. A black vee of honking geese headed for warmer climes.

Flora arrived at the cabin door as Peggy emerged, a pail in each hand.

"Hello, Flora! Come to the barn with me while I do the milking. I want to tell you something."

Flora followed her into the warm barn and dropped onto a pile of fragrant hay while Peggy settled herself on the milking stool.

"Do you remember how much Blossom frightened me when we first arrived?" she asked. "I was so afraid of her that I did the milking through the bars of the stall. And I squeezed for an hour to get a cup of milk!" She grasped the cow's teat and a stream of warm milk gushed out.

Flora laughed. "You couldn't call us greenhorns now."

"No, indeed. There have been a lot of changes since then." The milk squirted rhythmically into the metal pail. "And there's going to be another one, come spring."

"What is it?" Flora asked. "Are you getting another cow?"

"No, but I'm getting an extra three hundred and twenty acres. And a husband, to boot."

Flora sat bolt upright. "A husband! Are you joking?"

"No, Flora. I'm going to marry Percy Buckhorn."

"Marry Sourdough!" Flora was so surprised she couldn't find anything else to say.

"I know we didn't think much of him when we arrived, and he didn't have a high opinion of us, either." She smiled. "But underneath his rough exterior, he has a good heart."

"Yes, of course he does. Nobody understands that better than I do. I just never imagined that anyone would want to marry him."

"In spite of our independence, Flora, I'm lonely. I believe women should have their rights, same as any man, but a pair pulls better than a single horse. As it says in Ecclesiastes: 'Two are better than one, because they have a good reward for their toil. Again, if two lie together, they keep warm, but how can one keep warm alone?'"

Flora was still struggling with this remarkable news. Mr. Grey jumped onto her lap, but Flora ignored her. "I didn't think Sourdough was the marrying kind."

"He needed someone to remind him that he wasn't raised to live like an animal. If there's one thing I've learned out here, every ruffian is longing for a woman's love. Besides, Percy is an excellent farmer. His shack might look like a battle zone, but his barn and his fields are neat as a pin. The two of us can create something special together."

Flora studied her friend. She had seemed much happier lately, but Flora had assumed that was due to her bumper crop. Her eyes bright and her skin glowing, she looked ten years younger than when they had first met. Could she really be in love with old Sourdough? Flora wanted to pose the question delicately. "Peggy, how do you feel about him?"

The widow pressed her forehead against the cow's flank and wouldn't meet Flora's eyes. "I'm very fond of him, Flora. I might as well admit it—more than fond. I love him. I haven't felt this way since Alwyn came courting, seventeen years ago."

Flora was relieved that Peggy wasn't marrying him for financial security, although she would be the last one to cast that stone. "Have you told the children?"

"Yes, last night. They're keen on the idea. Jack needs a man's hand to guide him, and of course Percy simply dotes on the girls." She gave Blossom a final tweak and stood up, facing Flora with her chin high. "We might even have children of our own."

Flora was ashamed of herself. "I haven't congratulated you yet!" She stood and put her arms around Peggy. "I wish you and Percy the very best. We'll have to stop calling him Sourdough, since you're going to sweeten his temper!"

"Thank you, Flora." Peggy stepped back and wiped her eyes on the corner of her apron. "Your good wishes mean the world to me."

There was still one question to ask, and Flora dreaded the answer. With Jessie and the Chicken Ladies gone, she couldn't bear to lose the Penroses too. She had grown to love them all, and couldn't imagine herself alone in Ladyville.

"Where will you live?" Flora held her breath.

"Right here. Nothing could make me move into that shack of his. I'm so attached to my farm that I wouldn't trade places with Vanderbilt himself."

"Oh, thank goodness!" Flora's eyes filled with tears of relief. "I'm verra thankful that you're staying, Peggy. I couldn't manage without you and the children."

"There's no need to move, Flora. We'll be able to walk into the new town and it will have everything we want—a school, and a store, and even a church! And we can hop on the train into Lacombe without bruising our posteriors on that frightful trail."

"It does seem like a miracle, doesn't it?"

"As the old hymn says: 'God moves in a mysterious way, his wonders to perform; he plants his footsteps in the sea, and rides upon the storm.'"

Flora laughed through her tears. "Trust you to have a quotation for everything. Will there be room for Sourdough . . . I mean Percy . . . in your cabin?"

"When he turns eighteen, Jack will take over Percy's old place. In the meantime, we'll build an addition on my cabin with two bedrooms. It's time the lad had his own room, anyway. We can't get married until I earn my title, so we'll work on the house when the weather allows and marry next spring. You know the date as well as I do—May the ninth, God willing."

"We have earned our homesteads with the honest sweat of our brow, especially after all the abuse we suffered from that ghastly Sterling Payne."

Peggy's expression was scornful. "I'll spare you another quotation, but it appears that he's going to be punished for his wicked ways."

Payne was behind bars where he belonged. Following one too many drinks at the tavern in Lacombe, he shot off his mouth about getting rid of the females at Ladyville once and for all. His two companions in crime had readily agreed to testify against him in exchange for a lighter sentence. He was locked up in the Red Deer jail, awaiting his trial for arson.

As the two women headed toward the cabin, each carrying a pail of frothing milk, Peggy changed the subject. "What about you, Flora?"

"Me? What do you mean?"

"You're a young woman, and you should have a husband and children of your own. Nothing would make me happier than to see you find a partner in life. I don't think it's any great secret that Dr. Farraday is sweet on you. Don't you care for him at all?"

Flora braced herself for the Big Lie. "I don't plan to marry. I'm better off as I am. Besides, the doctor is stepping out with Clara Nelson."

"Ah, you're wrong there, Flora. Clara is engaged to a farmer north of Toddsville, or should I say Alix." Jokingly, she clutched her neck. "That name sticks in my throat, although I expect we'll get used to it."

Flora stopped walking. The day suddenly seemed brighter, as if the sun had broken from behind a thundercloud. "Are you sure? Where did you hear that?"

"Percy told me. He knows the young farmer well. So you see, the doctor is still single, and if he's like every other bachelor around these parts, he's pining for a wife."

CHAPTER FORTY-ONE

How do you tell a man you want to marry him? Flora wondered. Five months had passed since their magical day on horseback, when the doctor's proposal had been so emphatically rejected. She was painfully aware that was a long time, especially since she had given him no hope whatsoever. Even with Clara Nelson out of the picture, this eligible bachelor might have found someone else. Or perhaps his affection, starved of encouragement, had withered and died like a wheat field in a drought.

Flora agonised for several days before concluding that she had to take the initiative, however humiliating the outcome. She sent the briefest of notes to town with Beau, inviting the doctor to call when he was free.

The very next day, his palomino appeared over the hill.

Flora answered the door in an ill-fitting brown gingham dress that was too short in the hem and baggy in the bodice, one of the garments donated by the Women's Country Club. She knew from examining her reflection in her butcher knife blade that her face was pale and tired after several sleepless nights, but she tried to be fatalistic. Perhaps it was better that he see her at her worst.

"Miss Craigie, you asked me to come." He had reverted to calling her Miss Craigie, establishing a mood of formality between them again. "Are you ill?"

Flora hoped she might find inner strength in the great outdoors. "I'm perfectly well, Dr. Farraday. Shall we go for a walk?" She drew her tartan shawl around her shoulders and led the way toward the creek. It was cool and crisp, one of those October afternoons when everything seemed dusted with gold—the tips of the long grass, the late asters, the bullrushes.

When they reached the trees, Flora stopped and turned. She inhaled deeply, hoping to slow her runaway heartbeat. "I invited you to visit because I have something to tell you."

He dipped his head. "You're welcome to tell me anything, Miss Craigie."

After much internal debate, Flora had decided to confess the whole truth. She knew the doctor would remain in ignorance unless he heard the story from her own lips. Flora was aware that this upright citizen might find her story repugnant. He might even hand her over to the mounted police. But she would not lie to him, ever again.

Stalling for time while she summoned her courage, she turned away and pretended to admire the view. Beside them, the burned area had become a glorious field of vivid purple fireweed. A few leaves fell like golden tears from the bare poplar branches. Everything seemed sharper and brighter, as if her senses were heightened with apprehension.

She couldn't wait any longer. She took a breath and spoke in a voice thick with emotion. "Last spring, you did me the honour of proposing. I was forced to refuse. I had no other choice."

She glanced at him and saw that the doctor's face remained impassive.

"I was already married."

Predictably, his eyes widened in shock. He opened his mouth and closed it again, waiting for her to continue.

Scraping up her determination, Flora presented the bald facts: Her decision to marry a man she didn't love in order to secure a home. The attack on the train, followed by her frantic flight. Her fortunate meeting with Nurse Godwin, and the chance to homestead. She even suspended all maidenly modesty and forced herself to tell him about Hector's illness, and the fact that their marriage had never been consummated.

She stopped then, waiting for his reaction.

His face was unreadable, but he gave an encouraging nod. "Please go on."

Flora stared at the creek, avoiding his gaze. "Six weeks ago, my husband found me here. He told me he was dying, and then tried to strangle me. During the struggle one of my friends, it doesn't matter which one, accidentally shot and killed him. We knew that no one would believe us, so we buried his body."

She braced herself. Would he recoil in horror? Would he respond with his usual courtesy, and then ride away forever? The landscape was hushed, as if it, too, were waiting for his response. Surely he must hear her heart thudding in her chest.

The doctor turned his back and walked a few steps, as though he needed to put some distance between them. Flora clutched her fists under her shawl and stared blindly at the murmuring creek. A dragonfly the colour of lapis lazuli lightly touched her hair before flitting over the smooth water.

It seemed a long time before the doctor returned to her side. He didn't look angry or repulsed. Instead, he wore an expression of deep concern. "Miss Craigie, what if someone finds the body?"

"I swear to you that will never happen." Jessie informed them that she had ridden three days before burying the body so deep that neither man nor beast would uncover its bones. "I would not have confided in you otherwise."

He shook his head and blinked rapidly, as if unable to comprehend the magnitude of her ordeal. "I'm so sorry you had to endure this awful burden alone. I wish you had told me sooner."

"There was nothing you could have done."

Another silence followed before Flora spoke again. "Since you know the whole story, I must have the truth: Have your feelings about me changed?"

He didn't hesitate. "Yes, they have."

Flora bit her lip hard, desperate not to cry. She squared her shoulders, as though she were preparing to face the firing squad and wanted to die with dignity.

But the doctor wasn't finished. "I always thought you were one of the bravest people I know. Now I believe you're also one of the most honest."

Flora experienced a wave of relief that he didn't despise her. However, he still hadn't told her what she needed to hear. Apparently he was far too considerate to reopen the painful subject. It would have to be up to her.

"Was there any statute of limitations on your proposal of marriage?"

Confusion crossed his face like cloud shadows passing over the prairie before hope dawned in his eyes. "No, Miss Craigie. My offer stands as long as I breathe."

Flora exhaled in a rush. "Then I accept, with all my heart."

Two seconds later she was in his arms and he was squeezing her so hard that her ribs hurt. Breathless and laughing, she protested. He kissed her. A wave of desire poured through her with the power of a white-foamed breaker on the open sea. It was a good thing his strong arms were around her, because her legs would no longer support her weight. She leaned into his broad chest and felt herself opening to him like a flower facing the sunshine—not surrendering, she had come too far to surrender to anyone—but embracing her own vulnerability. It was terrifying, but at the same time it felt utterly right.

"My darling love. How soon can we be married?" he asked.

"The day after I get my title."

CHAPTER FORTY-TWO

I t was the eighth day of May, and the prairie was experiencing its annual rebirth. Flora and the doctor rode into Lacombe through fields of rippling yellow grass, jolting across mudholes and corduroy bridges, sitting close enough on the buggy seat to feel the warmth of each other's shoulders and thighs. Flora was so happy she wished the distance were longer. After all the weary months of waiting, she wanted time to stand still.

They dropped the horse and buggy at the livery stable in Lacombe, boarded the train to Red Deer, and checked into the Alexandra Hotel. Following an excellent dinner in the dining room and several lingering kisses in the deserted hallway, they retired to their separate rooms. "Two more nights," he said, and she knew what both of them were thinking.

Flora was up before dawn, and this time, she was first in line at the lands office. She watched the eager homesteaders queuing behind her and silently wished them luck. In the past three years, the land rush had turned into a stampede.

The heavy wooden doors swung open. The same officious clerk she had seen during her first visit was seated behind the counter. Flora passed him her

355

certificate, signed by the mild-mannered inspector who had replaced Sterling Payne. The new inspector had made a single visit to Flora's homestead and congratulated her on a job well done.

The certificate read, rather wordily:

I hereby certify that *Flora May Craigie* has complied with the provisions of law required to be conformed to, in order to entitle him to receive a patent for such Homestead, and that I have issued a recommendation of such patent.

Signed:
James Featherstone
Homestead Inspector

The clerk showed no sign of remembering her. Once again, he examined the certificate thoroughly, holding it to the light and checking the signature against another application signed by James Featherstone. In the end, he stamped and dated the certificate and handed Flora her title.

She met his eyes, and only then did she see his shock of recognition. She smiled triumphantly. "You once called me a landgrabber. You were wrong to think it, and wrong to say it. You are a disgrace to the office you hold."

Flora left him with his mouth hanging open below his moustache and sailed out of the office, clutching the document in both hands.

"She got her title," said one of the men standing in line. "If she can do it, it can't be that hard."

Flora laughed aloud, wondering how many of them would be broken on the wheel of homesteading.

As she approached the buggy, she waved the paper above her head. They could not embrace in public, but the doctor squeezed her hand as he helped her onto the seat. They drove away, Flora rejoicing over her title. She wished her parents could see her now. She wished everyone she had ever met could see her now. "May we drive straight to the hospital?" she asked. "Ach, I canna wait to show my title to Nurse Godwin."

"Maybe you don't want to marry me, now that you're a woman of property," the doctor teased.

Flora laughed again. "Maybe you don't want to marry a farmer. It isn't an easy life."

He smiled into her eyes. "I want any kind of life with you in it."

As the organist began to play "The Wedding March," Flora walked down the aisle of the little Anglican church in Alix. The pews were filled and guests lined the walls. Flora recognised a few faces, but most people were there to celebrate with their beloved doctor, who had helped them recover from illness or injury. When Samuel saw Flora approaching, his eyes shone with tears. She could feel her own happiness glowing like an inner flame.

Two months earlier, a letter had arrived from California. The Chicken Ladies had sent a five-dollar Canadian bill with a note: "For your wedding gown." Flora had ordered a length of white satin from the general store and sewn her own dress. The skirt was gathered at the waist and fell to the floor in the shape of a bell. Over her high-necked lace bodice, she wore a string of pearls belonging to Dr. Farraday's grandmother, sent all the way from Port Hope, Ontario. An embroidered headband held her frothy veil in place. It was too early for wildflowers, so she carried a nosegay she had fashioned herself from wild grasses and wheat stalks, tied with blue ribbon. When she reached the altar, Flora faced her groom. The heels on her satin shoes made them almost the same height.

As she recited her vows, Flora remembered the last time she had spoken the same words. She had made her promises dutifully, with every intention of being a good wife to Hector. She had hoped she might even come to love him in time. But she felt no sense of duty today, only an overwhelming rush of love for Samuel as she smiled into his green eyes, promising to honour and cherish him until death.

Reverend Crawley made a little speech about the sanctity of marriage. "Whither thou goest, I will go," he said, and Flora felt he was saying the words to her alone. She would follow Samuel anywhere.

Three years ago, a couple of indifferent strangers had acted as witnesses at her first wedding. This time, her dear friend Peggy stood beside her, wearing her good indigo dress and a new picture hat trimmed with a white ribbon rosette. Nellie and Jewel stood self-consciously beside their mother in matching pink flowered frocks, their hair beautifully curled in ringlets, topped with white bows the size of their heads.

On the other side of the groom, Percy was handsome in a navy suit and silk tie. He and the doctor had developed a friendship based on mutual respect during their campaign to secure the women's homesteads. As the minister read the service, Peggy and Percy never took their eyes from each other. Their wedding would be next.

Now Samuel and Flora were man and wife. As they walked down the aisle, Flora beamed at Nurse Godwin, seated in the back row, and the nurse winked at her. They went out onto the lawn where Nellie and Jewel, along with the other local children, pelted them with rice. Laughing and ducking, they ran to their buggy—bedecked with white ribbons and a sign that said JUST MARRIED—and drove to the newspaper office. Mr. Frederick was also the town's official photographer. Once again, he took her photograph. This time, she stood beside Samuel in the traditional pose designed to show off her wedding gown, while he sat beside her, looking terribly pleased with himself.

Then it was off to the new community hall. Luncheon was waiting, prepared by the Alix Country Women's Club under the direction of their president, Mrs. Parlby. The women had decorated the hall with spruce boughs and bullrushes and pussy willows. On the head table was a three-foot, three-tiered iced fruitcake, provided by Alix Westhead.

Mrs. Westhead herself did not attend, but she had an excellent reason—an important bull sale in Edmonton. Maisie, whom they saw more often since she had become Mrs. Dunne, had told Ladyville the salacious news about her former employer six months ago when Charles Westhead had propped a goodbye note on the mantel and departed for Vancouver, taking the handsome stable boy with him.

Deprived of her husband's monthly remittance cheque, Alix decided to manage the ranch herself. She took a correspondence course in animal husbandry from the University of Guelph, increased her herd of purebred Herefords, and was named the first president of the new Alix Agricultural Society. By all accounts, she was a great success. Her maid, Hattie, had been with her ever since Maisie left, setting a new record for longevity.

Flora thought she was too excited to eat, but when presented with plates full of dainty ribbon sandwiches and raspberry thumbprint cookies and date squares, her appetite returned. Samuel, too, ate heartily. It was the least they could do to repay the ladies for their effort. There were speeches, toasts, and telegrams read aloud from the Chicken Ladies and Jessie McDonald and the doctor's family in Ontario.

When Flora excused herself to freshen up, she found Irene Parlby in the hallway.

"Mrs. Farraday, may I have a quick word?" Mrs. Parlby asked.

Flora thrilled at hearing her new name.

"This isn't the time or place, but when I heard you speak in Red Deer, I was struck with how much you have to offer our country. And now you're a landowner as well! It won't be long before we get the vote, and it will come sooner if women like you form the advance guard. May I call on you to discuss the matter when you're back home?"

Flora agreed, feeling slightly dazed as she returned to her chair. Could she really assume a role in public life? She forgot the conversation five minutes later, when it was time to toss her bouquet. A group of giggling girls lined one side of the hall. Her little bundle of grass and wheat soared through the air and landed in the outstretched hands of Beau's girlfriend, Etta, who cast him a demure glance from the corner of her eye.

After the wedding cake was cut and passed around, Flora and Samuel looked at each other. It was spring, when every hour counted, and the farmers were eager to return to their fields, but they knew nobody would leave before the bride and groom. Samuel pulled back her chair, and they made their farewells.

"Will we always think alike?" Flora wondered happily.

They mounted their buggy to cheers from their guests. They would spend their wedding night in Red Deer, and board the southbound train in the morning. Samuel had booked three nights at the Banff Springs Hotel, the crown jewel in the Canadian Pacific Railway's hotel chain. Flora was eager to see the majestic Rockies. She had been so close, jumping from the train before it entered the foothills. This journey would end with joy rather than heartbreak.

As their buggy made its way across the prairie, Flora and Samuel chatted about the wedding and their future plans. On their return from Banff, Flora would move into the single room above Samuel's office. The cramped quarters wouldn't bother her, since she was accustomed to her shack, but she dreaded selling her farmland. It was a willing sacrifice, since her husband's practice must come first, but the loss would be heart-wrenching.

To avoid thinking about it on this happiest of all days, Flora told Samuel about Mrs. Parlby's suggestion that she become involved in local politics.

"That's an excellent idea," he said. "Women should have a greater voice in our new province. I'll stand behind you every step of the way."

"You wouldn't mind?" she asked.

"Of course not. I shall bask in the reflected glory. I'll be known as the husband of the famous Flora May Farraday."

"Samuel, you really are the most wonderful man." The doctor drew the buggy to a halt and they exchanged a passionate kiss that made Flora feel faint. Finally, he picked up the reins again.

As they approached the fork, he turned south from the Buffalo Lake Trail onto the track leading to Ladyville.

"Where are we going?" Flora asked. "Did we forget something?" Her valise with its carefully chosen wardrobe, including a peach silk nightdress handstitched by Peggy, was in the back of the buggy.

"I have a surprise for you." Samuel refused to say anything else.

Within minutes, they were clip-clopping down the hill, but the doctor startled Flora again by passing her property and entering the lane leading to the yellow house. They drove between the rows of budding maples, now proudly standing twelve feet tall, and up to the front door.

The house was more alluring than ever in the soft spring sunshine. Although the ladies had been gone for months, the house and yard were immaculate. The flowerbeds were raked, the bushes trimmed, and the stained glass window over the front door winked at them knowingly.

"Welcome to your new home." Samuel smiled, watching her.

"My new home! Whatever do you mean?" Flora stared at him.

"It's yours if you want it, Flora. The ladies have agreed to sell me their quarter section, but I wanted your approval first. You see, once the railway goes through, my services will be needed in the new town. I contacted a former classmate who will take over my practice in Alix. If we move out here, you can keep farming, and we can live close to our friends."

Flora stared in disbelief at the dear yellow house, and then back at the man who was mysteriously able to read her mind. She had not thought it was possible to be any happier, but her new husband had proven her wrong.

"I love you, Samuel Farraday."

He grinned, showing his crooked tooth. "And I love the way you say my name, Flora May Farraday. Our name. Promise me you will repeat those words every day for the rest of our lives."

And so she did.

A NOTE FROM THE AUTHOR

My inspiration for *Finding Flora* arrived like a bolt of prairie lightning when I learned that the Canadian government refused to allow single women to claim a free homestead under the 1872 Dominion Lands Act, even though the practice was common in the United States. The only exception to this ridiculously unfair law was for widows with minor children.

Determined to write about a woman homesteading alone, I searched for a legal loophole and found one: twelve Canadian nurses who had served in the South African War received scrip as their reward, entitling them to claim a free homestead. I decided that my fictional heroine, Flora Craigie, would meet one of these nurses and buy her scrip.

I chose Scottish heritage for Flora because my own ancestors were evicted—otherwise known as cleared—from their tiny croft in the Highlands, not far from the town of Dornoch in the County of Sutherland, Scotland. Lynne Mahoney, curator of the Historylinks Museum in Dornoch, helped me with my research and came up with the bright idea of Flora's freshwater pearl.

I then created Flora's circle of neighbours: a Welsh widow with three minor children; an American couple who were engaged in a "Boston marriage," as the cohabitation of two single women was sometimes called back then; and finally, a Métis woman. Together they formed a small community known as Ladyville. In reality, no such place ever existed, but it would have been near the location of present-day Clive, Alberta.

My Métis character, Jessie McDonald, is named after my own great-grandmother, who lived in Red River, Manitoba; "Half-Breed" was the legal term until 1982. Sadly, she died of typhoid at the age of thirty-seven, leaving behind seven children. It is through her that I claim my Cree ancestry, and I dedicated this book to her.

My fictional Jessie was inspired by a woman who lived near my current home in Invermere, British Columbia, in the early 1900s. She was Rosalee Kinbasket, a skilled hunter and horsewoman, and the beloved youngest daughter of Chief Pierre Kinbasket, the last hereditary chief of the Shuswap Band. Her extended family still lives in the area.

My Cree friend Julia Frank, member of the Sweetgrass First Nation in Saskatchewan, came up with the perfect name for Jessie's horse. Tipiskow means "night" in the Cree language.

Darcy McRae, historian and longtime member of the Métis Nation of Alberta, helped me research the cruel treatment of the Métis People.

My novel was edited for sensitivity by Rhonda Kronyk, an Indigenous editor in Edmonton, Alberta.

When my book begins in May 1905, Alberta and Saskatchewan did not exist but were part of the vast North-West Territories. I grew up in Saskatchewan, the granddaughter of homesteaders, and I still own land there in partnership with my brother Rob Florence, who operates the family farm near North Battleford. I would have set the book in my home province had I not stumbled across the fascinating story behind the naming of Alix, Alberta.

I included some real historical figures in my novel. However, many of their personal details and all the scenes in which they appear were entirely fabricated by me.

The following information is true:

Minister of the Interior Frank Oliver, publisher of the first newspaper in Alberta, was a huge booster for Edmonton and the entire province, but his sexism and racism are well documented.

Alice (Alexia) Hall Crofton Westhead, nicknamed Alix, was the first white woman settler near the Alberta community that bears her name. She eventually separated from her husband, Charles Westhead, who was not a remittance man. She ran the Quarter Circle One alone for several years, before returning to England, where she worked on the Rothschild Family Estate until her death.

Canadian Pacific Railway Chairman William Van Horne was an intriguing character who struck up a friendship with Alix Westhead during a transatlantic crossing, and he renamed the tiny community of Toddsville after her. While it was rumoured that they were more than just friends, I have no documented proof of an affair.

Irene Marryat met her husband, Charles Parlby, when she came from England to visit her friend Alix Westhead. She later became active in politics, was the first president of the Alix Country Women's Club, was elected to the Alberta Legislative Assembly, and became one of the "famous five" who had women legally declared persons in Canada in 1929.

Wherever possible, I also used the real names of lesser-known people and businesses. For example, Harold A. Snell owned the first jewellery store in Red Deer and sold it to Alexander Mitchell. After more than one hundred years, Mitchell & Jewell still exists.

As far as dates are concerned, I compacted them slightly to fit my three-year timeline from 1905 to 1908. The events depicted in my novel actually took place between 1900 and 1910.

The most delightful aspect of my research was learning more about western Canada's rich and varied history. If you are interested in some deeper background, I highly recommend the works of nonfiction and the riveting memoirs listed in the bibliography.

BIBLIOGRAPHY

Alix-Clive Historical Club. *Pioneers and Progress*, 1974; and *Gleanings After Pioneers and Progress*, 1981.

Binnie-Clark, Georgina. *Wheat and Woman*. University of Toronto Press, 2006.

Blackburn, John H. *Land of Promise*. Macmillan of Canada, 1970.

Broadfoot, Barry. *The Pioneer Years, 1895–1914: Memories of Settlers Who Opened the West*. Doubleday Canada Limited, 1976.

Carter, Sarah. *Imperial Plots: Women, Land, and the Spadework of British Colonialism on the Canadian Prairies*. University of Manitoba Press, 2016.

Carter, Sarah. *Montana Women Homesteaders: A Field of Their Own*. Farcountry Press, 2009.

Cavanaugh, Catherine. *Telling Tales: Essays in Western Women's History*. University of British Columbia Press, 2000.

Cormack, Barbara Villy. *Perennials and Politics: The Life Story of Hon. Irene Parlby, LL.D.* Barbara Villy Cormack, 1968.

Dehart, Shelagh Kinbasket. *The Kinbasket Migration and Other Indian History*. Shelagh Kinbasket Dehart and Dusty Dehart, 2006.

Hensley, Marcia. *Staking Her Claim: Women Homesteading the West*. High Plains Press, 2008.

Hiemstra, Mary. *Gully Farm: A Story of Homesteading on the Canadian Prairies*. Fifth House, 1997.

Holmes, Peggy. *It Could Have Been Worse*. Collins, 1980.

Hopkins, Monica. *Letters from a Lady Rancher*. Calgary: Glenbow Museum, 1981.

Knowles, Valerie. *From Telegrapher to Titan: The Life of William C. Van Horne*. Dundurn Press, 2004.

Kohl, Edith Eudora. *Land of the Burnt Thigh: A Lively Story of Women Homesteaders on the South Dakota Frontier*. Minnesota Historical Society Press, 1986.

MacGregor, J.G. *North-West of Sixteen*. Western Producer Prairie Books, 1977.

McClung, Nellie. *Clearing in the West: My Own Story*. Dundurn Press, 2005.

McGoogan, Ken. *Flight of the Highlanders: The Making of Canada*. HarperCollins Canada, 2019.

Milholland, Billie. *They Came: Pioneer Women of the Canadian West*. Friesen Press, 2018.

Minifie, James. *Homesteader: A Prairie Boyhood Recalled*. Macmillan of Canada, 1972.

Mitchell, Elizabeth B. *In Western Canada Before the War: Impressions of Early Twentieth Century Prairie Communities*. Western Producer Prairie Books, 1981.

Neatby, L.H. *Chronicle of a Pioneer Prairie Family*. Western Producer Prairie Books, 1979.

Roberts, Sarah Ellen. *Of Us and the Oxen: A True Tale of Pioneering in Alberta Around the Turn of the Century*. Modern Press, 1968.

Rollings-Magnusson, Sandra. *The Homesteaders*. University of Regina Press, 2018.

Rose, Hilda. *The Stump Farm: A Chronicle of Pioneering*. Little, Brown, and Company, 1928.

Silverman, Eliane Leslau. *The Last Best West: Women on the Alberta Frontier 1880–1930*. Fifth House Publishing, 1998.

Strange, Kathleen. *With the West in Her Eyes: The Story of a Modern Pioneer*. Adam Strange, 2019.

Young, Carrie. *Nothing to Do but Stay: My Pioneer Mother*. University of Iowa Press, 2000.

Zuehlke, Mark. *Scoundrels, Dreamers & Second Sons: British Remittance Men in the Canadian West*. Dundurn Press, 2001.

ACKNOWLEDGMENTS

Women's history goes largely unrecorded, so I was very thankful to find the research performed by Dr. Sarah Carter, Professor and Henry Marshall Tory Chair Emerita, Department of History, Classics and Religion and Faculty of Native Studies of the University of Alberta, who has written several wonderful nonfiction books, including *Imperial Plots* and *Montana Women Homesteaders*. Her work far and away had the greatest influence on this novel.

In researching the history of Alix and area, I am indebted to Elaine Meehan, volunteer at the Alix Wagon Wheel Museum in Alix, Alberta; and the Alix-Clive Historical Club, which published the book *Pioneers and Progress* and its sequel, *Gleanings After Pioneers and Progress*. Local history books are often a gold mine of information that can't be found in the larger museums.

Dr. Bill Waiser of Saskatoon, author and western Canadian history expert, gave me some great leads; as did Bill Mackay, former president of the Central Alberta Historical Society in Red Deer, Alberta. Staff at several institutions were most helpful, including Brittany Kerik at the Lacombe Museum and Archives, Alberta; those at the Lacombe & District Historical Society, Alberta; Andrew Webster at the Red Deer and District Archives, Alberta; the Provincial Archives of Saskatchewan in Regina; and Doug Thorne at the Canadian Museum of Rail Travel in Cranbrook, British Columbia.

I wish I were able to thank Red Deer, Alberta, historian Michael Dawe, who promptly and accurately answered all my questions. Sadly, he passed away in 2023 and took a lifetime of local knowledge with him.

I was warmly encouraged to write this novel by my friend, acclaimed Indigenous author Darrel J. McLeod. He joined his ancestors in 2024 and will be deeply missed by everyone who knew him. Three other generous friends read earlier rough drafts of this manuscript: Jo-Anne McLean, Donna Tunney, and Leslie Vass.

While navigating the choppy waters of publishing, my manuscript fortunately found its way into the hands of true professionals. I want to thank my editor at Simon & Schuster Canada, Adrienne Kerr, for her wisdom and her confidence in me, and book editor Laurie Grassi for making this novel so much better.

My heartfelt thanks goes to my husband, Heinz Drews, who made supper every night for three years even though he has his own successful construction career. Greater love hath no man.

Finally, I have a huge amount of respect for the women, both Canadian and American, who braved hardship and heartache in this new world to carve out a future for themselves and their children. Millions of us today are alive and thriving because of them.

ABOUT THE AUTHOR

ELINOR FLORENCE grew up on a Saskatchewan farm and earned degrees in English and journalism. She worked for newspapers in all four western provinces, spent eight years writing for *Reader's Digest Canada*, and even published her own award-winning community newspaper. Her first novel, *Bird's Eye View*, was a national bestseller, while the second, *Wildwood*, was named one of Kobo's Hundred Most Popular Canadian Books of All Time. *Finding Flora* was inspired by her own Scottish homesteading and Indigenous ancestors. She is a member of the Métis Nation of British Columbia and makes her home in the mountain resort of Invermere. Visit her at elinorflorence.com and subscribe to her monthly history blog, Letters From Windermere.

FINDING FLORA

Elinor Florence

A Reading Group Guide

1. Were you surprised to learn that the American government was more progressive than the Canadian government in allowing single women to claim free homesteads? Why do you think the law was different in Canada?

2. Irene Parlby went on to have a huge impact on Canadian politics. Women in the three prairie provinces were the first to be enfranchised, but not until 1916. Discuss how women in Canada must have felt not to have a vote.

3. The Métis People of Red River, Manitoba, were robbed of their land by an unscrupulous federal government. Were you aware of this historical injustice? Do you think their descendants are entitled to compensation?

4. Frank Oliver was a national figure who was the first newspaper publisher in Alberta and instrumental in the creation of Edmonton. However, he was an avowed racist and sexist. Do you believe that parks and monuments in his honour should be renamed?

5. The ignorance of European settlers who arrived in Canada with no knowledge of their new environment is staggering. Discuss what must have been their first impressions.

6. Winters were harsh on the prairie, with blizzards that lasted for days and temperatures falling to minus fifty degrees Fahrenheit. What is the worst weather you have experienced?

7. The isolation of people living in homesteads sometimes literally drove them mad. Do you think you could survive for months without contact with another human being?

8. Almost every settler family lost a baby or young child, sometimes several of them. Do you think people were more hardened to grief and loss in the past than they are today?

9. How do you think the residents of Ladyville, including the children, changed and evolved during the course of their adventures?

10. What was the most memorable scene or twist in the story? Do you think the women were justified in hiding Hector's body?

11. How well did the author blend historical fact and fiction in this book? Did you find the book accurate and authentic? Did you learn something new about the time and place in which it is set?

12. What do you think happened to the characters after the book concluded? Were you surprised by the ending?